The Roads We Take

Christy K Lee

Text copyright © 2023 by **Christy K. Lee**

All rights reserved. For information regarding reproduction in total or in part, contact Rising Action Publishing Co. at www.risingactionpublishingco.com

Cover Illustration © **Nat Mack**

Distributed by **Blackstone Publishing**

ISBNs:
Print: 978-1-990253-36-2
Ebook: 978-1-990253-37-9
Hardcover: 978-1-990253-90-4

FIC090010 FICTION / World Literature / Canada / Colonial & 19th Century
FIC035000 FICTION / Medical
FIC044000 FICTION / Women

Follow Rising Action on our socials!
Twitter: @RAPubCollective
Instagram: @risingactionpublishingco
Tiktok: @risingactionpublishingco

RISING ACTION

This novel was written on the unceded traditional territory of the Matsqui, Kwantlen, Katzie, and Semiahmoo First Nations

To my daughters:
May you always know that you are enough.
Ka nui taku aroha ki a koe
My love for you knows no bounds

The Roads We Take

Part One

Chapter 1

April 1885, District of Saskatchewan

THERE WAS JUST SO MUCH DAMN BLOOD.

Clara had to admit she felt a bit frantic. Despite Dr. Cameron's warning and the tourniquet tied tight around the man's leg, the flow made it difficult for Clara to see or even think clearly. She took a deep breath and held the heavy saw above the bone.

"There you go, Miss Thomas." Dr. Cameron's voice came calm and reassuring, with a slight Scottish burr. "Take your time. Nice and even, all the way through."

Despite the cool day, Clara struggled with the effort, sweat beading on her brow and nose. The saw wobbled as her arms grew tired—it seemed bones broke so easily in other circumstances. Finally, after a few minutes of intense work, a sudden release of pressure on the saw made her nearly stumble as the tool finished its grisly task. She hesitated before pushing the discarded limb away, her stomach giving a sudden lurch.

No. Do not retch, Clara. Not now. She swallowed the bile creeping up her throat and picked up the long pieces of horsehair laid beside her. Taking a steadying breath, she found the first artery in the soldier's lower leg and carefully tied it off with the hair, then did the same with the second.

"Excellent work, Doctor. Now, file down the bone and wrap the end with the excess skin you reserved. Don't forget to leave an opening for drainage," Dr. Cameron said.

The older doctor turned on his heel and made his way to the end of the surgeon's tent. A gust of wind and rain blew through the tent, Clara's patient groaning with the sudden chill. She quickly added a few drops of chloroform to the cloth over his mouth to give her time to finish her work. It took a few moments to file the severed bone smooth, and then she gently wrapped the leg in the patient's own skin.

"Clara! There you are. I've been looking for you every-where." Lieutenant John McKay burst into the tent, brushing the rain from his jacket before taking in the scene before him. She watched with great amusement as his face went pale, his carefully coiffed hair falling over his eyes. He was not fond of her doctoring, and the gore in front of her was likely turning his stomach.

"My God, Clara, what *are* you doing?" The air was filled with the sharp tang of blood, overtaking that of the spring rain. He came closer to her and then obviously thought better of it, taking a cautious step back.

Clara bent her head over her patient. This was her first chance to work with the surgeons, and she did not want to risk making any mistakes.

"Good morning, John. It's quite blustery out today." She flashed him a quick grin. "I could definitely use a cup of tea." The wind tore through the open tent again, and she shivered despite the thick woolen vest she wore over her dress.

When she was finally finished, she nodded to the orderlies who were waiting nearby. They came and carefully lifted the man out of the surgeon's tent. The orderlies would take him to the infirmary, where she would check on him later, along with the other soldiers in her care.

Clara moved along to the next amputation patient—the wounded men lay on tables down the length of the tent, their moans a gasping chorus. She anesthetized the man with chloroform and tightened a tourniquet around the affected limb. Biting her lip in hesitation, she remembered the instructions from Dr. Cameron and began to cut the first layer, taking care to save a flap of skin to wrap around the stump.

John followed her, clearly agitated, his deep blue eyes flashing. "Miss Thomas!" he hissed, rubbing his hands over his face in disbelief. "I thought you were working in the infirmary. This," he gestured to the white canvas tent, "is hardly the place for a woman. Your father—"

"Isn't here, John. Are you staying? Because I should warn you, it's about to get quite bloody." Clara pushed back her hair with a stained hand, feeling rather annoyed at John's intrusion.

"Clara." John moved close to stand right at her shoulder. Despite being posted in a military camp for the past few months, he still managed to smell good—his cologne reminded her of the evenings they had spent dancing together at society balls. "We had plans for dinner yesterday. I am assuming you forgot." A slight tone of resentment pitched his voice, and she held back a grimace. She paused, holding the Catlin knife in her hand. Once she cut through the muscle, she couldn't rest until the entire removal was complete. The dinner hadn't been forgotten. Instead, she'd gone to the privacy of her tent after a long day tending to the infirmary. It seemed she wouldn't be able to avoid John a second day in a row.

"Yes, it slipped my mind." She smiled as brightly as she could and turned to face him. "Come find me this evening."

Not waiting for his reply, Clara went back to her patient, her gaze resting on the man's face. He was no more than a boy, really, his complexion fair and rosy-cheeked. Knowing he was about to have his life altered forever, she said a small prayer as she took his arm.

A FEW HOURS LATER, Clara left the surgeon's tent, famished. Despite the overcast sky, it had to be around three in the afternoon, and the stodgy bowl of porridge that had been her breakfast was a distant memory. Even so, she wrinkled her nose at the thought of an evening dinner with John McKay. At least the food would be good. She knew John's intentions for dinner were more than friendly, his unrelenting attention to her making that abundantly clear. He had always pursued her, even when they were still children. And yet, while her parents would be happy with the match, she couldn't bring her mind to the idea of a lifetime with him.

She stepped through the mud of the military camp on her way back to the infirmary—the ruts left behind from the wagons had mixed with the heavy spring rains to create a sodden mess. When her father had secured the position for her, he had insisted that she work only in the convalescence camp, far removed from the front lines. It was a small uprising; the Métis peoples had stood up against the Canadian government over the loss of their land and livelihood. Now that the buffalo on these great prairie lands had been hunted nearly to extinction by the white man, the Métis were struggling to survive.

Clara didn't particularly mind being away from the front lines—she was just content to have work. Her six months at home after graduating from medical school had been quite miserable. Clara's mother was upset by—no, obsessed with—her spinster status. At the age of twenty-six, Clara shamed her family by remaining unmarried. Her only saving grace, her mother had announced one evening at dinner, was that Clara's looks and figure still turned most men's heads—married or not. It had been a great battle between her mother and father that she be allowed to attend medical school at all, but now that she was finished, they were both in agreement. *Marriage.*

"Miss?" a voice interrupted her thoughts. Joseph, one of the orderlies, stood waiting at the tent flap of the infirmary. He was tall and spindly, about ten years younger than her, with a sparse beard covering his youthful chin.

Much larger than the surgeon's tent, Clara had been assigned to the infirmary alongside another young doctor, but when he had been called to the front lines, she'd been left to care for the entire tent alone. It was always dreadfully busy, filled not only with soldiers and militia but the medical needs of the men and women serving the camp.

"Hello, Joseph. I'm sorry I was away for so long. What have we got in here?" The young man blushed at her words, and she smiled inwardly at his discomfort. Poor Joseph could hardly talk to her without turning several shades of red.

"It's quite busy, I'm afraid," he said, leading her inside. The stench of unwashed men was ripe, and she braced herself against the overwhelming smell. "A few men needing sutures, two with post-amputation fever, and that one," he said, pointing to a blond man in the corner, "got thrown from a horse."

She quickly scanned the tent and decided to start with the man thrown from the horse. Internal injuries could be tricky. But first, a meal. Her legs were unsteady, and her vision swam slightly.

"Joseph, could you please find me something to eat?" she called.

"Of course, Miss Thomas." Joseph's cheeks grew pink again, and he ran off in search of food.

The blond man in the corner gave a short laugh as Clara approached him. "Well, it looks like *he's* in love." He nodded at Joseph's retreating figure, then winced and held his side.

Clara ignored the comment, suppressing the urge to roll her eyes. "Let's take a look." She lifted his shirt, revealing a mottled purple patch of skin. Her fingers carefully touched the area, pressing but not too hard. He had definitely bruised the kidney.

"What happened?" She pulled his shirt back down and went to gather a bedpan from the supply table.

The man watched her from across the room. "I'm Brendan. Brendan Murphy. I was on the general's mare. Nasty temper on the ol' girl. We draw straws in the stable to see who takes her out for exercise every day. She threw me, and I landed on the fence." His voice had a strong Irish lilt, which was quite charming. He was handsome too, Clara noticed, despite the poor light in the tent; a small dimple accompanied his flirtatious grin.

"Well, Mr. Murphy, you've bruised your kidney, which can be quite serious, I'm afraid. I'll have to keep you here for a few days to check your urine for blood and keep an eye on you for fever."

Brendan's smile vanished, a slight scowl in its place. Before he could speak, a steaming bowl of stew appeared in front of Clara. She thanked Joseph and dug in.

Brendan watched her eat. "I can't stay. I need to work." He tried to sit up in the cot and leaned against the rounded metal frame. "I'm here with my sister, workin' our way west. She's ... she's in the family way. She's no' married, so it's up to me to provide for her and the babe."

Despite herself, Clara raised her eyebrows and leaned in closer to Brendan. Most of her patients didn't engage in conversation, afraid of being treated by a female physician. "She's pregnant?"

Brendan rubbed the stubble of a few days' growth on his chin, just a shade darker than his hair. "Aye. She won't tell me how it happened. Against her will, most likely. But it was here; I *am* sure of that." His fists clenched.

Clara swallowed thickly, her mouth going dry. Attacks of that nature were known to happen in military camps. Her father had warned her of the dangers while escorting her from their home in Ontario to this most recent resistance led by Louis Riel and Gabriel Dumont. When Lieutenant John McKay, the son of a family friend and her childhood friend, had been suggested as her chaperone, her father had agreed instantly.

"Where is your camp? I'd like to check on your sister," she offered, "but you will need to stay here until morning at least. Doctor's orders," she finished firmly, seeing a protest form on his lips.

"She's in the camp near the cook's quarters. All full of Irish folk." He gave her another smile. "Her name's Rebecca. I really appreciate that, Miss ...?"

"Dr. Thomas," she supplied. "But yes, Miss Thomas will do."

Clara added visiting Rebecca to the growing list of tasks for the rest of the day, as well as changing before dinner. Staying clean couldn't be expected while living in canvas tents outdoors, but she was a mess. She smiled to herself—it had been *quite* the day. She'd never been invited into the surgeon's tent before, but when Dr. Cameron had come looking for an extra pair of hands, she'd jumped at the opportunity to learn a new skill. She decided she might see what Dr. Cameron was up to again tomorrow.

CLARA HEARD the Irish camp long before she arrived, as the jovial voices thick with accent drifted in the evening air. She poked her head around the corner, watching them for a minute. They had built a little village of tents arranged in a circle, leaving a large open communal area in the middle. Most were eating their evening meal—a large pot of stew hung over the fire, filling the air with the fragrant aroma of hearty food. A hefty man with a red beard spotted Clara and raised his brows inquisitively.

"Can I help you, Miss?" He walked over with a friendly smile on his face.

"Yes. I'm Dr. Thomas. I treated one of your men here today, Brendan Murphy. I'm looking for his sister, Rebecca."

The man's thick eyebrows shot up at her introduction. "Ah, the woman doctor. We've heard of you around the camp. I'm Marty Byrne, and this here's Becca," he said as a blond woman came up to stand beside him. He put his arm around her shoulders. Rebecca was tall and willowy, nearly the same height as the man beside her.

"Rebecca Murphy." She frowned slightly, and Clara could see the resemblance to her brother in the intensity of her grey-blue eyes. "Is my brother all right?"

Clara smiled, hoping to ease her worry. "Yes. He has a bruised kidney, so I'm keeping him for the night. But he should be fine." Clara glanced around the camp for a place to speak with Rebecca alone. "Is there somewhere we can have a word, Rebecca?"

Rebecca's face paled, but she nodded, leading Clara out of the camp towards the barns. Both Marty and Brendan worked in the stables, she explained as they walked. The horses for all the company's men lodged there, needing care after days on the battlefield.

"And what do you do for work?" Clara asked. She knew that the women in camp worked just as hard as the men, providing cooking and laundry services for the soldiers and their own families.

Rebecca held out her hands, which were red and

chapped. "Laundry. Havin' your hands in water all day with the lye soap makes 'em sore. Most nights, they bleed."

Clara nodded and reached into her bag. She'd heard the same from many women on her rounds and had made a salve with the juice of a prickly-pear cactus that grew in the field behind the camp.

"Try this." Clara handed Rebecca the jar, who nodded her thanks. They had reached the stables, and Rebecca led her to sit on a log alongside the fence. Men still busy with work bustled around them, but the two women were far from the prying ears of Rebecca's camp.

"Miss? What's this all about?"

"Please, call me Clara. Your brother told me about your predicament. I promised him that I would check on you. It's too early to provide medical care for pregnancy, but he's worried about you."

Rebecca snorted. "I am no' so sure it's worry. More that I've put a kink in his plans." She crossed her arms over her chest. "But thank you, I'm fine." Rebecca began to rise, but Clara held out a hand to stop her.

"Rebecca, do you mind if I ask?" Clara hesitated, choosing her words with care. "I will keep it to myself, I promise. Is this ... a baby from a love affair?" She thought of Marty and the way he had put his arm around Rebecca protectively. "Or were you ... forced upon?" Clara needed to know whether a predator lurked in the camp.

Rebecca heaved a sigh. "Not love." She shrugged. "Maybe I should've fought harder. No' the first time this has happened to me." She shook her head, and her eyes held a response that Clara couldn't read. "I won't tell you who, so don't ask. Brendan will ... well, never mind. I suppose it's too late to ask you for a remedy to rid myself of it? I'm no more than three months gone."

Clara shook her head. Even if it was within the time frame, Clara did not want to risk herself with illegal activities. Women talked amongst themselves; she knew. Besides, such supplies needed to be found with an herbalist or apothecary, which would be in the next town.

"Clara! Miss Thomas, your dinner awaits!" a man's voice echoed through the stable yard.

Rebecca looked at Clara in surprise, and then a deep frown fell over her features. As John rounded the corner in search of Clara, Rebecca's face went stark white, and she stood abruptly, looking frantically for a way to leave.

"Clara, darling, you are the *most* difficult woman. I—" John's voice cut off in a sharp silence as he took in the scene before him. He stopped, frozen mid-stride.

As the seconds passed, realization struck Clara like a lash from a whip. Her eyes grew wide as she looked from John to Rebecca and back. The man who had violated Rebecca and put her in the family way was none other than her childhood friend and chaperone, Lieutenant John McKay.

Chapter 2

April 1885

BRENDAN MURPHY LAY IN THE INFIRMARY CONSIDERING his luck. He didn't share much of his past with folks, but if he happened to stumble into a conversation over a bottle of whisky, he might mention that good fortune had never been on his side.

From as early as Brendan could remember, his upbringing had been far from lucky. As a small boy, the *Protestant Orphan Society* in Belfast had been his only home. Around the age of five, Brendan realized that some of the children were told stories of the tragic fates of their parents. Some children were even blessed enough to be given a memento of happier times and people long gone: a faded photograph, a book, or a soft blanket. The children who had no such stories, like Brendan and his twin sister Becca, were defined by their shame: *unwanted, unloved, abandoned, bastard.*

When the children were twelve, their luck had changed.

Or so it seemed. A husband and wife who had never been blessed with children took them in. They were to move to the countryside outside of Coleraine to help with the farm and other household duties; they were warned it would be hard work. The couple were heathen, it was whispered, but kind. It would be a good life.

It had not been a good life. Within a month, Brendan learned to defend himself with his fists—the first time, he had been caught unaware, and it had cost him three of his back teeth. He learned that an empty stomach after a day of hard work was best warmed with a drink from a kind neighbour. Worst of all, Brendan learned that older men should not be trusted in the company of young girls like his sister.

They had lived there for only four months before they fled under cover of night, taking only the clothes and shoes they were wearing and some food stolen from the pantry. Catching a wagon ride from a kind farmer, they'd ended up in Londonderry, living under a bridge with a pack of other vagrant children. There were many street children then, hard times wearing on the families of Ireland. Brendan had spent those years defending his territory with his fists, numbing his hunger with bottles of drink.

Yes, it was true—Brendan had never counted much on luck.

At the stables today, Brendan had grumbled his way over to the general's mare. He had started to feel the melancholy rise in the last few weeks, depression coiling like a snake in the pit of his stomach. The same low spirits had plagued him for years—leaving, then returning with a vengeance he had come to dread. So, it didn't much surprise Brendan when the horse had reared at his touch, throwing him against the fence. He'd sat in the infirmary, his pain feeding the beast inside, when, like a flame in the night, luck had finally nodded her head in his direction.

He knew who the doctor was, of course. They all knew—stories had grown into a frenzy at the thought of a woman doctor working right here in this camp. He'd laughed along with the rest of them, conjuring an image of a woman so hideous and desperate she would take the occupation of a man. When she had entered the tent, her assistant tripping over himself to please her, he'd seen nothing of the ogre they'd imagined.

She was beautiful. Her skin glowed like a pearl against the copper of her hair, with flashing dark eyes and perfect pink lips. Although she was short, she carried herself with the height of a woman who knew her true measure. Most of all, he'd realized as she spoke with him, she was kind and nurturing like the mother he'd never known.

He'd spent an hour thinking after she left, both his pain and his low spirits soothed by their brief encounter. Brendan Murphy had found a woman he could marry.

JOHN MCKAY SAT across from Clara, plates from the general's kitchen in front of them: chicken with gravy, carrots, potatoes, fresh biscuits, and pie for dessert. Somehow, he had even managed to obtain a decanter of wine. Dinner hour was over, and as they sat in the corner of the mess tent, only a few men filtered through. As John made small talk, Clara mapped out her thoughts carefully.

He'd recovered quickly from the shock of seeing her with

Rebecca by the stables. Too quickly. Very smoothly. Whisking Clara away, he'd chattered about everything from the details of the battlefield, to bemoaning the endless rain, and to the news that Clara's sister was engaged. Clara had stopped at that, curious, and then felt sick at her betrayal to his charm.

As much as she longed to, Clara could not confront him. In dealing with men, particularly the ones she had studied with and learned from in medical school, she'd learned that she must negotiate with caution. To call John out would ensure a rapid trip home—and her days of independence would be long gone. Without him as her willing chaperone, she would be shipped back to her mother's lair of misery. Clara had spent the winter attending every event in society— endless cups of tea, elaborate dinners, and even one secret rendezvous with a politician's son. Even that had been tedious and boring, and she'd dreamed of holding her scalpel once again.

"... your father has already agreed. What do you think about that, Clara darling?" John was looking across the table at her, his dark blue eyes attentive.

Clara shook her head. "I'm sorry, I was just lost in thought. It was a busy day. What did you say?"

John sighed, folding his hands in front of him. "I was talking about marriage. Our marriage."

She choked on a mouthful of wine, though it wasn't really a surprise. It was true that in recent weeks she'd felt a growing affection for John. Fond memories of long summer days spent together as children had helped fan the idea of romance in her heart. But now ... surely, he'd noticed the exchange in the stable yard. He couldn't think of her as that stupid. Although, Rebecca was not yet showing her pregnancy. It was almost certain John didn't know about the baby.

Clara set down her glass. This was not going to go over well.

"No. I'm sorry, John, but I won't marry you." She refused to let him down easily. She may have resolved not to confront him about Rebecca, but he didn't deserve any pampering. It did not matter that he was a man of wealth and prestige. He had assaulted a woman against her will.

His eyes became like steel. "Your father has agreed."

"I heard that part, John. I do not wish to be married. I won't give up my medical practice."

John threw up his hands in exasperation. "Clara, you cannot possibly plan to waste your life away stitching up broken men on a battlefield. That is not a life for a woman of your position." He nudged his chair closer to hers. "I've waited for you, Clara. Four years since I first asked you, before you went away to medical school. It's time."

Clara's temper flared, blinding her previous resolution. "I hardly call having your way with unsuspecting women waiting, John. What of that laundress? Forcing yourself upon working women is not appropriate for a man in *your* position."

John started to rise from his seat, and for a moment, Clara felt her heart quicken in fear. "You're a child." His fist came down on the table, spilling her glass. "A spoiled little girl. Women like that are practically begging for attention from a man like me. Maybe if you hadn't made me wait for so long—"

"I'm sure my father will be interested in hearing all this.

He should be here any day now." She crossed her arms and glared at him.

John rolled his eyes and scoffed. "Oh, your father. It's a shame he's been so indulgent of your little doctor charade. If you were my wife—"

"This conversation is over," Clara interrupted him, standing. "I will never be your wife." She collected her coat and shrugged into the sleeves. She turned and ran directly into Dr. Cameron, who had been approaching them from across the mess tent.

"Miss Thomas. I hope I am not interrupting your evening meal." Dr. Cameron threw a wary glance at John, making her wonder how much of the conversation he had overheard.

"Thank you, Dr. Cameron. I was just leaving. I am rather tired after today's excitement." She smiled warmly at the older man, some of her anger dissipating.

"Ah, yes. Please, call me Ian. I have to say, Miss Thomas, I was pleasantly surprised today. I checked on all the men after you left, and your work was excellent." He smiled down at her, his face a story of lines and wrinkles.

"Well, I had a very patient teacher," Clara said, eager to please the doctor. She would take any opportunity to hone her skills and work amongst the men.

"It's those damn minié ball bullets." Dr. Cameron shook his head. "Pardon my language, but as a surgeon, I cannot advocate for anything that will shatter the bone completely. Such a shame."

"I would be happy to help you again, Sir, if you need it."

Dr. Cameron chuckled then, his deep laugh reminding Clara of her father. "I was thinking you might ask. Yes, please come over any time you have completed your regular duties." He glanced back at John. "Good evening, Lieutenant. Miss Thomas."

As Dr. Cameron took his leave, Clara came back to the table. John looked up at her in surprise, a glimmer of hope in his eyes. Without a word, Clara lifted her plate, still untouched. The food was now cold, but she didn't mind. She felt John's eyes follow her as she left the mess tent to enjoy her dinner.

Alone.

THE NEXT MORNING, Brendan was gone from the infirmary. Clara gritted her teeth in frustration at the discovery. She was admittedly cranky, as sleep had not come easily after yesterday's events. She'd mulled over John and Rebecca for quite some time, trying to distract herself by completing her medical journal for the day and then reading a novel by the poor light of the kerosene lamp. In the end, she'd succumbed to the thoughts, lying awake on her uncomfortable cot, staring into the darkness.

"Where is he?" she snapped at Joseph. The infirmary tent was full, and the air putrid. Some of these men might be dead before nightfall, and she didn't have time to chase Brendan Murphy around camp.

"Gone when I arrived this morning, Miss Thomas." Joseph shrugged. "But I saved this." He reached under the table and proudly presented a bedpan full of urine. The urine was tinged with pink, as she'd suspected.

Clara smiled, despite her frustration. Joseph was young

but a quick study. If she ever had the opportunity to open her own medical clinic, she'd offer him a job. She set Joseph to the morning tasks of emptying the bedpans, assisting the men with breakfast, and changing bandages. Joseph had learned, under her careful teaching, to check wounds for signs of inflammation.

She left the tent and walked briskly through the camp, hugging herself against the chill of the morning. As she passed the surgeons' tent, she glanced in. It was almost empty, a reprieve from the busy day before, and the doctors were seated at a table, playing a hand of cards. Clara prickled with jealousy. These surgeons would never come to help her in the infirmary. To them, she was nothing more than an orderly or a nurse. It had been much the same during her time at medical school, being treated as inferior to the other students in the program. She firmly pushed the stray thought aside—being busy in the infirmary was better than being idle at home.

She passed the Irish section at the midpoint of camp, heading straight to the stables. Clara marched past the log where she had sat with Rebecca the evening before and into the yard. Brendan was here; she was sure of it. She spotted him saddling a horse at the end of the riding ring. Passing the gates with her eyes trained on him, she nearly slammed into a massive man.

"Get out of here," he growled through a thick beard. "No one in my stable yard."

"I just—" Clara started, staring up at him. He was thick and brawny and completely intimidating.

The stable master leaned down. She could smell his

breath, foul with a mix of tobacco and onion. "You can have your lover's quarrel later, missus."

"I'm his physician. He—"

"Out."

She scowled as he pointed to the gate. It was obvious there was no arguing with him. Looking back into the yard as she left, she saw Brendan headed their way. After a brief conversation with the stable master, he met her outside the gate, where she waited, arms crossed.

Brendan laughed when he saw her. "I could feel your fiery disposition from across the yard. Are you sure you don't have a bit of Irish in you?" He nodded at her hair. "Though I don't know many Irish beauties with hair as lovely as yours."

"There's blood in your urine." She uncrossed her arms and leaned against the gate, though her heart warmed at his words. "You should be resting."

"Aye, you told me." He gave her an easy smile. "And I told you why I can't."

"I need to examine your side." She indicated for him to lift his shirt. Instead, he pulled the garment over his head, despite the morning chill.

She felt her cheeks grow warm as she examined the bruise on his side, now turning dark green and yellow. She had seen plenty of bodies during her medical practice, but there was something about the way he was standing—like he *wanted* her to look at his naked form. The hair on his chest and arms was a fine dusting of blond, and the lean muscles on his torso flexed as Clara touched his side.

"All right. It looks much better already," she said, standing back up straight, trying to hide that she was flustered from touching him. A glance into the stable yard told her that they had an audience; a few of the men had noticed her touching Brendan and were watching with interest. One gave a whistle.

"My turn next, sweetheart," he jeered, grabbing at himself lewdly.

Brendan quickly put his shirt back on and propelled Clara by the elbow around the corner to a small alcove, where women were busy scrubbing laundry in large tubs of water.

"Let's sit for a while."

"Just for a minute. It's busy in the infirmary."

He nodded and led her to an empty tub. He flipped it over, and they sat together on the small space. Clara caught her breath as their legs touched, her face heating once again as she glanced at the nearby women, wondering what they thought of her sitting alone with Brendan.

"So, a doctor, eh? Haven't met any lady ones before." He flashed a dimpled smile.

Clara laughed, finding his closeness comforting. His scent was different than John's, the aroma of a hardworking man. "Well, there aren't many of us."

And there weren't. Women had only been allowed to attend medical school for the past ten years, and the feat was not easily accomplished even now. If it had not been for her father's large financial contribution to the college, she would not have been accepted into the program. As it were, Clara had been constantly left out—the college had even refused to let her practice on a cadaver, stating firmly that it was no skill for a lady. Her colleagues had complained that her presence was distracting and they constantly questioned her ability to diagnose, claiming that her female emotions got in the way of her better judgement.

"And you? When did you come from abroad?"

He grinned, turning to face her on the tub, his leg brushing against her once more. "Well, I'm no' from anywhere fancy, like *abroad*. Just Ireland, m'lady. We came over on the boat last fall. We were hopin' to come the year before, but ..." he trailed off, looking embarrassed. He got up quickly, making the tub jolt.

"What?" Clara asked. She had been enjoying his company, much to her surprise, and didn't want it to end.

"Nothin' I'd best be gettin' back to work."

"Yes, me too."

He took her hand, helping her up. "Come for supper tonight. I want to see you again."

Clara considered his offer. Surely John would be looking for her around dinnertime, but ... "I'd like that, Brendan. Be careful with yourself today." She reached out and touched his hand again in a farewell.

CLARA WANDERED BACK to the infirmary, deep in thought over Brendan. A young girl waited outside the tent, impatiently hopping from one foot to the other. Her dress had been scrubbed down to the barest of fabric, and her face was filthy. When she saw Clara, she ran over and grabbed her hand.

"Please miss. It's my ma. The baby's coming, but Ma says something's not right."

Clara grabbed her medical bag from inside the infirmary

and hurried along with the girl to where her mother was waiting at the far end of camp. Here, the canvas tents were worn, with holes that had been patched over and over to keep out the rain and scorching sun. She knew that migrants followed the military wherever it went, setting up camp in hopes of earning a few extra dollars. They were not part of the company and, therefore, not part of Clara's duty, but she had treated a few of them anyway.

The woman was in the throes of heavy birthing pains as Clara approached. She leaned against a tent post, swaying from side to side, her voice low and throaty as she groaned. Clara waited until the wave passed before she spoke.

"How long have you been in pain?" she asked, feeling the mother's rigid belly. The baby was head down—a good thing

"Too long," the mother replied. "Since yesterday morning. But this is the eighth. It should be here by now." She started moaning again. The youngest of her children lay nearby on a blanket, just a babe himself.

Clara looked around the tent, noting a few wooden crates that the family used for tables and chairs. She nodded to the girl.

"Set some water to boil. Get three of those crates and bring them here." Clara arranged them in a triangle; one for the mother to sit on and two for her feet.

"Have your waters broken?"

The mother nodded, and Clara gently led her to sit on the crate. Clara removed her forceps from her medical bag—a long scissor-like instrument with a rounded clamp on one end. She doused them liberally with carbolic acid from her bag, prevention against the spread of germs and infection.

After she performed an internal exam, Clara unhooked

the forceps and carefully slid the first side of the clamp into the mother. Feeling inside the woman, she tried to place it around the baby's ear. Then she did the same with the other. Finally, she locked the device together.

"Stand behind your mother, and let her lean into you," she told the girl, who was no more than ten and rake thin. Clara hoped she could support her mother's weight.

Over the next thirty minutes, Clara helped ease the baby out, inch by inch. Her back and shoulders ached as she crouched down low to the mother. The woman was silent other than her grunts of effort, tears rolling down her cheeks.

Suddenly, thankfully, the head slipped free. Clara dropped the forceps, and with one final push, the baby was delivered. The infant was blue. She turned the baby over to pat her gently on the back, but it was as Clara had suspected. The baby took no breath, and no frantic wail pierced the morning air.

The baby lay still.

She placed the baby in the blanket she had prepared and helped the mother deliver the afterbirth. Neither of them spoke. Clara bit her lip to keep her tears at bay but instead busied herself cleaning up.

In the end, the mother refused to take the dead baby. She got up, taking her youngest son with her, and went to the farthest corner of the tent, where a pile of blankets on the ground made up their sleeping space.

"Take it away." Her voice was hoarse. "Take it away from here."

Clara swaddled the infant girl in the blanket, carrying her silently back into the busy hum of the main camp. Medical school had never prepared her for this moment—

carrying another woman's stillborn baby. What was she to do with the child?

Clara felt her throat close and her stomach churn. She walked aimlessly, not noticing where she was. Her thoughts raced, a jumble of mixed words and images swirling in her brain. Sweat poured down her back, though the day was still cool.

"Clara?" A strong hand clamped down on her shoulder, and Clara jumped.

It was her father.

Chapter 3

April 1885

Brendan stared into the crackling fire, his disappointment so potent he could taste it. The popping wood created a shower of sparks that illuminated the darkness around him. It was late, and the ever-present noise of the camp had settled into a soft lull. Voices became murmurs as families sang their children to sleep, and the occasional telltale moan of an amorous encounter filled the crisp night air.

He felt like an overeager fool. He'd spent most of the day filling his head with visions of a romantic interlude with the lovely doctor. He rolled his eyes—he didn't even know her first name. What was worse, he had told some of the men in the stable about his invitation to supper, and Marty had watched him sink into a humiliated temper as the hour came and went without any sign of her. When Marty had picked up his guitar to entertain the crowd with songs of Ireland— something Brendan usually enjoyed—he'd stormed off into the larger camp in search of a drink. He'd joined some men settled around a cask of moonshine, the vile liquor searing his throat and guts. He missed Irish whiskey—hell, right now, he even missed the damned country itself.

Brendan sighed and heaved himself off the log. He rummaged around the edge of the fire's light for a shovel, just about to bank the fire for the night when a movement caught his eye. It was *her*, standing near a tree a few feet away.

She came a bit closer. "I wasn't sure if that was you," she said, her voice low and husky. Brendan could see that she'd been crying, as her eyes were red and swollen. He frowned. He hadn't thought of her as a woman who was easily upset.

"Is everything all right? I was expecting you earlier. It's late for you to be walking through camp alone." He offered her a seat close to the fire.

"I know. How are you feeling?" She sat, hugging herself. "I'm Clara, by the way."

Clara. He smiled. The name fit her perfectly. He paused, taking her in. She seemed different from their previous meetings. Softer.

"Is everything all right?" he repeated, his gaze sweeping over her. "You seem ... upset."

Clara gave a short laugh and looked away, staring into the darkness. He reached out and touched her face, bringing her head back to look at him.

"You can tell me. I'm a fair listener." He wiped her tears away with his thumb. She startled at the movement, so he dropped his hand.

"My father is here. I have to leave. Go home."

He raised his eyebrows. "I don't understand. Why do you have to go home?"

She sighed heavily. "I have to agree to marry ... someone. If I don't agree to the engagement, I have to leave. Tomorrow." She kicked at the dirt with her boot. "The man he wants me to marry. He's ... well, he's not a nice man."

Brendan's heart hammered in his chest. Why had he thought a girl like her wasn't already spoken for? Of course, she was getting married.

He spoke, willing his heart to beat a little softer. "Clara, I don't know you very well, but you don't seem like the type of woman to ... give up without a fight."

She turned to look at him, her eyes sad and forlorn. Brendan fought back a sudden urge to hold her, to gather her in his arms.

"I don't know what to do. I've gone over it a hundred times. I don't want to leave. But ..." She shuddered, pulling her shawl close.

Brendan threw a few leaves into the fire, watching as they shrivelled in the heat, curling until they vanished into a memory. "Well, you could agree to the engagement and stay. Then call it off."

Clara nodded. "I thought of that. My father would be livid, but it could work." She nodded again, her face brightening a bit. "Maybe that's what I should do."

Brendan hesitated before reaching for her hand. She tried to pull away, but he grasped it firmly. "I don't want you to leave. We could try for supper again."

She looked at him for a long moment, and he reluctantly let go of her hand, a faint disappointment washing over him. He wanted her to feel as strongly about him as he did about her.

"Supper," she repeated. She started to say something else

but frowned and shook her head. "That sounds good. But now, Brendan, I should go. I need to wake early to speak with my father." She rose from the log, resting her hand on his shoulder momentarily.

"Goodnight, Clara."

Her figure melted into the night. As Brendan watched the space where she had been, his heart went too.

Clara.

CLARA'S HAND curled into a fist. She had never hit anyone in her life, but the smile on John McKay's face made her wish she could. She stared at the spot where she would get him, right at the corner of his mouth where his lips curled upwards in a sly grin. Clara had tried to speak with her father alone, but he had insisted on breakfast. With John.

"We will keep the news of your engagement to ourselves until after your sister's wedding," her father said, taking a gulp of coffee. He grimaced at the poor quality of the brew.

John nodded, sending Clara a smile that could only be described as a smirk. He reached across the table and took her hand, stroking the back of it with his thumb. It took everything in her not to wrench it from his grasp, but she could not help the scowl that settled on her features.

"Yes, that's best. I must report to the Thunder Bay military base in the autumn, though. I would prefer if we were married before I leave." He reached for his coffee cup, and she slipped her hand out of his, hiding it under the table out of his reach.

Clara had pleaded her case to her father the day before

to no avail. He had come on a routine visit, he insisted. He wanted to deliver the news of her sister's wedding in June to her in person. But she knew her father well. William Thomas was a businessman, and this was his latest transaction; he needed to see the contract to its completion.

She had tried to explain about Rebecca, even mentioning the pregnancy, but her father refused to be swayed. They had struck a deal, he reminded her, when he had agreed to allow her to take this job. She'd agreed to marry anyone of his choosing. Clara hadn't taken the promise seriously; her giddiness over the prospect of a position as a real doctor had clouded her judgment. She'd even taken the rail for the first time—the military had used the Canadian Pacific to gather men quickly from the east and transport them to the prairies when the Cree people and their sons and daughters of mixed descent, the Métis, had stood their ground against the Canadian government.

It was not going to be easy, Clara realized that morning, to weasel out of the engagement. She would need a solid plan and perhaps a great deal of good fortune. Her father and John seemed set on making it happen sooner rather than later.

Looking outside the mess tent, she spotted Brendan and red-haired Marty leading a group of horses through the camp. As they passed the table where she sat, Clara caught Brendan's eye. She gave him a slight smile, remembering his gentle consolation the night before. His gaze slid to her father and John, his face tightening and jaw clenching; he clearly understood the meaning of the meeting.

"Who's that, Clara darling?" John's voice was in her ear, and his hand found hers once again under the table. He squeezed it firmly to the point of hurting. Brendan had turned his head back to look at them, catching Clara's eye once again. He gave a slight nod, and she drew sudden strength from it.

"A patient from the infirmary. And speaking of which," she said, rising from her seat. Her father's eyes widened in surprise at her dismissal. "I have work to do. Seeing as this," she gestured around the table as if it encompassed her future, "is all arranged."

"Darling, that's enough." Her father's voice was firm, and his mustache stood straight out, as it did when he was displeased. "Sit back down, dear."

"I'll see you at dinner, Father." Clara's voice was just as firm. She had done her part and, in return, would stay until the rebellion ended. That was the deal. She gave the men a curt smile and went to work.

THE NEXT FEW days went by in a busy haze. The infirmary was always full, and Clara worked from morning until evening, day in and day out. Her father had departed that morning on his way to a local lumber mill to negotiate another acquisition. William Thomas had begun building his fortune with the waves of families arriving from abroad, hoping to settle and build homes in Canada. She'd been ten when he'd landed an exclusive contract providing lumber to the railroad. Now, he was constantly buying up smaller mills across the country, expanding his reach from coast to coast. Thomas Enterprises had become unstoppable, and her family was among the wealthiest in the country.

Clara made her way through camp back to her own sleeping quarters. It had rained all day, and she wondered if she would ever feel warm and dry again. Perhaps she was crazy—she could be sitting in front of the fireplace in her bedroom back in Ontario, reading a novel, while her maid Isabelle drew her a hot bath. Instead, she was covered in blood, pus, and other unidentifiable bodily fluids and soaked to the bone.

Finally reaching her tent, she ducked out of the rain. Her accommodations were small and held the barest of furnishings. A few wooden crates served as a table and chairs, a cot held blankets and a pillow, a kerosene lamp provided some light, and her personal items consisted of clothes tucked into a valise, her worn copy of *Jane Eyre*, and her medical journals.

A large brown leather case sat on a crate with an envelope on top. A gift from her father? She frowned, checking the envelope. No, it was addressed to Miss Thomas in a scrawling, unknown hand. Who had placed this in her tent?

Her curiosity would have to wait, as she needed to get out of her wet clothes. Clara stripped as quickly as her shaking cold hands would allow and sighed in relief when she was changed into a dry skirt and shirt. She had just done up the last button on her blouse when her tent flap flew open, and John burst in, the whole tent shaking at his intrusion.

"John!" Clara shrieked, appalled. Her hands flew up to cover herself, even though she was now fully clothed. "I've just gotten dressed! You shouldn't be here." Her face grew hot in anger and embarrassment. Her mind turned to

Rebecca, and the chill returned, though now with wondering in which circumstances John had cornered her alone.

He glanced down at the pile of wet clothes discarded on the ground and grinned, wetting his lips. "That's a shame. Came a moment too late." He sat on Clara's cot with no obvious intent to leave. "I've just come to find you for dinner."

She grimaced. She'd hoped to avoid dining with John. In fact, she'd hoped to avoid John altogether, but there were few places left for her to hide in camp. Apparently, her own quarters were no longer private either.

"What's this?" John reached over and snatched the envelope from the top of the brown leather case. "A love letter from an admirer?"

Clara thought of Brendan, warmth spreading inside her. She hoped the note wasn't from him—or maybe she hoped it was. She hadn't seen much of him during her father's stay, but he had come to visit her at the infirmary, and they had stolen away one day for lunch down at a nearby riverbank.

John opened the letter, reading it silently, holding it out of Clara's reach as she protested loudly. He rolled his eyes at the content, then handed it to her before flopping back down on her bed.

DEAR MISS THOMAS,

I hear that you are to be congratulated on your engagement. No doubt the Lieutenant will make a fine husband, and you a beautiful bride.

I've left you a rather odd engagement present—well, odd

to most people, but I think you, Miss Thomas, might rather like it.

This also comes with some news that I have to share. That is, of my retirement. I've been meaning to retire for the last fifteen years, since I served in the Great War Between the States. The thought of settling down in my old age and picking up a tame hobby rather makes me cringe, but my agility is not what it once was, so I must learn to be content with retired life.

I hope you enjoy the gift.

Sincerely yours,

Ian Cameron

GLANCING BACK AT JOHN, Clara opened the leather case. She laughed aloud, her joy filling the small tent. It was an amputation kit, the very one that she had borrowed from Dr. Cameron during her first time attempting the procedure. She picked up the Catlin knife, touching the edge with her finger. It had been sharpened many times, its long blade thin and lethal. She looked over her shoulder at John again. With this, she could force him out of her tent and maybe even her life.

"You should return that to the old codger, darling." He got up from the bed and took the knife from her hand. Clara wondered if he could hear its stories, the limbs that it had taken, the lives changed. He put the knife back in the box and closed the latch. "Darling, you know you won't be cutting men open anymore once we are married." He put his finger to her lips as she started to protest. "Oh, I don't mind the occasional suture or even delivering the odd baby or two, but no more of this." He patted the top of the case.

"And speaking of retiring," he said as he led her outside, holding his jacket over her to shelter her from the rain, "your father and I have discussed mine. I will be leaving the military."

She stopped, her feet landing deep in a puddle. The cold water seeped into her boots and stockings. She narrowed her eyes at John, his face no longer handsome. To her, he was just a snake. "Why on earth would you be leaving?"

John took her arm and propelled her out of the puddle. He waited until they were under the canopy of the mess tent before answering. "I'll work with your father. He wants to retire in the next few years, so your sister's husband and I will take over the company."

There it was. Her insides turned to stone, and her heart hardened even further. This was the life of a woman. She was expected to give up her practice as a doctor so John could advance his career with her family's money.

Clara tasted none of the food she ate for dinner. Her thoughts were singularly focused on one crucial notion: escape.

THE NEXT AFTERNOON, Clara left the infirmary early, feigning a headache. It wasn't a stretch from the truth. Her life felt like one awful headache indeed.

She carried Dr. Cameron's worn leather case through camp, walking like she had nothing to hide. She had already rehearsed the lie that she'd tell John if she ran into him. She was returning the kit to the retiring doctor, just as he had suggested.

As she reached the outskirts of the Irish section of camp, she hesitated, biting her lip. She didn't know Brendan well, as they'd really only talked a few times, but she felt that she could trust him with the safekeeping of her treasure.

She scoured the camp for any sight of him—perhaps he was still at the stables—when a firm hand grabbed her elbow and dragged her behind a nearby tree. Clara yelped in surprise, stumbling over a root, but managed to right herself before she fell.

It was Rebecca. "What are you doing here?" she hissed, her face tense with anger. "*That man* will be followin' you in here."

Clara pulled away from Rebecca's grip on her elbow and set her jaw. "Perhaps." She scowled at Rebecca and walked around the tree back into the camp. "My father has arranged our marriage. We're engaged."

"What?" Rebecca's mouth dropped open before quickly snapping it shut again, her mouth in a hard line. She raised herself to her full height and crossed her arms over her chest.

"I'm not planning to marry him," Clara explained, eyes searching the camp. "But I have to pretend for the time being. I'm here to ask a favour of your brother." Clara held up the leather case. "And he's invited me to stay for supper if that's no bother to you."

Rebecca frowned. "I don't think my brother is the right man for you. He's got some problems, and you seem a bit ... soft." She looked Clara up and down from head to toe.

Clara bristled. "I am *not* soft."

Rebecca gave Clara a long look, her jaw working with

unsaid words. "Well, don't say I didn't warn you," she said finally, glancing over Clara's shoulder.

"Clara! You're here. I hope you're staying for supper," Brendan's voice rang out. He and Marty came up behind her, Marty carrying a map. He had a guitar slung over his back. Brendan took Clara's hand and led her away from Rebecca and Marty. She smiled, a thrill shooting through her at his touch. He was so different from John. As they walked, Clara explained the amputation kit.

"You'll have to keep it out of the reach of children, of course. But do you mind?" Clara turned to him, her hand still in his. It was warm and rough; nothing like John's soft grasp.

"Of course, I'll store it for you. Let's go find a spot for it now." He brought her over to the tents, all marked with the Canadian Red Ensign on the flap. She released his hand as they reached his tent, preparing to wait outside. Instead, Brendan pulled her in. His tent was like hers, except his personal belongings spilled out of a rucksack leaning up against his cot. It was the second time she had been alone with a man in a tent in as many days, and she felt scandalous, though this time, her pulse quickened with excitement.

Brendan took the case from her grasp and nestled it under his cot, chuckling. "I'm no' sure what kind of woman you are, asking me to hide your knives under my bed." He brought her hand to his lips and brushed her knuckles against them. "But I would like to find out more."

Clara's breath caught as their eyes met. Brendan was unlike any man she had ever known, so forward with his affection. She moved a step closer to him, the tent creating a secret space for her quickening heart. She had never kissed a man like Brendan before, though a few had certainly tried. This time, she would allow it, a warm desire already pulsing through her body.

His hands slid around her waist and then up her back. Brendan pulled her close and leaned his face toward hers. His lips were gentle and soft and full of promise. Clara smiled against his mouth, inviting him to continue.

Brendan broke away with a grin. "You like me, don't you?" He touched her lips with his thumb. "I like you too, Clara Thomas. You make everything seem better."

He kissed her again, leaving her breathless, before opening the flap to the tent. "Supper?"

THE CAMP SUPPER WAS DELICIOUS. It was Irish stew made with barley, potatoes, carrots, and small morsels of meat. Clara had eaten what seemed like a thousand bowls of stew since her arrival in camp a few months ago, but none as tasty as Rebecca's. Or maybe it was the company. The Irish camp was lively and heartwarming, filled with laughter, jests, and friendship. After the meal was done, Marty carried his guitar to the fire and sang, his voice a deep baritone that filled the night air with the magic of comradery and love. Brendan held Clara's hand again, and she felt the stoniness inside her melt away.

She stayed late, sitting around the hearth with Brendan, Marty, and Rebecca. Clara listened to their talk thick with their brogue and Irish slang as they swapped stories. Marty left the fire for a moment, returning with a flask, which he passed to Brendan, along with the map Clara had seen earlier.

Spreading it out on the log, they explained their plans to Clara. They were heading to British Columbia, the most western region in the country. The rebellion had filled their collective pockets with enough coins to arrive before winter if they left by June. They would travel west by horse, crossing the districts of Saskatchewan and Alberta. Once they reached the range of mountains stretching from north to south, they would travel across them via the newly constructed railroad.

"Here." Brendan pointed to a spot in the far west, almost touching the ocean. "We'll settle here. Folks say it's the most fertile ground in the whole west, perfect for farmin' and raisin' a family." He threw a sidelong glance at Clara, and she couldn't stop the swell of happiness that bloomed inside her. It made her forget her troubles with John. A rebellious plan formed in her head.

Clara stared at the spot on the map, her thoughts racing. It seemed perfect. She looked back at Brendan, frighteningly aware that her whole future was about to change. *West.*

Chapter 4

May 1885

CLARA SAT UP WITH A START, BLINKING IN THE PITCH dark.

"Miss?" It was a voice that had woken her. "Miss Thomas?"

It was Joseph at the tent flap.

"Coming, Joseph." She lit the kerosene lamp beside her cot and rubbed the sleep from her eyes. She dressed quickly in only a dress and blouse —foregoing her corset and petticoat—with her jacket over top.

She stumbled through the darkness of the camp behind Joseph, the moon above doing little to guide her steps at the midnight hour. In the past weeks, she had been finding it difficult to concentrate, her thoughts circling in uncertainty. The decision to move west had excited her at first but had lately filled her with a foreboding sense of dread. Could she really leave her family behind? Be a homestead wife? She didn't know a thing about farming. Her domestic skills were embarrassing, as she could barely cook a meal. As the weeks passed and the departure date grew closer, her doubt became overwhelming. To add to her confusion and exhaustion, her relationships with Brendan and John monopolized her time —dinner with John each evening was followed by late-night visits with Brendan. Clara struggled to recall the last moment she'd had entirely to herself.

The sick man lay beside the open fire, the sheen of his fevered skin apparent even before Clara put down her bag. He groaned loudly, the smell of vomit pungent on his breath. Another man sat beside him.

"Were there no' a proper doctor?" the friend said to Joseph, the disdain visible on his face despite the low light cast by the fire. "I didn't ask ye to bring yer girl."

"Oh, for heaven's sake," Clara muttered, her mood souring by the second. She lifted the man's shirt and palpated his stomach. He groaned again when she pressed his right side. *Appendix. Damn.*

"Let's get him to the surgeon's tent," she ordered Joseph. "I need more light. And fetch Dr. Cameron too, please."

"Naw. I'll no' let him go with this witch." The sick man's companion spat into the fire, the saliva hissing as it evaporated. "She'll hex him or cut off his manhood."

"I am not a witch," Clara said, seething. "Your friend has an inflamed appendix. It must come out or he'll die." She nodded to Joseph, who disappeared into the night.

Clara took out her scalpel from her medical bag. She pressed the area again, and the man groaned. Perhaps she should begin without assistance. If the appendix burst, the risk of infection and death was high. She had never removed one, though, and the light was poor. She glanced over at the man's friend, who eyed her warily, reminding her of her colleagues in medical school whenever she had to perform for a group. Deciding to wait for Dr. Cameron, she slipped her scalpel into her jacket pocket.

It took more than twenty minutes for Joseph to return, and Clara had spent the entire time worrying—for the man in front of her, but mostly for herself. Her thoughts circled back to the looming decision to leave. Brendan had been ecstatic at her request to join them on their journey, of course. He'd even scrounged up a spare rucksack for her belongings, as her valise was entirely unfit for travel by horse for days on end. He'd whispered words of marriage into her ear, while stroking the back of her hand lovingly. For the first time in her life, she felt excited about the prospect of a husband.

"What seems to be the trouble here?" A doctor that Clara didn't recognize had returned with Joseph in tow.

She stood, brushing off her skirt. "Sir, I am fairly certain it's the appendix. It's causing him pain when I press in at the lower right side."

The doctor shouldered past her. "Take him to the surgeon's tent," he ordered two men behind Joseph. Clara followed closely behind, then stood in the corner of the surgeon's tent as Joseph lit kerosene lamps. The doctor did not hesitate at his first incision but soon let out a curse.

"Hell. Damn thing's ruptured." He glared over at Clara, who shrunk under his gaze. "He'll be dead by morning." Her stomach churned at his words as the chance to save the man had passed.

With that, the doctor stalked out of the tent.

FOUR HOURS LATER, Clara rode out of the military camp with John at her side. She'd tried to resist accompanying him, exhausted by the night's events, but John had arranged for them both to have a day on leave. When she pressed for more details, he said it was a surprise. Clara gritted her teeth—surprises from John McKay could prove treacherous.

There had been a moment of great discomfort when Brendan was assigned as the stable hand who helped her find a horse for the day. John had his own, of course, but Clara had arrived at camp by stagecoach with her father. Brendan found her a black mare with a saddle to match, working silently. The jealous anger rolled off Brendan in a manner that made her flush with unease. Their relationship had developed rapidly in the past couple of weeks; their kisses became frequent, and his hands caressed places she had never allowed a man to touch before. She found herself thinking of him when she woke in the morning, fingering lips that felt bruised by Brendan's increasing urgency.

"Where are we going, John?" Clara asked for the fifth time once they were out of earshot of the stables. She glanced back to where Brendan stood watching them, his eyes dark and narrowed.

John grinned at her, his enthusiasm making her smile despite herself. "Regina."

"Pardon me?" Regina was a three-hour ride away.

John laughed at her expression, tossing her a wide-brimmed riding hat. "I need to deliver a message to the General. The rebellion is over. We'll be returning home by the end of next week."

A wave of panic washed over Clara. Would she be ready to leave, too? Marty and Brendan wanted to wait until they had received their final pay before heading west, and then they would slip away, unbeknownst to John and her father.

John looked over at her, flashing her another lighthearted grin. "I thought you might like to do some shopping. There are a few shops there. Perhaps a souvenir to bring home to your sister."

And not much else, Clara thought. She'd stayed in Regina with her father the night before she started work at the camp, and the shops were not what she'd called well-stocked. Still, she might be able to find items that would be useful for her trip west. That uncertain fluttering rose again at the thought of frontier life, but Clara pushed it aside. If she did not leave with Brendan and his companions, she could forget about ever practicing medicine again. That thought alone bolstered her resolve, and she squared her shoulders in determination.

"You might also find a dress for our engagement party." John's voice brought her back to her current reality—engaged to a man with a vile secret, who was only interested in her father's money. Yes, it was certain that she needed to leave him behind.

Arriving in Regina at midday, sore and tired from the long ride, they lunched at the saloon, a welcome break from the repetitive menu of the mess tent. Afterward, while John checked in with the local military, Clara meandered down the main street of Regina. It was certainly different from the bustling streets of Toronto, which she missed dearly. Clara had enjoyed her four years at the Toronto School of Medicine, perusing the city in her free time, exploring the shops, and observing the busy lives of the people in Canada's ever-diversifying mosaic: wealthy and poor, whites, the Indigenous peoples, and Chinese; men and women from all backgrounds and walks of life.

Clara stopped in front of a medical supply shop, fingering the purse full of coins John had given her, as her own salary and allowance from her father were stored safely at the bottom of her rucksack. She had also sewn an emergency sum of bills into the lining of her jacket pocket —she reached in to check on it—and found the rounded stem of her scalpel. She had forgotten to remove it after last night. She made a mental note to put it away in her medical bag at camp before she accidentally sliced her thumb open.

Clara was pleasantly surprised by the supplies available in the shop. She bought bandages, gauze, new suturing needles, catgut thread, a bottle of chloroform, carbolic acid, some cocaine paste for topical pain management, and laudanum for more serious treatments.

She was about to head back to the dress shop when she saw a woman seated off the main road behind a small table covered with a variety of jars and sachets. Several children ran around her, and one bumped into the table. The mother scolded her children, but they were too enthralled in their game to pay her heed.

Intrigued, Clara walked closer to take a better look. Plants, roots, and herbs were stuffed into the jars. *Remedies.* Clara was overjoyed at the woman's collection. What luck!

By the time Clara was done, she had collected remedies for headache, indigestion, influenza, blisters, inflammation of wounds, and abscess of the tooth. The woman smiled wide when Clara handed her the coins, her weathered skin wrinkling around her eyes and nose.

Turning to leave, Clara spotted another larger bag on the ground. "What's in there?"

The woman looked down. Not meeting Clara's eyes, she murmured, "Remedies for women."

Clara understood her hesitation. Many women hoping to rid themselves of an unwanted pregnancy would use herbal remedies, but they were illegal and only used in secret.

"Do you have anything to prevent pregnancy?" Clara blurted out. She hadn't expected to ask, but ... she touched her lips. *If* she were to marry Brendan, she would need it, as she had no intention of travelling while pregnant. The journey would be long and arduous, and early pregnancy could make a woman feel rather ill.

The woman nodded, glancing carefully around to make sure no one else was nearby. "I have enough for about six months."

"I'll take it." She bought the entire supply and the woman's mortar and pestle. The woman packed everything up in a sack, tucking the female supplies at the bottom, away from prying eyes.

John was looking for her when she arrived back on the main street, and his eyes widened when he saw her carrying a burlap sack over her shoulder.

"Clara, what in heavens did you purchase? No, wait, I don't even want to know." He rolled his eyes but took the bag and packed it carefully on the back of her horse, which was tied to the hitching post in front of the saloon.

"Did you find a dress?" He smiled at her, his nose red from the long ride in the sun.

"I didn't look. But John, I am sure my mother will take care of all that." She was eager to head back to camp. It was a long ride, and she hated riding in the dark. Besides, Brendan was likely to be in a foul mood if they arrived too late.

John grabbed her hand. "Just a quick look. I want to approve, and I know your mother will have other ideas." He winked, and she laughed in agreement. Her mother was not known for her weak disposition.

He led her to a dress shop down the street. Lo and behold, in the window hung the most beautiful dress she had ever seen. John put his hand around her waist and drew her close, resting his chin on her shoulder. "See? It's perfect."

The dress fit like it was made just for her. It was light green, its fabric glossy and bright. There was a high slit in the side, where the white underlayer peeked through, making it seem as if Clara were floating on a cloud. The bust was low enough to be fashionable without being immodest. And the most exquisite detail of all: the dress was embroidered with tiny roses, and a small gem sat in the centre of each one. When Clara twirled, she sparkled.

John had paid the dressmaker before Clara finished changing. The woman packed the dress carefully in brown paper and tied it with a string.

"Congratulations." She smiled at Clara, her eyes crinkling at the corners. "You'll make a beautiful bride."

Clara felt a twinge of guilt. The dress was expensive, and she would never marry John McKay. She felt the woman's eyes on her—perhaps sensing the truth—as they left the shop.

❧

It was past dark when they finally arrived back at camp, the moon bathing them in its soft glow. Clara bade goodnight to John and carried her sack and dress to her tent. She packed the medical supplies and remedies into her rucksack, then laid the package containing the dress on top. Perhaps she would leave it behind, as he might be able to return it.

She heard a bang outside her tent, followed by a curse. *Brendan.* She lifted the flap of her tent. He was trying to right the cooking pot he had knocked off a nearby log. Oats were spilled over the ground. Likely someone's breakfast had just been ruined.

Brendan swayed as he walked over to her. "Clara?" he said loudly, scowling at her. He was clearly very drunk and grabbed onto the frame of her tent for support.

Clara left her tent and took his arm to steady him.

"You shouldn't be here," she hissed, though he had already likely woken everyone nearby. "And you smell like the bottom of a whisky barrel."

"Why are you so late?" he slurred, his sour breath washing over her. "I thought you hated that man."

"I do," Clara whispered, trying to hush Brendan. "But we rode to Regina and back. It's a long journey."

He let her walk him back to the Irish section of camp, and Clara led him to sit by the fire, which now burned down to glowing embers.

"I thought you'd run away with him," he slurred, slumping forward, too close to the fire. Clara pulled him back, settling him farther away against a log.

"Of course not," she said, her tone terse. The sleepless night before, followed by the long day, had caught up to her, the weariness settling into her bones.

"I love you. I know you think that's crazy, but I do." His eyes were glazed by the spirits, but he still managed to flash her a dimpled smile.

Clara touched him, her fingers running over the bristles of his unshaven face. Sometimes he reminded her of a boy wanting to be consoled by his mother. "I know." She leaned over to kiss him gently, ignoring the smell and taste of whisky. "I need to sleep. And ... you need to sleep this off." She turned to leave, then remembered. "The rebellion is ending. We'll be sent home next week."

He took her face in his hands and kissed her again. "I can't wait to start our life together. Just the two of us. Well, and Rebecca and the baby. And Marty, too, I guess." They laughed together before Clara got up.

"I'll see you tomorrow," she whispered.

She hadn't walked far when she ran directly into John. He stood, frozen, blocking her path, his arms crossed over his chest. Her mouth went bone dry, and a lick of fear unfurled in her belly. Had he followed her?

"You stupid girl." His face was as cold as the biting night air.

Before Clara had time to respond, she found herself face down in the dirt. Small rocks bit into her skin as John pressed his hand against the back of her head. She tried to cry out, but she couldn't move under his strength.

"A stable hand? That's low even for you, Clara," John's voice was thick in her ear as she struggled against him. "If you're willing to be with scum like him, you shouldn't mind rutting here in the dirt with me."

He pressed down harder on her head, sending her heart thumping into her ear like a horse's hooves thundering down a deserted path. He was going to rape her, right here in the open camp. Surely there had to be someone around to help her, despite the late hour. Gasping for air, she nearly choked down a mouthful of soil. The cool night air hit her thighs as he lifted her skirts and drove a knee between her legs, sending panic screaming through her body.

No! Clara summoned all her strength, fighting to roll away from him. John responded by shoving harder against the back of her head. At this rate, he was going to suffocate her. Clara forced herself to relax, feeling his hand release slightly in response.

She managed to suck in a shallow breath.

"That's a good girl." She heard the buckle of his pants clink open, his knee still firmly pressed between her legs. Her thoughts raced as she squirmed under the weight of his body. She couldn't scream with her face pressed to the ground. He was too strong for her to get away. If only she could find a rock to throw back at him or something sharp to …

Scalpel. It was still in her pocket. John's bare thighs pressed against hers. She only had a few seconds.

Her hand slid down the length of her body into her pocket. *Wrong pocket.*

Her movement had alerted John. He grabbed her hand with a vicelike grip.

Clara gritted her teeth against the pain and reached the other hand down. *Got it.*

She thrust her hand wildly back over her shoulder. *Please, God, let it hit him. Please.*

The scalpel hit something solid. John cried out; the pressure moved off the back of her head. Wasting no time, Clara lifted her head, inhaled as deeply as she could, and screamed into the night.

She managed to scream once more before John rolled her over to face him. Blood ran down his face. His fist clenched, and he spat at her.

His knuckles came at her fast and hard. Her world went black.

SHE WOKE SUDDENLY, gasping for air as if she had been underwater. Strong arms lifted her easily, wrapping her in a comforting warmth.

"It's fine, lass; I've got you." Dr. Cameron's eyes were close to hers, and his forehead wrinkled in concern. "I'm just going to set your nose."

Clara cried out as the doctor reached for her. It was excruciating, and the edge of her vision blurred again. Her face throbbed in pain, and the coppery taste of blood filled her mouth. Dr. Cameron glanced over her shoulder, where shouts rang out, and the sharp slap of fists on flesh resounded. She tried to follow his gaze, but a wave of dizziness had her sinking to the ground.

Then Joseph lifted her up, carrying her away. His face was pale, and his brow furrowed as he walked briskly through the camp. He carried her into her tent and set her gently on the cot, then disappeared back into the night. Returning with a bowl of water and a rag, Joseph lit a lamp, knelt, dipped the cloth in water, and gently wiped her face.

Dirt and blood came away with the cloth, and she hissed at the sting.

He looked up at her, his eyes worried. "Miss, did he—? Dr. Cameron needs to know."

She froze. When she was unconscious, had he ...

"No." She choked on the word, her voice raspy. She wasn't sore anywhere except for her face. "He tried, but no, I don't believe so. I ... I stabbed him with my scalpel."

Joseph raised his eyebrows and he laughed, before remembering himself. He set the rag down. "Miss, you should rest. I am sure the morning will bring ..." He stood, ready to leave the tent.

"Joseph!" she called. "Please, don't leave me alone." Her voice shook, hot tears trickling down her cheeks, making her nose sting. "Please."

He nodded and sat on a crate at the far side of the tent. "I'll be right here, Miss. Don't worry. Please rest."

She reached into her rucksack and found the bottle of laudanum. Turning away from Joseph, she uncorked it and took a shaky sip. The drug worked fast, and she felt the cot envelope her as she slipped away into a deep, dreamless sleep.

CLARA WOKE to the sound of voices outside her tent. She struggled to open her eyes, the lids glued together by a sand-like crust. Her face throbbed as the events of the night came rushing back to her. It was still dark, though the small kerosene lamp filled her tent with a flickering light. Joseph was asleep in the corner, his head resting in his hands.

"Clara ..." It was Rebecca, her voice tinged with anger. Where was she?

"No. I'm telling you, Becca; she'll be naught but trouble for us."

Clara stood, a little unstable on her feet, the laudanum making her limbs heavy. She lifted the lamp and went to the tent flap, finding Marty and Rebecca outside, locked in a heated discussion. Rebecca's hands were planted on her hips as she glared up into Marty's face.

"Clara." Marty stared at her and winced. Her face must look awful.

Rebecca didn't meet her eye, her gaze fixed on the ground. "We're leaving, Clara. Now. Brendan wants you to come."

"It's the middle of the night."

"Aye, and Brendan beat that lieutenant within an inch of his life. He managed to get away before they locked him up. But it'll be prison in the morning ... or worse."

Clara took a deep breath. That must have been the fist-fight she'd heard while Dr. Cameron set her nose.

"I'm coming," she resolved. "Let me get my things."

She turned to enter the tent when Joseph moved out of the shadows, likely now aware of the entire plan.

"What is he doing here?" Marty growled. "He'll alert the guard."

Clara looked cautiously at Joseph. He shook his head, his expression unreadable in the darkness. "Miss, are you sure? Your father—"

Clara nodded. She was sure. There was nothing this side of heaven that would convince her to stay with John. "Yes."

Joseph sighed in resignation, and Marty shifted impatiently behind her.

"Marty, I don't have a horse. I'll have to ride with one of you until I can purchase one." She frowned at the dilemma, as each of them had their own packs to carry as well.

Joseph's hand was on her shoulder. "Miss Thomas, take mine. Please, I insist," he added when Clara started to protest.

"Thank you, Joseph." She was overwhelmed at his generosity as he slipped off into the night to gather supplies. She bit her lip, swallowing back the tears. She could not appear weak in front of Marty, or he would change his mind about allowing her to come.

It was decided that Marty would take Clara's pack as Joseph and Clara snuck to the stables. Clara would meet Marty and Rebecca outside the migrants' camp. If she didn't show up within an hour, the others would know that she had been detained.

"Ready, Miss?" Joseph had brought her a canteen and, surprisingly, a pistol in a worn leather holster. He showed her how to attach the holster around her waist with a belt, the handle of the gun faced forward for an easy draw.

Clara nodded, grabbing the kerosene lamp to guide them on their way to the stable, its light falling in an eerie shadow around the tent. She'd placed the parcel with the beautiful green dress on the cot. She hadn't wanted to bring any memory of John with her.

She nodded again. "Yes, I'm ready." Then, on an impulse, she reached back down, taking the dress in her arms. She would make new memories. *Damn John McKay to hell.*

When they found Rebecca and Marty, silver streaks of light stretched over the horizon, the memory of night fading fast. Three horses were saddled and ready, another packed with their goods. Brendan was waiting for them, hidden in a forest nearby.

"Goodbye, Miss Thomas. Stay safe. Write."

"Joseph." Clara flung her arms around his neck, clutching at him. "Thank you. For everything." Lowering her voice to a whisper, she breathed into his ear. "We're going to Langley, near the Fort. Tell my father, please."

As they rode into the milky morning, Clara felt an uneasy calm settle over her. She fought back the tears and persisted forward, forging a hope that carried her into the day.

Chapter 5

June 1885

THE DAYS AND NIGHTS BLED INTO ONE ANOTHER AS THE four companions made rapid distance from the military camp. Marty pushed them to ride hard, concerned about being followed. After the first few days, Clara's back ached, her nose throbbed, and she feared she might lose balance on her horse from exhaustion. On the fourth morning, she voiced her concern.

"Marty, we need to rest today." She hobbled over to the fire where Rebecca was making a simple breakfast of oats.

"Aye. I'm with Clara," Rebecca said, stirring the pot hung on a makeshift hook. "Maybe it's a good day to head into the next town and be wed."

Clara agreed, glancing over to where Brendan still lay sleeping. It would be not a moment too soon—once leaving the camp, they'd coupled off in their sleeping arrangements. She'd been surprised to realize that Marty and Rebecca were physically affectionate and planning to be married as well.

Around the evening fire, Marty's hands would start to explore Rebecca's body, leaving a line of kisses down her neck. The two of them would disappear soon after, their giggles turning to sounds of a low, deep desire that left Clara feeling a little nervous, with a stirring that ran from her belly to her thighs.

Brendan's hands had started exploring too. Clara woke from her sleep to find him removing her nightdress, his mouth moving over her breasts with a nip and pull that made her look forward to being married, and quickly. The next night was more of the same, with his hands moving lower, demanding more. He wasn't going to wait much longer to be intimate, she'd realized. Although the incident with John was still fresh in her memory, she pushed her thoughts away. Everything would be different with Brendan.

She'd dug into her rucksack and found the herbs she'd bought from the Cree woman in Regina, a concoction of Queen Anne's Lace and smartweed that Clara would make into a daily tea. Used regularly, it would help to prevent pregnancy. She wouldn't tell Brendan, of course, as he would likely frown on her decision. Waiting until they were settled into their new life was the right thing to do, she'd told herself firmly. Truthfully, Clara viewed motherhood with a certain trepidation. It wasn't just the pregnancy itself—though she had seen plenty of danger and loss even in her short medical career. Perhaps it was her upbringing that tinged her feelings about having a baby. Clara's mother had never seemed to have much interest in children, even her own.

Their wedding was a small affair. They stopped in Saskatoon, a small town north of Regina, and although the minister gave Clara a dubious look at the sight of her bruised nose and face, with the help of a few coins, he married the four of them that afternoon.

"Let's celebrate," Marty said, digging into his saddlebag for some money, "with dinner at the saloon."

Brendan dug into his bag, too. "Clara and I are getting a room above. I'll no' spend my wedding night sleeping in the dirt." His anticipation of the night ahead was clear, and he grabbed Clara's hand with a grin. She grinned back, an eager warmth spreading over her. Although she knew that the first time could be painful for women, she had no doubt Brendan would be a kind and patient lover.

Sitting down to dinner in the saloon, Brendan ordered a bottle of whisky for the table.

"Brendan," Rebecca said, giving him a wary glance, "not today."

"Just to calm the nerves." He winked at Clara, wetting his full lower lip. "Look at my beautiful wife. She's enough to make any man feel nervous."

After the dinner of venison, fresh vegetables, and biscuits was over, the whisky bottle was half empty. Rebecca grabbed it, the amber liquid sloshing, and made for the stairs. "We'll just save this for tomorrow, then."

Brendan's fist came down on the table, reminding Clara of John. She stared at her now husband as he growled at his sister. Rebecca looked at Clara with pursed lips.

"Fine." She put the bottle back on the table with a *thud.* "Enjoy your night, then."

Brendan rolled his eyes. Clara looked at him with surprise—his usual mild manner was gone. Clearly, the whisky had taken hold of him. Unease crept into her gut. Surely, he didn't plan on consuming the whole bottle alone.

"Brendan," she said, taking his hand and giving him a charming smile. "Let's go upstairs."

Brendan ignored her, and his eyes fell on a group of men playing cards nearby. "You go upstairs. I'll be up in a while."

She frowned, her temper starting to flare. The hour was already late, and she was weary from the long days of riding in the summer heat. "It's our wedding night, Brendan. Maybe we should—"

But he was standing up, striding over to sit at the table with the men. Clara swallowed back her disappointment and headed upstairs to her room alone. She took her time getting ready for bed, still hopeful that he would come to join her, but after an hour, she went to sleep without him.

When she woke in the morning, she found the bed beside her still empty. Where had he been all night? A bitter resentment settled in her throat as she got dressed and made her way back down to the saloon. Brendan was asleep, slumped over on the tables where they'd eaten the night before.

"This yer man?" A plump barmaid came over to Clara, hands on her hips. "Owner wants him out. Ya might want to take 'im over to the river. He's been sick all over 'imself."

Clara heard Rebecca and Marty making their way down the stairs as the barmaid left. Her cheeks flushed with shame, and tears pricked at the corner of her eyes. It was certain they would know that she'd spent her wedding night in solitude.

Rebecca took in the scene with a knowing eye. She kicked her brother in the leg. "Get up, you drunk." When he didn't respond, she leaned down and grabbed his ear. Brendan woke with a yelp. "Get down to the river and wash. We leave in an hour."

After Brendan stumbled out the door, Rebecca looked at Clara and Marty. "Breakfast?"

❧

CLARA SPENT her honeymoon in town, setting up a temporary medical clinic outside the lone post office. The first day had been slow; people were reluctant to trust a woman doctor, especially one who looked like she had been in a fistfight at the local saloon. But after she'd extracted a particularly painful tooth for the mayor, word had spread.

Even Marty had been impressed by the goods she brought back. The mayor had been kind enough to pay her in coins, but most folks offered what they could: six eggs, two pike fish, a blanket, a small sack of oats, a sack of flour, some carrots, and even a jar of honey.

And so, it continued: they travelled west from dusty small town to dusty small town, resting for a day or two while they earned what they could. It hadn't been part of their plan to work and travel, and although it slowed their progress, it allowed them to keep the money they'd saved. Marty expressed his worries constantly about their pace of travel, how they would survive the winter on a homestead arriving so late in the season, and Rebecca's advancing pregnancy.

After their wedding night, Brendan had apologized for his drunken behaviour, bringing Clara a bouquet of wild-flowers he'd collected from a nearby riverbank. They'd consummated their marriage the night after in an open field under the stars. She'd forgiven him already, pushing the bad memory away as he made love to her in the gentle way she'd anticipated.

They stopped in the town of Medicine Hat, a small community just north of Fort Walsh. Like all the places they'd halted, it was made up of a few shops along a dirt road that made up the main street. Most had no resident doctor, only a barber who would pull a tooth or stitch a wound if necessary. Often, there was not even a grocer but farmer's wives and daughters who had set up tables selling corn, milk, eggs, and the occasional side of meat. Clara had started to realize that her city days were a thing of the past, and this was a vision of her life to come. It was just as well; she had caught sight of herself the day before in a mirror in the general store and had barely recognized the stranger that looked back. Her face was now healed from the altercation with John, but in its place were freckles that spotted her browned nose, cheeks, and forehead. Clara's secret vanity, her hair, no longer hung in its loose cherry brown waves. Weeks of rarely bathing and sleeping outdoors had tangled it into something resembling a lion's mane.

The day was incredibly busy. The farther west they migrated, folks were already anticipating her arrival. Word had spread about the travelling woman doctor, and although sometimes they just came to goggle at her, most of the time they came with their various ailments—rotting teeth, inflammation of old wounds, boils and blisters, insomnia, and chronic coughs and aches. It was a different pace from the infirmary, and Clara started to dream of setting up a permanent clinic once they'd settled in British Columbia.

One afternoon, as she turned the corner, on her way back from the market to where Marty had set up camp, Clara stumbled upon a thin, bedraggled girl curled up on an old feed sack. She was sleeping, but it was obvious she was severely malnourished. There was little flesh on her bones, her cheeks were sunken, and she had dark shadows circling her eyes. She had wares for sale spread out on the feed sack. Among them lay a small medical case. The size and shape of the case looked like it might be a set of syringes, which was something Clara didn't have in her collection of instruments.

Dropping the sack of potatoes she was carrying, Clara gently shook the girl's shoulder, who woke and sat up with difficulty. The girl, more of a young woman, was Chinese. Clara tried to hide her surprise. She'd seen many people of Asian descent on their journey— now that the railroad was complete, many were searching for jobs or migrating to new destinations, typically in families or as a couple. She had seen men travelling alone but never a woman.

The young woman squinted up at her, trying to focus her vision. "Wha d'you want?" she slurred with a thick tongue.

Clara squatted beside her, forgetting about the syringe set. This woman was severely dehydrated and on the brink of starvation. She took out her canteen, which was still half full.

"Drink this." The woman snatched the canteen and took several gulps. "Slowly," she added. "My name's Clara. What's yours?"

The woman shifted on the feed sack, and bruises showed through her tattered dress. There were even some on her neck. Clearly, she had been through quite an ordeal.

"Jo." The young woman nodded over at the sack of potatoes. "Is that food?"

Clara raised her eyebrows, this time not bothering to hide her surprise. Jo was not a Chinese name; in fact, Clara's middle name was Josephine. "Yes. Or no. I'll get you something to eat, but not that. Is Jo your real name?"

Jo shrugged, turning her face away. "That's the name they gave me. Before they made me leave."

Clara's frown deepened. She wasn't sure she wanted to know who *they* were and why they had made this poor girl leave. "Jo, I'd like to trade for that." She pointed to the medical case. "Do you mind if I open it?"

Jo narrowed her eyes but nodded. She passed the case to Clara.

Flicking open the latch, Clara let out a quiet shriek of glee. There were four syringes—glass barrels, oval plungers, and hypodermic needles. "I'd like to trade," she said, looking at Jo's thin frame, "for two days of meals. And some coins." Her companions might be upset at the loss, but Clara's daily earnings far surpassed what the men were able to bring in, and Jo needed the money more than they did.

Jo's eyes widened in agreement. Clara helped her gather her belongings and slowly walked her to their tent. Marty and Rebecca sat by the fire while Brendan lay nearby with his hat over his face, taking an afternoon nap.

Marty stood when they approached, a warning in his voice. "Clara. What's going on?"

Brendan sat up quickly, clearly alerted by Marty's tone. "No," he growled, taking in Jo, who stood beside Clara. "Whatever you're thinking, Clara, the answer is no."

Clara's ire rose at his quick dismissal. "I've already traded, I'm afraid." She held up the small case with her new treasure. "These are valuable medical supplies. I'll feed her with my own coins if I have to. I hardly need your permission, Brendan. Or money."

Brendan's handsome face turned dark with rage at

Clara's assertion. He marched over to her, glowering. "Don't speak to me that way. Take her back, Clara. Now."

"No. She eats here. I promised her two days." Clara stomped her foot, raising herself to her full height, which was only as far as Brendan's chest. She wouldn't let him stop her from helping Jo.

"Enough." Rebecca's commanding voice came from across the fire. She pushed herself awkwardly off the log and strode over, planting herself between them. Her belly had begun to swell in recent weeks, and Clara knew that riding made Rebecca sore and uncomfortable. "You two look like squabbling children."

She turned to face Brendan. "I remember being that hungry." She gestured at Jo, whose face was red from the heated discussion about her. "I know you do too, Brendan Murphy. She eats here."

"Fine." Brendan's face turned petulant at his sister's reprimand. "But don't expect *me* to." He picked up his hat, gesturing to Marty, and strode off towards town.

Marty looked up meekly at Rebecca, unsure if he should follow her brother.

"Aye. Go make sure he doesn't drink away all his coin." Rebecca rolled her eyes towards the sky, shaking her head. "Clara, go get the girl some stew. It'll be just us ladies here tonight."

Clara went to the hearth and filled bowls for herself and Jo. As she carried them back, she glanced up to the darkening sky coming in from the east. There was bad weather ahead.

~

THE NEXT MORNING, Clara woke early, chilled. Their makeshift tent had done nothing to shelter them from the rain, and she'd spent the night curled in a tight ball, trying to stay warm. The men had returned sometime in the night, but Brendan positioned himself at the far end, away from Clara.

Jo was next to her, oblivious to the damp conditions. Clara had given her some of her clothes—they were nearly the same height, although her blouse and skirt hung off Jo's skeletal body. Regardless, Jo had been overjoyed at the gift and the food. She'd eaten four bowls of stew, stretched out over the hours of the evening.

Carefully extracting herself from the tent, Clara went outside and found her rucksack stowed under a large oak tree, protecting it from the night's storm. Rebecca was up, starting the fire to cook breakfast, but Clara was desperate to bathe. It was a chilly morning, but she'd discovered a private nook at the nearby stream the day before. Unpacking some of her belongings, she found the bar of soap that she'd been using sparingly, as it was a treasure brought from home. She brought the soap to her nose and inhaled deeply—honey, lavender, and a faint whiff of jasmine made her sigh in pleasure. Clara had shuddered at the use of the vile lye soap in the military camp, a concoction of rendered animal fat, ash and water. She refused to wash and not smell clean.

Clara made her way down to the stream, carefully avoiding the mud that had appeared overnight. She stripped off her clothing down to her undergarments. Then removing her shift, she entered the stream. The temperature made her squeal as she plunged in up to her waist.

"Clara, it that you?" Brendan's voice came through the

clearing. He stood, watching her, his eyes roaming over her unclothed body.

"Brendan!" Clara's voice rose, surprised. She smiled before swimming in further to cover herself modestly. Husband or not, she still felt uncomfortable being undressed in front of him. "Are you coming in?"

"No." His voice was sharp, still angry from their argument the night before. Clara felt a sharp sting in the back of her throat at his rejection. "I've just come to tell you that we've decided to leave. Today. With the weather and all." He lifted his eyes to the clouds, which remained dark. "Becca's made breakfast for us and your ... friend. After that, we're packing up."

Brendan turned, leaving Clara alone to wash.

CLARA PUSHED the oats around in her breakfast bowl, knowing she had to say goodbye to Jo. She'd made up a purse of coins that she would give to her, but it still didn't seem like enough. There was nowhere for Jo to go, no one who would take her in. Once the money ran out, Jo would be in much the same situation, dying on the streets. She looked over at Marty, who was watching Clara carefully, his ginger brows furrowed. Finally, he sighed heavily and whispered in Rebecca's ear.

Rebecca nodded, her eyes finding Clara's across the fire.

Marty grabbed Brendan by the elbow, taking him around the oak tree, out of earshot. When they returned, Clara could feel their eyes boring into her back.

"What?" she said, turning around to face them. "What have I done this time?"

Marty crossed his arms and exhaled loudly. "Can she do laundry? Cook? Help out?" He looked over at Jo, who was helping Rebecca fold blankets.

Clara nodded, her heart alight in understanding. She threw her arms around Marty and looked to Brendan. He was standing with his arms crossed, giving Jo a wary eye. Clara bit her lip—clearly, he was still not pleased about the decision.

"She can come. Not live with us when we get there, mind you." Marty's voice was soft, and he was looking at Rebecca with love in his eyes. "Becca's going to need help. And, well, it's better than her wasting away here, all alone."

She looked over at Brendan again, who, to her relief, gave her a brief embrace. "Just this once." Brendan's voice was firm. "I'm your husband now. You need to learn to listen to me, Clara."

Marty smiled at them both. "Clara, she rides with you."

As they rode into the drizzling morning, now a party of five, Jo turned her head back to look at Clara. "Thank you," she whispered, "for saving my life."

Chapter 6

July 1885

IT WAS A SCORCHER OF A DAY. THE SUN LASHED OUT mercilessly, its rays unforgiving, drawing life force from both human and beast with an unrelenting determination. Even the crickets had stopped their damned infernal chirping.

They were mere days away from Calgary, where they would sell the horses and board the train west on the final leg of their journey. The heat had slowed them down considerably. For the past four days, they'd started at dawn and had been forced to stop at midday for the sake of both the horses and riders.

Brendan sat with his bare feet dangling in the creek, Clara's pistol in his hands. He stroked it, admiring its elegant beauty. The barrel and the stock were trimmed in gold, with an intricate engraving on the surface. It was an expensive weapon, something he would never have been able to buy in his lifetime. It suited Clara, though, because Clara was exactly that: out of his reach.

Brendan fingered the engravings down the barrel and then back up again. He spun the chamber with his thumb before cocking the hammer.

"Brendan. Put down the gun." His sister's voice was heavy, lazy with exhaustion. She was under the shade of a nearby tree with Marty, who sat, head bowed over his guitar. He'd plucked out the same damn tune so many times in the last week that Brendan had been tempted to steal the guitar and toss it on the railroad track.

Brendan ignored Becca's reprimand. He idly wondered if Clara would rescue him, stitch him up, and nurse him back to health if he accidentally shot himself in the leg. Or perhaps she was already fed up with him. Perhaps she would leave him to bleed out, as he probably deserved.

He took a long look down the dusty dirt road into town, where Clara had gone to mail her letters. She'd taken to writing by the fire each evening, smiling to herself as she jotted down her news. Brendan wasn't sure what she was writing or who she was writing to, but he always wondered if the letters were about him. After leaving the close community of the military camp, reality came to light, and he realized that he and Clara were nothing alike.

He had known, of course, that they were raised differently. Wealth oozed out of her; it was in the way she walked, talked, and even in the way she made love. Brendan sighed heavily, raking his hand through his blond hair. He knew their marital intimacy disappointed her. Brendan had never had a problem with the ladies before—he *was* dashingly handsome, after all—but with Clara, he was nervous from start to finish. He'd taken to disappearing at bedtime, to the saloon if possible, just to avoid seeing her careful pretense that she was, in fact, satisfied.

"Clara's coming back just now." Marty's voice pierced the haze of the sluggish air. He looked over at Brendan, a spry look in his eye. "Over you go, Brendan. Give that wife of yours a kiss."

Brendan sighed, reluctant at first, but then perked up. It was nice enough to sleep under the stars, after all. Perhaps he would steal Clara away tonight, down to the river.

He met her on the road, her excitement visible from a few paces away.

"Brendan! You won't believe it!" She waved a newspaper in front of her, face alight with exhilaration. "I'll wait ... let's discuss this with the others. Ooh, but here, I got us all something."

She paused in front of Brendan and put her finger to his lips, gently opening them. She popped something in, and suddenly his mouth was filled with the spicy sweetness of licorice.

"I know I shouldn't have spent the money," Clara admitted. "But it's so hot; I thought we needed a treat." She held up a bag full of penny candy. Standing on her tiptoes, she tipped her face up to his for a kiss. "Don't tell Marty," she murmured against his lips.

"Marty's no' the boss," he murmured back, pulling her close, his body responding to hers. She was so damn beautiful, and her curves fit perfectly against him.

They walked back together, fingers entwined. Brendan took the bag of candy, handing it around. When he got to Jo, hidden around the backside of the tree, he hesitated slightly but then offered her a chewy toffee.

"Not that candy," Clara interjected. "Her teeth are loose." She came and chose a hard lemon drop from the bag, instructing Jo to enjoy it slowly in the corner of her mouth. Taking Jo's hand, she led her around to where the others were seated.

A pang of resentment grew in Brendan's chest as the two women sat down together, side by side, their skirts spread out over the grass. Ever since Jo had joined their band a few weeks before, she and Clara had become inseparable. Even Becca had grown attached to Jo, giving her the affection of a younger sister.

"Look," Clara said with excitement, opening the newspaper and spreading it on the rough horse blanket Marty had set down under the tree. She looked up at Brendan expectantly, her dark brown eyes glittering.

"What does it say, Clara?" Brendan's cheeks grew hot at her presumption.

"It's right there, Brendan. About farmland for sale." She pointed again at the article, looking to Marty now. An uncomfortable silence blanketed them. As Clara continued to gaze at their faces, her own cheeks slowly flushed.

"You really are daft sometimes, Clara," Becca scoffed as she pushed herself off the ground with great effort. Marty stood quickly to offer his assistance. "We can't read. You don't see us writin' letters by the fireside. Lord knows we weren't raised posh like you, with all your fancy schoolin' and such." She paused, stretching her lower back to relieve the weight of her pregnant belly.

"I can read," Jo announced. Everyone turned to her in surprise. "And write." She pulled her knees up close to her chest, seemingly startled by the sound of her own voice. She rarely spoke to any of them besides Clara and certainly not voluntarily.

"I can read some too, actually." Marty sank back under the tree, a peach in hand, the juice landing in droplets on his beard. "Let's take a look." He reached down for the newspaper, but Brendan snatched it away.

Brendan held the paper in front of him, trying to make sense of the letters on the page.

"Do ya think I'm thick, Clara? Is that what your problem is? You married an eejit?" His voice rang loud and angry, and he saw Clara grasp Jo's hand once more. A fury started to build in his chest, hot and burning. His hands started to shake, the newspaper quivering noisily.

Becca stood up from where she had been rummaging through their food supplies. In an instant, she was at his side, gently taking the newspaper from him.

"Take a walk, brother," she said, reaching into the pocket of her dress. She handed him a single coin. "Go have an ale in town."

Becca turned to Clara and pointed to the pistol, now lying abandoned on the ground. "Put the gun away, lass. We wouldn't want that getting into the wrong hands, now, would we?"

CLARA SAT up from where she had been lying with Jo under the stars. She sighed before finishing her story. "... and then Fantine drew her last breath, leaving Cosette alone." She glanced over at Jo. It was dusk now, and her features were soft in the twilight.

"No. You can't stop there. I'll be wondering all day!" Jo sat up and took another handful of berries from the bowl.

It had become an evening ritual. After collecting the ripe berries after dinner, Clara would tell Jo another part of the story. She was relaying her favourite novel, *Les Misérables,* and Jo loved the story of Jean Valjean as much as Clara. The berries were part of Clara's diet plan for Jo, as she had seen the signs of scurvy: loosening teeth, darkening of the skin on the arms and legs, fatigue, and redness of the eyes.

"Sorry." Clara sat up to face her new friend. "I should go and collect Brendan from the saloon before it gets too late."

After having to pay the tab on Brendan's long nights at the saloon a few times now, Clara had taken to going over earlier to bring him back. It was a task she had begun to dread. Some nights, he would be exuberant, playing darts with the men or chatting with a pretty barmaid. On other nights though, Clara would find him slumped at one of the grime-laden tables, heavy with the burden of his sorrows. She wondered which man she would find tonight, swallowing back an ever-growing sense of loneliness. This was certainly not what she had anticipated married life to be like.

She walked Jo back to the tent, then took the pistol and belted it to her waist. Walking alone had frightened her ever since John's brutal attack in the military camp. She suppressed an eye roll at herself—she'd had to ask Marty how to use it, but its weight on her hip made her feel safe.

Clara pushed her way into the saloon, bracing herself against the stench of sweaty men and sour ale mixed with a hint of vomit and fornication. The saloon could be called the Great Unwashed, judging by the dirty glasses that littered the tables. A quick glance around told her that Brendan was not playing darts tonight. She'd probably find him near the back.

And he was, staring into a sweating glass of ale. Clara breathed a sigh of relief, noting that at least it wasn't whisky tonight. She slid into the seat next to him and put her hand on his back. Something troubled him greatly, and she longed to fix it.

He looked over at her, his eyes clouded. "Clara. I was just going to leave and find you. I wanted to see my beautiful wife."

"That would have been nice, Brendan," Clara said truthfully. She missed the Brendan she had met in the military camp, who'd seemed happier and loved her deeply. This man seemed like a stranger in the same body but miserable, full of remorse and regret.

He gave her a half smile, his blue eyes untouched by her attempt. "I think I'm broken, Clara."

"You're not broken." Clara rubbed the back of his neck. She wished she could steal him away and make love to him until his sorrows disappeared. "I just wish I understood what's troubling you." She took a steadying breath, calming her anxious thoughts. Brendan's distress seemed to delve deeper than anything Clara had ever known.

"I tried to end it once. This." Brendan gestured to himself. He suddenly looked much older, exhausted. "It was Becca and her damn bottle of ipecac that gave me another chance. But some days, I wished she hadn't bothered." He laughed dryly before drinking the rest of his ale.

Clara watched him silently, thinking back to what she had learned in medical school. Treatments for men and women with disordered minds would include solitary confinement in hospital, blood-letting, and cold plunge baths. She firmly pushed the thought aside. Brendan was not insane; he was only melancholic.

Clara stood, reaching out her hand. "It's time to sleep," she said firmly. "We'll be leaving early before the heat sets in."

As they walked back together, hand in hand, Clara wondered about Rebecca and her bottle of ipecac. Had that been what Rebecca had tried to warn her of way back when they first met? It seemed that Clara and Rebecca were overdue for a heart-to-heart talk. She needed to know more about this man she had married.

Marty stopped the group as they reached the outskirts of Calgary. It was early morning, but the sun was already blazing in the sky. Clara took off her hat to tuck her hair underneath—having it around her neck was sticky and uncomfortable. A trail of sweat already trickled down her back.

She looked over at Brendan with his hat tipped low to keep the morning rays from reaching his eyes. He seemed to be happier over the last couple of days, much to her relief. Hopefully, their marriage would have a chance to strengthen once their tiresome journey was over.

He caught her eye and gave her a smile. "Excited for the train?"

She nodded. Agreeing to ride double with Jo had been fine at first, but after weeks of sharing the same horse in the blistering heat, she was ready for some space.

"We're finally here." Marty grinned broadly. Clearly, Clara was not the only one excited to get off the road. Rebecca, too, beamed at her husband.

"Ladies, you'll need to wait with our belongings while Brendan and I sell these fine and faithful beasts," he said as he stroked his horse fondly. "Then, we buy our tickets." He glanced at Jo, raising his eyebrows slightly.

"I'll pay for Jo," Clara announced. "I have some money left over from my father." She had a bit left, anyhow. Paying Brendan's tab at the saloons along the way had drained her funds significantly. "I've hired her as my assistant for when I open my clinic. She can work off her passage."

Marty's eyes widened, and he looked over at Brendan, who'd lifted his hat to stare directly at Clara. The disapproval radiating off both men was almost worse than the heat from the sun. Having a working wife was nothing to be proud of, but she refused to succumb to their outdated ideas. She was a trained medical professional and would put her skills to good use for as long as possible.

"Don't argue," Clara cut off any objection from the men, shaking her head. "We won't last the winter without me working, and you know it. We're too late in the season to plant many crops."

Brendan cleared his throat. "What about our family? You'll be with child soon enough."

Clara caught her breath slightly. So far, only Rebecca had questioned her about the tea, and Clara had passed it off as a remedy to help with her monthly period. Now that they were nearing their destination, Clara's feelings about pregnancy hadn't changed, and she wasn't particularly eager to start a family once settled, either. She wanted to open a clinic, and having children would force her to stay home. Perhaps in another year or so, she would feel ready to have a baby.

"We'll talk about that when it happens," Clara said, sliding off her horse. "While you men are collecting a good price for the horses, I need to visit the apothecary." She might as well stock up on remedies while they were in a decently sized town. Calgary was larger than most of the places they'd stopped at along the way and was growing rapidly due to the completion of the railroad. From where they stood, the Hudson's Bay Company shop towered over the rest of the buildings. The former fur trading company still sold its wares in a large department store. Even the roads were in better shape here, as boards were laid along the sides for pedestrians. She could imagine that in a few years, Calgary would rival Toronto in size.

Leaving Jo and Rebecca to watch their supplies, Clara headed into town, relishing the moments alone. She walked briskly, knowing her time was limited. Apothecary shops were usually hidden deep in the crevice of a lonely alleyway and could be difficult to find.

Ten minutes later, she found herself lost, as she had turned off the main road after asking directions from a married couple. Instead of ending up at a small shop filled with oils, dried roots, and herbs, she was in front of a rather large hotel. She was just turning to make her way back to the main street when a familiar voice made her stop.

"Miss Thomas!" A man dressed in an expensive suit came barreling down the front stairs of the hotel. "I thought I saw you from the window. I must say, you look dreadful, my dear."

"Bonjour, Jacques," Clara said to her father's footman, fingering her tangled hair. A surge of panic rose in her throat. Should she run? "I suppose my father is looking for me."

"Indeed." Jacques gave her a dark look. He had been her father's man since Clara was a baby and knew their family intimately. "He's gone down to the railway station every day for the last three weeks, at noon and three o'clock. It's a shame such a busy businessman is frittering away all that time."

Clara bit her lip while Jacques snapped his fingers at the hotel concierge. Her father would be livid; there was no doubt. Perhaps she could see him, just to assure him that she was safe.

"We'll go to the station right away, Miss Thomas. To let him know you've been found."

Within a minute, the concierge brought around a stage-coach, ready for departure. As Jacques helped her into the coach, her heart was pounding in her ears.

"My friends—"

"Will have to wait, *Mademoiselle*. Or is it *Madame* now, as your father fears?"

Clara said nothing as she looked out at the city moving past her. Tears started to fall, hot on her cheeks. This was it, then. She would be whisked away without a trace, taken back to her family home and John. She wondered how long the others would look for her before giving up. Would Brendan be disappointed at her disappearance or slightly relieved? She couldn't answer that with certainty or determine her own feelings on the matter.

"And we've arrived." Jacques held his hand out for Clara, his mouth dropping open in shock at the sight of her hands.

"My dear, really, when was the last time you bathed? I have never seen you in such a state."

She looked down at her fingernails in dismay, imagining what her mother would think if she were here. One could not have tea with dirty hands and broken nails. Hopefully, her father wouldn't notice such things.

They walked into the railway station, where her father was sitting on a bench near the entrance, staring off at the door to the platform.

"Sir?" Jacques addressed her father. His head snapped towards them, and he jumped up from the bench. "Here she is, finally! Miss Thomas appeared on the street, right outside the Hotel Alberta."

Clara gasped as her father crushed her in his arms. Her tears, which had dried, once again fell freely as she breathed in his cologne, a blend he ordered from Paris every fall. All her grief and worry came pouring out at his familiar smell. For a minute, they stood in an embrace, then he pulled away to look at her.

"Clara—"

"Father, I'm so sorry. I shouldn't have run away. I can see how I've worried you." She sat on the bench, putting her head in her hands. She saw now that she had behaved rather childishly, running away with a man she barely knew.

Her father sat beside her and lifted her chin up. "My dear daughter, I am the one who is sorry. You told me about John. I ignored your fears about his character. I ... I am the one who led you to make such a rash decision." He shook his head, swallowing back his own emotion. "Dr. Cameron told me of the entire situation."

Clara wiped away her tears and held out her hand to her

father. Despite everything, she had missed him dearly. "And John?"

"Court-martialed. Honourable discharge." Her father scoffed. "As if that's any real consequence. When I am through with him, the man will have no position left in society. How dare he try to take advantage of you?"

"Sir?" Jacques interrupted them, "Should I send the carriage away? Or would Miss Thomas like to bathe at the hotel, perhaps?"

"My friends," Clara said, watching her father's reaction, "and my husband, are waiting."

Her father's face remained calm, but he pulled his mouth into a tight line. "Very well." He turned to Jacques. "We will pick up her companions on our way back to the hotel. They probably all need to bathe. And I should very much like to speak with this husband of my daughter's."

Chapter 7

July 1885

HER STOMACH TIGHT WITH NERVES, CLARA SAT ON THE settee in her father's suite at the Hotel Alberta, twirling her now freshly washed hair around her finger. Jo and Rebecca were still in the bathroom, trimming their hair and fingernails, chattering away like excited schoolgirls. They'd dressed in the cleanest of their clothing, although everything was travel-worn and dirty.

Her father was downstairs in the dining room with Marty and Brendan, with Jacques likely nearby, listening to every word. Clara had desperately tried to be a part of the conversation, but her father would not be persuaded, sending her to bathe with the other women.

What would her father say? Could she stand up to him for the life she wanted? And what exactly did she want? She wanted to be useful and take advantage of her medical training to help people. Her marriage to Brendan wasn't exactly everything she'd hoped for so far, but she didn't want to go home to the tedious life of a socialite, that was for certain.

There was a sharp rap at the door.

"Clara? Are you ladies finished?"

Clara let her father into the room, nearly swooning at the sight of a large carafe filled with coffee. She missed good coffee more than all her fine dresses and jewelry combined.

Her father addressed Rebecca and Jo, who had emerged from the bathroom. "Lunch is waiting downstairs for you and the men in the café. Jacques is waiting at the top of the stairs to escort you." He looked directly at Jo, whose brow was wrinkled. "Don't worry. I've informed the hotel manager that you will be joining them. He has secured a private lunchroom for your comfort."

Upon entering the hotel earlier, the concierge had frowned at them in their bedraggled state and had firmly announced that the hotel was for whites and people of fine upbringing only. Only when Clara's father had intervened did the concierge let them inside.

After Rebecca and Jo left, Clara's father held up a plate. "I've brought us scones with ham or cheese." He poured them each a steaming mug of coffee, added a dash of milk, and let Clara enjoy her first sip before he spoke.

"Darling, you are a woman now, and you must make your own choices. But that man downstairs is not your equal. It's not because he's poor," he added quickly, taking a bite of his lunch, "but because he's uneducated, controlling, and, I daresay, a bit lazy."

Clara said nothing and took another long drink of her coffee, wondering if her father suspected Brendan's fondness for whisky. She knew she would not get to voice her opinion until her father was finished stating his, so she took another sip, enjoying the steaming hot goodness.

"Truthfully, I see a lot of myself in you, Clara. You are determined, you have grit, and you like to see the best in people. But I've made mistakes, darling. And marrying someone to whom I was not equally matched was one of them."

He didn't need to explain—Clara had always known that her mother and father were stark opposites. Her mother only cared about appearances, while her father knew the value of hard work and good people.

"We can wrangle you out this, Clara, if you want. He seems determined to ... keep you, but, in my experience, a man always has a price."

Clara finally spoke, smoothing the fabric of her rumpled dress. Her palms were damp, and she willed her voice to remain calm. "I know Brendan has his faults, but I don't want to leave him. I don't want to return home and have my scandal talked about endlessly until I finally find another man, probably not much different from John, to marry. And I don't want to give up medicine. I am becoming a good doctor, Father."

She stood, drifting over to the window. Their travelling gear had been brought up to the room, and she looked directly at the amputation set from Dr. Cameron, lying on its side in the corner. She would not live a useless, mundane life.

"Yes." Her father cleared his throat. "I thought you might say that. If it were just me, I would allow you to set up a practice in Toronto, but I'm afraid I wouldn't win that battle with your mother. But farming is a hard life, Clara. I hope you understand that."

"Will you let me go?"

Her father didn't answer. He stood from the table and went to the safe in the corner of the room. He withdrew a rolled piece of paper.

"It's a wedding gift, I suppose. But," he added, his voice growing firm, "more importantly, it's in my name. It's yours."

Clara unrolled the paper he handed her and found a deed: one hundred acres of farmland in British Columbia. She threw her arms around her father.

"Thank you, Father. I hope you'll come to visit."

Clara's father pulled her away, a serious look on his face. He reached behind her and took out a purse of coins from his bag. He handed it to her, the weight of it considerable in her palm. "I will, dear. You can be sure of that."

FOR THE ENTIRE first hour aboard the Canadian Pacific train, Clara sat in solitude. Jo had been sent to the colonist car, as the regular cars were for white passengers only. Many Chinese men had laboured on the construction of the railway, some even losing their lives due to dangerous working conditions, and yet they were segregated. Clara wondered if Jo's family had been part of the railroad or if she had a family at all. Jo had not shared much about herself.

Brendan, Marty, and Rebecca had disappeared immediately upon embarking on the train. On the ride to the station in the hotel stagecoach, they spoke with each other but avoided eye contact with Clara. She realized from their silence that they hadn't known the extent of her family's wealth until meeting her father and that their relationship would now change. It didn't matter that she had given it all up to come and live with them; she would always be an outsider.

She had just closed her eyes for a rest when she felt someone slide into the seat next to her. Brendan's familiar scent mixed with the smell of the hotel soap was unmistakable. She took a peek, wondering in which state she would find him. He was staring straight ahead, fingers clasped nervously. No doubt, the conversation with her father had been difficult for him.

"Becca's feeling sick with the motion." He looked at her expectantly, but his grey-blue eyes were troubled. "Do you have anything she can take?"

"No, everything is in the baggage car." She frowned thoughtfully. "Do you still have that bag of penny candy?"

"Aye." Brendan reached into the pocket of his trousers. "A wee bit sticky now, though." He cracked a small grin at Clara, and she gave one back, feeling relief at the small gesture.

"A peppermint one. Or maybe the licorice. It should help settle her stomach. And she should face the direction we're travelling. A bit of bread might help, too."

"Aye. There's no dining car, though," Brendan said. "The weight is too much travelling through the mountains. Conductor says we'll stop to eat." He heaved himself back out of the seat, heading back to his sister.

After he left, Clara stared out the window at the changing scenery. Already they had started to travel to a higher elevation, and the vegetation grew sparse. The excitement of travelling through the mountains had been dampened by the farewell to her father. She had stitched a pocket into the insides of her skirts for safekeeping of the money he had given her. The coins weighed heavy on her lap, a pressing reminder of the life she had left behind. Her father had also brought her a rucksack with items from home—some practical clothing, multiple bars of her favourite soap, her coloured pencils, a fountain pen, a few fresh notebooks, and a bag of coffee imported from his travels. She blinked back tears at his thoughtfulness. Even in his worry, he'd thought to bring her a few of her most treasured things. He'd even gone as far as repaying Joseph for his horse and giving him a position at Thomas Enterprises.

Clara had promised to write her sister and mother and apologize for missing her sister's wedding. Lastly, she was to send a telegram when they arrived and set up a bank account. Her father would not allow her to starve, he promised. She had not yet told the others of her acquisition of farmland with a homestead, as she already felt embarrassed by how spoiled she seemed.

Brendan thumped back into the seat beside her, startling Clara out of her solitude. He offered her candy from the sticky bag. "I wasn't sure you were coming with us. I thought ... well, I thought maybe you'd had enough of me."

Clara turned back to the window, avoiding his eyes. There was truth in his words. "I wasn't sure you wanted me to come."

He reached for her hand. "Clara, of course I did."

Looking at him, she swallowed back the sting in her throat. Already her father felt a world away. She had made her choice, but if she was honest with herself, she wasn't sure now that it had been the right one.

"I love you, Clara. I know I have some problems, but that's goin' to change. No more whisky. I'm going to do right by you—and our family." He stroked the side of her cheek.

Clara sat up straighter in her seat at the mention of a family. "I love you too, Brendan. But ... why don't we wait to have children? Just enjoy ourselves? Get to know each other a little more?"

His hand jerked back suddenly. "Don't be absurd."

"I'm not. I only meant—"

"You don't understand." Brendan's voice was loud, and other passengers turned to look at them. "You have a family. One that obviously cares about you. I only have Becca. No mother or father. I want my own children, Clara, and I don't want to wait. I'm already thirty-one."

"All right," Clara said to stop him, her cheeks hot from the stares of the woman across the aisle.

They sat in silence, listening to the ghostly wail of the train speeding down the tracks.

"Are you barren? Is that why you wanted to run away from the Lieutenant? Hoped you could sucker some poor man into a childless marriage?"

Clara turned, furious. Tears came to her eyes at the hurtful accusation. "I am not barren. If you must know, John had many ... indiscretions. He had violated women before me. And he would not allow me to continue my medical practice. I couldn't live my life like that."

Brendan scoffed, shifting his body far away from hers in the seat. "Well, I guess the fine Lieutenant and I have that in common. You're hardly my first lover, Clara. Nor the best." He continued, oblivious to the tears that now streamed down Clara's face. "You *will* be minding our children. And the homestead. If you have time to doctor after all that, be my guest."

He pushed himself up from his seat with a huff, disappearing into the belly of the train.

AFTER SPENDING the night at the Glacier House Lodge, just outside of Roger's Pass, the group got back on the train, and the second day of the journey began. They travelled for another long day through British Columbia before lodging again. Finally, the last day of their journey began. While Brendan had come to Clara to make amends and even made the most of their private room in the evenings, she still felt the acute sting of his hurtful words days later. Had she made a crucial mistake? Perhaps her father had been right—she and Brendan were from very different worlds, and he seemed to have difficulty showing her real affection. Would he really make good on his promise to leave the whisky alone?

They were sitting as a foursome, pooling their remaining money. Clara was helping Marty create a budget in one of her new notebooks. It would be lean for the first winter, that was certain.

"One wagon ... cost?"

"Around $70."

"And how many horses?" This was the pressing question. They had sold five horses in Calgary at a fair price, but they would need other livestock for the farm.

Marty looked at Brendan for confirmation. "Two. Farm horses, not riding ones. Sorry, Clara. I know you had your heart set on a riding one for yourself, but I don't think we can afford it this year." He averted his gaze, staring down at his hands. "Unless ..."

Unless her father had given her money. Clara had not divulged the extra purse of coins sewn into her skirts to her travelling companions. She had carefully removed her clothes each evening, hiding them from her husband. She would not have the money for her clinic wasted on whisky. She could see it so clearly—shelves of medicines, herbs, and her instruments. Perhaps she would open a small apothecary on the side.

"Here." Clara showed Marty the deed she had placed in her travelling bag. "This should help. There's just one homestead. We can share for the winter, and then you can build your own in the spring." Then, remembering that they couldn't read, she added, "It's a deed for one hundred acres of farmland."

Rebecca and Marty examined the deed with great excitement while Brendan sat back in his seat, arms crossed. He obviously resented that her father had given her the land as if it were her father subtly putting Brendan in his place. She turned away from him, her own irritation hot in her chest.

Their conversation halted when the conductor's second-in-command burst into the car in a panic. "Is anyone a doctor? I need a doctor or a midwife. Or anyone experienced in women's affairs."

Brendan spoke up, gesturing over at Clara. "My wife is a midwife."

"Excellent." The man looked relieved. "There is a baby

on the way. Quite rapidly, I assume, from the mother's distress."

Clara rose, narrowing her eyes at Brendan. "I am *not* a midwife," she said, straightening her shoulders. "I'm a physician."

"It's just easier than having to explain and have folks asking all sorts of questions," Brendan whispered.

Clara huffed past him. "I'll need my assistant," she told the conductor's second. "A Chinese girl in the back. Goes by the name of Jo." The man paled at her request, but he sent the car waiter, who had followed behind, to the back of the train.

When Jo arrived, they were led to the conductor's private quarters. A small woodstove in the corner heated the room. A bed sat in the other corner, and a large desk was in the middle. The mother was already in the room in the arms of a rather concerned-looking man.

"This woman is a midwife. And ... her assistant."

"No. I'll not have the likes of her in here." The man looked at Jo with disdain as his wife clutched at him, starting the low keen of a birthing contraction.

"Yes, she'll stay," Clara spoke loudly over the woman's cry. "I need an assistant. Unless you would like to volunteer?"

The man started to speak but was interrupted when his wife started to squat down on the floor.

"She's close," Clara said before the man could respond. "I need blankets, clean cloths, some water to boil, a large pan, and your sharpest knife."

"And a bottle of whisky," Jo added from beside Clara.

Clara looked at her curiously, pleased with her assertiveness. "Yes, thank you, Jo."

The husband and other men vacated the room quickly, bringing back the supplies within a few minutes. Jo had already removed the woman's skirts and was talking to her quietly.

"It's my first time," the woman said tearfully between birthing waves. "I told my husband we shouldn't travel, but here we are, three hundred feet in the air on the trestle bridges. State of the art, he says, making me look out the window." She gave a hysterical laugh, then grasped at Clara. "It's starting again."

"I can see the head!" Jo exclaimed as she crouched near the mother.

Clara looked at Jo, smiling at the pleasant surprise. "This is not your first time delivering a baby," she said, disinfecting the knife with the boiling water and whisky. Her medical supplies were all in the luggage car. She should have known better than to let go of her case. From now on, she would be sure to always have it with her.

Jo shook her head while helping the mother-to-be move onto all fours. Clara moved to the front of the mother to offer support, trusting Jo to indicate if she needed assistance. It took some time for the mother to push, but Jo was able to deliver the baby, cut the umbilical cord, and care for the afterbirth.

The mother held a healthy baby boy in her arms. "His name is Joseph," she told them, stroking her newborn son's head. Clara smiled, thinking of her Joseph fondly, while she stitched where the mother had torn. A perfect name. She nestled the woman and her son in the conductor's bed and went to help Jo clean the room.

Jo was sitting on her haunches, collecting the soiled blanket, when Clara caught her hand, looking at her quizzically. It was an invitation to talk, to explain. She knew Jo kept to herself, but she wanted to know more about her new friend.

Jo glanced at the woman in the corner, then back to Clara, speaking in a hush. "After my father died, I was sold to a house of ill repute."

"A brothel?"

"Yes." Jo continued to collect the blanket, then carried it over to beside the pan that held the placenta. "Many of the women there fell pregnant, and I helped deliver their babies." She paused, looking at Clara carefully. There was shame written on her face. "Don't tell the others."

Clara shook her head vehemently, feeling a surge of affection for Jo. "Of course not."

"Sometimes, I helped them use a preventative. I know a bit about Chinese medicine. There's a tea. The same one you drink."

Clara felt her face grow pale, and her mouth went dry. "Jo..."

Jo reached out for her hand. "It's the smell. I would recognize the smell of that anywhere after drinking it every morning for four years."

Clara nodded, trying to calm her thumping heart. She was sure that Brendan would be furious if he found out. "Don't tell the others," she whispered.

"Never."

They stood in silence for a while, watching the mother feed her infant.

"How did your father die, Jo?"

Jo looked away quickly, hiding tears. Her father had been gone a long time, but Clara could see that the wound still ached. She didn't press any further but instead put her arm around her shoulder.

Jo looked up at her. "Do you remember how you asked if Jo was my real name? It's not. My name is Li Na."

"That's a beautiful name. I can call you Li Na if you'd like."

Jo shook her head, wiping the tears with the back of her hand. "No, that girl is gone," she said, her tone sorrowful.

Clara reached her other arm around her friend in an embrace. "Maybe you'll find her again someday."

The whistle erupted from the train as it began to slow its way into the station. The baby, startled by the noise, started to wail. They had arrived at their final station in New Westminster, British Columbia.

Part Two

Chapter 8

August 1885, British Columbia

GETTING OFF THE TRAIN IN NEW WESTMINSTER proved nothing short of chaotic. Their baggage had been thrown haphazardly on the station floor among the throng of passengers trying to disembark. Thank heavens Clara didn't have small children to contend with as well—the woman beside her had four clinging to her skirts while her husband frantically tried to elbow the crowd aside to gather their belongings.

It took almost an hour, but Marty and Brendan managed to find everything that belonged to them. Clara rummaged through her medical bag and rucksack to make sure nothing had been damaged, and, to her relief, everything seemed in one piece.

They stepped out of the station, greeted by a bustle of travellers and shoppers. In the distance roared the mighty Fraser River, named for Simon Fraser, the Scottish explorer who had charted the river in 1808.

Marty and Rebecca found a shop that sold fried fish, and the companions ate in silence, devouring their meal. It was served with bread and fresh tomatoes and was fried to perfection—salty, crispy, and delicious.

"Aye, that was tasty," Marty said, brushing crumbs off his beard. "Let's buy our tickets for the steamboat to cross the river. Our land in Langley is a wee bit farther yet, a day's ride or so. Once we cross, we'll look for some farm horses and a wagon."

They waited in line for the steamboat for nearly an hour, the hot August sun beating down on them. Finally, the steamboat arrived. It was for passengers only, and they carried their baggage, standing together as the boat rocked back and forth in the choppy water. The ride was only ten minutes or so, and soon they were on the other side of the Fraser, in a town named Surrey.

"I need to go to the apothecary," Clara announced, waving off the concerned looks from the others. "Don't worry, no surprise hotel visits this time. I'll take Jo to keep me out of trouble."

"Don't be long, Clara," Brendan said. "As soon as we get the farm horses and wagon, we'll be back on the road."

They found the apothecary quickly. It was a small, squalid place with a rather poor supply. The man behind the counter was seedy as well; tobacco juice ran down his wiry beard, and his silver eyebrows were thick and bushy, giving him the illusion of a grungy wizard.

"Do you have women's supplies?" Clara ventured after finding only a few of the other items she needed.

"No," the man barked. "Those are illegal items. They'll be no interferin' with God's plan for childbearin' in this shop." His eyes flitted down to the gold-plated pistol slung around Clara's waist. "I might be able to find you some to trade for that, though."

Clara scowled, putting her hand protectively over the pistol. "Well, do you have them or not?"

The door of the shop opened, and a man walked through, ushering in a young boy alongside him. He glanced at Clara and Jo, then addressed the man behind the counter.

"Tom, I see you're making friends with the ladies again," he said, sending a grin in Clara's direction. He placed a small stack of coins on the counter. "The usual, and add stinging nettle, cascara, and elderberry."

While the shopkeeper busied himself behind the counter, the man leaned over to Clara. "Don't mind him. He's just an old sourpuss. Not used to the company of beautiful women." He looked down into Clara's basket. "Are you a midwife?"

Clara cleared her throat, looking over at Jo, who smiled kindly. Brendan was right. It was easier to say yes than to explain her profession, but she hadn't worked so hard to become a doctor only to lie about it. "No, actually, I'm a doctor. Trained at the Toronto School of Medicine," she added as the man looked at her in surprise.

"Yes, I've heard that women are being trained now," he said, his expression turning into a smile. "Although you're the first I've met. I'm a physician, too. Well, a farmer first, as you can see." He gestured down to his clothes, which were common work trousers.

He stuck out his hand. "Joaquin Walker. And this is my son, Ben," he added, ruffling the hair of the boy who stood next to him.

"Wah-keen?" Clara repeated, unsure if she was pronouncing it as he had. She had never heard of such a name in her life.

"Yes, it's Spanish. It's spelled J-o-a-q-u-i-n, though, no W, as most Anglophones expect. And your name?"

"Clara Th— Murphy," she corrected, a pang of deep loss resounding in her chest at the change of her name. "My friend, Jo."

Joaquin smiled at them, then took his supplies from the shopkeeper. He plucked an item from his bag and handed it to Clara. "Here you go, Dr. Murphy. You'll be needing this. Best elderberry in these parts."

Clara blushed at the stranger's kindness. "Thank you. That's very kind of you."

He looked at her for a moment, like he had something more to say. Then he was gone, out the door, hoisting his son on his back before disappearing into the dusky shadows of the alleyway below.

ALTHOUGH IT WAS ONLY a day's ride to their new home in Langley, travelling by wagon was tedious and bumpy. Clara's back ached from the constant jostle, and she worried about Rebecca and the baby. After a while, the three women decided to walk behind the wagon on the road.

Finally, they arrived. The town of Langley Prairie was as quaint as Clara had envisioned. There was a church, a bank, a post office, a small grocer, and of course, the saloon. A few people milled about, but for the most part, the dirt roads were bare. Marty stopped in at the bank with the deed, as the bank manager would lead them to their new home.

Standing in front of her land for the first time brought tears to Clara's eyes. The five of them gazed in awe. Their land stretched as far as the eye could see, and the cloudless sky was alive with the chirping of birds. The first twenty or so acres had been previously farmed, and the rest remained untamed, with a thick layer of tree growth at the border. A stream snaked its way along the edge of the property.

"Your nearest neighbour is just beyond those trees," Mr. Murray, the bank manager, told them. "A single man with five children. He's divorced," he said, eager to share the gossip. "Wife took up with another man, if you can believe that. Nice enough fellow, though. Always eager to help with town affairs."

Mr. Murray pushed open the door of the homestead, and a musty odour wafted out to greet them. "Folks died of consumption about a year ago. Been vacant since then. It'll need a good cleaning, but there's all the basics in there. Pots, pans, linens, you name it. Good for you since you didn't come with much." He peered into their wagon, but Clara noticed he astutely avoided looking at Jo.

"Looks like the barn needs a fair amount of repair." Marty walked toward the dilapidated structure out back. "Might need to build it from the ground up," he called back.

"You'll need to arrange a barn raising," Mr. Murray said to Brendan. "Get the folks around to help. You'll need it soon, before the autumn sets in."

Mr. Murray made to leave, then walked back to them

again. "I near forgot," he said, shaking his head. "Which one of you is Clara?"

Clara felt her cheeks grow hot as the others stared at her. "That's me," she volunteered, knowing that her father had likely contacted the man ahead of their arrival.

"Ah, yes. William Thomas—"

"My father."

"Ah, I see. Well, your father sent over a rather fine horse for you last week from New Westminster. A high-bred beauty, I must say. I didn't know when you would arrive, so I lodged her at your neighbour's." He glanced at the barn with dismay. "You might ask to keep her there until you get that fixed up. And until you get some hay and feed."

"Unbelievable," Brendan muttered behind her. "You are so spoiled."

Clara shot a sharp look at her husband. "Yes, it's *unbelievably* nice of you, Mr. Murray, to arrange that. I'll have to bring something over to the neighbour to say thank you." Although what she would bring, Clara didn't know. Mr. Murray was right—they didn't have much. Even their food supply was dangerously low.

Rebecca read her mind. "I'll make some loaves of that wheaten bread you like, Clara. And a pot of thick Irish stew." She peered back inside the homestead. "Tomorrow, we clean this place up."

THE NEXT MORNING, Rebecca woke them at dawn. The night before, after taking an inventory of their new home, Clara and Marty had come up with a list of items they would need to purchase now, before the winter, and what could wait until spring. The most pressing cost was lumber for the new barn. Marty had hinted that she ask her father to supply the lumber, but Clara had shaken her head. She was on her own now. Her father might send her money to supplement her income, but she would not ask him for extra help.

After breakfast, the work began. Marty and Brendan hauled all the furniture outdoors, so the women could scrub the homestead from top to bottom. They washed the floors, the walls, and the cupboards, with the men hauling water from the stream. Next, they took down the curtains and mattresses and beat the dust from them before taking all the dishes and kitchen utensils down to wash in the spring.

The homestead would easily fit the four of them. There was a large sitting room and kitchen area downstairs, with a room off the side for sleeping. Upstairs was another, larger bedroom. It had been decided that Rebecca and Marty would take the primary with the expected arrival of the baby in a few months. Where Jo would lodge was still to be determined, but Clara would help her find something—her new friend would not be destitute again.

"I am bone-tired," Rebecca sighed, red-faced. She fell into a chair that was still outdoors. "And hungry."

"I'll ride into town." Clara was eager to scour the streets for a rental shop for her clinic. "I'll buy some food from the grocer for us until Marty and Brendan have the chance to go hunting."

Taking one of their wagon horses brought to mind her new horse, still in the neighbour's barn. She couldn't wait to meet her, hopefully later today.

Town was a ten-minute ride away. She rode along the

main street slowly, checking for any vacancies in the buildings. There was one—a sign hung from the window of a two-story shop. She tied the horse to the hitching post and peered through the window. There were shelves built into the wall and a desk at the back of the room. It looked perfect.

At the grocers, she bought a few staples to feed them for the next few days: more oats, some flour, a bag full of local vegetables, and some dried beans. She stuffed them into her rucksack and headed home.

Rebecca was scrubbing the hearth, she and Jo both sweaty with exertion, when Clara entered the homestead. The woman turned from her task. "Oh, there you are, Clara. Can you fetch some more water from the stream? Once I'm done cleaning here, we'll make the supper."

Clara went out and grabbed the large bucket for hauling water. She found Brendan in the back, turning over the ground for their garden. Although the summer season was at an end, they could still plant a few vegetables that would continue to grow through the fall and winter months.

She decided to be nice, broaching her husband with caution. Conversation between the two of them had been strained since the visit with her father.

"Where's Marty, Brendan? Did he leave you to it all alone?"

"Ah, he's just gone to order the lumber and some seed." He put down the hoe and went to his canteen for some water. "Nice piece of land you've got here, Clara." The resentment seeped into his tone, his eyes turning dark.

"It's our land. It belongs to both of us. And as far as I'm concerned, Marty and Rebecca, too."

"Ah. But it's your father's name that's on the deed. That

was his plan, wasn't it? To show that I'm not worthy of his daughter. I never dreamed I would be living off my wife's land."

Clara said nothing, as his words had hit the mark. That was likely her father's exact plan. She lifted the bucket, walked past Brendan, and made her way to the stream. Brendan was right about one thing—it *was* a beautiful piece of land.

"Hello!" A young woman walked towards Clara, appearing out of the thick growth of trees. "You must be one of the new neighbours. Father sent this over." She held up a basket. "He would've come over himself, but one of the heifers is birthin' her first babe, and he wanted to stay close by."

Clara opened the basket lid to find a collection of vegetables, eggs, milk, and butter. "Oh my, that's very generous, thank you. I'm Clara. Pleased to meet you."

"Anna." She brushed back her dark hair, which was loosely plaited down her back. Anna seemed to be a girl of about sixteen, and although she was plain-looking, she seemed confident and sure of herself. She gave Clara a wary look. "You look like a city girl."

"I suppose I am," Clara admitted, wondering at the girl's observation. She had bathed and changed into a fresh dress, but her clothing was ordinary—no bustle or gown. Was it so obvious that she wasn't prepared for farm life?

"Anna, can I come over to your place now? I'd like to thank your father for storing my horse."

"That'd be fine. Is that your man?" She nodded over to where Brendan stood by the garden, watching them.

"Yes, that's my husband, Brendan." Clara waved him

over, but he turned and headed inside the homestead. She blushed at his obvious spurn. "He's a little shy, I guess."

Anna led her into the forest, expertly making her way along a hidden path. It was cool among the trees, as their massive trunks and branches completely sheltered them from the warm August sun.

"Here we are." Anna led her out of the thick forest, and Clara gasped in astonishment. The house was beautiful. It stood tall, facing the fields, which were abundant and golden with the season's harvest. The house was a proper home, not a rough homestead like her own. It stood three stories high, with glass windows and a veranda that ran all the way around its lowest level. It was painted white with light green trim, and pink flowers adorned the steps to the front door. Clara was in love.

"Anna," a man's voice came from the front door of the house. "Are you back already? The calf's been born, a fast delivery." He stopped and peered down at them. "Well, hello. We've met before, I believe."

It was the man from the apothecary in Surrey. "Yes," Clara said, smiling in recognition. "You're the doctor."

"And the farmer," he said, coming down the front stairs to greet them. "Miss Murphy, if I recall?"

"Mrs." Anna interrupted, hands on her hips. "She's married. And a city girl. Look at her dress, Father. She was haulin' water in her church clothes."

"Anna." Her father admonished her in a stern tone, smiling apologetically at Clara. "Please be polite to Mrs. Murphy." He turned to Clara. "Are you the new neighbour, then?"

"Please, not Mrs. Murphy. Call me Clara. And yes, there

are four of us there. Myself and my husband, Brendan, his sister Rebecca, and her husband, Marty. And my friend Jo. But she'll lodge elsewhere." She paused, trying to remember his unusual name. "And your name is Joaquin?"

"Yes, Joaquin Walker. But, just Joaquin, please, Clara. No need to be formal with me. I am guessing you'd like to see your horse, then?"

The two of them walked together to the barn, and she was struck by his height. He was at least a head taller than either Brendan or Marty, and she felt tiny next to him.

"What are your plans for doctoring?" Joaquin led her through the doors of the impressive red barn. "About time this town had a proper clinic."

Clara stopped suddenly, realizing that he might have a clinic of his own. "Oh, I didn't even consider ... you doctor these parts, too. Will I be stealing your patients?"

"Oh no." He waved off her concern, smiling kindly. "I mostly just tend to emergencies and my friends over on the Indian reserve. I've got five mouths to feed, and this farm doesn't run itself." He nodded over to a pen filled with hay. "Look, it's the new baby calf."

The newborn was standing on shaky legs, sidled up against its mother. It was still covered in the white residue of birth, nudging against the mother, trying to navigate its first meal.

"Does it have a name? Do you name your cows?" Clara laughed at her own question. "Your daughter is right. I am very clearly a city girl."

"I do name them. Haven't named her yet, though. I'm thinking of Clara; what do you think?"

She looked over in surprise at his bold suggestion.

109

Joaquin grinned at her, a twinkle in his eye. "Speaking of names, I've been calling your horse Red all week. It seems that her colouring might match you exactly." His eyes roamed her face and hair. "She's been making all of my other ladies in the barn jealous."

Clara felt her stomach flutter unexpectedly. She was used to attention over her hair, but the barn suddenly felt very intimate. Thinking briefly of Brendan, she walked ahead, trying to hide the flush that had risen to her cheeks. "Where is she? I'd love to see her."

"Better yet, let's take her for a ride." Joaquin lifted a worn saddle from a hook and handed it to Clara. Mounting his own horse bareback, he patiently waited for her to saddle Red.

"It's a beauty of a day," he said once they'd left the barn. "Look at those mountains." Clara gave him a grin and urged her horse into a gallop, leaving Joaquin to catch up. They rode in a comfortable companionship, enjoying the splendour around them. It seemed that country life might suit her well, after all.

THE VERY NEXT DAY, Clara strode into the bank in town and set down her purse of coins on the counter with a *thunk*. "I'd like to inquire about the shop for rent."

"My dear." Mr. Murray looked perplexed. "Your husband should be the one inquiring. What does he need it for?"

"It's for me. I'd like to open a medical clinic." She braced herself for Mr. Murray's disapproval, but it did not come.

Instead, he looked at her with his brows furrowed but a curious twinkle in his eye. Brendan would not be pleased, but she straightened her back and met the bank manager's gaze.

"Well, let's go take a look then." He took a key that was hanging from a hook on the wall. "My brother owns it. Used to be the mayor's office, but he moved to something larger, in the town hall."

They walked down the road to the building Clara had peered into the day before. It needed a clean, she could see, and a paint.

"It's not much, but there's a tenant's room upstairs, which you could rent out to offset the cost," Mr. Murray said.

It was perfect for a medical clinic—not too large, and Clara was hoping to sweet-talk Marty into making a surgery table for her after she supplied some money to help pay for the lumber to repair the barn.

The room had a large bay window looking out to the street directly across from Milner General Store. Clara stepped out to look at the front of her clinic—yes, she would also ask Marty to make her a sign. The best feature of all, however, was the tenant's room upstairs. A door in the corner led up a small flight of stairs to the second floor. A lodger's room, complete with a bed, a small chest of drawers, and a washstand.

Jo's room.

"I'll take it," she said, her excitement growing. She could hardly wait to set up and open for business. Perhaps she would buy some paint today, too.

Mr. Murray looked her over. "Well, normally, I'd need your husband's permission to rent you the shop. But it seems that you are a woman of ... means. I'll need some collateral. How about the horse? I do believe it's a Morgan."

"Yes, of course." She walked back to the bank with Mr. Murray, who drew up the rental agreement and took enough money for three months' rent.

Clara walked the entire way home wearing a smile she could scarcely contain.

Finally, a clinic of her own.

Chapter 9

September 1885

Clara stepped out of her clinic for some air and leaned on the railing, looking out to the street. A stray burlap sack blew unattended in the wind along the vacant dirt road. A new sign creaked on a rusty hinge above her—Dr. C. Murphy, painted in her finest lettering. She sighed loudly, disheartened. Her clinic had been open a full week, and she hadn't had a single patient. A few townsfolk had stopped in out of curiosity, asking to see the doctor, their expressions incredulous when she told them that she was Dr. C. Murphy. She was prepared for their reactions, but it still stung when their looks of surprise turned to disappointment, or worse, disgust.

Perhaps Brendan and Marty were right. Renting the clinic was a waste of money. More than that, she couldn't afford the squandered time, as Rebecca had already begun to complain that Clara was not keeping up with the very demanding duties of homestead life.

She was about to head back inside when her neighbour, Joaquin, came across the street from the general store.

"Dr. C. Murphy," he said, nodding up at her sign above the clinic door, "how's business?"

"Busy. I never get to sit down." She gave a little laugh and threw her hands up in the air. She winced a little, as the disappointment was evident in her voice. "No one. Not a single person."

Joaquin stepped over to where Red was hitched to the post and gave her a fond rub. He nodded, not surprised at her answer. "Well, it takes time for folks to adjust to someone new. It'll come, don't worry."

"I wish I had your confidence." She sighed again, then looked over to take in his appearance. He was a handsome man, although a little unkempt. His hair grew longer than was normal for men, curling around his ears and chin. He neither had a full beard nor was clean-shaven but had a rough stubble that crept around his jaw. His face and neck were a deep tan from long days spent in the sun.

He broke the silence, giving her a kind smile. "You're welcome to lodge your horse in my barn for as long as you need. It's no bother to me."

"Thank you. That's kind of you. I've ordered some horse feed that I will bring over." She bit her lip, not sure what else to say, but wanted to keep speaking with him. "Your name is so unusual. How did you come to have it?"

"Ah." He nodded as if having answered the same question many times. "My father, or the man who fathered me, I should say, was Hispanic. Came up from California following the Gold Rush in '45. He had a secret love affair with my mother on the way through and on the way back. It was the way back that got my mother into trouble. She was just sixteen at the time. Named me Joaquin after him, but my grandfather refused to call me by that name. I was called John as a child."

Clara gaped at him—she had never met anyone who explained their parentage, or lack thereof, so frankly.

"Well, I think it is an interesting name," she said, mustering a smile. "Much better than John, anyhow." She thought of John McKay with a shudder. *Yes, much better than John.*

They lapsed into silence once again, punctuated only by the sound of Joaquin rocking his boot back and forth on the bottom of the railing.

Clara straightened up. "Did you want to come in?"

Joaquin grinned, jumped the rail, and went inside.

She followed, her eyes taking a minute to adjust to the bright sun outside. He went around the room, examining her tools and instruments. Self-consciousness crept in—despite her father's initial protests about Clara going to medical school, he had always made sure that she had the best equipment and the latest models. Somehow, she was sure that Joaquin's instruments were not as modern or expensive.

He stopped at Joseph's pistol, which she had laid on the desk, still in its holster. Removing it, he took it in his hands gently, examining it from all angles.

"This here's a gentleman's pistol. I think you would be more comfortable with something smaller, a lady's Derringer, perhaps." It was a statement, but it was loaded with questions.

"It was a gift," Clara said. John McKay was not a conversation she felt like having.

"From your husband?" he asked, his head cocked. He had come over to the homestead for lunch the Sunday before and met Brendan, Rebecca, and Marty.

"My friend, Joseph. My assistant at the military camp, where I was employed," she added, after watching Joaquin's raised eyebrows suggest he'd arrived at a scandalous conclusion about Joseph.

He put the gun down and continued around the room. When he saw the amputation kit Dr. Cameron had given her, he raised his eyebrows again. Clearly, the kit did not fit in with the rest of her equipment, as it was well-used and a bit antique.

Sitting at her desk, Joaquin opened her medical journal, a document she kept for every procedure she completed. "Do you mind if I have a look at this?"

She nodded, and he started from the beginning and read each entry, carefully looking at her sketches. Clara stood in the middle of the room, leaning against the surgery table, feeling very much like she was under inspection.

"Interesting. Do you have any more of these?" he asked, waving the journal in the air. His long legs were stretched out far underneath her desk.

She cleared her throat. "Not here. My father is sending the rest of my journals and books and a few other supplies from my home in Ontario."

Joaquin turned back to the pages that described the amputations she had done with Dr. Cameron. "And this? It's impressive for a young doctor to do these alone."

"I did them under supervision," she said. "Well, another doctor instructed me." She walked over to the desk to take her journal before he peppered her with more questions, though she was secretly flattered by the attention. Brendan had never asked about anything to do with her doctoring.

He smiled up at her, soft lines crinkling his face. His eyes transfixed her, as they were the most beautiful colour: dark honey. They reminded her of the caramel candies her father used to buy for her when she was a child, which she would eat in one sitting while reading a book under the shady willow.

Joaquin leaned in closer to her from his seat. "There seems to be a detail missing." He winked at her. "Did you retch?"

"No. Well, almost," she admitted, blushing.

Joaquin laughed loudly, standing up from the desk. It was a warm laugh, one that invited Clara to laugh along with him. It had been quite some time since she had laughed with someone, and it felt nice.

"Don't worry. I retched the first half-dozen times. It still makes me queasy, to be honest." Chuckling, he headed back outside.

Joaquin stopped at the door, looking back in at her, his large frame filling the space completely. "There's a pregnant woman on the Indian reservation that's nearing her birthing time. She lost the baby last time and very nearly died herself. I'm going to deliver her baby surgically. I could use your help with the procedure."

"Have you done that before?" Caesarean sections were a risky surgery that she had only seen completed once at a prestigious hospital in Montréal.

Joaquin nodded. "It will be my third time."

Clara hesitated. She was impressed, but even with his

experience, there was a high likelihood of infection. "Are you sure that's the best decision?"

"I do." He frowned as if surprised by her challenge. "She has a narrowed birth canal. I had to do a craniotomy last time to save her life, and I'd like to avoid that again."

"But there's no hospital. Surely—"

"No. But even if there were, they wouldn't take her." He stared at Clara intently as if trying to decipher her but then spoke again. "I really do need an extra set of hands, though. I made Anna help me the last time." He gave a short laugh. "She may never forgive me for that."

Clara laughed, imagining Anna's horror. "All right, I'd be glad to help you. When?"

"Tomorrow should do. Come over after your breakfast, and we'll head out." He ducked under the doorframe, lifting his hand in farewell.

MUCH TO CLARA'S ANNOYANCE, Brendan was insistent on accompanying her to the reserve.

"I'm not sure that's necessary." She sighed, watching him saddle the farm grey in their rundown barn. "You should be helping Marty prepare for the barn raising."

Brendan grunted. He looked tired, with dusky shadows under his eyes. They hadn't been sleeping well—the bed in the homestead was small, and neither seemed to want to touch the other. "Aye. And you should be helping Becca with the cookin' and cleanin'."

They walked through the forested area together in

silence, Brendan leading the horse behind him. Clara would saddle her own horse in Joaquin's barn.

As they reached the edge of the property, Brendan spoke again. "It's no' proper for you to be going to the Indian reserve, Clara. And with this man. He's divorced, for God's sake. Who knows what kind of morals he has?"

Divorced and *a bastard*, she thought but said nothing as they reached the house. She liked Joaquin—his eyes were kind. They walked up the front steps together, and Brendan knocked on the door. It flew open, and the young boy Clara had seen in the apothecary emerged, vibrating with energy.

"Father!" he bellowed into the house, surprising both Clara and Brendan with his volume. Peering up at her, he put his hands on his hips. "Are you going to take out my tooth?"

"I can," she said, grinning at his cheeky demeanour. "Does it need pulling?"

"Yes." He pouted, using his tongue to wiggle the loose tooth. "Father tried, but it hurt. He says maybe I'd prefer the pretty doctor do it instead."

Joaquin appeared at the door. "Just on time," he said, showing no surprise that Brendan had accompanied Clara. "Ben, your breakfast is getting cold. Inside," he added firmly when Ben started to protest. Joaquin shook his head, letting out an easy laugh. "It's like a madhouse around here."

They set off on horseback, with Joaquin leading the way. As they rode along the trail in the woods, Brendan asked, "Why do you help the Indians? I'm not sure draggin' my wife off to the reservation is entirely fittin'."

Clara sent Brendan a glare, her blood starting to boil. She

didn't need him to monitor her actions. If Joaquin thought the reservation was safe for her, she was sure it was.

"Well, firstly, they're my friends. We all grew up together. Back then, the Indians roamed this land freely."

"What happened?" Clara asked. She knew some of the history from reading her father's newspapers but wanted to hear it from Joaquin's perspective.

"The Indians were the first people on this land. The various tribes existed much as we do—warring for territory, hunting, fishing, and making a home for themselves. About twenty years ago, that all changed. Plans for the railroad started, and the Indians were forced off their traditional lands onto the reserves." He shook his head. "They've even lost their names. The Indian agents insisted they have English names."

"Don't they have their own healers?" Brendan asked.

"They do, but not for any complex surgical procedures," Joaquin explained. "Look, there's the old fort."

Fort Langley stood proud, just above the bank of the Fraser River. It had been one of the primary fur trading posts of the Hudson's Bay Company. This post had been built in 1827, after the previous location, downriver at Derby Reach, had flooded multiple times.

Once they arrived at the river crossing, they tied their horses and got into Joaquin's canoe, which he had tied to a post, to cross the Fraser. On the other side, the reservation was a buzz of activity. Men, women, and children were engaged in various forms of labour: canoe repair, wood carving, field dressing a deer, stripping thin layers from a fallen cedar tree, basket making, and hanging long strips of salmon to dry in the wind.

A group of women milled by a large garden, collecting plants in large baskets.

"Are they collecting for medicine? Remedies?"

Joaquin nodded. "Yes. Although now they grow what they need here instead of collecting in the wild. I have a small medicinal herb garden at home, as well."

Clara gazed with interest at the women as they passed on the way to the longhouse. Perhaps she could ask one of them to supply her with the herbs she needed for her special tea. Her supply was dwindling, with no more than two months left.

Joaquin led them to a canvas tent, not unlike the one Clara had stayed in at the military camp. "Here's where I keep the majority of my tools and supplies," he said, opening the flap so she could peer inside. There was a variety of medical instruments, as well as knives, bottles, and jars. In the middle of the tent was a cot with a blanket folded neatly on top.

Joaquin disappeared inside, then returned with the items they needed for the surgery: a bottle of chloroform, two large clamps, a sharp scalpel, another blunt one to gently open the uterus, and silver wire for the abdominal sutures.

"And this." Joaquin withdrew a large bottle of whisky from under the cot.

"No." Clara shook her head, taking the whisky from him and set it back inside the tent. "This is better." She produced two bottles of carbolic acid from her own medical bag and handed them to Joaquin.

"I'm not sure that's necessary, Clara. Whisky does just the same. That just smells bad."

Clara pushed the bottles into his hands. "This is a risky

procedure. Carbolic acid is better. You can keep these. I've ordered more."

Joaquin looked down at her, a grin pulling at the corners of his mouth. "All right," he said. "Let's get started."

Clara looked questioningly at Brendan.

"You go ahead; I'll take a nap on the cot," he said. Joaquin and Clara took the supplies and walked to where some men were assembling an outdoor surgery table—a large plank of wood set atop several sturdy tree rounds. A tarpaulin had been arranged for privacy. The men greeted Joaquin exuberantly, exchanging embraces and, much to Clara's surprise, words. Joaquin spoke with them in their native tongue of the Coast Salish people, although he spoke slowly. One of the men lifted his hands to Clara, which Joaquin translated as thank you.

"This is Clara," he said in English, bringing her into the conversation with his hand at the small of her back. "She's also a doctor."

The men spoke with a fury of gestures, and one made a shapely figure of a woman with his hands. Clara was amused to see Joaquin flush, the top of his cheeks and ears turning red. She smirked to herself; men were the same in any language, and no translation was needed.

While she prepared for the surgery by disinfecting the instruments, Joaquin brought the woman outside from the longhouse. She lay on the table, clearly nervous, her hands resting at the sides of her protruding belly.

Joaquin comforted the woman in her language, holding her hand gently. He put a few drops of chloroform on a cloth and brought it to cover her nose and mouth. Her eyes fluttered closed, and he stood, ready to begin.

"You should really invest in a Lister Sprayer for the carbolic acid if you are performing surgeries like this, Joaquin," Clara said. "I've seen them used. It mists the area around your patient and sterilizes the air."

Joaquin said nothing but gave her an amused look as he liberally poured the solution on a cloth to clean the woman's protruding abdomen.

"Really," Clara persisted. "I'll write my father and have him send one."

"Is your father William Thomas?" Joaquin surprised Clara with the question. He was about to make the first cut, transverse, just above the pelvic bone.

"Yes. How did you know?"

"The sale of the land. I looked it up at the land office. I was confused because there was no William or Thomas among you."

Joaquin pierced the skin and fat layers of the abdomen, and Clara gently inserted the clamps, prying the cavity open for him to see.

"So, your family is wealthy." It was a statement. He had seen her horse and knew about her land, so he didn't need to guess.

Clara opened her mouth to reply when a voice interrupted her. It wasn't the speaker that alarmed her but the cadence of his tone. It was Brendan. And he was drinking.

She whipped her head around, trying to see. She found him drinking from the bottle of whisky Joaquin had stowed in his tent.

"Clara. I need your eyes here, please." Joaquin's voice was firm, but when Clara turned back, his eyes, too, had travelled over to Brendan, who was wandering back into the depths of the reserve. Joaquin's features hardened—his eyes narrowed, and his mouth formed a thin line.

"I'm sorry," Clara whispered, her face flushed with embarrassment. Her husband was a thief and a drunk. It was not even noon, and he'd stolen the spirits used for Joaquin's medical procedures.

"Does he have a compulsion? For the drink?" They were at the uterine wall, but Joaquin paused, his eyes on Clara's face.

Clara lifted her gaze. "Yes, I think so," she whispered. It was the first time she had admitted out loud that her husband had a problem.

Joaquin closed his eyes briefly before speaking again. "Then I am the one who is sorry. My grandfather did as well. It's ... not easy to live with."

He made the final cut and reached into the womb, carefully extracting the baby, purple and covered with blood. Clara took the infant as Joaquin turned back to the mother. As she swept the baby's airway free of mucus, the miracle of life began again—the baby took his first breath, his skin grew pink as oxygen reached his bloodstream, and his shrieks pierced the morning air.

CLARA RODE BACK to the homestead alone, the wind from the speed of her gallop drying the tears of humiliation and fury as quickly as they fell. Brendan was somewhere behind her, slowed by both the calibre of his mount and his intoxication.

She burst into the homestead just as Marty and Rebecca

were sitting down to their midday meal. Jo stood at the hearth, pouring tea for the three of them.

"You." Clara pointed at Rebecca, her whole body shaking in anger. "Why didn't you say something more? He's a liar? A thief? A drunk? Anything else? What else have you kept from me?"

Rebecca paled, putting her hands to her rounded belly protectively. "I—"

"Why do you carry a bottle of ipecac, Rebecca? Did he try to drink himself to death?"

Marty rose from the table and came to her, putting a gentle arm around her shaking shoulders. He motioned for Jo to bring her some tea. "What's happened, Clara?"

She sank into a chair at the table, putting her head in her hands to calm her speeding heartbeat. She drew a few steadying breaths before replying. "He stole a bottle of whisky. Right out of Joaquin's tent. Drank most of it while we were performing the surgery."

Marty shook his head, frowning. "Clara—"

"No." Clara scowled across the table at him. "Don't even say it, Marty. This has nothing to do with me working outside of the home. Besides, I was very clear with Brendan about that since the beginning. I am a *doctor*." Even as she said the words, Clara saw the consequences of her own decisions: she had only met Brendan mere months ago. She knew nothing of his character before they were wed.

Marty put his head in his hands. "He'll be accused of being a thief, and we'll all be tarred with the same brush."

The homestead fell into a tense silence as they considered the situation. If Joaquin labelled Brendan a thief, treacherous gossip would make their adjustment to the new town a difficult one.

Rebecca drew a shaky breath, tears rimming her eyes. "He's not always right in the head, Clara. I think you can see that. But it's only for a spell, and then he's fine again. He's ... he's not a bad man."

Marty shook his head. "The drinking's got to stop, Becca. He's—"

They were interrupted by the sound of retching outside. Rebecca stood quickly. "I'll tend to him."

"No." Marty stood, catching his wife by the arm. "I'll deal with this." He turned Rebecca to look at him. "Things have got to change, Becca. The babe will be here soon."

Clara felt a fondness for Marty at that moment—he cared about his wife and her well-being, even though he knew the baby wasn't his child. Meanwhile, Clara's husband didn't seem to care about her well-being at all. She swallowed back the surge of loneliness that had started to fray the edges of her heart.

∼

CLARA WOKE to the sound of a faint tapping at her bedroom door. The light outside the window had begun to fade.

Clara pushed herself out of bed and went to the door. It was Jo.

"I've slept away the rest of the day, Jo. I didn't realize I was so tired." She was glad that Brendan had gone into the barn. The smell of whisky on his breath beside her would have utterly repulsed her.

"I've brought you something to eat." Jo held up a tray with soup and biscuits.

Clara sat on the floor, her back leaning against the bed. She ate the soup with as much enthusiasm as she could muster, then pushed the tray away.

"I think I've made a mistake, marrying Brendan without really knowing him." Clara looked at her friend, who nodded sympathetically. "I'm wondering if I should just take the train home."

Jo tucked her hair behind her ears. "That's a big decision. What about your medical practice?"

"Do you think I should even carry on with it? I've had no one come to my clinic, and I'm not sure I'll make a good homestead wife." And she realized she wasn't willing to spend a lifetime with Brendan. Rebecca was right. She was too soft.

Jo got up and retrieved Clara's hairbrush from the chest of drawers. Removing the pins from Clara's hair, she brushed for a while before speaking. "If you do leave, I'll come with you. You won't have to go alone. But," she said, as the strokes from the brush continued their rhythmic pull, "my father used to say this to me as a child. 'It's better to light a candle than curse at the darkness.'" She turned Clara towards her. "You are a candle, Clara. You see good in everyone, even a dying girl on the street. I think this town needs you."

Clara looked out the window at the encroaching darkness. She heard the truth in Jo's words, but her heart remained heavy. She needed a candle, too.

Chapter 10

September 1885

BRENDAN WOKE WITH A CURSE. ICE WATER SLUICED down his face, into his shirt, and even into his trousers. He hadn't even managed to open his eyes properly when the second assault hit; this time, the water went straight into his nostrils, sending him spluttering into a stance, fists clenched, prepared for the third.

It was Becca, her face as red as the devil's wrath. Though the pain threatened to split his head in half, Brendan groggily recalled the events of the day before. He had passed out in the barn, but not before Marty had given him a piece of his mind—and a fist to the mouth.

"You drunken sot. Get your sorry self over to the spring for a wash," Becca seethed. "Folks will be here to raise a new barn in an hour, and you smell like horseshit." The third bucket came then, although thrown empty.

Brendan deflected it before it hit him. "Calm down,

Becca." As soon as the words left his mouth, he knew they were a grave mistake.

"*Calm down?*" Becca moved with a speed that seemed impossible for a woman of her current girth. She grabbed him by the collar of his dripping shirt. "I came to this country for *you*. You begged me to leave Ireland, where I would have been perfectly happy to live out my days, so you could find happiness somewhere else. Guess what, brother? We're here. And yet not much has changed, has it?"

She left the barn, her rounded frame disappearing around the corner, then came back a little while later, holding a steaming mug. "Clara made this for your hangover. Though I suspect she doesn't have much affection left for you, not after yesterday." She shook her head and pulled a crate to sit next to him. "You damn fool."

"Clara needs to learn to mind her place," he said, though his stomach tightened at Becca's words.

Becca gave him a knowing look. "Don't you want happiness, brother? You seemed to have it for a minute, and now ..." She shook her head. "I'm trying to be happy, at least. I won't let you ruin it for me. Not like last time."

Brendan fell silent, taking a sip of the tea. He grimaced; it was a vile concoction that tasted like the cod liver oil the headmistress used to administer daily at the orphanage. He did want to be happy, of course, but he wasn't sure he could find it with Clara. She was so *much*, so demanding.

"Why couldn't I find a woman who is content to just *be?* Clara's so difficult." He took another drink of the tea. His headache seemed to have tamed a bit, though he needed a good breakfast.

"Aye. Well, just be careful, brother. She's a beautiful

woman. And you ... well, you need to take on the task of making that beautiful woman happy again."

Becca left in her slow, awkward gait. Brendan thought of his wife, of her full breasts and shapely figure. *Aye.* He would take on that task.

〜

THE FIRST DAY of the barn raising had been a success. Families had come, the men and boys ready to work, the women and girls ready to socialize. The women brought food from home—fried chicken, corn on the cob, potato salad, coleslaw, biscuits, and pies for dessert. Rebecca had Clara and Jo busy in the kitchen, preparing pitchers of cold tea.

Although it would take a few more days for the men to put together the siding and the roof, the laborious task of laying the foundation and posts was complete.

Clara had watched the men work, and they were deftly practiced at the seemingly impossible task. Although Marty had not attended a barn raising before, he was an eager worker, laughing jovially with the other men. Brendan, who had come to fisticuffs with Marty the day before, worked alone, preferring to saw boards off to the side.

Joaquin arrived with his three oldest sons, Will, Jesse, and Drew. Even Ben, the youngest at eight, was eager to help, handing tools to his father and brothers. Anna had stayed on the ground with the women, helping to set the large tables and chatting with Clara and Jo. Although she was just sixteen, she was definitely interested in boys—Clara saw her cast not-so-subtle looks up at the young men working atop the roof of the barn.

After they'd ceased work in the late afternoon, Brendan had been stuck to Clara's side like honey. He had come in freshly washed from the spring that morning and taken her into his arms.

"I'm so sorry," he'd whispered into her hair before dropping kisses on her neck. "Please forgive me, Clara."

Marty and Rebecca had looked relieved at their short encounter, pretending not to watch as they bustled around, preparing for the workers about to arrive. Jo, the guardian of Clara's inner turmoil, had turned her face away.

Joaquin approached them after the meal, his children waiting in an impatient gaggle behind him. Clara noticed Jo chatting with Anna and Will. She smiled at the idea that perhaps Jo would make some friends her own age.

"Mr. and Mrs. Murphy." Joaquin greeted them formally, his face impassive. A pang shot through Clara's chest. He must still be angry about the stolen whisky. She enjoyed Joaquin's company and his professional advice, and it was devastating that her husband's behaviour might ruin things for them all.

Brendan stuck out his hand cordially. "Thanks for helping today, Joaquin."

An uncomfortable silence fell, and Clara prayed that her husband would apologize to their neighbour. He did not, and finally, Brendan cleared his throat and looked away.

Joaquin turned his attention to Clara. "Clara, I went and checked on our patient at the reservation this morning. I was hoping you'd do me the favour of doing so again tomorrow. We'll need to go next week to remove the silver wire sutures as well."

Brendan shifted beside Clara. "No. I—"

Clara cut him off, plastering a smile on her face. "Yes. That's the least I can do, Joaquin.

Joaquin smiled back at her, ignoring Brendan completely. Then, his face dropped. "Oh no," he groaned softly. A woman, dressed rather formally for a barn raising in a stiff-looking black gown, joined their trio. She peered at Clara, her pinched eyes sweeping Clara's figure, then landed back on her face.

"Hmm. This will not do at all. A female physician? We'll have all the men and boys in town having wayward thoughts in no time."

Joaquin sighed forcefully, his eyes rolling skyward. "Clara and Brendan Murphy, please meet Martha Davenport. Martha and her husband Jonas live over by Murray's Corner." He dropped his head closer to Clara's. "Not nearly far enough away," he muttered.

Martha wagged her finger at Joaquin, the tight curls piled on the top of her head bobbing up and down. "Enough from you. I'll have you know that my hearing is excellent, and I'll not be talked back to by a bastard child."

Joaquin laughed dryly. "I'm no longer a child, Martha. I'm a man of thirty-eight with children of my own."

"Hmmm." Martha's gaze turned to his children, who were now scattered across the yard, before turning to Brendan. "You seem a nice enough man. Though why you've allowed your wife to doctor is beyond me." Clara's eyes widened at her bold remark while Brendan shifted uncomfortably beside her.

Martha's scathing attention came back to Clara. "Will you be attending to the women and children only, then? Surely your husband doesn't allow you to touch other men.

You're a pretty thing, dear. Men will be getting the wrong impression if you're tending to their *ailments* and such."

Clara flicked her gaze to Brendan, whose face was etched with horror. Clearly, the idea hadn't crossed his mind until now. "Mrs. Davenport, I can assure you—"

"Dear, you should come to our Tuesday quilting circle. We'll get you started on a baby blanket or two." She glanced down at Clara's trim waist. "Unless working outside the home has already polluted your womb."

Damn. Joaquin was right—the old busybody didn't live far enough away.

"Martha, that's hardly how conception works. New studies have shown—" Joaquin started.

"I bore my Jonas eight children, and two gone to the Lord too soon. Speaking of the Lord, I haven't seen you at church the last few weeks, Mr. Walker. Those scoundrels of yours need to hear the word of God, as I have no doubt the morals in your home leave much to be desired." Martha and Joaquin met each other's eyes with even stares.

"Excuse us, Mrs. Davenport." Brendan cut into the conversation abruptly. "My wife has a headache. I was just taking her into the house to lie down." He whisked Clara away, his hand firmly at her waist.

Brendan led her to the homestead and ushered her into their bedroom. He closed the door.

"She's right, you know." He crossed his arms over his chest with a serious look. "I did have wayward thoughts when you attended to me in the infirmary." He pointed to the bed. "Get undressed."

Clara drew back in shock. "What? Now?" She looked

out the window to where people were still milling around their yard.

"Aye. I'm ready just now. And I realize we need to attend to the task more often if you're to become pregnant. I haven't paid enough attention to you lately, Clara, and I'm sorry."

Clara stared at him as he turned his back to allow her to undress. He turned to her a minute later to find her still fully clothed.

"Ah." He walked across the room and closed the shutters on the window. "There you go. A little privacy. Now, into bed."

She left at dawn, pulling on her riding jacket to keep out the morning chill. It was a morning as Clara had never seen; the hue of summer had been replaced by the vibrant thrum of fall, and the air was gloriously crisp.

She made her way into the forest at the edge of her property, threading her way along the dark path that had now become familiar. She planned to take Red out of Joaquin's barn for a leisurely ride before visiting the reservation, put in a few hours at her clinic, and then head home to the chores.

The house stood as majestic as ever in the pale morning light, the railing dewy to her touch. Her eyes scanned the windows, wondering which rooms were whose. Clara decided it was Anna who slept at the very top—as a young woman, she would very much need the private space away from her four brothers.

Going into the barn, she heard the splash of milk hitting the bottom of a wooden bucket. Someone was up with the cows. She found Joaquin sitting on a wooden stool, his shoulder resting against the hind leg of the animal, while his hands squeezed, one and then the other, to express milk into the bucket. There were four other cows in the pen, and one lowed loudly at her arrival.

"Clara. You're up with the birds this morning, I see." Joaquin's smile was welcoming, and she found herself sitting down on a nearby crate.

"Yes. I couldn't sleep. I thought I might ride."

He smiled again as the sun began to stream in through the seams of the barn. A calico kitten came swishing toward Clara for attention.

"I've been thinking." Joaquin cleared his throat before continuing. "You should keep Red here for the winter. She's made herself at home."

Clara laughed as a rapid warmth cascaded through her body. "Well, I don't blame her. You have a beautiful home." She knew she should protest; feeding and caring for her horse was not a burden he needed, but there was something in his expression that stopped her. Looking away from his gaze, she picked up the kitten and stroked it.

"My great-grandfather built this house. He was a bit of a romantic, I guess. One of the first settlers after the Hudson's Bay Company sold off their land." He stood, pushing the cow gently away. "I was just about to make coffee, if you'd like."

The morning ride forgotten, Clara followed him into the house, helping him carry the buckets of milk from the five cows. At the entrance, there was a hallway going back, a room on either side, and a winding staircase that led up to the second floor. Joaquin led her to the left, into the kitchen and sitting room.

"I have something for you," he said, taking her coat as they entered the kitchen. He reached up high and produced a tin box. Inside were two guns, small enough to fit in his palm.

Clara did protest this time. "Oh, I don't need that. I've stopped wearing the other one."

"These were my mother's," he said, closing the box. "And you *should* carry one. You're alone in your clinic. The other one is for your friend, Jo. My eldest, Will, can show you how to use and clean them tomorrow afternoon."

The conversation closed, he started to make the coffee, moving around the kitchen with ease. She studied him, wondering about his wife. Why had she left him for another man? Clara couldn't see any obvious faults.

He turned as if noticing her watching him, so she moved to browse the room. It was cozy and tidy and made Clara's heart ache with an unexpected wave of loneliness. She missed her family, her father especially. Maybe she would visit in the spring. Clara's glance fell to a book on the table near the settee.

"Oh!" she exclaimed excitedly. "Is it good? I've wanted to read this." She held up a copy of *The Adventures of Huckleberry Finn*.

Joaquin came, handing her a cup of coffee. "I'm not sure yet," he said. "I always judge a book by the ending. Come with me. I think you'll like this." He led her out of the kitchen and down a hallway towards the back of the home. Pushing open a door, his eyes twinkled down at her. "The library."

"Oh, my." Clara gazed at the most beautiful room she had ever seen. Her father had an impressive collection of books, but nothing like this: books were stuffed into shelves, haphazardly it seemed, and there was a wood stove in the corner next to a reading chair. The window overlooked the farm, with the mountains in the distance.

"I want to live here," she laughed, settling into the reading chair. "Yes, this will do very nicely."

Joaquin cleared his throat, his cheeks pinking. "You're welcome to borrow whatever you like. Or read here."

"Thank you. My father will send some of mine, as I am getting rather tired of re-reading *Jane Eyre*."

"Oh, *Jane Eyre*." Joaquin scoffed, moving to stand near the window. "I hated that book. Rochester was so cruel, really."

Clara laughed, her heart lifting with the conversation. A kinship had grown between them, now fueled by a love of books. "You've read *Jane Eyre*?"

"Unfortunately." Joaquin grinned at Clara before turning his eyes towards the ceiling, grimacing at the terrible thud from above. She could only presume it was his children, out of bed, getting ready for the day.

"I wanted to ask you, Clara, about your friend, Jo," Joaquin said as they walked back to the kitchen. Anna was preparing breakfast in the kitchen, and Will and Jesse headed outdoors for their morning chores. Clara greeted them, although Will shot her a surprised look, likely at her being there so early in the morning.

"Do you think she would be interested in helping Anna with the housework a few days a week? I hired a woman in the summer, but she's moved. It's too much for Anna to do alone. I can't pay much, but there are three meals a day and a small stipend."

"I'm sure Jo will love that. I'll ask. You don't mind? About her being Chinese?" Clara wondered if Rebecca would be put out at losing Jo's help. She would ask them both.

"Not at all. I know a thing or two about being different."

They walked out to the barn again, and Joaquin handed her a shovel to clean up the horse dung. Clara stifled a giggle as she took the shovel. Perhaps he was tired of taking care of Red after all.

He went into a stall and filled the water trough. Clara picked the stall next to him and started to shovel the horse mess into a large bucket just outside the partition.

"And you? You didn't blink an eye when I asked you to come to the Indian reserve." They switched stalls, and he flashed his easy smile as they passed.

"No. I never thought I would be healing whites only. I don't know why," Clara admitted. She thought of Brendan and his resistance to both Jo and the Indigenous peoples. "Although others seem to have a problem with it."

He nodded, and they worked in silence for a while. When they finished, he took the shovel and handed her a soft horse brush. He took another, and they went to Red's stall.

"How did you meet Brendan?" he asked, looking at her over the top of the horse. "I just ask because you seem to come from very different backgrounds."

"At the military camp we were both working at. Marty and Rebecca, too."

"The same camp where you were gifted the pistol?" Joaquin brushed Red's cherry brown coat in long, even strokes, raising an eyebrow at her.

Clara sighed softly. He wasn't going to leave the pistol alone until he uncovered the story.

Taking a deep breath, she blurted out the details. "I was

engaged to a Lieutenant who was also posted at the camp. A family friend." She paused as he stared over at her, hooked by her sudden revelation. "He attacked me, shoved me down, and tried to violate me in the dirt. And broke my nose." She closed her eyes briefly against the violent memory. "My friend Joseph gave me the pistol when we fled."

Joaquin's eyes widened, but he looked away without further inquiry. She could see that he had many questions, but she didn't elaborate. Just the mention of John had made her feel sick to her stomach. They moved to the next horse, the weight of Rebecca's story heavy on her tongue. "He's also the father of Rebecca's baby. By force," she added, not wanting to tar Rebecca's character.

Joaquin leaned on the horse, his arms folded on its back. It was his mount, a shiny black steed. "Well, he sounds like a charming fellow." His face was serious. "Does Marty know?"

"He knows it's not his child, but not who the father is."

"Ah." Joaquin was silent as he processed the revelations. "Well, Marty's a good man, then. It was not easy growing up fatherless in this town. And no man would look twice at my mother. How did you come to marry Brendan?"

She smiled. He was persistent; she would give him that. "We had already started a courtship, so I came west with them. We were wed only two months after we'd met. I didn't realize he had a problem with the drink." She shook her head in a rueful manner. "I'm afraid I sound rather foolish. And impulsive," she added, coming to her own realization.

He gave her a wry smile, handing her the saddle for Red. "You're talking to a divorced man. I know all about mistakes and regret," he said, avoiding her eyes.

Clara put a blanket on Red, then buckled the saddle,

mulling his words in her head. Joaquin left the barn briefly, then came back with two apples, a mix of yellow and pink. He gave one to Red, handing Clara the other before helping her on the horse.

"My friend will meet you to help you at the reservation. He speaks English well, so you can ask him any questions you have. And use anything you need from my tent. Thank you for your company this morning, Clara. We'll make a farm girl out of you yet."

His smirk made Clara laugh, and she rode off into the morning lightly, as if relieved from a burden she hadn't known she was carrying. *A farm girl, indeed.*

Chapter 11

October 1885

THE NEXT FEW WEEKS WENT BY AT THE SLOW PACE Clara had come to associate with small-town life. Their routines fell into an easy rhythm, and they started to enjoy events outside of homestead and farm duties. Marty brought his guitar to the minister's wife, who played the organ at the church, and they soon became a duo. Clara and Rebecca joined the quilting circle in hopes of getting to know some of the other women in town. The others there were thrilled with the quality of Clara's running stitch and backstitch.

Jo started to work at the Walker farm three days a week and came to Clara with accounts of Joaquin and his children. Many seemed to include Will, Joaquin's oldest son. Clara had seen them together after church, chatting with Anna and a few of the older teens in town. Jo and Will seemed especially interested in each other's company. Jo's cheeks glowed with a flush Clara had never seen on her friend's complexion. She'd caught Joaquin's eye over the church crowd as he noticed them too, and they'd shared a secret smile over the young flirtation.

Only Brendan had not found any activity in the community, though some evenings he meandered down to the saloon for ale and a game of cards with some of the men. Clara breathed a sigh of relief on those nights when he was away, though she felt guilty for not enjoying her husband's company. She'd started to read again in the evenings, helping herself to the plethora of books in Joaquin's library, and it was easier to concentrate when he wasn't home.

The clinic had started to be busy as well. Clara had a steady stream of women and children who came by, mostly with superficial needs and a few minor emergencies. She had not yet treated any men, although Joaquin had assured her it would just be a matter of time before they came, too.

Joaquin came through the clinic door carrying a large parcel on a busy Wednesday morning. He wore a heavy plaid overcoat and gloves, as the last few days had seen a cold snap.

"I just came from the post office, and this was there for you. Looks like it's from your father," he said as he set the parcel down and leaned against Clara's desk, crossing his arms over his broad chest. Lately, Joaquin had been dropping by the clinic every few days for some reason or another, and they ended up chatting for a while before he headed home to the farm. She enjoyed their time together and found herself peering out the window, wondering when he would come by next.

"Thank you. I just don't know what I'd do without you." She hesitated, checking outside for any nosy townsfolk, before coming over and perching close to him on the desk. It was true—he was always offering to help, both at the clinic and at the homestead. Last week he had fixed the stairs going up to Jo's room, as two were soft and one had broken through altogether.

"Actually," she said, biting her lip, "I was hoping to ask you for a favour."

Joaquin's face lit up. "Absolutely. Whatever you need, Clara." He took off his gloves and laid them on the desk, smiling at her.

"I want to learn more about plant medicine. Do you think your friends at the reserve could teach me?" This was also true, although she was hoping to ask one of the women if they had a concoction that would help her prevent pregnancy. She knew she risked Brendan finding out or thinking that she was indeed barren, but she could not come to terms with the idea of carrying his child just yet.

"Of course. I'll have to come with you to translate, but I'm sure I can spare an afternoon or two. There's less to harvest in the winter months, but we can continue in the spring and summer too."

Clara frowned, letting out a sigh. She needed the remedy sooner than the spring, and she was hoping to ask the women directly. It would be awkward to ask Joaquin and try to explain to him that she did not wish to become with child.

Joaquin noticed her expression. "What's wrong?"

"I just ..." She decided to tell a half-truth. "I need some women's supplies, and I was hoping to speak with one of them directly."

"Ah." He was quiet for a moment. "I *am* a physician too, Clara. Nothing you ask is going to frighten me."

Growing uncomfortable under his gaze, she made her

way over to the lancet she'd used for piercing a patient's boils earlier and cleaned it. She felt his eyes follow her and heard a disgruntled sigh.

Finally, he came over beside her. "Why did you become a doctor? It couldn't have been easy for you at medical school."

She gave her own sigh, glad he was changing the subject. Joaquin had a fondness for probing her for details about her life before moving west. "I'm afraid it wasn't a very noble reason. After my debutante season, I was bored to death with all the afternoon teas and society functions and decided I couldn't live up to my mother's expectations of becoming a socialite wife." She looked up to find amusement on his face. "My mother wouldn't speak to me for six months when my father allowed me to go. And medical school wasn't so impossibly hard. The men treated me as inferior, but I expected that. It was no worse than doctoring is now." She gestured around her humble clinic. "What about you?"

Joaquin raked his hand through his unruly hair. It seemed to be longer every time Clara saw him, and she wanted to offer to give it a trim. "Not so much different than you. I needed to leave home for a while." He paused and turned to face the window, hiding his face from her. "I wish I could have known you then. Before. I ... think I would've been very interested in getting to know you."

Clara's stomach somersaulted as he shot her a sidelong glance. A bold statement, but that had been happening lately, too. Every time he came by the clinic, he seemed to make her flustered. The problem was that she didn't mind.

"Well," she managed, her voice weak, "you're getting to know me now."

He smiled kindly, putting her at ease once more. "And enjoying it immensely. But I want you to tell me what you need, Clara, from the Indian women. Please. Just trust me."

Clara drew a steadying breath. She did trust him, even though she had known him a short time. "I want to prevent becoming pregnant."

His eyes flickered before he walked over to the other side of the room and gathered his gloves. She watched as he put them back on, his movements sharp and terse. He seemed to be upset at what she had revealed to him.

"All right. I'll likely be able to find you something. A brew made with the leaves and stem of the blueberry plant might be best." He walked to the door, the wooden floor creaking under his boots.

"Joaquin—" Clara started but stopped. His shoulders were square, and his stance rigid. Was he angry with her? He seemed to be open-minded about most things, but perhaps she had gone too far in trusting him with her secret.

"I'll see you a bit later, Clara. I've got some errands to run before Ben and Drew get home from school. Anna's away visiting her mother right now."

Clara stood at the door after he left, blinking away sudden tears. Refusing to cry in public, she flipped the clinic sign to closed, early for the day. Perhaps she would lodge Red in her own barn tonight.

Joaquin was used to being alone. In fact, most of the time, he preferred it. He liked to spend time in easy silence, working the land, relishing in the ache of his muscles. It

145

wasn't that he was simple in conversation, but quite the opposite—he rarely found people that stimulated him. It had been at the centre of how he'd failed his wife, Laura. He'd had nothing to say to her and had become resentful of trying.

Lately, however, his solitude had become an enemy, his thoughts treacherous. It came slowly at first, with memories of Clara's smile or wondering how she was faring at the clinic. Then it grew with speed so wicked he felt sick with its persistence. *Clara.* For reasons he didn't fully understand, he couldn't get her out of his head. It wasn't just her beauty, but something more. He'd even noticed his sons watching her as she moved about their home, asking questions and touching things, feeling blankets, books, even their dishes. Her fingers were always exploring. It was how she learned, by touching and doing. He found himself running his hands along the same surfaces when she was gone, wondering what she thought of their home, of him.

Joaquin came out of the barn to find Jo churning butter alongside the house. Shaking his head, he laughed. Butter churning was Anna's least favourite chore—of course, she had delegated it to Jo. Anna usually joined the other women in the community for the task, but he suspected that most would be wary of a Chinese girl among them.

"Let me take a turn there, Jo. Give your arms a rest." He took the plunger from the girl, who wiped the sweat from her brow. Jo was a lot like himself, a quiet observer. Glancing at her again, he wondered if she would tell him more about Clara.

Jo met his eye with a humorous glint. She was pretty, with a small nose, full lips, and shiny black hair that fell down her back. He saw why his son was attracted to her and hoped Jo would agree to a courtship. But his oldest son was on the serious side and would never confide in his father about such things.

"What is it you want to know about her?"

He was taken aback and stopped churning for a moment to stare at her. "Is it *that* obvious?"

Jo gave a soft chuckle. "I haven't known her long, but I've never seen her laugh as much as she does when she's here. And you watch her. Like a hawk."

He sighed, rubbing his face with his hand. It was obvious then. He probably looked a fool. "She's married. I want to stop, to leave her alone, but ..."

"Yes. But she's not happy with Brendan."

The question burned on his tongue and twisted his guts. It had for a while now, but even more since she'd asked him for help with the herbal remedy.

"I just need to know one thing. Does he ... does he hurt her? Does he lay his hands on her?"

Jo took the churn back from him, frowning. Her hesitation made him feel sick that the answer was as he feared. Finally, she answered. "Not that I've seen. But ... he's not kind to her. She's been talking with me about returning home."

Joaquin felt his stomach plummet. "Home."

"Yes, to her father's estate in Ontario. Away from Brendan."

Away from Brendan, away from here.

Away from me.

Jo became silent again, drawing the wooden stick up and down into the churn, but he could tell she had more to say. "The day Clara found me, I'd been violated and beaten by the worst kind of man. She fed me, clothed me, and befriended me. She brought me here. I owe her everything."

Joaquin nodded. He hadn't known, but it wasn't hard for him to imagine. A Chinese woman left alone would be an easy target for despicable men.

"Clara isn't happy over in that homestead. But she deserves to be happy because she's a caring soul." Jo looked at him, directly in the eyes, with wisdom much older than her seventeen years. "I think *you* can make her happy."

"You think I should ...?"

"Yes, Joaquin. I think you should." She gave his arm an encouraging squeeze. "You're a kind man. You deserve happiness, too."

Joaquin smiled, though he wasn't convinced. He had put his children through enough with the divorce. They didn't need their father adding anything else to their social burden. And yet ... when Clara laughed, his heart lifted in a way he'd never known. He would do anything to make her happy.

It was Monday, the most dreaded day of the week. Sunday was so perfect, with church and picnics, followed by a relaxed afternoon at home, but Monday lurked in wait, with its insurmountable task—laundry. The entire community shut down on Mondays. Clara's clinic closed, and the men knew to prepare their own meals from Sunday's leftovers. The women gathered with their neighbours at the closest spring or river with their bundles of clothing.

She imagined it wasn't so bad in the summer when it was warm and the rain stayed away. But now, in late October, the weather turned cold and miserable, and the laundry never fully dried. The women dragged out all the clothing from the week, including the bedding, to the stream. There, they would set pots of water to heat over a fire before pouring them into large wooden tubs. Then, the back-breaking work would begin. They would scrub the clothing up and down the washboards with harsh lye soap and then rinse them, wring out the extra water, and hang them to dry. Marty had constructed a set of lines that ran zigzag to allow the clothing to dry as quickly as possible in the sun or wind. But on days like today, when it was raining, it all seemed pointless.

"You don't have it so bad. I have four brothers and a father," Anna said. "I swear Drew rolls in the pig slop just for fun."

"Oh, stop your grousing," Rebecca snarled. "At least your belly isn't the size of a heifer's. Here, Clara will take some of yours." She grabbed a handful of clothing from Anna's basket and deposited it into Clara's.

Clara looked over at Jo with a suppressed grin. Rebecca was *cranky*. They had been avoiding her for the last week, but they were stuck together now that it was laundry day. But she couldn't blame Rebecca. Nearing the end of pregnancy looked very uncomfortable.

"How was your time at your mother's, Anna?" Clara asked. She was incredibly curious about Joaquin's former wife. A small pull of guilt tugged at her for wondering, as her thoughts strayed more often to her neighbour than her husband.

"Fine. Boring. Well, except Sunday." Anna's colour rose suddenly. She went back to scrubbing clothing furiously, leaving the other women raising their eyebrows at each other.

Rebecca rolled her eyes. "Just tell us what happened, Anna. We don't need to play childish guessing games."

"A boy kissed me."

The women stopped their scrubbing and stared at Anna. Uneasiness prickled Clara's neck. Joaquin would not approve of his daughter kissing boys.

It was Jo who managed to speak first. "What kind of boy, Anna?"

"A boy from church. I didn't mind. He's handsome."

The women went back to their task, awkwardly avoiding looking at each other, unsure of what to do. Clara looked down and realized she was washing one of Joaquin's shirts. She fingered the collar and wondered if he was still angry with her. They hadn't spoken since she had asked him for the herbs a few days earlier, and it bothered her.

"Ahh!" Rebecca gasped suddenly, looking down. "My water's broke, Clara. No! Not with Marty gone." Marty had left that morning for New Westminster to pick up an order of farm equipment and seed and wasn't due back until the next morning.

Clara hurried over to her sister-in-law's side. "He might arrive on time, Rebecca. First babies often take their time arriving."

Rebecca clutched her belly. Clara left Jo and Anna to finish the laundry, instructing Jo to meet her at the homestead once they were done. She ran to catch up to Rebecca, who lumbered along, wincing every few minutes with a contraction.

"Do you want Brendan to stay with you?" Clara asked. "I need to ride to the clinic for my medical supplies." Rebecca nodded gratefully as she made her way indoors.

Leaving Rebecca alone in the homestead, she went to find her husband. Brendan was in the barn, busy hiding clay bottles under the hay. She stared at what she was seeing in disbelief, swallowing hard.

"What on earth are you are you doing, Brendan?"

"Dammit, Clara. Go back into the house."

"Your sister is having her baby. I came to ask you to stay with her while I ride to the clinic." Narrowing her eyes, she marched over to where he was furiously trying to conceal the remainder of the bottles. She picked one up and uncorked it, the powerful aroma making her cough. *Spirits*.

"What is this, Brendan? What happened to no more whisky?"

"Uhh ... McGregor over in Glen Valley gave me a good price on this corn mash. It's no' a crime for a man to have a drink. It'll be cheaper than the saloon."

She threw the bottle down in the hay with disgust. "Where did you get the money for this?"

He looked away, hiding his face. "I traded the pistol for it."

"*What?* The pistol? It's not even *mine*, Brendan! How could you?"

"All the more reason it needed to go. Another man giving my wife a gift."

Clara shook her head incredulously. Fury nearly overwhelmed her, but Rebecca couldn't be forgotten.

"Go into the house. Your sister is in labour and doesn't want to be alone. I'll be back shortly."

Brendan reluctantly left the barn and trudged to the house. Clara stared at the bottles, a hard knot sitting in the bottom of her stomach. Finally, she saddled Red and left for the clinic.

CLARA AND JO WORKED TOGETHER, and the baby was born the next morning, red and squalling. Once they determined the baby was healthy, Jo left for the day to do the chores at the Walker farm.

"What's his name?" Clara asked, wiping Rebecca's brow. It had been an easy birth, with no complications, though Rebecca likely didn't think so, as she was clearly exhausted.

Still, Rebecca grinned, elated with the adrenaline of delivering a child. "Patrick. Patrick Byrne. After Marty's father. He's promised to raise the child as his own."

"Marty's a good man, Rebecca. You're lucky to have him."

"Aye." She looked down at her baby fondly, who was suckling at her breast. "I am."

There was a bang at the door. "Is it done? Has the babe been born?"

Clara let Brendan in with a glare, the spirits in the barn still searing in her mind. During the long hours spent tending to Rebecca, her resentment had grown. How dare he trade her pistol? And for liquor. There would never be an end to his drinking, no matter what he promised.

Brendan came over to the bed, tripping over a pair of boots left on the floor. He had opened one of the bottles while waiting; the smell trailed after him, and he swayed in his steps.

"Ah. Not a ginger, then." He peered at the nursing baby.

"Of course, not a ginger." Rebecca's voice was hot. "I told you it wasn't Marty's child from the beginning."

Brendan shrugged. "Just a bastard then."

Rebecca's eyes widened with a ferocious look. "You bugger!" she screamed. "You're a good-for-nothing drunk. Even your wife hates you." Spit flew from her mouth, and she struggled to get out of bed.

Clara rushed to hold her down. "Rebecca, you really should stay—"

There was a loud crash as the chamber pot flew across the room and smashed into the wall. Rebecca rose from the bed with effort, blood soaking the front of her shift. Her face was red with fury as she stared at her brother.

Clara took the baby. He was barely an hour alive, but she needed to take him outdoors, away from the fight. She ran around the side of the homestead with baby Patrick, hot tears blinding her vision. The hell continued inside—Clara could hear them both screaming, their Irish accents thickened in anger. It was too much. It was always too much with Brendan. She sobbed, covering her mouth with her free hand, as the exhaustion of being up all night coupled with the overwhelming disaster of her marriage.

"Clara? What's the matter?" Joaquin ran towards her from across the field. She frantically tried to wipe her tears away, but it was too late. He had seen. He gathered her in his arms, the baby between them. He held her for a moment, and she rested her head ever so briefly against his chest.

"Anna told me Rebecca went into childbirth." He stopped suddenly, pulling back. "Is Rebecca all right?"

Another smash came from the homestead, followed by a string of curse words.

"Brendan called her son a bastard. He's drunk again." She looked up at him, her eyes again full of tears.

Joaquin sighed heavily and pulled her to him once more. It started to rain, the cold pelts hitting the back of her neck. "Here. Give him to me." He took the baby and put him under his coat, and they made their way to the barn.

"I noticed that you've kept Red here these past few days." His voice was quiet, and he furrowed his brow.

Clara was too exhausted to lie. "I thought you were angry with me. About the remedy."

Joaquin came to sit beside her on a bale of hay. Patrick fussed, missing his mother's milk, but he rocked the babe like a seasoned parent. "I'm not angry with you. I ... I'm worried. What happens if he finds out? He could report you to the law. Or worse."

"I don't care anymore." She turned to him, putting all her trust in him. "You won't tell?"

"No, of course not."

"I've made a mistake, Joaquin. I don't know what to do." She put her head in her hands, blinking back more hot tears. Leaving. It was the only way out. Her father would fix it, though she would have to swallow her pride and admit her fault.

"Everyone makes mistakes, Clara." His voice was soft but firm, and she lifted her head to look at him. His eyes held something in them that made her pulse begin to race. "You just need to leave your mistakes behind and move forward."

He gently pushed the hair that had fallen into her face away. "You're becoming a great doctor. And you've got friends. Me. Jo. And other folks in town, I'm certain. Are those things you want to give up?"

"No," she whispered, leaning against his shoulder, so solid and reassuring. "I don't."

They sat in peaceful quiet, with only the sounds of the animals and the rain outside, until Joaquin finally stood. He took Clara's hand and led her, with the sleeping infant, back into the house.

Chapter 12

November 1885

JUST AS JOAQUIN SAT DOWN TO BREAKFAST, BEN YELLED from the front door. "Father!"

The noise from five children was enough to drive anyone mad.

"Just let her in!" he hollered back. It would be Clara. She was always early, never late.

Her voice filtered into the kitchen. "Good morning, Ben. How are you?"

Joaquin leaned back in his chair for a sight of her down the hall, reprimanding himself even as he did it. Jo was with her, and they hung their coats on the hook by the door. Clara turned to smile at him—her hair was down today, braided in a plait down her back rather than pinned up, as she often wore it.

"Ladies. Please, eat." He got up and helped Anna prepare them a plate of eggs, potatoes, and thick slices of back bacon. Clara came around the table and poured the coffee, sidling up next to him.

"Thank you," she said, only loud enough for him to hear. "For coming with me to McGregor's."

"I just don't want you to be disappointed, Clara. He may have sold the pistol already or could refuse to sell it back. He's an unsavoury man, at best."

"I know, but I'd like to try all the same." They sat together at the table, Clara taking the seat next to his. They were quiet for a while, and he watched her eat out of the corner of his eye. He found it amusing, the small ways in which her refined upbringing came through. Eating was one of them, her knife and fork always carefully poised.

"What happened with the corn liquor that Brendan stashed in the barn?"

"Marty dumped it. Brendan is furious. Especially with me for telling."

Joaquin glanced over at Jo, whose face remained still. She had promised to inform him if Brendan laid a hand on Clara. It was a worry that wouldn't leave him, one that kept him awake at night.

"Nothing good ever came from corn mash. It was my grandfather's drink and turned him into a mean devil." He paused, deciding to reveal more details from his childhood to gauge Clara's reaction. "He turned his fists on us all, especially my grandmother."

She looked at him with an expression that made him want to forget everyone in the room, take her in his arms, and kiss her over and over. She reached for his hand, which he took, and curled it into his, just the way he liked it. Their touches had become frequent, and it filled him with cautious hope and desperate longing, despite knowing he was coveting another man's wife. Will had seen them in a parting embrace yesterday. He'd raised his eyebrows but said nothing. Jo had probably told him of his father's affection, as the two of them were inseparable these days.

"Joaquin," Clara said his name, but with purpose. She wanted something. "It's ... your hair. Jo and I were discussing this on the way over. It needs a cut. I'm going to do it for you before we leave."

He looked at them, eyes wide. It did need cutting. He just wasn't sure he could handle her hands in his hair without his body reacting.

"Oh yes. Please do, Clara. Here, I've got soap to wash it first." Anna's voice came from the kitchen, and soon the three women were scurrying around, arranging the water basin and scissors.

"No. I'll visit the barber in town—" Before he knew it, he was leaning back in a chair with his hair wet. Then it was just he and Clara, as Jo and Anna had gone upstairs to start the morning chores.

Her hands were firm and brisk as she washed. He should've known they would be, as any great doctor needed steady hands. You could have all the knowledge in the world, but without calm nerves and a strong resolve, it would be for nothing. He took a couple of deep breaths, relaxing into her hands.

"Did he hurt you? Your grandfather?"

He looked up at her backwards and smiled. "No. Not really. My mother and uncle protected me."

She was quiet, biting her lip, as she pulled his head back down to rinse. "What are their names? Your mother and uncle?"

"Beth and Eddie. Eddie was more like a brother, really. We're only five years apart. I'm going to visit him soon, actually. His wife is pregnant again, and she's lost the last two, so they want me there for the delivery." Joaquin wished he could take Clara along. He wished she was his. A bittersweet pang grew in his chest. If only he could rid himself of these feelings, but they had evolved into a consuming desire that plagued him.

"And your mother?"

"She died six years ago. From the pox. My grandmother died in the same week."

She was quiet again, and he knew she was feeling his grief. "That must have been devastating."

"It was."

They lapsed into silence as she started to cut. She took her time, trimming his hair evenly. After a while, the *swish* of the scissors lulled him into closing his eyes.

"Why did your wife leave you for another man?" she asked quietly, almost under her breath.

His eyes shot open, jolted by her question. He should have known it was coming, though. It was only fair that she wanted to know about Laura.

"Let's save that for the ride, Clara. It's a fair way to McGregor's, and we need to leave."

It had been a longer ride than Clara expected, and for most of it, they hadn't spoken. Joaquin had made her take one of his horses, as he'd said Red would make McGregor think she had money. She'd shaken her head at the entire ordeal. Brendan certainly knew how to make her life complicated. She desperately wanted the pistol back, as she was determined to return it to Joseph one day.

The unanswered question hung between them, growing stagnant. Clara had begun to wish that she'd never asked it. It was his business, after all. But something about his demeanour made her wait before broaching a different topic. It seemed like he was choosing his words. They'd been riding for about forty minutes when he pulled over and slid off his horse. He took her reins and helped her down.

"That's McGregor's right there." He pointed to a large home, not unlike his own. "Listen to me, Clara. I want you to let me do the talking in there. He's not the type to listen to a woman."

"All right," she replied, then smiled upon noticing his red cheeks and nose. It was cold, and although they both wore hats and gloves, they were stamping their feet to keep warm.

"Come, you're shivering." He opened his arms, and she slid in, nestled against his chest. It had been happening a lot lately, both finding any excuse to touch the other. She knew in the back of her mind that it wasn't right, but she found herself not caring. Brendan barely spoke to her these days, and Joaquin provided the comfort she desperately needed.

"I've thought about your question," he said, rubbing her back with his gloved hand. "And I will answer it. But I have one, too."

Clara looked up at him, eyebrow cocked. This was going to be personal.

"Why did you marry Brendan? Was it love? I don't understand how a beautiful woman from a wealthy family ended up with a man like him."

Clara laughed, though her stomach fluttered at his words. She nudged him playfully with her elbow. "The one time I ask you a question, you answer it with a question. No. You first." It would give her time to think. Did she still love Brendan? Had she ever? Somewhere inside her, she had a memory of perhaps loving him, but it was deeply buried.

Joaquin laughed, too. "All right. Let's get this done first."

They walked their horses onto the property and tied them near the gate. Joaquin knocked on the front door. No answer. He knocked again.

The door opened, and a young girl appeared. She was beautiful, with golden blond hair that was braided intricately around her head. Her dress, a pretty shade of pink, was covered in blood. Joaquin grabbed Clara's waist tight as she gasped at the sight of the girl.

"We should go," he whispered hotly in her ear.

It was too late. An older man, who Clara could only guess was McGregor, came down the stairs into the foyer. "Ahh. If it isn't good ol' Georgie's grandson. You look nothin' like him. Must be the taint of the Spanish blood in ya." His eyes fell on Clara. "My, my. Well done on your woman though."

"We're here for the lady's pistol. This here's Mrs. Murphy. Her husband traded you a pistol for some mash."

"Murphy, eh? Sorry, I don't recall."

"Brendan Murphy. An Irishman. Blond."

"Ah. That wee scoundrel from the saloon. Didn't know he had such a pretty wife, though."

"Do you have the pistol or not, McGregor? It has a fine engraving on the side."

McGregor looked them over, running his tongue over his

teeth. "I do recall you're a doctor. I'm in need of some medical assistance just now. For the pistol."

Joaquin grew still beside Clara. "We'd just prefer to pay. The lady's brought some money."

"Hmm. Sorry, I just remembered the pistol's been sold to a trader that came through." McGregor went to close the door.

"I can do it." Clara blurted out. The pistol was there, she knew it. "I'm a—nurse," she finished lamely. McGregor didn't seem a man to trust a female physician. She heard Joaquin inhale sharply beside her.

The door opened. "Get inside."

McGregor took them upstairs. Fine rugs and expensive furniture filled the house, though everything seemed to be covered in a fine layer of dust. She guessed that McGregor had done very well with his illegal moonshine distillery.

In a room on the second floor, a blond woman lay in bed. She was the girl's mother, it appeared, as the resemblance was striking. She had not one but two arrowheads lodged in her leg. Clara's mouth hung open. Nerves threatened to overtake her—she had never removed an arrow but had heard it was treacherous.

"Are you happy?" Joaquin hissed in her ear. "I told you not to say anything."

She turned to him. "What—"

"Don't ask. For heaven's sake, Clara. We'll just remove them and get out of here." He cast a suspicious look around the room. "McGregor's got a lot of dealings with criminal types."

As if on cue, McGregor came back into the room. He held Clara's pistol in one hand and a knife in the other. The woman stirred slightly, moaning in her unconscious state.

McGregor handed her the knife. "Whisky's in the drawer." He cocked the hammer of the pistol and kept his place near the door. "Get to work. She dies, so do you."

Clara froze, staring down at the barrel of Joseph's pistol. She shot a glance at Joaquin, whose face grew dark and thunderous.

"I'll need a tourniquet," she said as she looked around the room. She spotted the ties holding the curtains back. "This will do."

As she tied the tourniquet above the arrows, Joaquin came to her side.

"I'll do it, Clara."

McGregor shook his head. "No. I'm remembering just now what happened the last time you took out an arrowhead, lad. Your grandfather bled out all over my front lawn if I do recall. Let's take our chance with the lady."

Clara looked at Joaquin in horror. His grandfather had died here?

Joaquin blew out a heavy breath. "Clara, you'll need to cut around the head. Do not yank on the wooden shaft. The animal sinew that attaches the head to the shaft tends to dissolve in the body, so you'll end up having to dig if you pull it off."

He pulled a chair up to the bed as Clara tightened the curtain sash around the woman's leg. She did her best to ignore McGregor, who still had the pistol pointed at her.

She had no doubt this man would shoot them both if she failed.

"Laudanum?" she asked. The woman would be in excruciating pain once Clara started to cut.

The older man shook his head. "Whisky."

"Joaquin—"

"I'll hold her down." He stood, giving her the chair and positioning himself to hold the woman's leg. Clara drew in a breath and made the first cut.

"Stoppe! Nei! Stoppe!" The woman opened her eyes, crying out in a language Clara had never heard. Her keening wail filled the room for an interminable hour as Clara worked feverishly to remove both arrowheads.

CLARA AND JOAQUIN stood by the window, watching the sunset. The woman was alive but was moaning in pain from the bed.

"She really needs some laudanum," Clara said, walking over to check her for fever. "She can't rest for the discomfort."

She went back over the window and put her hand on Joaquin's back. "I'm sorry. Please. We're stuck in here all night. I can't bear for you to be upset with me still." When the arrowheads had been successfully removed, McGregor had left, locking the door behind him. He'd shouted through the door that they were to keep the woman alive overnight, and he'd let them out in the morning.

"I'm not upset with you, Clara. But spending the night at McGregor's is hardly ideal."

Clara sighed. "Maybe we can climb down on the roof."

Joaquin gave a dry laugh. "I don't want to get shot and die on McGregor's land." He still faced the window, leaning his arms high on the glass. "Not like my grandfather."

She leaned against the window frame, trying to catch a glimpse of his face. "Everyone will think—"

"Yes. It will be all over town by tomorrow. They won't care about me so much. I'm already a stain in their eyes. But they will talk about you, to be certain. Spending the night with another man. Martha Davenport will never let that die; you can be assured."

She thought about his words. Even if they tried to explain themselves, the gossip would be damaging. Not just to her but Rebecca and Jo, too. Had she condemned them to loneliness?

"We'd best not see each other for a while after this," Joaquin suggested.

"No. Joaquin—"

He turned to her, his face serious. His clothing covered in the woman's blood, the same as hers. "You're a married woman and a beautiful one. I'm a divorced man. Their words will not be kind."

The sun was gone, and the room was dimming rapidly. Clara went and flopped onto the settee, not caring that her bloody clothing was likely staining the furniture. "I really am sorry, Joaquin. I should have listened to you and let you talk with McGregor."

He sighed and moved from his post at the window to sit beside her. "Well, you need to think a little more carefully before you act." He shook his head. "But at the root of it, it's not your fault. You shouldn't have to be chasing your possessions that were sold for spirits. I just don't like to be involved with McGregor."

Joaquin sat back on the seat and brought her into his open arm. She came, her head resting against the inside of his shoulder, his hand curling at her waist.

"We should stop doing this." His voice was husky, and in the darkness of the room, Clara heard something else: his aching loneliness that matched her own.

"You're not a stain." She turned her face up to his, feeling his heartbeat against her cheek. "You said you were a stain in their eyes, but you're not."

He looked down at her, their faces almost touching. "I'm a bastard, Clara. From the second I was conceived, that was already determined. The other children weren't allowed to play with me. My grandfather had to pay a large sum to my wife's family for me to get married at all. I had enough smarts to go to school, but I had to lie on the paperwork to get in."

"You're smart. Kind and gentle and a good father. A good friend. You're not a stain. Not to me, anyway."

He gave her waist a squeeze, and they fell into a momentary stillness. The woman had gone quiet in the bed, and Clara hoped she was asleep.

"My wife didn't leave me for another man. Well, she's married again now, but that wasn't the cause." He took a deep breath, and Clara sat up, out of his embrace. "That's the only grounds for divorce, adultery, so that's the story we decided to tell."

"Oh." Clara didn't know why it bothered her so much, but her stomach was in knots. It sounded like maybe he had been the one to blame.

"There was nothing between us from the start. Which

isn't so unusual, I guess. Folks get married with no feeling for each other all the time. Around the time our second youngest, Drew, was born, it started to go awry. With all the stresses of managing a farm, my medical practice, and raising the children, it just got worse. We could barely stand the sight of each other. She was right angry when she got pregnant with Ben. And then my mother died, and I was a mess." He heaved a sigh. "I hated the man I was around her, in the end."

Clara's cheeks burned, and she was grateful for the pitch-black of the room. She had visions of Joaquin and his wife, intimate in the bed of their marriage, creating their babies. It made her chest tight with jealousy. She got up and walked to the window, grateful for the coolness that came through the glass. She thought of Brendan, wondering if he was looking for her now.

"Your turn." He stayed at the seat, sensing her need for space. Or maybe he needed the space; she wasn't sure.

"Yes, I loved him. Or I think I did. I'm not sure. It all moved so fast, and I realize now I didn't know him at all." She leaned her head against the frame, staring out into the darkened field. "I was running. Not just from my fiancé but from my life as a socialite. My father wanted me to return, as was our agreement. But I couldn't live that life, going to tea parties and never doing anything useful. It's never been me. Never."

"Will you stay with him?" His question was heavy, loaded with a thousand unsaid words. A question she knew he would never have asked in the light of day.

"Women don't get to choose to leave their husbands, Joaquin. You know that."

"No, but money is your ally, Clara. You can do whatever you want."

Her mind raced. She knew her options well: leave Brendan, go home. Her father would not allow her to stay in the West alone. If she went home, she would likely remarry someone of her father's choosing and never practice medicine again. If she stayed, she might keep her freedoms, but at what cost? She turned to look at Joaquin, who was watching her from across the room. If only ...

He came up behind her, his body close, and she could feel it all: their connection, their desire, their love. It was frightening and intoxicating. He was everything she could ever hope for.

She turned to face him, wishing that his lips would find hers, take her away, out of her predicament, into his bed. But no, he would never do that. He would never compromise her.

Instead, she found her place in his arms once again. They sat together on the settee and talked. She told him of her father, mother, sister, and of her happiest memories. He told her stories of his children and his friends on the reservation. They talked until the morning rays lit the room and, settled in Joaquin's arms, Clara fell asleep.

Chapter 13

November 1885

CLARA WOKE WITH A START. SHE WAS SITTING ON THE settee in McGregor's home, her head resting on Joaquin's chest. There was another *thump,* and she tried to get up, but his arms held her firmly against him.

"They've been banging and hollering for a while," he said as she turned her head to look at him. "McGregor went down there to speak with them about twenty minutes ago, but he hasn't come up here yet. Probably enjoying a leisurely breakfast, the old coot."

"Who's outside?" she asked, resting her head against him again. He was warm and safe, with a comforting smell of the farm that lingered in her nose.

"From what I can hear, it's my son." He paused, his arms tightening around her slightly before adding, "And your husband."

Brendan. Clara wasn't sure she had the strength to tolerate whatever temper he was likely boiling to outside.

"I dozed off," she said, trying to take her mind off her husband.

Joaquin chuckled, the vibration rumbling under her ear. "Yes. I was telling you about my time at medical school when I was interrupted by your snoring."

She started to defend herself, stating that she absolutely did *not* snore, when the door of the room flew open. McGregor stalked in, coming over to the woman on the bed. He checked her breathing and looked at her leg. He raised his eyebrows at Clara and Joaquin on the settee, then barked, "Get out."

After making their way downstairs, McGregor gave the pistol to Joaquin, who looked at Clara.

"I'm keeping this for now," Joaquin said, emptying the chamber before putting it into his overcoat.

She nodded. Although she was exhausted from a night with hardly any sleep, she had a nervous quaking in her stomach. They'd shared so much with each other in the dark hours before dawn, and now everything had changed.

Joaquin put his hand on the knob of the door to stop McGregor from opening it. "We'll see ourselves out," he said, giving the old man a look. McGregor smirked but made his way upstairs.

"I'm going to leave you alone for a while," Joaquin said quietly, avoiding her eyes. "Until this whole thing blows over. I leave next week for my uncle's, and I'll be gone two weeks, maybe more."

Clara said nothing, but her heart sank. That would be December.

"I like your company, Clara." He looked down at her, his eyes sombre. "I like it too much. I wish ... I wish things were different, but they're not. This is probably for the best."

"It's not." Clara blurted out, reaching for his hand. On the other side of the door was her husband. On this side was a man she was falling in love with, a man she trusted with her life.

He closed his eyes, and she could see that he was fighting back his own swell of emotions. There was another bang at the door, startling them both. Without another word, Joaquin let go of her hand and opened the door. Will stood waiting, Jo by his side.

"Clara!" Brendan ran over to her as she came down the front stairs. He grabbed her behind the head and kissed her deeply before pulling back, a scowl on his face. "What the hell? Why did you come here with him?" he asked, glaring at Joaquin, who had stalked past them. "Did he—"

In an instant, Joaquin was back beside her, his face enraged. He took Clara by the shoulders and moved her aside. Then he drew back his arm and swung, his fist landing squarely on Brendan's jaw. Brendan stumbled and fell.

"First, you stole my whisky. Then, Clara's pistol. Now you've compromised both of our reputations by having us come *here*." He looked back at the house with disdain. "You're an ass, Murphy. I don't like you. Not one single bit."

Joaquin strode back to where they had tied the horses the morning before. "Let's go, son," he said, motioning to Will. Jo and Will rode over, and the three of them left. Marty, shaking his head at Brendan, joined them.

Clara stared down at her husband. His face was red where Joaquin had hit him and would likely swell and bruise. How did he always manage to say the wrong thing?

"Well, did he?" Brendan glared up at her as he picked himself off the muddy ground.

"Of course not." Clara walked away, hiding her face in case her true feelings showed. Joaquin hadn't done anything untoward, but if he'd tried, she wasn't sure whether she would have stopped it.

Clara got on the horse she had borrowed from Joaquin the day before. As they rode out of the property and onto the trail, she tried to look for Joaquin, Will, Jo, and Marty, but they were already gone, nowhere in sight.

They'd ridden about halfway home when Clara spoke. It was time she was honest. Perhaps Brendan would agree that their marriage was a mistake. Still, her mouth was bone dry when she spoke.

"Brendan, maybe it's time I leave. Go home to my father."

He looked over at her with a frown. "For a visit?"

"No, I mean for good." She shifted on the saddle, breaking out in a nervous sweat. "Maybe it's time to end our marriage. We ... don't really seem to be good for each other."

He was quiet for a minute. "That's not what *I* want. Although I can see that Joaquin's been filling your head with all sorts of immoral nonsense."

"This has nothing to do with Joaquin." She felt her pulse quicken with her lie. "You and I are nothing alike."

Brendan sighed. "I'm no' a bad man, Clara. I just drink too much on occasion, maybe. I can change. I *will* change. You're so beautiful, and I want to make you happy."

Clara said nothing but let out a sigh of frustration. She was starting to wonder if Brendan only liked the *idea* of her, if he'd ever seen her for anything except her beauty. The belief that he was going to change had vanished the minute she'd seen him trying to hide his stash in the barn.

They'd come into view of the homestead, where Marty was waiting, when Brendan turned to her, his mouth set in a hard line. "If you leave, I will hunt you down and bring you back. I'm no' scared of you or your father, Clara."

Her heart pounded as he rode ahead, taking the horse to the barn. She wasn't sure if she believed his threat, but it made her stomach churn.

Marty greeted her at the front of the homestead. "I'll take your horse back over," he said, helping her off the borrowed animal. "And I've brought Red back here, where she belongs. *You* need to stay where you belong too, Clara."

"Marty—"

"I'm not blind. Joaquin's a lonely man, and you have the doctoring in common. I think he's taken with you. Best leave that alone, Clara, before Brendan notices, too."

Clara glanced into the grove of trees that separated the two properties. Joaquin was so close but now felt so very far away.

It was Rebecca who saved Clara's reputation, who tamed the gossip before it caught fire. She dragged Clara to the quilting circle on Tuesday, coaching her along the way.

"I've dealt with my fair share of scandal. You just need to keep your head high. You haven't done anything wrong, so there's no need to hide."

They walked to Murray's Corner, enjoying the twenty-minute stroll in the brisk air, Patrick bundled on Rebecca's back.

"Do you think he looks like *him*?" It was the third time Rebecca had asked Clara if her son bore any resemblance to John. "I hope there's enough Murphy in him so no one questions if Marty's the father."

Clara looked at the baby's face, which had been growing rounder by the day. It was too early to tell, really, if he resembled John McKay. "No, I see a bit of Brendan in him, actually. In the cheeks and nose."

Rebecca looked relieved. She narrowed her eyes thoughtfully, then spoke again. "It's comin' again. His melancholy."

"Brendan's?"

"Aye. There are signs. He sleeps too much, eats too little. Drinks too much."

"Oh. What do we do? Maybe I can find a remedy to help."

"Aye, maybe. Sometimes it's mild, and other times ... well, other times have been hard."

Clara stopped walking and turned to Rebecca. "Tell me."

Rebecca kept walking. "It's mostly the drinkin'. But on a few occasions, he's had bouts of anger. Ones that he doesn't remember later."

Clara felt a sudden chill, colder than the frigid air. "You're a good sister to him, Rebecca." A much better sister than she was a wife.

"Aye. I'm happy he has you now to help share the burden. For a long time, it's been only me helpin' him through."

The women reached the front of Mrs. Davenport's house. Clara wanted to leave. The idea of explaining her night away from home to the town gossips filled her with dread. Brendan and Marty had searched the town for Clara, asking folks about her whereabouts. Now, everyone knew she had spent the night with Joaquin.

Rebecca grabbed her hand firmly and dragged her through the front door. They were greeted with the usual bustle of the quilting circle—scraps of fabric covering the sitting room, women drinking tea and eating biscuits, and of course, sharing juicy stories.

"Mrs. Murphy, Mrs. Byrne, come in. Here, let me take your coats. Oh, little Patrick has grown so much since last week!" Martha Davenport greeted them at the door, her pleasantries accompanied by a narrow-eyed stare at Clara.

The women made their way to their usual spot, next to the fire, to keep the baby from the winter chill. Clara dutifully picked up the quilt she had been working on, a child-sized one that Mrs. Davenport insisted she make. Would she ever need it?

Mary Williams, a younger woman with an often-malicious tongue, was the first to broach the subject, "Clara, we've heard about you spending the night with Mr. Walker all the way over in Glen Valley."

"Aye. Clara and Joaquin were called to tend to a medical emergency at McGregor's," Rebecca piped up, giving Clara a firm look. "Their surgery went late into the evening, so McGregor offered them their own rooms."

"Yes. One of McGregor's housemaids had a nasty accident in the kitchen. It was quite a complex procedure. Very bloody." Clara added to the story, hoping that the mention of gore would turn the women off from more questions.

"But why the both of you?" Mary pressed as the entire room listened in.

"I'm still learning," Clara explained. That was the truth, at least. "And McGregor paid us well. Twenty dollars apiece." She wanted to laugh at her own lie. Anyone who knew McGregor would know that wasn't true.

"Aye. Clara's husband, Mr. Murphy, was mighty happy about that. We need the money, seeing as we arrived here so late in the season. No crops to get us through." Rebecca finished the tale with flourish before helping herself to a cookie from a nearby plate. She passed one to Clara.

"I like Mr. Walker," one of the other women said. "And I heard his wife ran from him in the night. Just packed her bags, no goodbye. Must be hard on a man, raising five children all on his own."

"I wonder why she left," another mused. "He's a handsome man, tall and strong. Maybe he was unkind."

"Oh, I don't think so. I remember when they were first married, Laura told me that he was very attentive. Especially in the bedroom." A third woman waggled her eyebrows.

Martha Davenport cleared her throat loudly at the front of the room. The conversation had gone too far. She focused her gaze on Clara, whose cheeks had warmed, and not from the fire. Clara bent her head and worked quietly on her quilt. When she looked up again, Mrs. Davenport was still watching her, apparently not convinced.

THE NEXT FEW days went by in a sluggish way that agonized Clara. She kept herself busy cleaning the clinic from top to bottom, helping Rebecca out more than usual at the homestead, and taking plenty of outdoor walks with Patrick to ease him to sleep when Rebecca needed a break. But her eyes were always drawn to the trees that now seemed like a fort wall, standing in the way of Joaquin's smiling eyes, his easy demeanour, his warm embrace. She understood why they needed to be apart and that she should push the thoughts aside. But guarding her mind was exhausting, and she found her thoughts drifting, always, to him.

Her clinic had closed for the day, and she was finishing up the sweeping when Jo burst through the door.

"Oh good." Jo was out of breath like she'd been walking briskly. "I thought you might be gone."

Clara put away the broom and gathered her coat from the hook. "Just about. How was your day?"

"Not very busy, actually. Joaquin took the children to their mother's in preparation for his going away. So, it was just Will at the house today."

Clara raised her eyebrow but did not prod any further. Her friend had not yet confided any feelings she had for Will, although it seemed obvious to everyone that the two were courting.

Jo blushed at Clara's expression. "Will's asked me to marry him."

Clara hung her coat back on the hook, a grin spreading across her face. "What?"

"Well, not in an official way, but we've talked about it. Maybe in the spring."

Clara gave her friend a hug before pulling back to look at her. "Does he know? About ... before?" She imagined it must be hard for a man to know his wife had worked in a brothel.

Jo nodded. "He does, though he says he doesn't want to know the details."

Clara silently agreed. Details could be damaging. She thought of the women at the quilting circle speculating about Joaquin being an attentive lover to his wife. It was just speculation, but even so, the jealousy threatened to drown her.

Jo shoved a piece of paper at her. It was plain writing paper, folded carefully into a square. "Joaquin sent this for you." She paused before adding. "I read it."

Clara felt herself blush at her friend's admission. She had also not revealed her feelings about Joaquin to Jo. How could she? As a married woman, it was quite immoral. Hopefully, there was nothing revealing in the note.

C –

Leaving in the morning for my trip. Will's home, so if you need anything, ask him.

– J

Nothing revealing at all. Clara felt a little disappointed at the brevity of the note. Why had he even bothered? She put it in her desk drawer before taking her coat again and putting it on.

"So, will you go?" Jo crossed her arms, leaning against Clara's desk.

"Go? Where?"

"In the morning. To say goodbye."

Clara frowned. "It didn't say that."

Jo shrugged. "No, I guess not. But you could."

Clara looked at her friend, wondering if Joaquin had suggested she come. Or perhaps Jo could see right through her and the connection she had with her neighbour.

"You should bring a gift," Jo said, opening the door that

178

led up to her room. "Something for his uncle. That's the neighbourly thing to do." She turned and gave Clara a wink.

As Clara left and locked the clinic door behind her, her heart gave a small dance. Yes, it *was* the neighbourly thing to do.

JOAQUIN KNEW what he needed to pack. He'd done it scores of times. His rucksack with clothing, his shaving supplies, and food and water for the road. A sleeping roll and blanket —Eddie's place was a three-day ride through a mountain pass. There were no hotels, not that he would stay in one anyway. His medical bag. And he'd bring his oilskin travelling coat. The weather seemed fair, but any local knew it could change in an instant, and he'd be drenched through.

He packed with an unhurried pretense, contemplating his choices, while Will stared at him with a dubious look from the kitchen table. When he was finished, he'd carted it out to the yard, loading the horse with a heavy heart. She wasn't coming. He hadn't been clear enough in his note— how could he have been? It was highly inappropriate for him to write at all, never mind asking a married woman to come say goodbye.

Or maybe she simply didn't *want* to come.

It was nearly seven. He needed to leave, or he'd be making his way through the mountain terrain at night. Really, he should have left an hour ago. He rested his hands on the horse's back, ready to mount, when he heard a rustle in the trees. He looked back to see a hare on her way out, probably looking for her breakfast in his garden. He shook his head, pushing away the dismay and climbed onto the steed.

Then she was there right in front of him, on her own horse, probably on her way to the clinic. He caught his breath—her hair was luminous in the morning light coming through the trees, and the mist of the autumn air had pulled curls around her face. His whole body suddenly lit on fire, like a torch to the tinder-dry summer grass. All the effort he'd made this past week to push away thoughts of her evaporated into nothing. *Damn.*

"I came to say goodbye," she said, her voice tight with forced casualness. "Have a safe trip." She sidled her horse up to his and held out a package wrapped in brown paper. "This is for your uncle and his wife. It's coffee. From my father's travels," she added, her cheeks turning pink with embarrassment, as they did when she acknowledged her wealth.

He had difficulty finding his voice. "Thank you, Clara. For the gift and the well-wishes." The trip that he'd been looking forward to seemed like a duty now. He would be away for so long.

He held up the package. "Would you like to have a cup now? I've never had coffee from abroad before. And there's a new book on the shelf." He knew he needed to be on his way, but the thought of spending a little time with her was too enticing to ignore.

"Yes, please. That sounds lovely." She grinned, and they both slid off their horses at the same time. He caught her by the waist, their bodies pressed too close between the animals. His hand moved up to her hair, his eyes on her lips. For a second that dragged into eternity, his heart pounded as he thought about kissing her. Then he let her go.

"What's the new book?" Her voice was breathless as they walked to the house.

"Henry James' *Portrait of a Lady*. Have you read it?" He'd read it, and it made him think of her.

"Not yet. But I will by the time you return." Her smile was soft, and he imagined reading it to her, curled up the by the fire, in an evening that stretched into night.

The coffee was delicious, as he knew it would be, and the company even better. When he left an hour later, the package tucked snugly in his rucksack, he knew what he'd already suspected. He was in love.

Chapter 14

December 1885

IT WAS THE RAIN, THE ENDLESS RAIN, CONSTANTLY drizzling outside his bedroom window, that really got him down. It'd been the same in Ireland—long winter months of an endless piss that made everything murky and grey.

Brendan was awake, though he pretended to be asleep. Clara was up, quietly moving around the room with only the dim light of a single candle on the chest of drawers. He watched as she changed, her slender back falling into the rise of her buttocks, down into the length of her legs. He supposed he should feel aroused watching her. His body should be ravaged with the kind of lust that Marty and Becca still had for each other, even more so now that the baby was born. He could hear them in the wee hours of the morning, their moans echoing down the stairs and into his sleepless nights.

Clara blew out the candle and left without saying good-bye. She'd been even more distant than usual lately, ever since she'd mentioned she might leave. He had thought about it for a moment when she'd brought it up. It would probably be easier. But then everyone would talk. He'd become no better than the neighbour next door, not man enough to keep his wife.

A thudding on the stairs indicated Marty had also risen. Brendan closed his eyes tight lest Marty see him awake. He wasn't up to the torture of clearing the fields, not today.

The door of the room flew open.

"Get up."

Like the morning last and the one before that, Brendan didn't answer. The mattress dipped as Marty sat down next to him. "You stink. When's the last time you bathed?"

Brendan ignored him.

Marty pushed him onto the floor. "I said, get up. Runnin' a farm is a lot of work, in case you hadn't noticed. I'm sick and tired of doin' all the work around here."

Brendan peered up at Marty with a scowl. There was a pressure in his head, a pressure that refused to leave. He needed a drink.

"I'll be out in five minutes." He nodded to the door, and Marty left, heading outside. They would work for an hour before coming back in for breakfast.

He went over to the corner of the room and pried up the floorboard with a knife he'd stashed under the mattress. Inside the floorboard were three clay jars full of McGregor's corn mash. He'd hidden seven more under a floorboard in the barn and buried another ten in the yard, close to the forest, where no one would notice the disturbed land. He'd been more careful this time, especially since he'd had to pay extra to have McGregor's son Andrew deliver it.

He took a long pull from the bottle and then another. One more, and he corked it again. He waited a minute for the calm, the heady rush that would get him on his feet and outside.

Marty talked as they walked out to the fields. They were aiming to have the first fifty acres of the land cleared before spring planting—the few acres that had already been cultivated held their winter crops: turnips, carrots, collards, squash, and more.

"You need to take a turn with the axe today. My back is killin' me. I'll dig up whatever you get loose." It *was* backbreaking work, chopping up the roots, stumps, and growth that had been left behind when they cleared the thick forest.

Marty stood there, lording over him, watching him work. It made Brendan so angry, the way Marty thought he was better than him, always telling him what to do.

"You know," Brendan said, feeling a satisfied revenge before the words had even left his mouth. "You're no' Becca's first."

Marty looked up in surprise before setting his jaw. "I never thought I was."

"Aye, but what I mean is, you're not her first love."

"Get to work, Brendan."

"His name was Seamus. They worked together. And they liked to *be* together. All night long, in the daytime, too. I never slept for the sounds of her moanin' out his name."

Marty threw down his shovel. "You're sick; you know that, Brendan? Sick in the head."

Brendan threw down the axe. "I'm no' sick in the head."

"Aye. Ya are. And that pretty lil' thing of yours that you *say* you love? She sees it, too." Marty leaned in close to Brendan, right in his face. "I sure don't hear her moanin' out *your* name in the night. Better watch out before someone takes the job for ya."

Brendan felt the fury rise, starting in his chest, closing his throat, and blinding his eyes. His hands balled into fists, and before he knew what was happening, they made contact with Marty's face, and he pummeled him over and over.

"Clara is mine!" he shouted, spit flying. "I'll kill any man who dares to lay a hand on her."

When his rage ended, he looked down at his friend—the one he'd met on the boat to Canada, the one who'd made his sister happy again, the one who'd believed in him when he'd fallen for a woman far outside his means—lying on the ground. And Brendan did the only thing he knew how—he ran to the barn for a drink.

CLARA WAS APPLYING wild honey and gauze to the arm of little Tommy McCarthy, who had burned himself on his mother's stove, when Marty stumbled through the clinic door. His face was severely bruised and cut, with one eye completely swollen and blood running freely from his mouth.

"Marty!" she shrieked, covering Tommy's eyes from the sight.

Tommy's mother ushered her son out the door, throwing her payment on the patient table in haste. Clara shut the clinic door and drew the curtains closed, feeling sick to her stomach.

"Can you speak? What happened?"

Marty mumbled through swollen lips. "Your husband."

Clara felt her stomach heave. What had possessed Brendan to leave his best friend in such a state? Pushing back her horror, she looked inside his mouth, checking for loose teeth. Most of the bleeding seemed to be coming from his lip. It also looked like his nose might be broken. She had him hold a cold, damp cloth to it and another to his swollen eye while she lifted his shirt to check his torso. Nothing. A relief.

"I'll need to clean your face and suture this cut on your lip. Marty, tell me."

Marty yelped as Clara set his broken nose. "We argued. Well, he pushed me to argue, truthfully. Said some things about Becca. I said things back. About you," he said, looking slightly guilty. "Though he got the best of me. Not sure he's banged up at all."

Clara started to thread the suture needle with catgut, swallowing back impending hysteria. "What will you do?"

"Becca and I decided he should stay in the barn till his melancholy passes. She's concerned for you. It's the damn liquor he can't stay away from." He paused as Clara started to stitch a gash on his forehead. "You know, I'm not like them. I have a family, a loving one. I came here to make a better livin', own some land. Eventually, I'd like to bring my folks over as well."

"You're a good son, Marty. And a good husband. Rebecca's lucky to have you."

"Aye. When I met them on the boat, I thought Becca was the most beautiful woman I'd ever seen. All I could think about was what it would be like to kiss her. Then, when she was violated, I thought my chances were over. But I thought to myself, no, Marty, if you love her, you love all of her. And I do. I love Patrick the same as if I'd fathered him myself."

Clara bit her lip. She didn't love all of Brendan, that was certain. If she was honest with herself, she didn't even like him anymore.

Marty continued. "We'll be buildin' our own homestead in the spring, Clara. If your father agrees to sell me the back fifty acres, we'll still be close to you. But we might buy our own and be farther away." He paused, looking at her with his one good eye. "You're a fine woman. I wasn't sure about you at first, but I've come to know you and admire you. Your clinic's doing well, and you've learned a lot about homesteadin' these past few months. But ... Brendan won't be able to support you. He can't—not the way he is."

Clara sighed. Life with Brendan had become intolerable. What if he became violent with herself or Rebecca? Or, Lord forbid, with baby Patrick?

"All I'm sayin' is maybe it's time to ask your father for help. Whatever kind of help you need."

There it was—even Marty saw the futility of her future. Rebecca and Marty would leave, and she would be alone with Brendan. The letter to her father was already written, sitting in the drawer of her clinic desk. All she needed to do was mail it. And she should, except ... she had tried not to entertain the thought, especially in his absence, but she wondered what Joaquin would think of her leaving. The idea of never seeing him again made her keep the letter in the drawer.

The clinic door opened, and Anna walked in, much to Clara's surprise. Joaquin had only been gone a week, and she thought the children would stay at their mother's for the duration of his trip.

"Mr. Byrne!" Anna's face screwed up in disgust at the sight of Marty. "What in heavens happened to you?"

Marty looked at Clara, who shrugged. It was doubtful he wanted to tell the truth about his injuries, least of all to a fifteen-year-old girl.

"I'll be off then, Clara. Thanks for your help." Marty scurried out the door, his hat pulled low over his eyes to hide his face from the town. Luckily, it was a dreary day, and not many people were about.

"Is your father home already?" Clara asked Anna, a flutter in her stomach. Maybe he had come back early.

"No, we've just come for the day to visit Will. They want to meet Jo," Anna added in a whisper, even though they were the only two in the room. "Mother says she's not sure it's right for him to be courtin' a Chinese girl. They're just out there, waiting."

Clara looked out the clinic window to see Jesse, Drew, and Ben waiting on the street with a woman and an older man. The woman turned into view, and a twinge ran through Clara. She was taller than Clara, with a trim waist and a shapely figure. Her features were attractive, and her chestnut hair was pulled into a fashionable style. She could only be Joaquin's former wife, Laura.

Anna's voice pulled her back into the clinic room. "I need a tonic for her *husband*. He's having stomach troubles."

Clara looked at the girl with an insight into her feelings. It must be hard, being a young girl navigating two families. "I don't have any made up right now, Anna. It will take me a few minutes. Maybe send them on their way? You can catch up with them."

Anna nodded and slipped out the door to tell her family. They agreed to the suggestion and were soon on their way out of town. Clara wondered what Joaquin thought of them coming to his home while he was gone. She shook her head to clear the thought. It was really none of her business, and she had no claim to him or his home.

Anna watched closely as Clara crushed the ingredients for the remedy in her mortar and pestle: slippery elm, mint, and ginger. "Tell them to boil this for twenty minutes before drinking. He should feel better within an hour."

"When did you know you wanted to be a doctor?" Anna took a turn with the pestle, twisting her wrist to crush everything into a paste.

Clara smiled. "I didn't really: I just knew I wanted to do something useful. I was good at math and the sciences, so I chose doctoring. It was challenging as a woman, though. Still is."

Anna nodded. "I've been keeping up with my studies in the evenings. Well, my father insisted. He helps me with the hard parts."

Clara felt a surge of affection at Anna's words. Joaquin was such a good father, a good man. She could never imagine Brendan doing that. She blinked back tears at the stark foresight of having a daughter with Brendan. She would fight to have her daughter achieve her own dreams, and Brendan would want nothing of the sort. Her heart ached in a way she had never known—the loss of raising a child with a man who understood her and who had the same values and dreams. Someone like Joaquin.

189

"... in Victoria." Anna looked up at Clara expectantly.

"Sorry, Anna. What did you say?"

"I said, I was thinking of writing the entrance exam for teacher's college. Rosemary Murray did last year. There's one in Victoria."

"I think that would be wonderful, Anna. What does your father say?"

"I haven't told him yet. But do you think I can do it? Pass the exam?"

Clara smiled at her brightly as she poured the tonic into a jar. "Yes, Anna. You can do anything you put your mind to."

Anna took the jar in hand, making her way to the door. "All right, I will."

CLARA RODE home from the clinic, panic rising in the back of her throat. She couldn't get the image of Marty's bruised and swollen face out of her mind. What kind of villain had she married? One that would beat his friend over a slight altercation, apparently. For the first time, she found herself afraid that Brendan might hurt *her* one day. As well, seeing Anna had left her with an intense longing that sat uncomfortably in the pit of her stomach. She never had in her life missed someone as much as she missed Joaquin.

The sour stench of vomit pervaded the space as she came to the barn door. Taking a deep breath, she walked inside, leading Red to her stall. Then she followed the sound of retching to find Rebecca hunched in the corner, holding a bucket. Brendan lay curled on the floor, his head over the bucket. A bottle of ipecac, used to induce vomiting, lay beside them on the floor.

"Rebecca?" Clara announced her presence, though she wasn't sure why. It would be easier for her to just sneak back into the homestead unnoticed.

Rebecca's head snapped around. "Just go, Clara." Her words were sharp and biting.

"Is he...?" She didn't know what to say. There were three empty jars of corn mash laying nearby. This was more than just a compulsion. It was a disease.

"Leave." Rebecca sat down on the dirty barn floor, pulling her legs up to her chest. "Unless you want to clean him up, just leave."

Clara blew out a breath. The smell of alcohol and vomit was so pungent it stung her eyes. She sat down on the floor next to Rebecca and took her hand.

"I'm sorry," she whispered to Rebecca.

Rebecca looked up at her, her features softening. "This is not the first time and certainly not the last. It's just the way he is." Rebecca shook her head, trying to hide the glossy tears in her eyes. "I'm so afraid Marty will leave."

Clara's eyes widened. She hadn't even considered that Marty would be angry with Rebecca.

"It happened before, you know. I was engaged to a wonderful man in Ireland. Seamus. But Brendan drove him away. He drives everyone away."

Unable to find words, Clara pulled Rebecca into an embrace, rubbing her back in a small, circular motion. She looked at her husband, who was now slumped on the floor, snoring loudly. What would she do? She couldn't live with this forever.

Joaquin helped himself to another cup of coffee and looked out the window at the snow. He took a sip, savouring the rich, aromatic taste. *Coffee from her father's travels abroad.*

Uncle Eddie's wife, Charlotte, waddled into the kitchen. "I think the baby's coming today, Joaquin. I can feel it."

He smiled at her kindly, knowing that it would not be today. The babe had not yet dropped, and her mood was still too cheerful. Babies always knew when you were in a rush— or wanted to return home. He'd been away a week and a half already and could barely sleep for missing Clara. The harder he tried to push his feelings away, the worse he felt.

Eddie slapped him on the shoulder in a way that only family could. Even though they were uncle and nephew, their close age made them more like brothers. "Don't rush the baby, Char. More time for Joaquin to help me around the place. We'll whitewash the barn today and get to repairing the roof tomorrow."

Joaquin gave him half a smile as he put on his coat and boots. He had no qualms about helping Eddie, but today he was tired. He wanted a moment's peace from thinking about her. It was driving him mad.

"Joaquin, what's going on?" Eddie stood in front of him, blocking the entrance to the barn. The snow fell heavily; the winters were colder here in the interior.

"Let's get inside, Eddie. It's freezing." He tried to push past him into the cozy warmth of the barn. Away from his uncle's prying.

"No. Not until you tell me what's going on."

Joaquin laughed. There was no way he was telling Eddie. What would he say? *I'm madly in love with a married woman.* It sounded ridiculous, even to him. "Nothing's going on."

Eddie laughed back at him. They were similar in appearance—broad-chested and tall, with long, straight noses. Despite Joaquin's Spanish heritage, he was the lighter of the two, with light brown hair that picked up tints of gold in the summer, while Eddie's was dark, almost black.

"Even Char's picked up on it. You haven't been this quiet since you were thinking of leaving Laura."

Joaquin picked up a handful of snow and shoved it down Eddie's shirt. "It's nothing."

Eddie came back with his own snowball, landing expertly on Joaquin's forehead. "It's a woman."

Joaquin sighed in resignation. It might be good to talk about it. Maybe Eddie had some tips for forgetting about her. "Yes. A woman. And she's married. My new neighbour." He used the advantage of surprise to slip past Eddie into the barn. Once there, he found a long bale of hay and laid on it, arms behind his head. Whitewashing would wait.

Eddie pulled up his own haystack. "What's this? I've never seen you glance at another man's wife before."

"Clara's different. We have so much in common. She's even a doctor."

"Oh. So, you fell in love over an appendix?"

Joaquin said nothing. It had been surgically delivering a baby. But he didn't love Clara just because of that. Or her mind. Or her beauty. Or her acceptance of him, just as he was. He'd tried to pinpoint exactly why he loved her but couldn't. It was as if he'd been possessed by an unknown force that was unrelenting.

"I've never been in love before, Eddie. Not like this. I feel sick."

Eddie shifted his weight, chewing on the side of his lip. "You really love her? Or maybe it's just been too long since you've been with a woman."

Joaquin glared at him. "I think I know the difference."

"But a married woman?"

"Her husband is ... despicable. Just like grandfather. A thief, a liar, and a mean drunk. She's miserable with him."

"Oh no." They both knew how despicable that was. Eddie had moved far away just to escape his grandfather, who'd made their lives hell.

"Does he ...?" Eddie didn't need to finish the sentence. They'd both watched Joaquin's grandmother become a shell of a woman, beaten into submission by her husband's drunken rages.

"Not yet. But they haven't been married long, maybe six months at most. But the violence is there. I can see it, lurking."

"What will you do? If he does?"

Joaquin sat up on the bale. "I'll kill him."

Eddie shook his head. "No, you can't. You'll go to prison. Or be hanged. You have too many strikes against you already, being a bastard and divorced. It would never be a fair trial. Not to mention you have children to provide for. Besides," he added, stroking his charcoal beard, "if you do, you'll never be able to be with her."

Joaquin listened. It was good advice. "What should I do? If he does?"

Eddie got up and gathered the supplies for the white-wash. It was a tedious job—moving the animals to the far side of the barn while they cleaned and applied the solution, then bringing them back to do the other side.

"You can't kill him," Eddie mused. "But I know someone who will. For a price."

"Who?"

"McGregor."

Chapter 15

December 1885

THE SKY HAD JUST STARTED TO CHANGE, GOLDEN GLEAMS of sunlight fading behind the trees, when Clara locked the clinic door. It had been the strangest of days. The morning had been slow, with only Mrs. Williams bringing her daughter in for a sprained ankle, but the afternoon had kept her running.

First, Johnny Samuels had broken his arm, slipping on the steps down to his cellar. Then, she had been called away to the birth of Mrs. Smith's seventh daughter, who arrived like a tornado—swift and fierce with red fists clenched tight. Clara had arrived back to the clinic, preparing to leave for the day, when Sven Weber had arrived with his farm hand, who had taken a blow from his horse. Despite her fatigue, she craved the busy clinic hours. It filled her with a sense of purpose that she'd only ever dreamt of.

Clara glanced across the dirt road to the post office, desperate to mail her letters. She'd just finished them off that morning and had been hoping for a chance to send them out. She darted across the road and caught Mr. Williams just as he was packing up the till.

"Too late?" Clara asked, holding up her envelopes and giving him her sweetest smile. Mr. Williams sighed but took her letters and put stamps on them.

"Mrs. Murphy," a voice said behind her in a Scottish accent that made her stiffen.

"Mr. McGregor." Clara turned with reluctance to the older man.

McGregor laughed, showing a row of stained teeth. "My dear, no one calls me Mister. And rightly so. I'm hardly a gentleman."

Well, at least he knew the truth. "I'm just on my way to supper, McGregor. If you'll excuse me." She tried to move past him, eager to be out of his sight.

McGregor grabbed her arm. "I'll need you to pay your husband's debt, Mrs. Murphy. He already owes me fifteen dollars. After his next delivery, it'll be thirty."

Clara stared at him. "Delivery?"

"That's right. He's ordered twenty bottles of my liquor every month for ten dollars. Five dollars extra to be delivered to your homestead."

Her stomach sank. Brendan had been drinking in secret again. "I'll need you to cancel that next order, please."

McGregor laughed in a way that made her pulse quicken in fear. She remembered the woman, crying in agony, as she'd cut the arrowheads from her thigh.

"I don't take orders from a woman." He leaned in close— she could see the grunge on his teeth, and the odour of his body hit the back of her nose like an uppercut. "I'll need the money by Friday. I see that nice clinic o' yours across the street. It would be a shame to see it go up in flame."

She had pressed herself up against a shelf, away from McGregor and his threat, when a movement outside the door caught her attention. Joaquin stood outside the post office. An unexpected warmth spread through her body, making the anxiety about Brendan and McGregor wash away. Joaquin was finally back! Pushing past McGregor, she quickly left the shop.

"You're back from your trip." Stepping outside, she gave Joaquin a welcoming smile, resisting the urge to throw herself in his arms. Instead, she clasped her hands firmly in front of herself and kept a decent distance away.

Joaquin smiled back, his gaze sweeping over her, but then frowned back through the shop window at McGregor. "What did *he* want?"

Clara gave an internal sigh. There was no use in holding back the truth. "Brendan's been having more bottles delivered. McGregor told me I need to pay the tab." She touched his arm briefly before drawing her hand back. "When did you arrive home?"

"Just today. Actually, I need a favour," he replied, his eyes still following McGregor inside. "I went to the homestead, but they said you hadn't arrived home yet."

He gestured down to his leg, which had been tied around the thigh with a long strip of white cloth soaked with blood. "I caught it on an overhanging rock edge on the trail. I think the bleeding has stopped, but I wondered if you would suture it for me."

"Of course. I'm just glad you're home safe. Let's just pop across to the clinic. I can do it there."

"What happened to Marty? His face was quite bruised," Joaquin asked as they crossed the dirt road together. Clara gritted her teeth together at the question. Joaquin was not likely going to like the answer.

"Brendan. They had a fight over some farm work," she said dismissively, darting a nervous glance over at him. Truthfully, she hadn't seen anything of Brendan in the last week except when she retrieved Red from the barn. Even then, he'd been hiding in the loft of the barn, not speaking to anyone except Rebecca.

The sun had now set, and she fumbled with the lock on the clinic door. Joaquin waited a step behind, giving her space to find the kerosene lamp in the dusky twilight. As she lit the lamp, it bathed the room in a soft glow, illuminating the angles of her desk and softening the dark corners of the small room.

"Can you?" She indicated to his blood-stained trousers and turned her back, hiding the furious blush on her cheeks by busying herself with gathering the supplies. She heard him shimmying out of one pant leg, grunting in pain as he moved the fabric away from the wound. When she heard the creak of him sitting on the chair, she turned around.

She brought over a small stool and the lamp and sat beside him. He had gashed it a few inches above the knee, and the wound was angry and inflamed. She gingerly touched the area, and he flinched, drawing his leg suddenly to the side.

"I'm not going to hurt you." She grinned up at him teasingly, then stopped. His gaze was intent, his caramel-coloured eyes glowing almost golden in the dim light of the room.

Clara handed him the lamp, her heart racing once again. What was it about him that made her so flustered? After gently cleaning the wound, she picked out the stray pieces of fabric and rock, then doused the gash in carbolic acid, pouring too much from the bottle with tremoring hands.

"Dammit, Clara." He cringed. "You should warn a man before doing that."

"Sorry."

He seemed tense, and not from the pain.

He exhaled loudly. "No, it's me. I'm just so worried. That's quite a beating Marty took." He reached out for her hand, giving it a squeeze. "What's to stop him from hurting you?"

Clara said nothing, taking a steadying breath before starting the sutures. Brendan had never directly threatened to hurt her, but she hadn't thought he would hurt his friend, either. Letting her thoughts drift, she fell into a rhythm of pulling the curved needle under and over, watching the wound slowly close.

"He's a damn fool, your husband," Joaquin whispered, making her look up briefly from her task. His eyes had fixed on her, and it made her stomach tighten, sending a jolt through her entire body. Suddenly, all she could sense was him—the warmth of his leg under her hand and the sound of his breathing, which had become heavy and slow.

Then his hand was in her hair, like the morning he left, and he raised her face to look at his. His voice was husky. "I missed you. I know I shouldn't have. But I did."

"I missed you, too," she whispered back. "So much." She turned her face towards the palm that was cupping her face and hair and closed her eyes.

His whole body tensed—from where she had her hand rested on his thigh to the fingers that now dug deep into her hair. She didn't dare move—if she did, she would end up kissing him. They were in the clinic, and any passerby in the night could look in to see them alone in the flickering lamplight.

When Clara felt his fingers ease, she turned back towards the sutures. Her heart was pounding loud enough for him to hear, she was certain. She worked quickly, not risking a glance at him, afraid of what might happen if she did.

"You're pretty good at that." His voice interrupted her fervent work. He was looking at the neat row of x's running just above his knee.

Clara laughed, relieved at the shift in mood. "Yes. Thanks to my mother insisting I practice embroidery for hours on end. I always spent the entire time wishing I were reading."

He chuckled. "I can see that, actually. You, stabbing away with a vengeance."

She smiled. "Yes, like *The Three Musketeers*."

"Oh, *The Three Musketeers*," Joaquin said, a fond memory in his voice. "I must have read that ten or fifteen times as a boy."

"*Les Misérables* was my favourite," she said, speaking the title in practiced French.

"I can see you liking that one. You want to save the world, Clara." His voice was soft, and she thought about what his lips would feel like on hers. Warm and gentle. Or maybe fierce and wanting. She craved both.

"Saving the world one stitch at a time," she joked, trying

to hide the unsteadiness in her voice with laughter. She finished the last suture and clipped the end with her clinic scissors. After inspecting her work, she stood, stretching her back. "All done, soldier."

She left the clinic so he could dress, shivering in the night air. When he joined her, she locked up, and they rode off together, him leading the way in the dark.

"I forgot to ask," Clara said, remembering, "about your uncle's baby."

"A girl." He grinned back over his shoulder. "Julia, like your sister."

Too soon, they were at her homestead. Joaquin dismounted and helped her down off her own horse, his hands lingering too long on her waist. "Thank you, Clara, for the stitches."

"Goodnight, Joaquin." He mounted his horse, and Clara watched him turn away, his broad back disappearing into the inky darkness. Her heart gave a strange lurch at his departure as she turned to her own front door.

That Sunday, Jo grabbed Clara's hand on the way home from church. It was the third Sunday that Brendan had stayed home, and she'd hurried out the church door to avoid the questioning from the town gossips. Marty and Rebecca still lingered, chatting with friends.

"I need your help." Jo's voice was a whisper, and Clara turned to see Joaquin and his family not far behind her. Light snow had begun to fall, the first of the season.

"What's the matter, Jo?" Much to Clara's amusement,

her friend's cheeks had taken on a blush. It must be about Will.

"I don't know what to wear ... to the Christmas social. Will has asked me to go." They turned to glance back at Will, who grinned, his nose red from the frosty air. He was almost the same height as his father, although narrower in the shoulders.

"Anna's picked a few of her dresses that I can borrow, but I am not sure they're right. I think you're probably the best person to ask. Can you come and help me choose?"

"Now?" Clara asked, though she realized it didn't matter. Rebecca and Marty would probably enjoy the afternoon alone together. Without Brendan in the house, she felt almost like she didn't belong.

"Sure. They always have flapjacks for Sunday lunch. Easy to make, delicious to eat."

Jo ran back to join Will, and Clara waited for Joaquin. "Jo's invited me for lunch at your place. I hope that's all right."

He gave her an easy grin. "You know it is. Hope you like flapjacks. Ben wouldn't forgive me if we changed the menu."

"Jo wants help choosing her dress for the Christmas social." Clara glanced back at the couple, who were walking with her arm on his. "Looks like things are getting serious."

"Yes. I think my son is in love." Joaquin threw a sidelong glance at her, and she swallowed hard, keeping her eyes straight ahead. "It will be hard for them, though, as a couple of mixed race. People will talk."

Clara nodded, looking back at them again. "But they look so happy. Who can deny them that?" She felt Joaquin's eyes on her once more, and she darted a glance up to meet them. Imagining a life with him was happy too.

They passed her homestead without speaking, and Clara looked to the barn, where her husband stayed. If she were a good wife, she would bring Brendan some lunch.

"It won't stop, you know." Joaquin's voice broke the silence. "He'll say he's not going to drink, that he's sorry, that he'll do better. But it won't stop. I don't think he can."

"I'm starting to realize that. And I'm not sure how I'm going to pay McGregor's tab. That's all I make at the clinic in a month." She could use her allowance from her father, but there was no doubt in her mind that her father would not approve. Besides, she refused to indulge in Brendan's poor decisions any longer.

Joaquin led her into the trees, taking her hand and sliding his fingers into hers. The children barreled ahead, excited by the snow, planning snowball fights and snowmen. Clara smiled—there was hardly enough to cover the ground, but their dreams ran free.

"In the spring, I'll help you plant a garden for your remedies. That will help with some of the cost of running the clinic. I've always wanted to open a supply shop for herbal medicine, actually. Maybe in a year or two, we can open one together. Lots of folk coming in on the railway, and we need one in town."

"Joaquin." She stopped him right before the edge of the clearing. "I'm not sure I'll still be here by spring."

"What?" His other hand found hers, and he brought them both up to his chest.

"I've written a letter to my father. I ... I just haven't mailed it yet. But ..." She shook her head. "Marty will break off from us in the spring. Build a homestead to farm his own land. I just don't know how I can do it all. Brendan's not capable of taking care of the land. He can't take care of me. And to be honest, I don't want to live with his affliction forever."

Joaquin dropped her hands and crossed his arms. "And what happens to you when you leave?" he asked, his voice low.

She shrugged, toeing the ground with her boot. "My parents will cover up the scandal. I'm sure my mother will have a new husband lined up for me before I even get off the train."

"And your medical practice?"

"I'm not sure. I guess that will depend on my new husband."

His jaw was set, the hurt in his eyes evident. "What if you left him, but you didn't leave? What if there was someone here who didn't care about the scandal? Someone who very much wants to take care of you?" He took her hand again, and she gasped as he pulled her against his body.

She wanted that. So very much. "You have five children, Joaquin. I can't expose them like that. And ... I'm not sure Brendan wouldn't try to get revenge. He might be violent."

She imagined a fire engulfing their house at night. Joaquin shot in the barn. Herself, dead in her clinic.

"Father?" It was Will. He took in the whole scene: Joaquin's hand at her back, holding her close against him. Too close for friends.

She expected Joaquin to let her go, for him to be embarrassed, but he kept her close. "Son, I'll be a minute. Clara and I are discussing something important."

As Will ambled away, Joaquin chuckled. "I'm sure I'll get an earful about that."

Clara smiled but had not forgotten the conversation. He wanted a life with her. It sounded so wonderful. They were pressed close, and his hand was travelling up her back. How good it would be to belong to him, to be touched without worry.

His voice rumbled softly in her ear. "Don't leave. Not yet."

"I—"

He put a finger to her lips. "Think about it. Just know you have another option."

He led her out of the trees by the hand and into the house. They made the flapjacks together, testing out the role of a couple on a Sunday afternoon. It fit. Perfectly.

Joaquin shrugged into his plaid overcoat, heading out to feed the animals in the barn. The sticky remnants of their lunch remained: dishes on the table, pools of blackberry syrup left on the plates. He liked to give Anna the day off on Sundays to let her be a girl for the afternoon. He'd clean up when he came back in from the barn. Maybe Clara would help him. He smiled, listening to her giggle from upstairs, where the girls were trying on dresses for the Christmas social.

A knock at the door drew his attention. A stranger stood on his porch. It was a man with a thick mustache dressed in a long, charcoal grey overcoat and top hat. Glancing down at his shoes, a fine pair of leather Oxfords, Joaquin realized exactly who this was.

"You must be looking for Clara," he said, taking the man by surprise.

"Ah, yes. I'm her father, William Thomas. Rebecca said she's likely over here."

"She's just upstairs with my daughter. I'm Joaquin Walker. Please, come in. I was just headed to the barn, but I'll call Clara first." He felt slightly ill at the unexpected arrival of her father. She might be gone sooner than the spring.

"Hmm, I think I'd like to speak to you first, if you don't mind. I can join you in the barn."

Now it was Joaquin's turn to be surprised. Why would her father want to speak with him? He looked down at William's shoes and reached behind the door for a spare pair of boots. "You might want to change those."

Her father laughed, and Joaquin found himself smiling at the sound. Their laugh was almost the same. William removed his Oxfords inside the house and slipped into the boots. "Much obliged, Joaquin."

They made their way out to the barn, his thoughts racing. Had someone in town alerted her father to their night at McGregor's? Was her father here to avenge the reputation of his daughter? Once inside, Joaquin handed him the shovel, smiling to himself. It was his secret way of testing a person's character—silently asking them to clean up the horseshit. Clara had passed the test months ago now. He remembered the morning clearly; she'd looked so beautiful, like everything he'd ever wanted.

William smirked. "I think you'd make a fine businessman, Joaquin. Asking a stranger to clean up after your horses. Shrewd, indeed."

Joaquin laughed, deciding he might like William Thomas. "Remind me never to play cards with you, Mr. Thomas."

They started the work—Joaquin feeding and watering the animals while William dutifully shovelled. It was quiet, but he wanted to let the man start the conversation on his own.

"From the sounds of it, my daughter likes to spend time here quite often. Her letters are full of tales of you and your family."

Joaquin felt his pulse quicken. "We enjoy her company as well. She's a good friend."

William nodded, leaning on the shovel. "Especially when things aren't great for her at her own home." It was a statement, but Joaquin knew he wanted confirmation.

"Yes. Her husband's a drunk. He steals to pay for his compulsion and is putting Clara in debt." He wasn't going to mince words. William might take Clara home regardless, and Brendan didn't deserve protection.

William shook his head. "Oh Clara, what have you done?"

Joaquin returned to his work, unsure of what to say. He wanted to beg William not to take her home, but as a father himself, he knew the worry that must be pumping through his blood. Suddenly, he had an idea. "Are you staying, then? To visit with Clara?"

"Yes. I was planning to spend Christmas, and maybe into the new year. A few weeks."

"Why don't you stay here? The traveller's lodge is far, and you'll spend all your time riding back and forth."

"I couldn't—"

"It's really no bother. I have a spare room if you don't mind my noisy children. And it will give you a place to speak with Clara alone."

William nodded. "All right. I think that sounds lovely. As long as you let me help out around the place." He held up the shovel. "Manure duty included."

They chuckled together and finished the chores before heading back into the house. Clara stood, face pale, staring at her father's shoes in the foyer.

"Hello, Father."

Chapter 16

December 1885

By the time Clara and her father made their way through the forest and to their homestead for dinner, Brendan was sitting at the kitchen table, freshly washed and sober.

"Brendan, you're home," Clara said brightly, trying to hide her anxiety. Her father's surprise visit might very well be a strained one. She suspected he had already gathered information about the situation from Joaquin.

"Where else would I be, Clara? Did you enjoy your afternoon?" His face looked paler than usual, but he seemed fine otherwise. "Becca's left dinner on the hearth."

Clara went to gather the dinner, waiting for her husband to greet her father. He was silent, looking past him as if he wasn't even in the room. Finally, her father sighed and sat next to him at the table.

"Two lots of land, one for you, one for your sister's husband. Nice farming land, farther east." Her father cut right to the heart of his deal. He was offering to buy her freedom.

Brendan looked at Clara, his eyes hard. "No."

"Complete with homesteads and a couple of nice riding mares."

"I said no."

Her father looked at Clara, and she knew the conversation was going to get tense. From his expression, he wanted her to leave the room. She stayed.

"And two hundred dollars."

Brendan stood, his fists clenched. "For the last time, no."

"I refuse to let my daughter pay your debt to this McGregor. You're on your own, Mr. Murphy."

Brendan sent her a glare that gave her goosebumps.

Her father stood, pushing his chair aside. "Let's go, Clara."

"No." It was Brendan again, though softer this time. "You're right, Mr. Thomas. I will pay my own debt. And there will be no more."

Clara stood by the hearth, dinner bowls in hand. Had Brendan just admitted he was wrong? She looked at her father, who was also staring at him in surprise.

Both men sat back down at the table, and Clara brought over the bowls and spoons with glasses of water. She also sat, though with no food. Her stomach had been churning since she'd seen her father at Joaquin's house. Was she indeed going to leave with her father and return to Ontario?

"I love my wife. I'm no' willin' to give her up for money or land, Mr. Thomas."

"Joaquin says you've got a problem with the drink."

Brendan grimaced at the mention of Joaquin's name.

"I've just gone through some melancholy, is all. That's passed now, and I'm back to work. I'll spend some days workin' on McGregor's farm to pay back the debt."

"Hmmm." Her father pushed his bowl away, untouched. It looked like he had no appetite, either. "I'd best get back to the neighbouring farm. I don't want to be out too late." He gave Clara a kiss goodnight before making his way to the door. "I'll come to see you at your clinic tomorrow, Clara."

After he left, she made her way into the bedroom. It was early, but she had a sudden headache. Much to her annoyance, Brendan followed her into the room.

"You can go now, Brendan. He's gone. I know you've got drink hidden in the barn somewhere that you want to get to. I just want to sleep." She was exhausted, but not in the way that sleep could fix.

"Did you know he was comin'?"

She shook her head.

"Why is he stayin' at the Walker farm?"

"Joaquin invited him to. I don't know anything about it." It made her nervous. She was afraid her feelings for Joaquin would be very difficult to hide from her father.

"I'm not goin' back to the barn."

"I really think you should."

He sat down on the bed next to where she was lying. "Your father may own this land, but I'm your husband. I say what happens between us, not him. If I want to stay in the barn, I will. If I want to sleep in my bed, I will. If I want to make love to my wife, I will." He reached down and undid her blouse, reaching his hand inside.

Clara jerked and took his hand away. When he persisted,

she squeezed her eyes shut. She didn't want him to touch her, not anymore. Another man's touch filled her thoughts and dreams now. After Brendan had had his way with her, Clara rolled to the edge of the bed, listening to Brendan snore beside her. Joaquin's proposal came to calm her. She imagined leaving Brendan and going to stay with him. It was insane, and it would never be permitted by the town, but the idea made her happy. She fell asleep with visions of her life in that beautiful house. Tending to the home and garden, maybe a child or two doing schoolwork in the library, and Joaquin's arms wrapped tight around her when they slept at night.

Jo CAUGHT up to Clara the next afternoon when she was walking home from the clinic. It was a fair day, with no rain in sight, so she'd left Red at home and decided to walk for the exercise. The walk did nothing to clear her mind, though, which was fraught with so many worries—McGregor, Joaquin, Brendan, and now, her father.

"Did you decide what you're going to wear?" Jo asked as she caught Clara's hand. She was asking about the Christmas social, which was the next day.

"I don't think I'm going to go, Jo. Rebecca's staying home with the baby. I think I'll just stay with her to keep her company." Marty had volunteered to play his guitar for the evening at the social, and Rebecca didn't want to bring the baby to the event. Clara did want to go, but the idea of spending the evening with Brendan, her father, and Joaquin made her reluctant.

"No. Your father was talking to Joaquin today at lunch. They're both going. You *have* to go."

Clara sighed, her stomach already in knots over the whole ordeal. "I'll wear some church clothes, then. Maybe my blue one."

Jo stopped walking. "Clara, this is *the* event of the town. All the ladies have ordered new dresses. You can't wear your church clothes."

Clara giggled. "The social is in the Murray's *barn*, Jo."

Jo laughed along with her. "I know. But it's being decorated. And the dress is formal."

"I do have a dress, but ..." But it was the dress purchased by John McKay the day that he tried to attack her. She hadn't unwrapped it, even once.

Jo sensed her hesitation. "I'll come over and look at it with you."

They made the rest of the walk home quickly, and Clara breathed a sigh of relief to find the homestead empty. She reached under the bed, where she'd stashed the package when they'd arrived back in the late summer.

Jo gasped as Clara undid the dress from the brown paper cover. Its shimmery green fabric fell in loose waves, and the gems inside the embroidered flowers twinkled. It really *was* beautiful.

"I suspect it's too fancy," Clara said, knowing it would be. The dress was worth what most farmers made in a year or maybe even two.

Jo gave her hand a squeeze. "Well, you're fancy. In a good way, I mean. And," she said, giving Clara a meaningful look, "there's a certain man who would love to see you in that dress."

"I'm not sure Brendan cares about fancy dresses, Jo." Clara willed herself to speak calmly. What was Jo saying? Or maybe Will had told her what he'd seen in the tree grove a few days before.

"You know that's not who I mean."

"I'm married to Brendan."

"But you love someone else." Jo sat on the bed. Her voice lowered. "And he loves you, too. He asks me about you all the time. And he always watches you. He thinks about you."

Clara took a deep breath, the dress still in her hands. "Does everyone know?"

"No. But you two can't help yourself around each other. You both look ridiculously happy."

Clara smiled, despite her worry. It was true. She thought back to when they had made the flapjacks, how his fingers had grazed hers more often than they should, how he'd looked down at her so closely when she'd flipped the pancakes, their eyes never wanting to leave each other.

"Have you kissed?"

"No! Jo, I'm married." Clara's cheeks burned at her friend's question, though not completely from embarrassment. She wanted to, and she thought he did, too.

Jo chuckled at her. "But, you'll wear the dress?"

"I will."

"Do you have affection for my daughter?"

The question caught Joaquin off guard. Luckily, his face was turned away from Clara's father, his shoulder resting against the flank of the cow he was milking. William seemed like a decent man, but admitting to loving his married daughter might be too much. Clara was also much younger than he was—she hadn't even begun to start her own family, and he was thirty-eight with his oldest son intending to be married. Not to mention his divorce and heritage.

William came around the front of the animal and pulled up a crate. "I see the way you look at her."

He kept his expression flat. "And how's that, Mr. Thomas?" He couldn't bring himself to deny his feelings when even the mention of her name sent a jolt through his body.

"I've asked you to call me William."

Joaquin smiled and stood up from the stool, carrying the full bucket of milk over to the ledge and taking a new one. "What makes you think I have affection for her, William?"

"You look at her like ... well, I don't know exactly. I've never seen anyone look at her the way you do. And she ... she looks at you the same way. I'm not quite sure what to make of it, to be honest."

Joaquin's stomach fluttered, and he smiled again, despite himself. *She looked at him the same way.* She was the woman of his dreams, though painfully unavailable.

William stared at Joaquin, his forehead furrowed. "Aren't you going to say anything?"

Joaquin sat down and started to milk the next cow. "Yes. But it's more than that."

William's mouth fell open. "More than that? Are you—?"

"No, not that." Joaquin stopped milking and looked up sharply. "I would never compromise your daughter, sir. I just meant that it's more than an infatuation." He took a deep breath. "I love her. She's everything to me."

William was quiet, watching the milk shoot into the pail. "Does she return those feelings?" His voice was only above a whisper, his face creased into a frown.

Joaquin cleared his throat. "She hasn't said the words, but yes. I am certain." He decided that this was his chance and continued. "I know you want her to leave. Brendan is not a nice man and lacking as a husband. But … if you allow her to stay, I will watch out for her. And maybe, one day …" He wanted to tell William that he hoped to make Clara his, but he knew that would require a miracle.

Her father nodded. "Yes. Maybe one day." He stood as Joaquin finished the milking. "Let's go inside. There is much to discuss."

CLARA GAVE a nervous laugh when her father picked her up the next evening. Marty had hitched the wagon, and her father had decided to ride along with them, as Joaquin's wagon was already full.

"Father, we're going to a social. In a wagon. In a barn." She loved her new life in a small town, but the irony of her father coming with her was too much. They were both used to Christmas balls held at grand estates or fancy hotels.

"Yes." Her father laughed along with her. "I'm sure your sister will be quite amused when she hears the story."

Brendan came outside, interrupting their laughter. He was in his Sunday best, not owning any fancier clothing. He took in her gown and her father in his suit and top hat.

"Don't you think that's a little too fancy, Clara?"

"Probably, but I like it." She decided she wasn't going to

let him ruin her evening. She looked nice, and it felt good to dress up and go to a party.

"Actually, I have something to go with your lovely gown, darling." Her father reached into his jacket pocket and produced a small box. Inside were earrings—a circle of diamonds with an emerald inside. "Merry Christmas."

Brendan rolled his eyes while Clara gave her father an embrace. "They're beautiful, thank you." She put them on, enjoying the small bit of luxury.

Marty came around the side of the homestead with the wagon, and soon they were on their way. Brendan rode in the front with Marty while Clara and her father took seats in the back.

"How is Julia?" Clara asked. She and her sister had written letters back and forth, but she knew Julia was still angry that she had missed her wedding in the summer.

"She's with child. Around four months gone. You'll be an aunt in the new year."

"Oh, she must be so happy." Clara knew her father must wonder about her state of childlessness but was too polite to ask. At this point, it was a blessing that she had continued taking her remedy. How would Brendan support a child?

"And Mother? She didn't mind you coming to spend the holidays with me?"

Her father was silent for a minute. "She spends her Christmases with another companion these days, Clara. It's been that way for a few years now. I thought you knew, but I realize you were away at medical school."

"Oh." The noise of the wagon kept their conversation private, but she wasn't sure how much he wanted to reveal. "Will you—"

"No. She's discreet, and we attend many functions together throughout the year for appearance's sake. She's happier this way."

"Are you—"

"No. I've been busy with the company and chasing my daughter across the country. I'm not looking for my own companion."

Clara was quiet for a few minutes, grimacing at the jostle of the wagon over the bumpy terrain. She didn't think she'd ever get used to riding in a wagon. She would've preferred to take Red, but riding in a gown was not at all practical.

"Is it anyone I know?"

Her father gave a dry laugh. "You could say that. It's Charles McKay. John's father."

She raised her eyebrows at him, then looked down at her gown, rubbing one of the gems under her thumb. Her mother, in a companionship with John's father. No wonder the arrangement for her own marriage had been made. No one would've questioned the two families spending time together frequently. Did John's mother know? Closing her eyes, Clara imagined what her first Christmas as John's wife would have been like. Much different from her current reality, that was certain.

Pulling up on the Murray's land, Clara saw that Jo's prediction of the festivities was correct. Wagons scattered the field, with couples and families all dressed in their best, milling towards the barn. The sun hung low in the sky, but lanterns lit the way—at least a hundred—strung up with rope as a guide.

"Hello, Mrs. Murphy. Mr. Thomas." Joaquin appeared at the back of the wagon. He stood with his hand outstretched, offering to help her out. Accepting his hand, she smiled at his appearance. He wore a black suit, no tie, and his hair slicked back, though curls were escaping around his ears.

"You look lovely as usual, Clara." His voice and face were carefully neutral as he reached up to help her father down as well.

"Yes." Brendan came up beside them, grabbing her possessively around the waist. "My wife is the most beautiful woman in these parts." He leaned down to kiss Clara on the cheek, and she stilled, trying not to wrench away from his grasp.

"Where are the children, Joaquin?" Clara made conversation as she walked with the four men into the barn. She wished Rebecca had decided to come, as it felt rather like she was being escorted by her own private guards.

"They're inside already. David Murray always dresses up as Father Christmas and gives gifts to the children. They've been talking about it all day." He grinned at her. "I think Jo and Will might have a Christmas announcement as well."

"Oh, do you think he'll propose? How exciting!"

Brendan caught up with them, joining the conversation. "I'm no' in agreement of their pairin'. Folks should stick to their own kind."

"Well, I think they're lovely together." Clara shot a look at her father, and his expression made his thoughts clear. She and Brendan were not of an even pairing, either.

As they entered the barn, Clara smiled at her father and Joaquin. More lanterns hung from the loft, bathing the barn in a romantic glow. A large Christmas tree rested in the corner, decorated with popcorn and berries. Tables and chairs sat in long rows, with wreaths carefully placed along the middle. Outdoors, large fire pits roared, with extra seating in circles around them. The Murray women had been cooking for two days—dinner was roast turkey with stuffing, gravy, potatoes, and carrots, and the other women in town had contributed baked goods for dessert.

Jo waved everyone over to a table while Marty left to find the rest of the band. Clara sat between Brendan and her father, with Joaquin, Jo, and Will across from her. The rest of the children ran around the yard. Brendan sat restlessly beside her, bouncing his leg and looking around the room as if waiting for someone. *He's looking for a drink.* Her father and Joaquin had fallen into an easy conversation, discussing her father's business, but she knew Joaquin was watching her out of the corner of his eye and keeping watch on Brendan.

Brendan grabbed her hand with a ferocity that startled her. "Let's walk."

"Brendan, I prefer—"

He leaned down to her ear. "I said, let's walk."

Clara caught Joaquin's eye as she rose from the table. His face was hard, his eyes flashing. Gone was the careful neutrality.

She walked with Brendan in silence to one of the outdoor firepits, pulling her shawl close. Her dress was beautiful but not warm, and the December air was frigid.

"That man is always sniffing around you like a dog in heat. He's still looking at you, even now."

She didn't need to ask who Brendan was talking about. She glanced over her shoulder—indeed, her father and

Joaquin had eyes on them. A nervous sweat broke out on her brow.

"I'm sure you're imagining things."

Thankfully, Brendan was distracted, watching a group of men at a firepit farther away. "There's McGregor. Let's go." He started walking, but she stopped, letting him get a few feet ahead.

"I'm not going. I have no desire to speak with that man. I'll meet you back at the table."

Brendan stomped back to her side. She could see his temper rising to the surface. He grabbed her by the upper arm, his fingers digging deep into her flesh. "I said, you're coming with me."

"Stop," she hissed, glancing around at the other party-goers nearby. "That hurts."

His fingers tightened, and she cried out in pain. He pulled her along over to McGregor's fire. When she resisted the last few steps, he yanked. She stumbled and fell, her knee hitting a rock. Brendan sneered at her. "Get up."

"Let her go, Murphy. Now." Joaquin stood behind them, arms crossed over his thick chest. His expression became menacing, his eyes narrowed, and his jaw clenched.

Brendan laughed, grabbing her arm again and hauling her to her feet. "I think it's time for you to find your own woman, Joaquin. This is my wife. My property."

"Not if I have anything to do about it." Clara's father stood on the other side of Brendan.

"Let her go, Brendan. I'll not stand by watchin' you hurt Clara." It was Marty behind them. The three men circled them, and Brendan dropped her arm with a sullen expression.

"My, my," McGregor's voice pierced the dusk. "What a tangled web we have here."

Brendan looked around into the crowd that had formed. The townsfolk were all staring at them. Clara rubbed where he had grabbed her, a dark bruise already forming. She spotted the town constable heading their way, his dinner interrupted. Hot tears of humiliation pricked her eyes.

"Is there a problem here?" Sergeant McDonald looked sternly at the group.

"My son-in-law was just headed home." Clara's father spoke up, his anger visible from the light of the nearby fires. "I'm going to escort him."

"Have Becca set him up in the barn, Mr. Thomas." Marty's words were hot and irate.

The crowd dissipated as Joaquin took her father and Brendan over to the wagon. Marty returned to the band, and everyone around Clara resumed their conversations. Soon she was standing alone in front of McGregor.

"Mrs. Murphy. That's quite a lovely gown. If you'd like, I'll take it off your hands next week and clear your debt."

She laughed. "McGregor, this gown is worth well more than thirty dollars."

"Ah, you're right. A few hundred more. But it seems the gown is a bit of a bad omen. Who bought it for you? Not your husband, to be sure. A jilted fiancé, perhaps?"

A chill ran down her spine. Surely the old man was guessing. She frowned, peering closer at McGregor. Past his hardened expression, there was something familiar about him, but she couldn't quite place it ...

He leaned in closer to her. "I find you curious, Mrs. Murphy. Diamonds in your ears and a poor Irishman by your side. Yet, every time I've seen you, it's the Spanish bastard whom your eyes are focused on."

Clara swallowed. He seemed to know everything about her.

His face was too close for comfort, and she could smell the spirits on his breath. "It seems to me that you have a lot to lose." He raised his eyebrow, giving her a malicious grin. "Will it be your money, your husband, or your lover?"

With that, McGregor disappeared back into the crowd of men. Clara watched him for a minute before making her way around the back of the barn. She found her way by the light of the moon and sat on a log, away from the party, away from the people. What a tangled web, to be sure.

Chapter 17

December 1885

JOAQUIN BREATHED A SIGH OF RELIEF WHEN HE FINALLY found Clara twenty minutes later. She was behind the barn on a log, barely visible in the night.

"There you are," he said softly to himself. As he came close, he saw there was a bruise spreading on her arm, purple against the white of her skin, illuminated by the full moon. *That ass, Brendan.*

He gave her the jug and glasses he was carrying and took off his suit jacket. The night was cold, but the jacket was for more than warmth. He knew she wouldn't want people looking at the bruise when she eventually emerged from her hiding spot.

She let him put the jacket over her shoulders before she spoke. Her voice was husky, and although her eyes were dry, he could tell the tears were there, close to the surface. "Just leave me be, Joaquin. Go to your children. I'm sure you don't need any more of my ... complicated life. I can't even come to a Christmas party without everything going wrong."

Without replying, he poured her a glass from the jug, then poured one for himself. Fighting back the urge to take her in his arms, to let her weep against his chest, he took a sip.

"What is this?" She'd taken a sip too, and her surprise made him grin.

"It's Martha Davenport's famous Christmas wine. She only makes it once a year for this social, though people beg her to make it all year round for weddings and such."

"Martha Davenport makes wine?" she asked incredulously, taking another sip. "It's delicious. Is that cranberry?"

"And oranges. It's pretty strong, though, so don't drink it too fast." He paused, trying to choose the right words for what he wanted to say. "I'm sorry if I embarrassed you, Clara. But I'd do it again. I won't let him hurt you."

"Stop, please." Her voice trembled, and she tried to collect her emotions before continuing. "I don't want to talk about it. At all. Please. I'm going to drink enough of this wine so I forget about it completely." She reached for the jug and poured herself another glass.

He looked around to make sure they were still alone, then took her hand. He wanted to take her mind off Brendan and cheer her up. "Ask me anything."

"What?"

"You can ask anything, and I'll answer. But then you have to answer the same question."

She turned to smile gently at him. She was so beautiful tonight, especially under the moonlight. He wished her father would take the wagon to the nearest cliff and drop her husband into the abyss. But alas, the damn Irishman would still be around in the morning.

"What's your favourite colour?"

He looked down at her dress, then up at her. "Green. Or ... the colour of your hair. Yours?"

She laughed and moved closer to him on the log. "Also green. And the colour of your eyes. They remind me of honey." She paused, thinking of her next question, taking another drink. Her second glass was already half empty. "Where would you go if you could travel anywhere?"

That was easy. He'd had that dream since he was a boy. "I'd go to California, where my father was from."

"You should."

"Maybe I will, someday. You?"

"My father has already taken me lots of places, so I'd like to go to California with you."

He poured them both another glass, emptying the jug. "I'd love that."

"What do you want for Christmas?"

He laughed, heady from the wine. She must be, too, as she was not used to drinking and much smaller than him. "I can't answer that."

"Why not?" She was so close, and her body was free from the earlier tension. She'd let go of his hand, and her fingers drifted across his chest.

He let out a hot breath, stilling her wandering hand with his own before he lost all self-control. "Because, Clara, I've never wanted for anything in my life. Now I want it all. And it's not mine to have."

They sat quiet, sobered by his words. The party continued inside, with music and laughter drifting through the barn wall. Clara shivered against the cold, drawing his jacket closer.

"We should go. It's getting late." He drained his glass and stood, helping her up. She slid her arms into his jacket. "I'll tell Marty I'm taking you home."

She was unsteady on her feet and grasped his arm. He considered taking her around the back way to the wagon before collecting his children. People might wonder why they were emerging from the darkness together.

"You didn't ask me." She leaned against him, wrapping her arms around his middle. The wine had made her very affectionate. He couldn't take her back into the party, that was certain.

"What do you want for Christmas, Clara?" Despite his reservations, he revelled in the moment of their closeness.

"I want you to kiss me." She stared up at him, her eyes wanting.

He reached out and put both hands around her waist, pulling her away. It was taking everything in him to do so, as just the suggestion of a kiss had set his body aflame. "I want that too. I think about it every day. Maybe a hundred times a day. But ..."

"But, what?"

"If I do ... then I'll never stop wanting you. I'll never stop asking you to leave him. And I need that to be your choice. You need to be sure."

He didn't let her reply. She was drunk, and if she tried to kiss him, he wouldn't stop her. But there were people everywhere, and she didn't need another tale to fuel the town gossips, not tonight.

He spotted Will by the edge of the barn and called him over. Jo came too, flushed with excitement from the party.

"Can you take her to the wagon? She's—"

"Drunk. I'm drunk, Jo."

While Jo took Clara, Joaquin walked back to the party with Will to find the rest of the children. Turning the corner, he came to a halt. Anna stood at one of the outdoor fires and was kissing one of the local boys.

"Anna?" His stomach filled with dread, followed by overwhelming guilt. She was only a child. He should have been watching her instead of being with Clara.

"Father?" Her eyes were glazed, and he saw a wine glass beside her.

"Oh, hell." As he cursed, the boy ran off into the barn. Will came over with Jesse, Drew, and Ben in tow.

"Your sister's been kissing a boy out here, and none of you noticed?"

The boys looked at their feet. Only Ben piped up. "She's always kissing boys. At mother's place or after church."

"What?" He stared at his daughter like she was a stranger.

"Father, let's talk about this tomorrow at home." Will said, no doubt eager to get back to Jo, and the night was cold. Besides, they didn't need to cause another scene for everyone to talk about.

"Joaquin!" It was Marty, striding across the lawn. "Have you seen Clara?"

"She's in my wagon with Jo. I'll drop her off, Marty."

"Ah, much obliged. I've promised the Murrays that I'll help clean up here. Mr. Williams will take me back."

They bade each other goodnight, and Joaquin made his

way back to the wagon, his hand at his daughter's back. She'd been playing with dolls just yesterday, it seemed. Now there were boys to deal with.

"Father?" It was Will, again at his side.

"Yes, son?"

"I'd like to walk with Jo."

Joaquin sighed. He should say no, that they needed to be chaperoned. He knew his son was yearning to be wed in the way that most young men did. Well, not just young men, he thought ruefully, remembering Clara's hand on his chest. He was yearning, too. "That's fine, son. Just don't stay out all night, please."

Jo jumped down from the wagon when they approached, and Will offered her his arm. Jo was wearing Joaquin's suit jacket, and Clara was now wrapped in a blanket he'd left in the wagon for the ride home. He thought of her—in that dress that revealed much more of her soft skin than he'd ever seen—under the blanket. He'd better take the fastest route home before his wanting got the better of him.

CLARA BRACED herself as the wagon wheel bounced through a pit in the field, grateful not to be in the back. Anna looked quite ill, and Joaquin's mouth was set in a grim line. Something had happened between the two of them, and the mood was tense.

She pulled the blanket tight around her shoulders, wondering what her father had done with Brendan. Her father would likely ask her to return home with him, especially after tonight. She glanced at the man beside her, who had become her best friend in town, save for Jo. Could she say goodbye to him for good? Her mouth filled with a bitter taste, like the worst kind of medicinal tonic.

Joaquin's eyes were on her as they exited the Murray's field and drove onto the main path, but he didn't speak. That was one of the things she loved about him most, she realized. He always held the quiet for her—creating a safe space in which she was free to be alone with her thoughts.

"They're asleep," he whispered about ten minutes later, looking over his shoulder. She glanced back and smiled. The four children were all curled up under blankets, eyes closed. How they could sleep with all that bumping and jostling, she would never understand.

The wagon suddenly veered off the main path, into the trees, following an even rougher trail. "Where are we going?" The darkness of the tree cover enveloped them, but the horses continued on, sure-footed.

"Off the main road for a while. I'm cold. Share that blanket with me." His voice had an edge to it, and she thought she might get her Christmas wish after all. Her pulse raced at the thought.

He opened his arm, and she scooted inside his embrace, wrapping the blanket around them. Instead of settling on her waist, his hand stroked her bare shoulder and arm. As the wagon came into a clearing, he pulled the horses to a stop.

Both of his arms were around her then, holding her close. She leaned her head against his chest, breathing in his now familiar scent. "Your father spoke to me today about us."

"What did he say?" She let her hand travel up to where his shirt was unbuttoned at the top. Her fingers undid one more, and she slipped her hand inside his shirt, feeling the hair there, much thicker than Brendan's. She looked up at him, leaned up, and kissed him on the jaw.

"Clara, stop." Desire was heavy in his words, his breath thick and heavy. "I'm trying to tell you something important."

"I'm listening." And she was, though her hand moved up behind his neck.

"Yes, but I can't talk with you doing that." He removed both of her hands, and she sat up, out of his embrace. He gave a laugh. "I'm not sure if that wine was a good idea."

She pouted, and he pulled her back into his arms. She laid her head on the inside of his shoulder. "I love you, Clara," he whispered in her ear.

"I love you too, Joaquin." There was no hesitation in her words.

"I've never loved anyone before. Not like this. I think, of all the women in the world, you're the only one who sees me, understands me."

"I feel the same way. It's like we've known each other for years." She took his hand, rubbing the back of it. These hands that healed, never harmed. "What are we going to do?"

"Your father asked if I was in love with you. Or rather, he asked if we were in love with each other."

"What did you say?" She could hear his heartbeat, slow and steady, under her ear.

"I told him everything. About Brendan stealing the whisky on the reservation, about the night at McGregor's, my grandfather. Even about my divorce."

"And?"

"And, if he ever manages to get you untangled from Brendan, he's given us his blessing."

She sat up. "Joaquin. That's—"

"The untangling will be difficult. Your father says Brendan has refused any offer of money or land. He can try with lawyers, but it will take time. Years. Or might never happen." One of the children stirred in the back of the wagon. Joaquin stopped speaking for a moment until he was sure they had settled back to sleep. "I've given it some thought. You should go home with your father for the time being."

"No. I won't leave you." She couldn't. Being apart for even a day seemed too long.

He picked up the reins again, and they jolted into a start, back onto the path. "In a year or so, I'll sell the farm and come to be with you. We'll start over. Change our names if we have to."

She was silent, digesting his words. "You'd give up everything ... for me?"

His eyes were steady on the trail. "For us. And I won't be giving up anything." He gave her a quick glance. "If you'll have me."

She took the reins from him and stopped the horses. They were in the forest cover again, and it was pitch-black except for a sliver of moonlight coming through the trees. "Of course, I'll have you. Kiss me, Joaquin."

His mouth was on hers in an instant, warm but not gentle. It was urgent, like she might disappear if he let her go. His hands were in her hair, then down to her shoulders, before cupping her breasts. His mouth followed, kissing behind her ear, down her neck, to the low cut of her dress. He stopped then, letting out a low groan.

"I ache for you, Clara." He leaned his forehead against hers. "With my body and my soul."

"Oh, Joaquin." She took his face in her hands and kissed him again. "I won't leave."

"I'm so scared he'll—"

"No. I won't run. Not again."

They kissed, softer this time. It felt like home.

He picked up the reins once more, and they came through the woods back onto the main road. She sat apart from him, even though the hour was late, in case there were any townsfolk still coming from the party. He reached out and rubbed his thumb across her lips.

"Merry Christmas," Clara whispered, just loud enough for him to hear.

"The best I've ever had."

THERE WAS a banging at the door, pounding like her head. Clara sat up with difficulty, then lay back down again. She was so dizzy, and her headache threatened to make her vomit.

The noise at the door continued.

She slowly got out of bed and made her way there, barely able to stand. It was Joaquin.

"Are you ill?" His face was sheened with fever, and he squinted with pain. "We're all sick. Your father, myself, the children."

"Aye." Rebecca came down the stairs, carrying Patrick.

"You're all ill. It's been three days, Clara, since you've been in bed. I've made some broth. Take some to your home, Joaquin."

"Thank you, Rebecca, for your kindness." He took the tin pail of broth, looking at Clara. He wanted to say more to her but couldn't. She gave him a nod and shut the door behind him.

Once he was gone, she managed half a bowl of broth and some water before falling back into bed. Rebecca came in sometime later with a cool cloth for her forehead. She touched Clara's bruised arm.

"Did my brother do that to you? Is that why your father brought him home early from the party?"

Clara said nothing, rolling over away from Rebecca's question. That whole night seemed like it was weeks ago. All she wanted to remember was her time with Joaquin.

"Brendan's in a bad way right now. Sick with this fever, but also from the whisky shakes. I don't suppose you've got anythin' to help? Medicine or a remedy?"

"Why?" Clara croaked, and Rebecca gave her some water. "Why do you keep putting up with him, Rebecca?"

Rebecca chewed her bottom lip. "He's family, I guess. And for so long, we only had each other." She helped Clara to the chamber pot. "He told me you want to leave."

"I honestly don't know why he doesn't want to let me go. He doesn't seem to even like me, let alone love me." Clara made her way back to the bed, then sipped more water. The more fluids she had, the sooner the fever would leave.

"Aye. Brendan has a hard time lovin' himself, so how can he love another?"

Clara heard the truth in Rebecca's words. She'd seen that

when Brendan was low in his depression. Part of her ached with sympathy for him, but another part knew that she deserved to be loved, too.

Rebecca cleared her throat. "Do you love Joaquin, Clara? Because Brendan thinks you do, and I'm startin' to think so, too. You and he are as thick as thieves."

Clara broke out in a hot flush. She grabbed the cloth and dunked it in the cool water again.

"I can't say I don't understand why. He's handsome and kind. Your father seems fond of him, too."

"Yes," Clara finally said, her voice croaking. "He's a good man."

Rebecca nodded, though her eyes were wary. "Have you coupled with him? Is that why you want to leave? You've given your body to another man?"

Clara shook her head. "Never. He wouldn't."

Rebecca heaved a sigh and sat down on her bed. "I don't want my brother to be left alone, Clara. And I want my own life, too. Marty and I are tryin' for another babe, one of his own. Brendan is no' easy for me either."

Clara understood. Looking down at the bruise on her arm, she found the words for her own truth. "Rebecca, Joaquin and I have a chance at true happiness. One that doesn't come along more than once in a lifetime. What I see you and Marty having. A real life."

"So, you'll leave then? With your father?"

"No, I won't leave just yet. But I will, eventually." Getting out of Brendan's grasp would be smart. But the idea of abandoning Joaquin, Jo, and the clinic made her decide to stay. She could always return home in the spring. Perhaps her father would be able to wrangle her out of her marriage sooner than he thought.

Rebecca put the cloth on Clara's forehead and tucked her back into bed. "Aye, I figured you would. From the beginnin'."

She closed the door. Clara wanted to ponder Rebecca's words, but the fever pulled her back into a dreamless slumber.

CLARA WOKE to sunlight streaming through the window. Her mouth felt dry, and the water cup beside her bed was empty. It looked like Rebecca hadn't been back to tend to her since their conversation.

She pulled on her robe and left the room. Her father sat at the table with Brendan, Rebecca, and Marty, eating some of Rebecca's delicious Irish stew. Clara was suddenly famished and helped herself to a bowl from the hearth.

"Ah, there she is," her father said, grinning. "And with an appetite, too."

Marty set his spoon down and took a long drink of water. "Aye, it feels like I'm awake from the dead."

"How long have I been sleeping?" Clara asked.

"It's been nearly a week since we fell ill," her father replied.

Clara wanted to ask about Joaquin and the children but didn't know how, given that Rebecca was now aware of her feelings. Her father read her mind and supplied the information. "Everyone is recovered at the other house. Jo took a little longer than the others, but she's up and about now.

Joaquin brought her over there early on, so he could mind her, too."

She smiled gratefully. He really was a good man.

"Clara." Brendan looked at her across the table, then down into his stew bowl. "I'm sorry about the party. I'm sorry for hurtin' your arm." He glanced at Rebecca, who nodded in encouragement.

"No." Clara's voice was loud and surprised her with its force. "You don't get to be sorry, Brendan. It's just something you have to live with." There was no excuse for his actions, and she would be a fool to continue to let it go on.

Her father looked at her, and she saw admiration in his eyes. He would let her stay for now. She resumed eating, then suddenly dropped her spoon with a clatter. Everyone looked at her.

"A week?" She was counting, frantically counting.

"Yes. Six days. Today is the seventh." Rebecca gave her a quizzical look.

Six days she'd not had her remedy tea. No, seven. She'd forgotten the night of the party, too wrapped up in thinking about Joaquin's kiss.

Nine days since Brendan had last come to her. She was sweating, perspiration making her hair damp.

She stretched her mind back, trying to remember when her monthly was due. A week from today.

She put her head in her hands. It was close. Too close.

"Clara?" Her father sounded concerned.

"I'm still feeling ill, Father. I'm going to lie down again for a while."

JOAQUIN FINGERED the note from Clara in his pocket as he waited. He'd read it twenty times since Jo had given it to him the evening before. His stomach clenched each time. It had been weeks since they'd kissed in his wagon after the Christmas social, and when they'd spent time together, he'd noticed she seemed distracted.

I need to speak with you alone. A private matter. It's important.

He'd sent a note back that morning, giving her instructions to a secret cove in the forest between their two properties.

C –

Meet me after supper. Follow the stream on your side until it grows narrow. When you see the fallen cedar tree covered in moss, go into the forest. I'll be waiting.

– J

He used to hide here as a child when his grandfather was drunk and mean, escaping into books and stories to push the sound of his grandmother's screams from his ears.

There was a rustle in the trees, and Clara appeared in front of him, her face drawn. She fell into his arms, her chest heaving with unshed tears—something was wrong. He ran over all the possibilities in his head, each worse than the last: Brendan had threatened her, she had decided to return home, she was with child, she no longer wanted his affection.

"What's wrong, my love?" The words rushed out of his mouth, but he was breathless and lightheaded.

She tipped her head back to look at him, anguish in her eyes. "I'm—"

"Pregnant." He finished the sentence for her, and she nodded tearfully.

He took in a deep breath and blew it out slowly, holding her tighter against his chest. He inhaled the scent of her, trying to calm himself before he spoke. The idea of Brendan's hands touching her, of him *inside her*, was more than he could bear.

"... I'll understand." She had been talking, and he wasn't sure what she'd said.

"What's that, my love? Say it again."

"If you ..." She bit her lip. "If it's too much for you, for us, I understand." Her body trembled under his touch.

He shook his head and pulled her to sit on the log in the middle of the small clearing. "No, Clara. I love you. This changes nothing."

"But—"

"Every child is a blessing. You mustn't resent this one. My mother had every reason to resent me, but she did not. I would be a different man today if she hadn't loved me the way she did." He turned and cupped her chin with his hands, lifting her gaze. "I won't lie and say that I don't wish the babe was mine. But what I feel for you is not something that will fade."

"But how do we move on from this, Joaquin? It feels impossible."

He gathered her close once more. He could not break; she needed him to be strong.

"Together. We move on together, my love."

Part Three

Chapter 18

April 1886

Brendan fiddled with his glass of ale. He sat across from McGregor in the saloon on a Tuesday afternoon. It was planting season, and every other man in town was busy working the farm. But Brendan had other plans—plans of going into business with McGregor.

"Not sure about that idea, Murphy. There's plenty o' other men makin' their own illegal brews from here to Vancouver."

"Look, my father-in-law is a wealthy businessman. I was listenin' to him explain it to Marty. You have yours here. We need another in Vancouver and one in between. We can deliver between the three, then buy up smaller brewers."

"Hmm..." McGregor sat back in his chair, a skeptical look on his weathered face. They were sitting at the front of the dark public house, looking out over the street. Both men were well into their third stout. Brendan watched as Clara came out of her clinic, a few doors down. She had barely spoken to him in the last four months since the Christmas social. Marty and Becca were also keeping to themselves. It seemed McGregor was fast becoming his only friend.

"Is your wife with child?" McGregor waved the barmaid over to indicate another mug.

Brendan squinted out to the street to look at Clara more closely. "Nay. I think she's barren."

McGregor peered at Clara. "I don't think she's barren, Murphy. Take another look."

Brendan swallowed the last of his beer just as the barmaid set down a new glass. He didn't want to look at Clara. The last time he'd touched her had been before the Christmas party. If she was with child, it was likely the bastard's.

"What do you know about Joaquin?" The question was out of his mouth before he'd really even considered it, and it sat there like a skunk ready to spray.

McGregor gave him a look that confirmed his worst suspicions. It seemed clear to everyone that Clara and Joaquin were fond of each other. He hadn't seen much of the bastard lately, but Clara would disappear for long periods of time, refusing to answer where she'd been. Becca said she wasn't, but Brendan was sure Clara was bedding the neighbour.

"I've known him since he was born," McGregor said, leaning back in his seat and crossing his arms. "His mother was a beauty. It was a damn shame she couldn't keep her legs closed."

"Mmm." Brendan had nothing to say. He was thinking the same thing about his wife.

"He was a quiet boy, always readin'. But I suspect the

readin' was his way to escape. His granddaddy was a fair wicked man. No one crossed ol' Georgie. Joaquin and Eddie played with the Indian boys, mostly, as there were only a few settlers here then. But then he grew up. Decided to make his own path. He's done well, considerin' where he came from. I don't have anythin' bad to say about him, except ..."

"Except, what?" Brendan's ears were perked.

"Well, there was the incident when his grandfather passed. Georgie got into some bad debt, you see, and couldn't pay it back. He was shot with an arrow."

Brendan sighed. He didn't want to hear about the bastard's grandfather. He wanted some dirty gossip to tell Clara.

"Joaquin came to tend to his granddaddy's wound. He was a new doctor, then. Well, I saw him out the window."

"Out the window? This was at your place?" Unease grew in Brendan.

"O' course, Murphy. Who else do you think he'd gotten into debt with? He had a likin' for the mash, like yourself." McGregor took a long drink of his stout. "Dangerous stuff, that raw liquor."

Brendan sent him a glare. "Finish the story."

"Ah, yes. Well, I saw him through the window. He got the arrowhead out, but he didn't stitch him back up. Let him bleed to death, you might say."

Brendan crossed his arms. "This does no' help me, McGregor. I need somethin' I can use. Somethin' to win my wife back." He'd said it out loud.

"My, my. It's true, then. You think she's carryin' his child?"

245

Brendan shrugged. He didn't know what to think about anything except having a drink.

"Well, you need to go into his house. While he's not there, o' course. Look around. If they're fornicatin', you'll find something of her's there, for sure. In fact, you should go now. The children are visitin' their mother for a few days, as I heard Joaquin sayin' down at the feed store. Just the oldest is home, helpin' in the field."

Brendan sat up straight. He reached into his pocket for coins to pay for the stout.

"Don't worry about the stout, Murphy. I'll add it to your tab."

Brendan grinned, then stood and put on his hat. He had a mission to complete.

BRENDAN WALKED UP to Joaquin's farmhouse in a deliberately casual manner, like he'd been invited over for tea. He'd stopped for a few nips of the liquor hidden by the forest before coming, for courage. It was perfect timing— Marty had gone into their house for lunch, and he was able to walk through to the neighbouring property without suspicion. Now to make sure the bastard or his son weren't in, having theirs. He went over to the barn and took a quick look in. It was quiet except for a few stray mice. Next, he made his way along the edge of the walls until he could see out into the fields. Yes, he could see them both, quite far out, hard at work.

Brendan strode to the door of the house and let himself in. He'd never been inside but figured he'd start with the main floor. To the right was a formal sitting room, which he passed right by, as it looked like it was hardly ever used. He walked down a long hallway and found a bedroom. Going in, he quickly decided it was a spare room, as the chest of drawers was empty. The next room was a library full of books and a reading chair. He paused for a moment. Clara probably loved that room, but then he remembered his mission—looking for signs of lovemaking. He should head to the bedrooms. Passing through the kitchen and main living area, he stopped to rifle through a cupboard stuffed with knickknacks and papers. There was a tin box on the highest shelf that looked interesting; he reached up and pulled it down, then opened it. Staring back at him was Clara's gold-plated pistol.

He took it out and opened the chamber, sliding the bullets back inside. Putting the empty tin box back in its place, he made his way out of the kitchen, carrying the gun.

The stairs led up in a half-circled spiral to one level and then the next. He checked the rooms on the first level. Two narrow beds in each. Children's rooms. He moved quickly up the next set of stairs, one creaking noisily under his weight. Upstairs were another two rooms, smaller than the ones below. He checked the first, finding a dress laid on the bed. The girl's room. He pushed open the door to the last room.

It was small and sparsely furnished: a bed with a small end table, a chest of drawers, and a high-backed chair facing the window. He looked out—up this high, he could see over the tops of the trees.

Brendan took a careful look around the room. There was a book and kerosene lamp on the table next to the bed, some men's shoes on the floor, and a few coats for the winter hung on hooks. The drawers were filled with clothing, washed and pressed. There was nothing of Clara in this room.

As he was leaving, disappointed that his adventure had revealed nothing, something on the top of the chest of drawers caught his eye. It was small, but its sparkle made Brendan's stomach clench. He picked it up, rolling it between his forefinger and thumb before placing it back down. It was a gem. A gem from Clara's damn Christmas dress.

The door opened downstairs with a bang. Brendan froze but then made his way quickly down the first flight of stairs. If he was going to get caught, he didn't want to be in the bastard's bedroom.

"Joaquin?" It was Clara, her voice calling up the stairs from the doorway. She'd heard his footsteps. Brendan stood still, barely breathing. He could only just see her through the railing.

"I'm just here, Clara." The bastard's voice came from outside. He soon joined her at the door. She squealed, throwing her arms around his neck.

"Let me wash first. I'm sweaty from working outside." He took her arms down and moved inside the house.

"I don't care. I miss you." Her arms were back, pulling him down to her. Brendan watched with disgust as the bastard leaned down and kissed Clara passionately. He ran his hands down her body, his thumbs grazing the sides of her breasts as they passed.

A fire burned hot in Brendan's chest, and the pistol grew heavy in his hand. He would end this. He would end it, now. He cocked the hammer.

"... the herbal garden." They were leaving.

"I love you," he heard Clara say as their steps echoed on the porch. "Thank you for my garden."

As soon as they were out of earshot, Brendan flew down the last set of stairs. He leaned the top half of his body out the front door. They were walking down the path to the side of the house. He trained the pistol at the bastard's back.

No. It's murder. He stopped himself, coming back inside.

He took a deep breath but then remembered the bastard's hands, touching Clara like she belonged to him. There might be a baby, *the damn bastard's baby*, growing in her belly. The baby she had not wanted to give him. The rage became hot once more, flooding his senses and tightening his muscles. Sweat poured down his head and into his eyes. He wanted them both dead.

He leaned out the door again and saw a figure walking on the path. He lifted the pistol with shaking hands, pulled the trigger, and fled around the other side of the house and into the trees.

He was already out of sight when he heard Clara's scream, followed by the bastard's shout. He froze as the words were clear. *McGregor.*

CLARA'S HANDS pressed down on McGregor's shoulder as Joaquin carried him into the house. They hurried into the spare room, where they laid him on the bed.

"My medical instruments are at the reservation." Joaquin handed Clara a towel to help slow the bleeding.

"The clinic key is in my pocket. I'll stay here with him."

Joaquin grabbed the key and made his way to the door, where he paused. "Who shot him? He might still be here. Maybe I should stay."

"Go. You're wasting time."

Joaquin gave her a look of concern but ran out the door. McGregor groaned under her. He had lost consciousness from the initial shock but was now coming to. She checked the gunshot wound in his shoulder under the towel. The bleeding had already slowed, and it wasn't spurting. He would likely live, but it would be a painful recovery. Very painful.

His eyes fluttered open—a white film covered most of the pale blue iris. She wondered how much of his sight he had already lost.

"Mrs. Murphy," he managed, his voice weak.

"McGregor. We meet yet again. But please, I think it's time you called me Clara."

The corner of his mouth lifted in an attempt at a smirk. "When a beautiful woman asks you to call her by her first name, it's usually trouble."

She ignored his jest. "Why are you here, McGregor? I can only assume you know how you got shot."

"Aye." His Scottish burr, which was normally quite mild, had thickened with the pain. "I gather it was your husband."

Clara felt only a mild shock at this revelation. Brendan's unpredictable behaviour failed to surprise her anymore.

"He came here to see if he could find evidence. Of your affair with the Spanish bastard."

"Joaquin. His name is Joaquin. And I'm sure there was nothing to find."

"Whose baby are ya carryin' then, Clara?" He said her name with a sneer.

Clara put her full weight on the wound she was pressing. McGregor gasped. Since becoming pregnant, her tongue had become bolder, sharper. She was no longer afraid.

"Why were *you* here, McGregor?"

"Do you have anythin' for the pain?"

She shrugged. "Whisky. Laudanum is going to cost you." Neither was within her reach, but she remembered the woman with the arrowheads in her nightmares.

He laughed then. "I suppose you think a sip of laudanum is going to clear your debt. It's now over a hundred dollars."

She narrowed her eyes. The older man didn't deserve an ounce of her kindness. "I'd say, McGregor, that you owe me much more than that. I am holding your life in my hands, after all."

His face grew serious. "Am I going to die, then?"

"Gunshot wounds are often fatal. If not initially, then from infection after."

He was quiet, and she did not press him further. She had learned from watching Joaquin that most people spoke if they were given enough time.

"I got to thinkin', after he left the saloon. That he might try to harm ya, if he found what he was lookin' for. Then I saw you leave your clinic, and I came to make sure he didn't."

Clara raised her eyebrows. It was likely a tall tale. McGregor didn't care about her safety.

"It's Brendan's baby, though I'm not sure how you know. I've only just begun to show."

McGregor nodded. His breathing was laboured, and she

knew he was in agony. "I had thirteen of my own. There are subtle changes, even from the beginnin'."

"Thirteen?"

"Aye. Eleven survived, but they've all left now, save for Andrew. They scattered as far as they could, away from their ol' man."

The front door banged open, letting a gust of wind in with it. Joaquin had returned from the clinic. She heard him washing in the kitchen and went to meet him.

"I'm leaving," she said. "I need to speak with my husband. He's the one who fired the shot."

Joaquin shook his head, a dark line of worry furrowing his brow. "No. Wait for me."

She reached up and smoothed the line with her thumb. "It's better if I go alone. I'll meet you in our spot at eight o'clock tonight."

She returned to the room and opened her medical bag that Joaquin had brought from the clinic, found the laudanum, uncorked it, and leaned down to McGregor.

He took the sip she gave him without hesitation. Licking the last of it off his lips, he looked up at her with his watery blue eyes. "Mrs. Murphy, it seems our roles have reversed. I am now in debt to you—for a life."

Clara found Brendan at the kitchen table of the homestead, the pistol strewn on the table, Rebecca rubbing his back.

She looked up at Clara in alarm. "What in the devil is

goin' on? There's blood all over you, and Brendan's refusin' to even speak."

Clara sat down at the table. "He shot McGregor. But he meant to shoot Joaquin. Or maybe me." She turned to Brendan with a hiss. "You tried to murder me. I should report you to the authorities."

"What?" Rebecca sat down and snatched the pistol off the table. "This is stayin' with me from now on. I can't trust either of you."

Clara was so angry she couldn't look at her husband. She spoke to Rebecca instead. "I'm with child." She blurted out the secret that she had kept for so long. "Brendan, you're going to be a father."

Brendan raised his head from the table. His eyes were red. "I saw you ... with him. Don't try to make a fool of me, Clara."

"I'm not. I'm four months along. I would have gotten pregnant at Christmas." She looked at Rebecca, whose face was oddly sombre. She thought Rebecca would be happy at the news of a baby, at least.

Brendan was staring at her. "It's really my child?"

She nodded. "I haven't bedded anyone but you." Her cheeks flushed. She wanted to be intimate with Joaquin—desperately—and he did too, but they had refrained.

Rebecca looked at her knowingly. "What are you going to do, Clara? You can't keep carryin' on like this."

Clara looked down at her hands. Her sleeves were stained crimson with McGregor's blood. It could just as easily have been Joaquin's or her own. Or the children's. Her husband was not right in his mind, and her choices would risk them all.

"You need to break it off with him. For good." Brendan grabbed her hand. Clara tried to wrench it away, but he held on firmly. "I don't want to harm you or our child, Clara, but I won't hesitate to shoot the bastard dead."

Her insides clenched at his words. It was time to contact her father at last. Her husband was a dangerous man. She would need to warn Joaquin that it wasn't safe for them to see each other for the time being.

She finally nodded at Brendan, keeping her eyes down. "All right, I won't see him anymore."

"Aye." Brendan nodded but gave her a wary eye. "I don't expect you will."

Brendan left for the barn, leaving Clara alone with Rebecca. Rebecca busied herself in the kitchen, continuing her preparations for the evening meal.

"Don't be thinkin' you're goin' to run off, Clara. Not with my brother's babe in your belly."

Clara stood, her temper flaring. "He tried to kill me, Rebecca. Even you have to see the futility of this marriage."

Rebecca heaved a heavy sigh, coming back to sit at the table with Clara. "Aye." She pulled the pistol out of her apron pocket and held it out to Clara. "Perhaps you want it back?"

Clara shook her head. "I can't stop loving Joaquin." Her voice was a whisper. "So, I should go home to my father, where it's safe."

Rebecca was silent for a long while. "Aye," she finally whispered, more to herself than Clara. She turned to Clara with resolution in her eye. "Stay, for now. I'll protect you. You and the babe." She stood, and her hand fell to her own stomach. "I promise with my life."

Chapter 19

April 1886

JOAQUIN PACED, HIS STOMACH CHURNING. CLARA WAS late. She was never late.

The clearing in the forest had become their meeting spot these last few months, as it offered a thick screen of privacy, both from the outside and the inside. But he couldn't see if she was coming, and his hands shook with worry.

A light bobbed in the forest, and Clara burst through the trees straight into his arms. She was sobbing, almost hysterical. His heart tore then, too, for he knew the conversation they were about to have. He'd known since she'd told him, pale-faced in January, that she was carrying Brendan's child. It might be impossible for them to continue on, despite their love.

"My love," he murmured into her hair, trying to calm her. "It will be all right. Everything will be all right." He didn't know how, but he needed to hope. He led her to their sitting spot on a log, where he had set down his own kerosene lamp.

She curled up on his shoulder, and he stroked her hair and back while she continued to cry. How was it possible to love someone so much only to be kept apart? He ached with need for her, day and night.

"He tried to kill us today." Her tears subsiding, she looked up at him. His heart broke into a thousand pieces at the sight of her, so distraught. He clenched his teeth against his own swelling emotions, determined to be strong for her.

"I know, my love."

"It could have been one of the children, Joaquin."

He kissed her forehead. He knew that, too.

"I'll need to leave, after all. Go home to my family."

It wasn't a surprise, but his stomach still seized. Months on end without her. Maybe years. She wiped her face with the back of her hands and took a shaky breath. "I'll stay until Jo and Will's wedding. Then I'll go."

He frowned. That was months away, at the beginning of October. "I think you should go before then. For safety."

"No. He'll be suspicious and may follow me. Rebecca already is. I've ... I've told him I'm breaking it off with you tonight." Her voice caught, but she continued. "After the wedding, I'll leave under the pretense of taking the baby home for a visit. But I won't return."

He was quiet, thinking. "Clara—"

"We shouldn't see each other anymore, Joaquin. It's too dangerous. McGregor's been whispering in his ear about us." She paused, looking up at him. "I ... I understand if it's too long for you to wait. Or if you've changed your mind about selling the farm. The children might not want to move."

"No." His voice cracked then, and he pulled her into a kiss. "My love for you will never change, Clara. I tried to forget you in the beginning. But it was no use." His laugh was tinged with sorrow. "I'll speak with the children. Perhaps they might choose to stay with their mother."

They sat together quietly then, turning to each other for an occasional kiss. He tried to hold her as close as he could, memorizing the feel of her, the smell of her.

She put her hand on his chest. "Make love to me, Joaquin."

He swallowed back the yes that came to his tongue. "One day, we will have each other. But that day is not today. This is not goodbye."

She cried again, though only for a minute. He gave her one final kiss before helping her to her feet. Holding her face in his hands, he spoke. "We must be strong. For each other. For the child."

She nodded, swallowing thickly. "I love you."

"And I love you. Go now."

She clung to him a minute more, burying her head in his chest. Then she left, back into the trees the same way she'd come, taking what felt like most of his heart with her. Joaquin sat alone for a long time, his head in his hands. In all his life, he had never been one to complain, to think that his lot in life was unfair. But tonight, the heartbreak was bitter, and it was almost impossible to swallow.

It seemed to Clara that as soon as she revealed the news of her pregnancy, her belly began to swell. One day there was barely a bump, only noticeable to her, and the next, she was having difficulty fastening her skirt. As the weeks went by, her condition was visible to everyone.

Mrs. Davenport and the ladies at the quilting circle had given her middle an appraising look.

"It looks like the Lord has blessed you after all," Martha had said n front of everyone at church. Clara had smiled politely, but she'd noticed Rebecca turn away.

Her heart was heavy every day, from the minute she woke, remembering Joaquin, to the hours she lay awake at night, trying to forget him. But for the most part, during the day, she was busy. Very busy. The spring had brought waves of new settlers, coming in on the railroad, buying up the farmland, or building homes in a row on the outskirts of town. Langley had started to grow, and her clinic was bursting at the seams.

Clara had started ordering monthly medical supplies from a catalogue to keep up with the demand. The dream of having a busy clinic was finally coming true, and she was going to have to leave it behind.

Jo came into the clinic one afternoon, catching her in a rare moment alone. Clara looked up from the desk, where she was updating her medical journal.

"Hello, friend." Jo came over and gave her an embrace, rubbing Clara's growing belly fondly. "How's baby?"

"The baby's good. Hungry, as I always seem to be eating." Clara laughed, surprising herself with the sound. Laughing seemed like a distant memory, a luxury of happier times.

Jo handed her the book she was holding. "He sent this. For you."

It was a copy of *Jane Eyre*. "He hates this book." A lump came to her throat, thinking of the morning when he'd first shown her the library. She'd loved him, even then.

"Look, here." Jo opened the book to the first page. Down the margins of the page, Joaquin had written his own commentary in pencil.

Jo read aloud from the book itself. "Jane, I don't like cavilers or questioners. Be seated somewhere, and until you can speak pleasantly, remain silent."

On the side, he'd written: *I'm imagining you as a child, especially when embroidering under your mother's gaze.*

And further down the page: *Poor Jane. It's going to get worse before it gets better. But it does get better. It will get better, my love.*

"He wants you to write in Chapter Two. You can leave it locked in your desk when you're done, and I'll take it back. I won't read it, don't worry."

Clara gave her friend another embrace. "Thank you, Jo."

Jo shook her head. "He's miserable. Will can barely stand to be around him."

Clara sighed, about to lament her own misery, when the clinic door burst open. It was Anna, and to Clara's shock, her mother, Laura.

Jo's eyes grew wide, and she slipped out the door with only a quick nod to the woman. Her future mother-in-law seemed to frighten Jo. Though they had accepted Will's choice, there was still some uncertainty that Jo and Will were a proper match.

"Anna tells me you're a doctor." Laura's mouth was firm, her face tight.

"That's right. Can I help you, Mrs.—?" Clara wiped her

palms down her clinic apron, trying to hide the tremble in her hands. How much had the children told their mother about their father's relationship with her? They hadn't tried very hard to hide their affection from them.

"Mrs. McIntosh. The children say you're the neighbour."

Clara breathed a sigh of relief. "Yes, I—"

Laura pushed Anna forward. "Tell her."

Anna's eyes filled with tears, and she held her hand to her mouth to cover her sob.

"What is it, Anna? Are you hurt?" Clara's thoughts raced. Perhaps Anna *had* told her mother, and these were tears of guilt.

"I ..." Anna shook her head, unable to speak the words.

"She's with child." Laura stood with her hands on her hips. "Around three or four months gone."

Clara gasped, putting her hand to her own stomach. She looked at Anna's midsection, which looked flat under her dress and petticoats. "Are you sure?"

Laura answered. "She says she hasn't bled since the new year. And yes, she's starting to show." She shook her head. "A boy from church. Don't ask me when or how because I don't know, and she won't answer."

Clara took a deep breath. "Have you told—"

"No. I'm not in favour of speaking with my former husband. I was hoping you would do that."

"Me?" Clara looked to Anna, who nodded, a plea in her eyes.

"Yes." Laura reached into her bag and withdrew a purse of coins, which she set down on the patient's table. "This is from my husband. For Anna's medical care throughout the pregnancy. It will be more appropriate for you to deliver the child than her father. If we could afford to send her away, we would, but this will have to do."

Laura reached for the door handle. "Goodbye, Anna. I'll see you when it's done. It's best you don't travel back and forth for now." With a swish of her skirts, she was gone into the street.

Clara stared after Laura before reaching for Anna's hand. "Let's go do this now. It's lunch, and your father will be in from the field."

Anna paled but nodded. "I'm so scared."

Clara squeezed her hand. "Me too, Anna. But your father is a good man. He might be angry to start, but he won't stay that way. Did your mother speak with the boy's family?"

"No, she says it's up to Father to defend my honour. But there's nothing to defend. It was my choice. And ... it was more than once."

Clara sighed. It was no wonder she had ended up pregnant. Most mothers did not speak to their daughters about sexual matters until they were engaged to be wed. Laura did not seem to be an exception. Clara's own mother had never spoken to her, but she had learned of it in medical school—both in her schoolbooks and from her male colleagues.

They held hands on the way, walking through town and then past Clara's home. She could see Brendan and Marty in the field, hauling water to the crops. They didn't notice as she and Anna slipped into the trees. Her heart started to race as the house came into view. She hadn't seen Joaquin at all since their departure a few weeks before. He hadn't even come to church. She understood why—seeing each other was too much to bear, and an alter-cation with Brendan seemed imminent. Now, she was finally about to see him, and the news she brought was unfortunate.

He had his back to them, tending to the garden he had planted for her. There were rows of medicinal plants—elderberry, blue vervain, nettle, arnica, and echinacea, to name a few. Her heart ached when she saw him, and she wanted to run to him, to kiss him. But she must share Anna's news without allowing her affection to get in the way.

"Joaquin?" Her voice was loud, startling herself. He turned quickly to her, his face etched with the same longing she felt. There were dark shadows under his eyes, and the hair on his face had grown thicker than normal. It was all she could do to stay where she was, to not embrace him.

"Clara?" His eyebrows raised in surprise, then creased in concern. He began to walk to her, then stopped, likely only now realizing Anna wasn't supposed to be home yet.

"Anna? I'm not due to collect you from your mother's until tomorrow. What's going on?" His face folded in a frown as he looked between the two women.

Anna burst into tears. Joaquin walked over quickly, taking her in his arms. He looked at Clara quizzically.

"She's with child," Clara blurted out, wanting to unburden the news as quickly as possible. "Around three or four months gone."

Anna's tears turned to sobs in her father's arms. Joaquin's face crumpled too. Anna was the same age as his mother when she'd fallen pregnant.

Clara couldn't stay away any longer. She came to him, and he held open his arm for her. The three of them stood there: Anna crying, Clara with her head turned to Joaquin's chest, and Joaquin with his chin resting on Clara's head. He gave her a small kiss on the forehead.

"Anna," he said finally, having gained control of his emotions. "Everything will be all right. Every child is a blessing. This one will be welcome in our family as well." His embrace tightened around them.

Anna nodded and lifted her head, wiping her face with her sleeve. "Father, I'd like to go lie down in my room for a while before I start making the dinner."

Joaquin's gaze followed her as she headed into the house. He looked down at Clara, who was still in his arms. "What happened? How did you come to bring her here?"

Clara didn't answer, shaking her head and staying close to him. She needed the comfort of his body, of his embrace.

He took her into the barn. They climbed into the hayloft, away from prying eyes. They lay on a pile of hay, and their lips found each other with urgency. The weeks apart had only increased their wanting, and their breath grew ragged with desire. Clara finally pulled away—not because she wanted to, but because they needed to talk about Anna.

"Your ... Laura came to the clinic. She paid me to take care of Anna during her pregnancy, including the delivery. Then she left, telling Anna goodbye until the child is born."

Joaquin sighed, pulling Clara closer again. She rested her head on his chest. It felt so good to talk with him, to touch him. "Who's the father?"

"A boy at church," she said. "I guess it's up to you to speak with the family."

Joaquin made no reply, his hands rubbing her back and side. One came and settled on the swell of her belly. "What am I going to do, Clara? I can't let her life be ruined like my mother's was."

"She's just made a mistake, Joaquin. You need to be supportive. The rest will sort itself out."

He brought her head up to look at him. "Perhaps, when we ... move, we can raise the baby as ours. They would be close enough to pass off as twins. I don't want her to have to marry a boy she barely knows."

Clara leaned up and kissed him in agreement. Now that she was in his arms again, she could dream about their future. It had been too hard to think about, alone in her homestead. "I hate this, being away from you. But thank you for the messages in *Jane Eyre*. I'll enjoy reading them and writing back."

"I needed to talk with you. I need to know that you're safe, Clara. I'm so worried."

"I'll start a second book. That way Jo will have one to bring every day."

Joaquin sat up suddenly. "I'm going to hate myself for asking this, Clara, but I need to know. Does he come to you still, in your bed?"

"No. Not since ..." She wrapped her arms around his middle. "And even then, I didn't want to."

"Good. Though, you shouldn't stop him if he tries. He might get ... he might try to hurt you." He kept his back to her, and she could hear the tense edge to his voice. "I hate him. I hate him with every part of me, Clara. I hate that he gets to live with you, to speak with you, to hear you laugh. He doesn't deserve that."

She leaned her head on his back. "No, he doesn't. You're

right. But we have to stay strong, Joaquin, as you said. And you need to stay strong, for Anna."

He turned to her with a small smile. "Come. Another kiss before you leave, my love. They sank back down into the hay, his hands once again settling on her growing middle. "I think of the baby as mine, even though I know it's not. I hope it's a girl."

Clara smiled against his lips. "So do I."

Joaquin kissed her again. "What will you name her?"

Clara laughed, feeling happy for the first time in days. "Jane."

Joaquin laughed, too. "No, not Jane. Poor Jane."

Their laughter echoed in the hayloft and down into Clara's heart. It *would* get better, she believed.

REBECCA WAS WAITING for Clara on the other side of the forest when she emerged.

"Clara," she hissed. "What in heavens are you up to? You said you were finished with that man."

Clara looked at her with an even stare. They both knew that Clara was not finished with Joaquin. She couldn't take back her love. "Anna's pregnant. Her mother brought her to the clinic. I came with Anna to help her tell her father."

"Oh no."

"Yes." Clara sighed. "It's unfortunate. She's so young."

Rebecca suddenly burst into tears. Clara was taken aback and stood awkwardly beside her. She had never seen Rebecca cry, not once.

"Rebecca, what's wrong?" She put her arm around her sister-in-law, and they sat together on a nearby rock.

"It's been over six months, and Marty and I can't fall with child." Rebecca wiped away her tears with a brisk hand. "I know it can take some time, but Marty's startin' to become troubled. Maybe somethin' happened to me when that man had his way with me. Maybe my womb is closed because of the sin."

"I doubt that," Clara said, consoling Rebecca. "I'm sure a baby will be on the way soon."

"We all thought you were barren, and now you're with child. Do you have somethin' I can take?"

"Yes. I can prepare something that might help." She would make a tincture of evening primrose oil and red clover for Rebecca the next day at the clinic.

They stood, Clara rubbing her aching back, and started the walk back to the homestead. Before they went inside, Rebecca spoke again. "I believe you, you know. About it bein' Brendan's child."

Clara sighed. "You should. I'm not lying."

"Aye." She looked back over at the forest. "But it's more him. Your Joaquin isn't the kind of man to sit by if he thought it was his babe in your belly. He'd be claiming you as his own, married or not."

Clara looked longingly into the trees. "Yes, he would."

Chapter 20

May 1886

CLARA WAS WALKING HOME FROM CHURCH WITH Brendan and Rebecca when Brendan turned to her. Their conversations were few and far between these days.

"We're going to McGregor's this afternoon after lunch." He scowled at her, then picked up his pace to walk ahead.

Clara crossed her arms in defiance. She did not want to go to McGregor's. Her back was sore, and she was looking forward to writing a letter to Joaquin in *A Tale of Two Cities* that afternoon. It was the highlight of her day when Jo arrived from the farm, giving her the book. She pored over it at the desk in her clinic, memorizing his words. Most days, his tone was light, making jokes about the book or its characters, but other days it was sombre, writing about his love for her. She had those days, too, wondering if it was all worth it, if they would ever actually have a life together. So many things could go wrong with their plan.

Brendan had been on edge. She'd been watching him

cautiously as he spent his evenings pacing the homestead. Marty had begun to build a new home on the land after he'd spoken with her father at Christmas. They had chosen a spot far enough away for privacy but not too far, Clara was glad to note. She didn't want to be alone with Brendan all the time.

"He's wantin' a drink," Rebecca observed of her brother, shifting Patrick to her other hip as they walked. Marty had stayed home from church, opting to work on their new homestead, but it was likely also due to the strain between the two that Clara had noticed.

"Going to McGregor's is not my responsibility," she told Brendan once they'd reached the homestead. "I'd like to rest this afternoon. And Rebecca is teaching me to make bread." In preparation for living on their own, Rebecca started to teach Clara to make the meals. Clara didn't love to bake, but she preferred it to visiting McGregor.

"Aye, it is. I haven't spoken with him since he was shot. And that was your fault, the way I see it."

Clara put her hands on her hips. "It was not my fault. You were trying to shoot me."

"Aye, it was. I saw you touchin' that filthy bastard. It would've been well within my rights to take things into my own hands. I still could. Imagine what the quiltin' circle ladies would think to know it might not be your husband's babe in your belly."

"It's your child, brother." Rebecca came up behind them. "Let's not start that again. Clara, take a quick trip with him to visit the ol' bugger. Then come back and have a wee rest. We can bake the bread a bit later."

Clara sighed, rolling her eyes at Brendan. She didn't want him to drink at all, but he seemed on the verge of detonating. If going to McGregor's made him calmer, she should go.

After a lunch of barley soup and biscuits, they were on their way to Glen Valley. It was an unusually warm day, and Clara felt uncomfortable in the heat, even in her lighter riding skirt. The baby kicked, and she put her hand to her belly with a smile. If it was indeed a girl, she had come up with the perfect name.

She and Brendan rode in silence, not having anything to say to one another. She longed for the easy conversations with Joaquin, their friendly banter. She missed his voice and the way he said her name.

"Once the babe is born, you're going to close the clinic." Brendan's voice was hard. Hatred for him rose like bile in her throat. He was trying to start an argument; she could see his temper bubbling under his words. She *would* be closing the clinic, but not for the reasons he hoped.

"I've made arrangements to visit my mother after the baby is born. She's insisted I come for a few months. You're welcome to come along, Brendan." She was calling his bluff. He had heard enough stories about her mother to frighten him into staying home.

He frowned. "You're going to travel alone with the baby?"

"No. My father will come to escort me. The whole trip is only five days by rail. Then a few hours by stagecoach to my parents' estate. Actually," she continued, deciding to elaborate in case she needed to leave earlier, "it might be a good idea for me to go beforehand. That way I can deliver in a hospital or with my family's private doctor. Unless you want

Joaquin to deliver it, as he's the only other doctor around here."

Brendan's frown deepened. "No, I won't have him touchin' you. Aye, that's a good idea, Clara. You'll send a telegram when the baby arrives?"

She smiled at him, trying to look like a caring wife. "Of course."

The sight of McGregor's house in the distance brought memories flooding back, and she swallowed back the sharp sting of unshed tears. She remembered the last time she had been here, months ago. The night she'd spent talking with Joaquin. The night she'd realized she loved him. Now, it had been so long since she had even seen him.

They hitched their horses to the gate and approached the front door. Brendan knocked. No answer. He knocked again.

"Let's check the barn," he said after they'd waited for a minute. As they walked through the pasture, Clara noticed a rope strung from the house to the barn. This was common practice for farmers in the winter when a storm or heavy snowfall made it difficult to navigate the way to the barn. But it was May, and the weather was fine. Unless ... Clara remembered noticing McGregor's deteriorating eyesight when he'd been shot. Perhaps he needed the guidance even in the light of day.

They found McGregor in the barn, working alone. He lifted his head when they entered. His eyes narrowed at them.

"Mrs. Murphy. Are you alone, or did you bring that Irish scoundrel with you?"

"I'm here, McGregor. I've come for some spirits. My delivery didn't come last month or this one."

"Ahhh. Well, that's because Andrew's decided to up and leave. Gone to live with his brother over in Surrey. Not to worry. My great-nephew is comin' to stay with me in the fall, all the way from out east. Lost his job and his woman, and he's lookin' for a fresh start."

"How's your shoulder, McGregor?" Clara asked. Brendan shot her a glare. She frowned back, screwing up her nose at him. It was not as if McGregor had forgotten about it.

"Clara, go wait outside. I'll just arrange a few things with McGregor here, and we can head home."

Why had he made her come in the first place? She left and started to walk back through the pasture but then heard Brendan say her name. She crept back and peered through a crack in the barn wall.

Brendan was sitting on a haystack, a cup of drink in his hand. McGregor was busy hauling out bottles of the mash from a hidden compartment in the floor. How Brendan was thinking of getting them home, she didn't know.

"So, she's up and left the Spanish bastard then?"

"Aye. Right away. Came running back into my arms. As it should be. How anyone could love a bastard is beyond me."

Clara saw McGregor stiffen at Brendan's words. She raised her eyebrows—perhaps Joaquin wasn't the only father-less son in town.

"She even told me today that she won't let him deliver the babe. She's leavin' town, to have it at her folks' place."

"Leavin' town, eh?"

"Aye."

McGregor turned away from the bottles and sat down on his own haystack. "Can I ask you somethin', Murphy?"

"Aye, what is it, McGregor?"

271

"Would you have shot her? Your wife, I mean. The day you hit me."

Brendan was quiet for a moment, draining his cup. He got up and poured himself another. The tight edge was gone from his walk, eased by the alcohol entering his bloodstream. "Aye. I would have. I still will if I catch her with the bastard again."

Clara held her breath outside the barn. She had visions of herself, broken and bleeding in Joaquin's arms. Her hands went over her belly protectively. It might be his child in her womb, but she would never allow him to hurt her baby. Brendan was poison.

McGregor rubbed his shoulder where Joaquin had removed the bullet. Clara had no doubt that it still bothered him. Wounds took time to heal, especially at McGregor's age.

"Why don't you just let her go, then? After the baby comes? You can keep the child, tell everyone the missus passed durin' the birth. It seems to me that the two of you might be better off apart."

Brendan looked at McGregor with a stare that sent chills through Clara. "Because she's my wife, McGregor. The other men in town look at me with envy when we're together. I won't find that again with some country girl. Clara will come 'round. She's just been indulged by her father for far too long. In another year or so, I'll have her shaped exactly the way I want."

"Hmmm. Well, in my experience, it doesn't serve well to keep kin on a tight rein. I tried. Lost all my children that way. They don't even speak to me no more."

Brendan laughed. The mash had changed his voice, his

demeanour. "You're an ol' codger, McGregor. O' course they're gone." He drained his second cup and went for a third. "Clara will do what I want. Even if it's my fists that do the talkin'. I'm sure she'll understand that."

Clara put her hand over her mouth to keep herself from crying out. Her husband was nothing but a cruel man. Even McGregor seemed to have a bigger heart than Brendan.

She turned, strode through the pasture, and climbed up on Red. Brendan could find his own way home.

It was an afternoon at the end of May when Rebecca came into the clinic. Clara looked up with surprise. Rebecca didn't often leave the homestead except for the quilting circle and Sundays at church. She had certainly never visited her at the clinic before.

Rebecca put Patrick down on the clinic floor. He was seven months now and sitting up well. And, Clara had noticed, looked a lot like John. There were parts of Rebecca in him too, but the pout of his lips was exactly like John, as well as his eyes.

"Joaquin's just come by the homestead. There's a medical situation at the reserve that he needs your help with. He needed to attend to the emergency right away, so I said I would fetch you."

"Oh." Clara felt her cheeks grow warm. It had been almost a month since she'd seen Joaquin, and it now felt strange to think of helping him.

Rebecca noticed her flush but said nothing. "You should

leave now. It sounded urgent. And ... don't worry, I'll tell Brendan you were called away to a birth."

Clara thanked Rebecca and mounted her horse. She rode as fast as her pregnancy would allow, making her way there in twenty minutes. Joaquin was waiting for her, ready to take the canoe across the river. His face broke into a smile when she arrived, and he helped her off Red.

"You're so beautiful," he whispered in her ear as they climbed into the canoe. Shivers ran down her body at his words. People milled around; although the Fort was no longer used by the Hudson's Bay Company, the area was still a hub of activity, with many shops and businesses thriving.

They passed the canoe ride in silence, enjoying the simple company of each other. Joaquin rowed with even strokes, and in a few minutes, they were across.

He took her hand and led her into the forested area of the reserve. They were only a few steps inside when Clara found herself against a tree. His mouth was fierce against hers, and his kisses moved everywhere, down her neck and behind her ear. He pulled at the buttons of her blouse, and his mouth moved along the top of her loosely tied bodice, his thumbs stroking her nipples through the fabric. She gasped at the heat that burned between her legs and moaned when he stopped, his forehead pressed against hers.

"You come to me in my dreams, Clara." His voice was hoarse. "I feel like a young boy again, waking with memories of your touch."

She leaned into his embrace, breathing him in. It was the smell of him that always left her first, fading soon after they were apart. As they stood together, a lump grew in Clara's throat and, pressed against his chest, she started to cry.

He kissed her again, wiping away her tears with his hands. "I know, my love, I know. But just think of how happy our life together will be. By this time next year, we can be together."

"I'm sorry." She buried her face once again in his chest. "It's the pregnancy. I cry over everything." It was then she remembered what Rebecca had said. "What's the medical emergency? We'd better get started."

He laughed, the deep sound filling her heart. "There's no emergency. There's a party. It's the first salmon of the season and, well, it's also my birthday."

She reached up to touch his face. "I didn't know. I would have brought you a present."

His mouth was against hers. "Everything I want is right here." His hands cupped her now round belly. "How's our baby?"

"I can feel her kick now." She placed her hand on top of his, and their fingers slid together. "How's Anna?"

"She fine. I went and spoke with the family, but they wanted nothing to do with her. Anna's parents are divorced, and her father's a bastard. I'm afraid it's going to be awfully hard for her now. I'm keeping her home, trying to keep it quiet."

"Joaquin, you are the best man I've ever known. Please stop calling yourself a bastard. I know it's a part of you, but such a small part. You're strong, smart, kind, and caring. There are so many wonderful parts of you that you give to everyone else."

He kissed the top of her head and led her into the reserve, where rows of salmon were cooking on long cedar planks over the fires. "Let's eat, my love."

FAR TOO SOON, it was time for Clara to return home. As he rowed them across the river, they were quiet again, but this time mourning their departure.

"I've written Eddie," he said as they rode their horses toward home. "I've shared with him everything between us."

"I'd love to meet him someday." As much as she wanted to be far away from Brendan and start a life with Joaquin, she was going to miss her life here very much. She didn't want to leave.

"We've decided that instead of selling the farm, Eddie and Charlotte will come here to live with their children. Then, after I collect you from your father in the spring, we'll go to live at their place. It's about a three-day ride from here."

"I told Brendan about my plans to give birth. He agreed that my father can escort me home to visit for a few months. But must we wait until the spring to be together again, Joaquin? I don't want to wait that long."

He smiled at her. "Maybe not. Perhaps you might consider telling Brendan the baby passed? He might be less likely to follow you."

She put a hand to her belly as if protecting the future child from the thought. "Yes, that might be a good idea."

Just before they came to the clearing that would lead them on their separate paths home, Joaquin slid from his horse and helped her down off hers.

"I don't want to go." She pressed her face against his chest, the tears once again threatening to fall. "It might be weeks before I see you again."

He was quiet, holding her close. "I want nothing more

than to take you home with me, Clara. It seems like it would be a dream. All day, I think only of the next time I'll see you again, and even then, I know that it's worse after I do."

She looked up at him. He was right. Tomorrow would bring only a painful memory of today, knowing that it would be so long until their next touch. "Tell me," she whispered. "Tell me what we would do if you brought me home."

He laughed into her hair. "It wouldn't be to sleep."

She leaned up to kiss him on the jaw. "No, I didn't think it would be."

Joaquin met her lips with his. "I'll write it to you. I want to make sure I get every detail right, my love."

THE LETTER CAME the next day when Jo delivered the book. It was written on a loose-leaf paper in an envelope, tucked inside the chapter where he'd also written his usual banter.

C –

I've sat here for an hour, trying to compose the right way to describe what it will be like, when our bodies first touch. To be perfectly honest, I will be as nervous as hell. I've lived on this farm my entire life, and you've lived a life I can only imagine. It seems that we would be opposites, but from that first day we met, when I saw you giving old Tom in the apothecary a piece of your mind, I've wanted you in my bed.

When we arrive home, I will put the horses away and get the barn settled, while you make us some tea. Then, I'll read to you. I want to read every book in that library, over many evenings, with your head resting on me and your hand touching my chest. After a while, you'll start to feel sleepy, so we'll retire to our room.

I can only imagine what your naked body will be like, but I know it will be a sight to behold. Not because you are different from other women, but because you will be my Clara. I will want to explore all the parts, from your arms to your shoulders and back, your breasts and nipples, your calves, knees, thighs, and the place that I most desire. Once I am inside you, I fear that I may never want to leave.

I can only pray that there comes a day when I can take your love for granted, when my hands will know your curves as well as my own body, when I can say your name in the night, and you will answer, right next to me. I will never stop wanting you.

All my love,

– J

Chapter 21

June 1886

A FIRE HAD BURNED THE ENTIRE CITY OF VANCOUVER TO the ground. It had started as a clearing burn outside the city and spread with ferocious fury. More than one thousand homes had been lost, and the people of Langley were stepping up to help.

The town council had called an emergency meeting in the church. It was packed to the brim, with standing room only. Clara stood with Rebecca, Marty, and Brendan in one corner. Joaquin, Jo, and Will stood in another. Clara could barely concentrate on the meeting as Brendan stared down Joaquin, who was looking straight ahead, not once glancing at her.

"We'll need to house as many folks as possible, possibly up to two hundred if we can." The mayor spoke from the front of the room. "It's expected that they'll need accommodation for a month, maybe two. Spare rooms are appreciated, but it will be even better if you can clear out a section of your barns so entire families can lodge together. Please report to the table outside with how many you are able to house."

He paused, taking a drink of water. The temperature in the church was stifling. "Doctor Walker and Dr. Murphy, if I can speak to you here at the front before you leave."

Joaquin looked over then, catching her eye across the room. Clara pushed her way to the front, Brendan following closely behind.

"We've been asked to set up a triage tent. All the major mishaps have been attended to in Vancouver, but these folks are coming with minor burns, smoke inhalation, and other injuries caused by the panic." The mayor glanced at Clara's belly, which had grown to a large size. "Dr. Murphy, maybe you should let Dr. Walker handle this. It might mean a lot of standing on your feet in the heat."

"Aye," Brendan jumped in.

"No, I'll be fine," Clara answered at the same time. She knew that if she were at home under her parent's care, she would be confined to her bed at this point of her pregnancy. Living in the West afforded her some personal freedoms, at least.

The mayor looked from one to the other, his eyebrows raised.

Joaquin cleared his throat. "I would be grateful for the help. I still need to tend to the farm and my own children. I can make sure Mrs. Murphy gets enough rest."

"Excellent." The mayor smiled at them both before Brendan could get in another word. "They'll arrive this afternoon."

"I think we should have everyone come through triage. Sometimes smoke damage can be hidden and can cause heart problems if not tended to." Clara glanced at Joaquin for his opinion.

"Agreed. That's a good idea, Mrs. Murphy."

The mayor grinned at them. Brendan left, stomping his way back over to Rebecca and Marty.

Clara smiled back at him. "We'll need as much honey as folks can spare and clean rags to be used as bandages, Mr. Mayor."

"As well as large pots of water to hang over a fire. I'll prepare a nettle tea with elderberry for the smoke damage."

"And I'll make a lavender rub."

"Well, it sounds as if you two make a fine team. I'll get some men to prepare the tent and have Mrs. Davenport spread the word for the supplies." The mayor left, his attention pulled to the line at the table outside.

Brendan was waiting at the back, his ire clearly raised. "Keep your filthy hands off my wife," he muttered as Joaquin strode past him. Joaquin kept walking, not bothering to acknowledge the remark.

"Brendan, for heaven's sake, don't make a scene." She was fed up with his surly attitude. She would be happy never to see him again. "We're helping people who are suffering from a fire and have lost their homes. Go home and help Marty clear out a space in the barn."

Clara left the church and found Jo. "Can you come with me to the clinic? My key is at home, and I need to gather supplies."

The women walked across town to the clinic. "Joaquin's told me about your plan to leave." Jo shook her head. "I can't say I blame you, but I will miss you. Will wants to stay here to continue on the farm with Uncle

Eddie. Will's building us a new house next to the farmhouse."

"I know. I'm sad to leave, really. I hope one day we can come back. Hopefully, you can visit us." Clara unlocked the clinic door. "The material for your dress has arrived. Do you want to see it?"

Jo gave her a shaky smile. "Yes. I'm getting nervous, though."

Clara laughed. "You're getting married, Jo. And I wouldn't miss it for the world."

"Only ten more weeks. And fourteen until you become a mother. Our lives are changing, Clara."

"Yes." Clara put her hand to her rounded middle. She had hesitations about giving birth but was less apprehensive about motherhood than she thought she would be. In fact, she might be looking forward to it.

Clara reached for the package on her desk and unwrapped the bolt of fabric. It was exquisite—the ivory satin was so soft in her hands.

Jo gasped, touching it gently, her eyes wide.

"It's from my father," Clara said, smiling. Clara had already given them money to help with the building of Jo and Will's new home as a wedding gift. "We'll pay Sarah O'Connor to sew it for you. She really has the best eye for it."

"I can't believe I'm actually getting married. Do you ... do you think you'll get to have a wedding with Joaquin?"

"No. Not unless Brendan agrees to a divorce, which he's been dead set against so far. We'll just have to pretend to be married. Joaquin says he knows a man who will draw up false papers." She gathered her stethoscope, carbolic acid, and her entire supply of bandages and gauze. She would have to be creative until her next order came in.

"It sounds like you have everything planned to leave." Jo reached up for the dried lavender on a shelf and started to crush the lavender in the mortar while Clara found the rendered animal tallow she kept in a jar. The fire victims would rub the mixture on their chests to help alleviate the effects of the smoke.

"My father will arrive shortly after your wedding. It's close to the end of my pregnancy, but the trip only takes five days. And he'll be with me in case something happens on the way."

Jo nodded. "And then Joaquin will come to get you. I wonder what Brendan will think then, when you don't return and Joaquin leaves."

It was the one part of their plan that might go awry. "I'm hoping Brendan doesn't follow me. He doesn't have the money for the rail ticket, and travel in the winter will be next to impossible otherwise."

They gathered the supplies in their arms, and Jo stopped to lock the door. "I just wish ..."

"What?"

"I just wish something bad would happen to Brendan," Jo whispered. "Maybe I'm awful for saying it, but it's true."

Clara said nothing but smiled sadly at her friend. In her darkest hours, she had thought the same. She had imagined a tragic ending for her husband, where she would be free to marry Joaquin and stay in the town she had grown to love.

～

THE TRIAGE HAD BEEN BUSY, but Clara loved every moment. Mrs. Davenport had dropped off a bounty of supplies, and Clara and Joaquin had worked side by side all afternoon. They were quick and efficient, almost able to read each other's thoughts.

Joaquin grinned over at her from where he was treating a woman with a burn. "I like this, working with you."

Clara smiled back. She was examining all the patients without obvious injury in order to send them on their way to their host home. "We should open a clinic together."

Joaquin looked around to make sure no one they knew was in sight. "Yes, or I'll build one off of the house. It might be more convenient with the two babies and tending to the farm."

"I like that idea even better."

The man she was examining peered up at her as she listened to his heartbeat with the stethoscope. "A husband-and-wife doctor team. My wife is a nurse. We talk about blood and pus around the dinner table, too." He chuckled and stuck out his hand. "Doctor Michael Adams. Pleased to meet you."

"Oh, nice to meet you, too." She blushed at the man's assumption of their married status. She didn't know how to correct the mistake. He had heard them talking openly about their future.

Doctor Adams stood. "I would be happy to help you out today. You may want to take a break." He lifted his pant leg to reveal a wooden leg. "I know about needing to sit down every once in a while."

"That's kind of you, Dr. Adams, but—"

"Clara, go have a rest. You've been on your feet for

hours." Joaquin reached out and briefly touched her back. He nodded to some chairs at the end of the tent.

"All right, I will, thank you."

Sitting in one of the chairs, she watched Joaquin and Dr. Adams work. They laughed over a joke, making Clara smile. She'd never had the chance to just watch Joaquin before. He was so friendly with everyone, and for the hundredth time, she found herself grateful to have found such a kind man. His hair fell into his eyes as he worked. It looked like it was time for another haircut.

She startled as someone sank into the chair next to her. McGregor. She could smell the too-sweet scent of opium smoke mixed with spirits.

"McGregor, what are you doing here?"

He was gazing over at the two male doctors with a glassy stare. She might need to ask Joaquin to send him home, as he seemed far gone into an opium haze.

"I'm fine." His words were clear, not slurred. "My faithful steed is just yonder." He nodded over to a horse tied to a nearby tree. "She'll ride me right to my front door." He reached into his pocket for a coin and held it out to Clara. "I've come for some medical advice."

"Keep your coin, McGregor. I can't help you. It can't be reversed." It was his eyesight he was here for, she guessed.

He nodded as if he expected her answer but still held out the coin. She took it, putting it in her pocket. It could go to one of the families from the fire.

"Six months ago, it started. Just a hazy white at the edges o' my sight. Now I go to bed every night wondering if this day will be the last I ever see. I can only just see the shadow of your Joaquin over there. I know it's him because you are sitting relaxed and smiling. Mr. Murphy makes you on edge."

Clara gave a dry laugh. "You're confused by your drug, McGregor." He may be going blind, but she still didn't trust him.

"I'm not confused. Though my tongue gets loose, I will admit." He paused before continuing. "I had no daddy, same as your lad over there. Well, rumour was that my granddaddy may've been my daddy, but that's another story."

She'd been right about his reaction in the barn. He was born out of wedlock, too. "I'm not sure why you're telling—"

"Difference is, Joaquin's mammy, she loved him somethin' fierce. She may have only been a child herself, but she was a good mother. Turned him into a good man. My mammy, well … you ever heard of the name Eunan?"

"No."

Joaquin's eyes were on them, concerned. She waved him off, back to work.

"My mammy named me Eunan. Means little terror." He laughed, a rusty sound that came from the back of his throat. "Guess I just grew up to be what she thought I would be. A terror."

"You're not—" Clara tried to think of something kind to say. She wondered how many people McGregor had revealed this story to. Probably not many.

"Aye, I am. I've been terrorizin' this here town for as long as anyone can remember. Say the name McGregor and folks will walk the other way."

"Well—"

He laughed again. "I do appreciate your fine upbringin', Mrs. Murphy. Always tryin' to find somethin' polite to say.

Nah, it's true. I've spent my days makin' money off weak men and their families. Men like your husband."

Clara was quiet. Was he threatening her again? No doubt Brendan had racked up new debts with his most recent travels to McGregor's farm. He had no way to pay, no money of his own. Clara had been careful to keep her own money in the bank and hid her valuables, like the diamond earrings her father had given her for Christmas, at Joaquin's house.

"I guess there's always time to change, McGregor," she said finally, placing her hand over her belly where the baby was moving. "You could always live out the rest of your days being a good man, like Joaquin."

"Hmm. I'm not sure about that. But I am rootin' for you, you know. For your happy endin'."

Clara looked over at him in surprise. Perhaps it was the opium talking, but she was starting to feel as if McGregor liked her just a little. Over his shoulder, Brendan approached. The sway in his walk told her he was drunk.

"Ish time to leave, Clara," he slurred, making her grimace. It was only supper time, and he was three sheets to the wind.

"All right." She knew better than to argue with Brendan when he was intoxicated, and it would only create a public spectacle. "Good night, McGregor." She caught Joaquin's eye across the tent. His face hardened, but he lifted his hand in farewell.

"Mrs. Murphy. Until we meet again." McGregor was back to squinting over at Joaquin. Clara left with Brendan, her thoughts consumed with the story of Eunan McGregor.

JOAQUIN GAVE the other doctor a pat on the shoulder. "Thanks for your help, Michael." They had made their way through all two hundred patients before they lost the light in the sky.

"It was a pleasure, Joaquin. Do you happen to know of any small towns like this one where they might need a doctor? The wife and I were thinking of moving out from the city, and now that we've lost our home, it seems like the perfect time."

Joaquin raised his eyebrows. As it was, this town would be needing a doctor soon enough, as the two it had would be leaving.

"Well, I think Clara will be closing her clinic after her baby arrives, and I can't doctor full time with the farm. So, if you like it here, you might want to stay."

"Oh, I thought the two of you ran the clinic together."

Joaquin cleared his throat. "She's just a friend, Michael. And the clinic belongs to her." He wished he could call Clara something more. He could only hope that one day he would.

Michael shook his head. "I thought I heard you say ..."

"No. You didn't hear anything." He cut the doctor off as his eyes fell on McGregor, who still sat at the end of the tent. "Looks like I have one more patient. I'll see you around, Michael."

He made his way down to the end of the tent and sat in the chair that Clara had occupied an hour ago. Before her drunk husband had come to collect her. *That ass, Brendan.*

"McGregor. What are you still doing here?"

"Ah, Spaniard, I'm just thinkin' on my life." McGregor took out a flask and held it out. Joaquin took a sip, the spirits searing down his throat.

He grimaced at the taste. "That's awful. How do you ever sell that?"

McGregor gave a chuckle. "It's easy. I sell to men like your granddaddy and Brendan Murphy. Men with no control—and no soul."

The comment filled Joaquin with a flood of panic. He hated every second that Clara was with Brendan. Every moment of every day. He swallowed back the fear with a sudden resolve.

"McGregor, I've got a fine dairy cow in my barn with your name on it. I don't have much in the way of coins, but I can find it if that's what you need."

"No, Spaniard."

"I just ... I need him gone. I need her." His voice was so raw with the need it frightened him. He was trying to make a deal with the devil just to have her.

"No. I'm turnin' over a new leaf just now. And you won't want his blood on your hands. She might hate you for it."

Joaquin lowered his eyes, staring at his boots. "I love her. And she loves me. It's not something a man like me finds, McGregor. I can't ... I can't lose her." He had no idea why he was pouring out his heart to this older man, except that the burden was so heavy. The ache exhausted him so.

"Well, men like Murphy always self-destruct. I've seen it a hundred times."

"That could take years."

"Aye. Or it could be tomorrow. Or it could be just in the

nick o' time, Spaniard." McGregor heaved himself off the chair. "Help an ol' man over to his mount, will ya?

Joaquin helped McGregor over to his horse and came back to the tent. He picked up his medical bag, ready to leave, when he noticed a scrap of paper slipped inside.

Meeting spot. Eight. – C

He cast his eye to the setting sun. It was past eight, closer to nine.

JOAQUIN HURRIEDLY TIED his horse to a tree and made his way into the thick forest. He didn't have a lantern, and it was now dark, so he felt his way in through the trees, hoping that she wasn't already gone.

She was sitting there, waiting for him. Her hair was completely undone, hanging in waves almost to her waist. She wore only her shift, and his eyes fell on the outline of her body through the thin fabric, illuminated clearly by the lamp she had placed on the log behind her. He looked up from the shape of her legs to the roundness of the child she carried. Taking a step closer, he could see her breasts, the nipples hard and dark against the white of the cotton. Finally, his gaze took in the whole scene—behind her, on the log, was her clothing, a blanket, and a book.

"You're late. I—"

He cut her off from speaking, crushing himself against her. He needed her more than the air he breathed. His mouth found hers, and she moaned as he ran his hands down her body. He reached to her behind and cupped it in his hands, pulling her even closer.

"I need you," he whispered in her ear. His voice sounded like a stranger to him, so desperate with longing. "I need all of you, Clara."

"I need you, too. Please. It might be months—"

He reached for the bottom of her shift and lifted it over her head.

She stood there as he took her in—all of her. He gently turned her around, his gaze moving down her back. She was beautiful.

His hands reached for the buttons to his own clothing, and soon he was standing before her, exposed, with his arousal stiff against his thigh. He held out his hand, and when she took it, he brought her gently to the blanket she had laid in the clearing.

Their bodies came together frantically, furiously, with a hunger fueled by a desire that pulsed rapidly through his entire body. His mouth found her breasts, and he felt a shudder run through her as he ran his tongue over her erect nipples. He reached down between her legs and slipped his fingers inside to find her slick with the same longing he felt for her every day and night.

"Joaquin." His name escaped her lips as she moved her hips against his hand, her pleasure almost at its peak. He watched her as she reached it, clinging to his neck with her eyes closed.

She opened her eyes again as he entered her, gently easing himself in. Then he closed his own eyes as his need overwhelmed him. He moved inside her rapidly, still careful of the child between them, his groans loud in the otherwise quiet forest. He needed all of her, again and again, over and over.

When he was finished, he gathered her in his arms, his heart pounding. "My Clara, my love." He moved her hair out of the way to kiss her neck.

"Forever and always yours." She snuggled against him, her bare breasts against his chest.

They lay together in the comfort of their skin against skin, her hand exploring. Their desire grew once more, and they came together again, slowly, relishing the movements of their bodies as one. Then they dressed, exiting their meeting place together with caution, kissing a final farewell before going their separate ways in the night.

Chapter 22

Late September 1886

Jo stood at Clara's door, an infectious grin on her face. It was just ten days before the wedding, and they were taking a trip to Surrey to visit a community of Chinese stores and merchants. Jo wanted to buy ingredients for red bean soup with sticky rice balls and Chinese tea to serve at the wedding reception, which would be a small and intimate affair of friends and family only.

"We're ready." Clara moved slowly from her perch at the kitchen table. Brendan was in the barn, saddling the horses. Upon hearing that Jo was heading to the Chinese market, Joaquin had suggested that they visit a traditional medical shop to stock their supplies. Brendan had reluctantly agreed but insisted on accompanying them.

"Is everything all right?" Jo noticed Clara's slow trudge to the barn.

"Yes, it's fine. I'm just sore." It was a half-truth. She was sore, but she had also been up most of the night with cramps.

Braxton Hicks contractions were normal in the last month of pregnancy, but she knew she should be relaxing instead of taking a trip into the next town.

Joaquin and Will rode up just as she was bringing Red out of the barn. Joaquin slid down, coming to help Clara onto the horse. He said nothing, but their eyes met as his hands slipped around her waist. His touch brought a shiver of arousal. They had started to spend many of their lunch hours hidden away in their meeting spot, learning the shape of each other's desire. It was risky, but they just couldn't stay away.

"I miss you," he breathed against her ear before lifting her gently up. She grimaced as she eased her way onto the saddle.

"This autumn heat is unbearable," Jo said, mounting her horse beside Will.

"I agree." Clara gave a short laugh, then stopped as the cramping in her belly peaked again. She winced slightly and put her hand on it, pressing against the discomfort.

"Clara?" It was Joaquin, concern written on his face.

"Just the baby kicking." She smiled, although the cramping had left her breathless.

Brendan came around the corner on his horse and glowered when he saw her next to Joaquin. "Clara. Come ride beside me."

She gave him a glare but moved back beside him. Her mood was on the verge of foul, and Brendan's comments made it worse.

The dusty road loomed ahead, long and arduous. The porridge she'd made for breakfast sat like a solid lump in her belly, her back ached, and the cramping in her womb continued to get worse. She took another drink from her canteen and tried to swallow back nausea.

As they rode, Jo and Will fell behind, deep in a conversation about their new home. It wasn't quite ready for them to move in, so they would be staying in the farmhouse for the first month of their marriage. Clara rode flanked by her men on either side. Neither of them spoke, but she could feel them eyeing each other over her.

Another wave of cramping started—deep and strong and concerning. It was still a few weeks until the baby was due, but Clara was starting to think these were birthing pains, not Braxton Hicks. At the peak of the pain, she fell behind the two men. Her breathing laboured as she tried to concentrate on staying on her horse.

"Clara?" Joaquin had immediately dropped back to her. "Are you all right?"

"I think so." She forced herself to smile through the pain. "I need some water. My canteen is empty." She would tell him her suspicions if the pains continued this strong.

He passed her his water, his brows furrowed in concern. Brendan looked back from where he was still riding ahead. "We're just a few minutes away." Joaquin's gaze was penetrating. "I think we need to find you a tea shop or a restaurant, so you can rest."

She nodded. Resting sounded perfect.

They had tied their horses at the east end of town and were walking towards the first set of merchants when the next contraction hit. She stopped, unable to keep walking. A groan escaped from her lips, and she leaned against a nearby hitching post.

Joaquin's hands were on her belly, his expert touch moving low to feel the baby's head.

"What the hell?" Brendan ran right into them, nearly knocking Clara to the ground. Joaquin grasped her firmly, strong arms wrapped around her. "Get your hands off my wife, bastard!"

"Stop!" Joaquin pushed Brendan away. "I think she's having the baby, you ass!"

"What?" Jo's hand came to her back. Clara moaned again as she hit the deepest part of the pain. She felt like she could barely breathe. Jo led her to a step to sit down as the contraction continued.

As she came out of the agony a minute later, she became aware of the chaos around her. Jo was speaking in Chinese to a nearby merchant. Brendan was leaning on a nearby hitching post with his arms crossed, glaring at Joaquin, who was scrambling around the market, looking for any medical supplies he could use. Will was standing with his hands in his pockets, looking very uncomfortable.

"Let's head back then," Brendan said as the others came back to Clara.

"No. Her contractions are too close. I'm guessing three minutes now." Joaquin looked at Clara. "When did they start?"

"Last night."

"What?" Jo, Brendan, and Joaquin all spoke in unison.

"Why didn't you say anything?" Jo asked, her voice gentle.

"I didn't think it was—" She stopped. Another wave was starting. They were almost on top of each other now, and fear was starting to creep in. Delivering her baby on the street was far from her idea of a hospital.

"We need to get her inside," Joaquin said.

"I've spoken with that merchant. His wife runs a tea shop just down the street. They live above, and he said we can use their room." Jo's concern was palpable.

"I'll try to gather the supplies. I should have brought my medical bag," Joaquin said.

"No. I'll no' let you touch my wife. You'll no' deliver my child."

There was a loud shuffling, and Clara looked up, still in the throes of the contraction. Joaquin had pushed Brendan up against a post, his hands around Brendan's throat.

"Do you know how many women *die* in childbirth? I'm your best bet for both Clara and your baby surviving." He let Brendan go, shaking his head as he walked away. Brendan came back at him, fists swinging.

"Stop!" It was Jo, her normally quiet voice a loud command. "I'll deliver the child. I've delivered twenty, maybe more. Joaquin, you can be nearby in case something goes wrong. But we need to get her inside, and quickly. There's no time for you two to squabble."

Jo held her hand as they made their way to the tea shop a few blocks away. They had to stop halfway when another contraction came. It was fierce and painful, and Clara cried out, alarming some of the closer people on the street. Jo's hands on her back were solid and reassuring, but she longed for Joaquin's arms. She managed a glance at his face, creased with worry, and knew he wanted to comfort her, too.

It seemed like an eternity, but they finally arrived at the tea shop. Jo spoke to the woman in Chinese, and the woman led them up the stairs. Jo supported Clara as she climbed the stairs with difficulty.

"I have some coins in my purse," Clara told Jo. "Leave them for this kind woman, please."

Jo left Clara in the room for a moment while she helped Joaquin gather the things she needed for the birth. Clara swallowed back her fear and looked at the space. It was a simple home with the barest of furnishings. Nothing like the room she would have birthed in at her father's estate.

Jo was back. "The men are in the kitchen, downstairs. Let's hope they don't kill each other before the baby arrives."

Clara didn't answer, as another contraction had started. Ready or not, she was about to become a mother.

Joaquin sent Will home to fetch their wagon, as Clara would not be able to ride after the birth. The owner had requested that they stay in the kitchen so as not to disturb the customers. But the last thing he wanted was to wait out the birth with Clara's ass of a husband.

Reluctantly, he made his way to the kitchen. Brendan sat at the table, an ale in hand.

Joaquin shook his head. "Unbelievable. Your wife is giving birth, but you've managed to find a drink." He gave a crazed laugh. "Actually, I am not surprised. You don't care about Clara one bit."

He could hear Clara's cries coming through the ceiling. It wouldn't be long before she started to push, judging by the sound. It was taking everything in his body not to run up the stairs and take her in his arms, to stroke her hair and rub her back. Every time he heard her cry, his guts twisted for her. Why in the world she had agreed to travel with them while in labour was beyond him.

"Aye, but you do. You care about the well-bein' of my wife an awful lot. *My* wife, bastard. Mine."

Joaquin wanted to smash the glass of ale over his head. Every word that came from this man's mouth was abhorrent. The fact that he had ever touched Clara at all disgusted him.

"You don't deserve her. You're a selfish coward through and through. No one in town likes you, Murphy." His voice was a growl. He was finished trying to be peaceful.

"You're just jealous because she's mine. Your pecker gets hard every time you see her, but it's me who gets to bed her."

Joaquin's hand curled into a fist. If only the drunkard knew the truth. "From what I've heard, your cock barely does the job, you Irish bugger. No wonder she fell into my arms."

Brendan's fist smashed on the table. "You goddamn son of a—"

The door of the kitchen flew open, and the woman who owned the restaurant came in with a torrent of Chinese. He couldn't understand a word, but clearly, they were about to wear out their welcome.

After the woman left, the two men stared at each other across the small room. It was hot, with boiling pots of tea simmering on the stove, and sweat trickled down Joaquin's face, back, and chest.

"This place is a hovel. It's because of you that she's delivering our child in this rat-infested shack."

Joaquin turned away. He wouldn't even dignify that comment with a response—these people were generous beyond measure, letting a stranger birth in their bed. From what Clara had told him, Brendan's own birth and upbringing weren't likely much different.

Brendan probed again. "Are you after her money, then? Fancy yourself friends with her father?"

Joaquin laughed at him. "I have all I'll ever need." It was true. Clara was his, with both her heart and her body. He didn't care one ounce about her money, and he would spend the rest of his days working to provide for her and their family.

Brendan heard the affection in his voice and frowned. "I won't let you have her. I'll kill you both."

Joaquin's response was drowned out by the sound he had been waiting for—an infant's cry from the room above.

Joaquin took the stairs, two at a time, to the top of the landing. He knocked. "Is everything all right?"

Jo's voice came through the door, giddy with excitement. "Yes! It's a girl. I just need a few minutes to clean up."

A girl. Sudden emotion pulled at his heart, and he felt tears well in his eyes. He would raise this daughter as his own when he and Clara started their life together.

Brendan came trudging up the stairs. "Is it a boy?"

Joaquin's happiness dissipated. Brendan would ruin this moment for her, for them. Joaquin wanted nothing more than to crawl into bed with Clara and gaze lovingly with her at the new baby. He wanted to watch the baby feed at her breast, to help her during the first trying weeks of parenthood.

The door opened. Brendan pushed past him into the room, his arms outstretched for the baby. Joaquin caught Clara's eye from his post at the door. They both smiled, a silent acknowledgement of their love. He mouthed the words *I love you* across the room to her.

"It's a girl," Jo told Brendan as she handed him the swaddled infant.

"Ah well, she's bonny. We'll name her Sarah."

"Actually, Brendan, I've already named her," Clara said, her voice firm despite the exhaustion in it.

Brendan looked at Clara with surprise. He shrugged. "All right. But I will name our son the next time."

Clara's eye's flitted over to Joaquin before going back to Brendan. "Her name is Beth. Bethany Rose."

Joaquin caught his breath with an audible gasp. Jo coughed suddenly, likely to cover the sound. He had only told her once, he was sure. His mother's name. *Beth.*

His hands shook, and he didn't trust his voice. When Brendan sat at the edge of the bed and handed the baby back to Clara for her to feed, she caught his eye once again. She had given him the greatest gift of all—a part of her child.

Chapter 23

October 1886

CLARA HAD NEVER KNOWN THIS KIND OF FATIGUE. EVEN in the strenuous exam period at medical school, she had been reasonably well-rested and alert. It seemed that Beth never slept, especially not at night.

"Is she hungry again?" Clara whispered, whimpering at the thought. Her nipples were chapped and raw from the baby's constant suckling.

"Aye, I'm afraid so." Rebecca brought over a warm cloth to ease the pain. "It's not always so painful. Just the first few weeks."

Clara grimaced as she brought the baby to her breast. She had known childbirth would be difficult, but no one had told her how trying it was to navigate life with a newborn on no sleep. Brendan was no help, but that didn't surprise her. When she was nursing in the midnight hours, her thoughts drifted to Joaquin. He would be sleeping, of course, his long legs spread out on his bed, his wavy hair askew on his pillow.

The thoughts of him were bittersweet. It was now only ten days until she would leave, to be distanced by the vast expanse of the country.

"After she's done feedin', I'll take her so you can get ready for the weddin'." Rebecca was always eager to take Beth off Clara's hands, doting on her constantly. Rebecca's own belly remained flat, and she had once again confided in Clara her worst fear: John McKay's baby would be her only one.

Marty came downstairs, dressed in his Sunday best, with Patrick on his hip. "It sure is a fine day for Jo's weddin'. Would never have imagined, when you brought her to us, all bedraggled and starved, that she would find a match."

Brendan grunted from the kitchen table. In true form, he was hungover. Fatherhood had not changed his habits in the slightest.

Clara discreetly switched the baby to the other breast. Again, the pain was fierce as Beth latched on.

Rebecca watched her, wincing in sympathy. "Perhaps now that the babe is born, you might delay your trip home, Clara. Just until you get more settled with her."

Clara shook her head. She wanted to leave. Leaving meant that her life with Joaquin could begin. "No, my father is too busy with the company. This is the only time he can escort me."

"When will you return?" Marty smiled.

"Before Christmas." It was her plan to delay the trip through the holidays and then hope Brendan did not follow her during the winter months. By that time, she would be back in British Columbia, hidden away in a new life.

Brendan looked up from the table. "Christmas? I thought this was a short trip, Clara."

"Oh, my mother has already arranged so many social engagements. Tea parties, charity functions, that sort of thing. She wants to show off her grandchild." Truthfully, Clara had no idea how her mother would react to her arrival home. Once the news came out that she was running away from her husband to start an immoral union with another man, her mother would be scandalized. Not that Clara would pay her mind—her own mother was doing much the same with Charles McKay.

"Here, let me take Beth now. You'd best get ready, or we'll be late. The church reception starts at two." Rebecca's eager hands took her niece.

Clara went to her room and took her dress off the bed. It was new, but she'd had to beg the local seamstress to alter the fitting, as it had been made to fit her pregnancy. Now she had almost returned to her normal size. Her hips were wider, her stomach still a bit rounded, and she couldn't yet get back into the clothes she had worn before. She shrugged to herself. Her mother would have an entire new wardrobe made for her upon arrival; that was one thing she was quite sure of. Her daughter, scandal or not, would not be paraded around society in farm clothes.

Her new dress was a deep emerald green, with a high bustle, white gloves, and a matching fan. She smiled to herself, remembering the Christmas social. Her first kiss with Joaquin. She ran her hands down her own body, longing for his sensual touch. She was looking forward to their new life in the bedroom as well.

They decided to walk to the church, as the weather was

fine. When they arrived, Brendan pulled Clara aside. "If I see you talking with that damn man, I *will* make a scene. You want that for your friend's wedding, Clara?" She shuddered at his words. Whatever had passed between Brendan and Joaquin during Beth's birth had not been pleasant. The tension was thick in the air, and she could barely stand it.

Jesse and Drew met them at the door, dressed in their suits. "Good afternoon, Mr. and Mrs. Murphy," Jesse said, leading them to sit next to Rebecca and Marty, near the front of the church, on Jo's side. It was nearly two o'clock, and the ceremony was about to start. Clara scanned the rows for Joaquin. He was in the front row on the groom's side, seated next to his former wife, Laura, and her husband. She ached with jealousy at seeing them seated together. It was so hard to continue to pretend when she wanted to be beside the man she loved.

Piano music started, and the back door of the church opened. The guests stood and faced the back, ready to welcome the bride. Clara snuck a glance over her shoulder. Now Joaquin was watching her and Brendan. She caught his eye and smiled before turning back to the procession.

Jo was beautiful. Her glossy black hair was piled on her head in loose curls, and a lacy veil covered her face. Her dress, however, was what everyone was staring at—the bodice fit like a glove, with an elegant bustle behind.

Clara's heart nearly burst with joy as she watched her friend pass. Tears came to her eyes as Jo smiled at her, then secured her eyes on her husband-to-be at the front of the church. The ceremony went off without a hitch, save for when a frog escaped from the pocket of one of the young boys in the audience. Clara caught sight of Rebecca wiping away tears during the vows and felt a surge of regret for everyone she would leave behind.

After the wedding, the guests walked to the reception held in Joaquin's yard. Clara stopped by the homestead first, to nurse and change the baby. She made her way through the forest, wondering if this would be the last time she crossed through. She gazed up at the light trickling through the trees with regret. There was something she loved about emerging from the dark tree cover and bursting through to the view of the beautiful farmhouse.

The backyard was full of family and friends, mingling and visiting. Some were seated at tables, eating. Jo and Will made their way around the crowd, receiving well wishes and gifts. Brendan and Marty stood chatting with some of the other men in town, and Rebecca was holding a friend's new baby, born just after Clara's.

"Clara!" Joaquin said, walking briskly across the yard. He stopped just short of her, something flashing in front of his face, as he suddenly remembered not to give away their romance in front of all their guests. Yes, it was a good thing she was soon to be on her way. It was getting harder and harder to resist the pull between them.

"Mrs. Murphy, how are you?"

"I'm just feeling sad about leaving," she said softly, only loud enough for him to hear. She swallowed back the lump in her throat. "I've really grown to love it here."

His expression said much the same. "Can I hold her?" He held out his arms for Beth. "She'll be so much bigger in a few months."

She handed the baby to him and shot a quick glance across the yard. So far, Brendan hadn't noticed them.

Joaquin smiled down at the infant, who was gurgling. "She's beautiful, Clara." He took a step closer to her. They gazed at the baby together, shoulder to shoulder. "Little Beth, take care of your mother. I'm going to miss her very much." His voice was husky, and he was no longer looking at the child.

He looked away, bringing the infant up to his shoulder and rubbed her back. She belched loudly, and Clara let out a giggle. "She likes you." Then more seriously, she asked, "Will I see you at Christmas? I thought maybe we could spend the holidays together at my parent's place before going to Eddie's."

He nodded but then glanced out at the lawn and took a large step away from her. Both Laura and Brendan were headed their way.

"Oh, I see your baby has been born!" Laura arrived, taking the baby from Joaquin's arms. She gazed down at Beth, her expression soft. "I remember when ours were this little, don't you?"

Clara looked up at Joaquin for his reaction, but his eyes were on Brendan, who had entered the conversation, his face red with fury.

"What—?" Brendan started.

"Oh, are you the father?" Laura's coos over the baby stopped Brendan's angry intrusion. "What's her name?"

Brendan's expression softened somewhat, though he kept his eyes on Joaquin. "Her name's Beth."

Laura's eyes widened in surprise, and Clara suddenly realized the grave mistake. Of course, Laura would have known the name of Joaquin's mother. She should have kept the baby's real name a secret for now. Joaquin stiffened beside her as he realized the same.

"Why, that's your—"

"How's Anna doing?" Clara blurted out. She lowered her voice so others around wouldn't hear. "She must be only a few days away from having her own baby." She knew Anna hadn't attended the wedding, wanting to hide her condition from the vicious town gossip.

Joaquin looked up to the top floor of the house. "I think she's quite upset today, missing her brother's wedding. Why don't you head up, Clara? I'm sure she'd love to meet the baby."

Clara took Beth and darted out of the conversation, grateful for an excuse to leave. She couldn't imagine what kind of rage Brendan would unleash if he realized that Beth was named for Joaquin's mother.

Clara found Anna on her bed, lying on her side. "Anna? It's Clara. I thought I'd introduce you to my baby."

Anna sat up, her eyes red and swollen. Pulling her patch-work quilt around her, she peered at Beth. "Is it hard? Caring for her?"

"It's tiring," Clara admitted, not wanting to give the girl too many frightening details. She would know for herself soon enough. "If I'm gone already to visit my parents, Jo will deliver the baby. And Rebecca can help you learn to nurse."

Anna nodded, then lay back down and turned on her side, away from Clara.

"Anna, what's wrong? Are you upset because you missed Will's wedding?"

Anna shook her head. "Not only that. Will brought me a letter from the post office yesterday. It's in my chest of drawers."

Clara went over to look. It was a letter from the teacher's college in Victoria. Anna had been accepted into the program. "Oh, Anna."

Anna sniffed back fresh tears, gazing past Clara out the window. "Now I'll never go."

Clara sat down on the end of her bed. She didn't know how much Anna knew about her relationship with her father. Or if she knew Joaquin was planning to raise her child as his own.

"Have you told your father?"

Anna shook her head but sat up again.

Clara handed Anna the letter. "I think you should. Just see what he has to say, Anna."

"Do you think so?"

"I do." She handed Beth to Anna. "Here. Her name's Beth."

Anna raised her eyebrows. "That was my grandmother's name." She stroked the baby's soft hair. "She smells nice."

Clara leaned over and gave Anna a hug. "I can't wait to meet your baby, too. They'll be playmates."

Clara sat with Anna for a few minutes longer, then headed down and back outside. She touched the doorknob of the house in a silent farewell.

JOAQUIN COULD HARDLY REMEMBER when he had seen such a storm. It was five days after his son's wedding and five short days until Clara would leave, but today, that was not his pressing concern. He stared out the window of the library, where he had been pacing for the last hour. The heavens raged—sheets of water fell from the sky, pushed sideways by the torrential winds. Debris from the forest flew everywhere, and he was worried about the last of the season's crops. But what plagued him most were memories from his childhood—storms would always set his grandfather into a violent disposition.

It was Jo who came to him at last, knocking timidly at the library door. "You should go."

He whipped his head around to look at her. "No, she's fine. I don't need to disturb Brendan even more. Her father arrives so soon." But he wanted to go, desperately. Just to know she was safe.

"Then I'll go." Jo left the room.

"No, Jo, it's dangerous out there." He followed her into the kitchen, his decision made. He found his oilskin coat and shrugged into it. As he reached for the doorknob, he hesitated, remembering his letter. Going back into the kitchen, he retrieved it from under the tin box on the highest shelf. His last letter to her. They had decided that writing would be too risky. Mr. Williams at the post office was a smart man, and a trail of letters would be too easy to follow. The letter went into his inside pocket, and he braced himself for the storm.

The wind whipped his hair into his eyes, and the rain soaked his skin. Clara wouldn't have gone to the clinic, not with the new baby. But the idea of her caged in the homestead with Brendan set his teeth on edge. He darted through the forest. The old growth was being snapped by the vicious winds, and to be struck by a tree could be fatal.

· · ·

THUD. His fists hit the homestead door. *Thud.* "Clara!" he called, now desperate. He hadn't considered that she might not be home. A flood of panic swept through his veins, and he pounded the door again.

"Joaquin!" She opened the door, grabbed his arm, and pulled him inside. "What on earth are you doing out in this weather?"

He scanned the homestead. It seemed empty. He came in and closed the door behind him.

"The three of them are at Marty and Rebecca's place." She took his jacket and got a towel for his face and hair, then wiped the floor where he had left a large puddle. "They invited me, but Beth is sleeping, and I couldn't stand being stuck inside for hours with them."

He sighed in relief, then pulled her close. He was still wet, but her hands drifted up his neck and into his hair. God, he would miss her.

"I'll make some tea. I'm so happy you came."

"I needed to make sure you were safe." He didn't let her go to make the tea. This could very well be the last time he held her for months.

"You won't need to worry much longer. I'll be waiting for you."

He kissed her neck. "I'll be there. I can hardly wait, Clara. Will is going to take the children to Eddie's when Anna is able to travel. Once I collect you, our family will be complete."

She pulled away, and he let her go. Once she had set the kettle on the hearth, she turned to him, her face creased. Something was on her mind. A trickle of unease crept into his head. Had she changed her mind?

He sat in the chair by the fire, letting her have the time she needed to tell him what was bothering her. She came and sat on his lap, her arms around his neck.

"I'm a horrible cook," she said, burying her head into him. "I'm quite embarrassed about it, actually."

He laughed, the worry he'd held on to for so many months melting away. She smiled back as he continued to laugh, burrowing his head into her neck to muffle the sound. "I love you, Clara, so much. Can I start calling you my wife? Mrs. Walker?"

Her lips met his with passion. "Yes. A thousand times, yes."

As she got up to tend to the tea, he remembered his letter. Retrieving it from his coat pocket, he held it out to her. "Don't read it now. Wait until the train."

She took it, smiling at him. "I have one for you, too." She reached between two books and pulled hers out before sliding his letter in its place. "Sealed with a kiss. And now," she said, selecting a book from the shelf, "will you please read to me?"

He knew what the book was before he even saw the cover. *The Three Musketeers.* They settled down, and he read for an hour, his voice filling the room and their hearts with stories of swords, treasures, and dreams come true.

Chapter 24

October 1886

JOAQUIN KNEW IT WAS A DREAM, BUT HE WAS ENJOYING it just the same. Clara was on top of him, her hair hanging over her bare breasts, parted just enough for him to see. Eyes closed, she was moaning out his name. The scent of her arousal was musky in the night air.

Then she was gone, and a voice permeated the vision. Someone was calling him. It was a weak sound, barely audible through the haze of sleep.

"Father!" Will bellowed. Joaquin sat up, his entire body rigid. Something was wrong. Very wrong.

He dashed to the door of his room, not caring that he was still bare-chested. Will met him there, breathing heavily.

There was a cry from the bedroom next door that turned his blood cold. *Anna*. He ran into the room, fumbling with the kerosene lamp twice before he managed to get it lit. She was on the bed, clutching her stomach. Between her legs was a red pool of blood.

Both Jo and Will were at his shoulder. Jo cried out and then covered her mouth to quell the sound. But it did not matter. For they all knew what lay before them.

"Get Clara." His voice was not his own—it drifted to his ears as if floating from another time and space. "Jo, take the children outside."

They left, thudding down the stairs. Anna was barely conscious now, but her face was twisted in fear. "Father, help me," she gasped.

Joaquin put the lamp on the chest of drawers and climbed into bed beside her. His hands shook as he gathered her in his arms and stroked her hair. His only daughter. "Will's just gone to get Clara, my sweet Anna. We'll just wait for her here." He kissed her forehead, tasting the tears that were running down his cheeks. It wouldn't be long now.

∽

When Clara and Will arrived at the farmhouse, they were panting with exertion. Clara had come in her nightdress, only pausing to put on her coat and grab her medical bag. They'd sprinted across the yard, the air still fragrant with the aftermath of the previous day's storm.

The children and Jo were outside, and Jesse was lighting a fire in the outdoor hearth. Clara grabbed Jo, leaving Will behind. Jo started to sob as they entered the house—it was deathly still, with only a flickering light at the top of the stairs. Clara grabbed her friend by the shoulders.

"I need you to be steadfast, Jo. Joaquin needs us now."

"There was so much blood, Clara. I don't ... I don't think she'll make it."

314

They climbed the stairs quickly but with trepidation in their steps. Clara shook as she tried to keep back her own cries. Was it possible Anna was really gone?

Joaquin was lying with Anna on the bed, weeping into her limp embrace. They were both covered in her blood, making it difficult to see where she ended and he began.

"How long has she been gone?" Clara forced her voice to sound sure and brisk as she'd resolutely pushed aside the impulse to scream and weep alongside her love.

Joaquin didn't look up. He didn't seem to realize she was there.

"*How long!*" Clara yelled, rousing him from his trance. Time was of the essence.

He saw her then and heard her question. "Not long. A few minutes at most." He nodded, realizing her plan. "Please try, Clara. Try to save the baby." His voice caught, and he rocked back and forth, holding his daughter.

She grabbed him by the arm while Jo got another lamp from his room. "You need to leave. Go outside." She pushed him out the door, not daring to fall into his embrace, or she would shatter into pieces.

She rummaged around in the medical bag for her scalpel, praying they had enough time. Clara checked Anna briefly with her stethoscope. There was no heartbeat, no breath. Anna was gone. It must have been a placental abruption, tearing away from the wall of the womb. Pushing aside her clothes, she spoke to Jo. "I'm going to cut through the skin, fat, and muscle. You need to hold it open. It will be wet and bloody, but it's important so I can see."

Jo nodded, bravely wiping away the last of her tears. "I'm ready."

"Skin. Fat. Abdominal muscles." Clara struggled with the muscle. It was tougher than she thought. "There. Bladder and intestines aside. Uterus." As Clara made the last incision into the womb, she prayed, she begged. When Jo reached to pull the uterus aside, Clara put her hands in.

"Baby. Support the head and neck. Shoulders. Hold the buttocks. Out. Over." Clara flipped the tiny purple body over, rubbing its back and supporting its neck. She reached her fingers into the baby's mouth and tried to remove any mucus.

"Please, God. Please. Breathe," Clara whispered. She gave the baby a soft thump on its back. Suddenly, to her disbelief, the baby let out a feeble cry. It was weak at first but shortly turned into the frantic cry of a newborn first exposed to the frigid air of its earthside home.

Jo cried out in happiness and jumped up to fetch a blanket. Clara handed her the baby and cut the cord that attached her to Anna, clamping it quickly. A granddaughter, with thick dark hair. Clara's shoulders began to shake, and tears poured down her cheeks. Jo put an arm around her, and they cried together.

"Take her out to Joaquin, but make sure he and the others don't come in. I need to clean this up." She didn't want those boys coming in to see their sister cut apart.

Clara took her time, carefully restoring Anna's body. As she did, the tears started to fall, blurring her vision. She replaced the bladder and intestines as best as she could and stitched up every layer. She found a cloth and some water and washed away the blood from Anna's body and dressed her in clean garments. Then she rolled all the blood-stained items into a ball and stuffed them into a laundry sack. There was still blood staining the floor, but there was not much she could do about that. She spent a moment holding Anna's hand, allowing the last of her tears to run free before she collected herself to go outside.

Taking a deep breath, she left the farmhouse. The outdoor fire was blazing. Jo and Will stood in an embrace, and Joaquin sat on a log, holding the baby, with his children around him, their eyes fixed on the newborn, who fussed, looking for her mother's breast.

Then Joaquin gave Jo the baby and came to Clara, pulling her hard against his chest. Sobs wracked his body— silent at first and then louder until the voices around her hushed in reverence. She stroked his hair gently, and the grief pooled inside her until she, too, wept with him.

"I love you," she whispered into his ear, the solitary condolence she could offer. His arms tightened around her in response. It was the only way he could speak through his anguish, but it was enough.

It had been three days since Brendan had partaken in a drink, and he felt unwell. Tension built in his jaw, and tremors had started in his hands. The pressure in his head, building behind his eyes, was threatening to send him over the edge.

That damn bugger McGregor had refused him any more credit. Brendan didn't know what had gotten into the old goat, but now he needed to find money or something to trade.

"What's the point of bein' married to money if I ain't got none?" he muttered to himself. Clara had been called away in the night and had still not returned. He hadn't cared then, but now he held a hungry baby, and his wife was nowhere to be found.

He carried Beth back to his sister's home, storming through the door without knocking. Becca was on Marty's lap, locked in a passionate kiss. A ravage, jealous lust tore through him—he hadn't touched his own wife in nearly a year. He should've never married her in the first place.

"Where's Clara?" he demanded as if they would know. "She left in the night and hasn't come back."

Becca's eyes widened, and he hated her for what she was thinking. That Clara had fled and run away with her lover. Left him to raise a child alone.

"Was it a medical problem?" Marty let Becca go and stood, ready to head out to the farm.

Brendan shrugged. He had heard the urgent voices in the night but slept through the details. He needed a drink. Damn McGregor.

"I'm sure it's just a birth. Some women labour for a day or more." Becca reached over to take the baby. "I'll watch little Beth while you track down Clara." She glanced at Marty, who was perched at the door frame. "Marty, bring me some milk from the goat for Beth. She needs somethin' while we wait for her mama."

Brendan left, walking back to his own homestead with a thoughtful trudge. He'd already looked around for anything he could trade for liquor but had come up short. After he'd taken the pistol the first time, Clara had hidden everything away.

The clinic! He quickened his pace, pleased with his idea. She wasn't often gone from both home and the clinic, so this was a perfect chance. He was sure he could find something of value to McGregor there. He flung open the homestead door. His gaze fell to the bookshelf, where she most often left the key. *There.* As he reached for it, he noticed a letter hanging out from between two books.

He opened the letter, not able to read it. But it had no envelope, no stamp. It was not from her family. Was the damn bastard writing her letters? He stuffed both the key and letter into his pocket and headed out the door.

Clara paced in the kitchen. Will and Joaquin had been in the yard for an hour, digging a grave for Anna. It seemed so soon, so fast. She would be buried in the family plot beside Joaquin's mother, Beth.

As soon as dawn had broken, Joaquin had ridden to the Indian reservation with the baby, who would stay with a breastfeeding mother there until weaned. He took the youngest children there, too, away from the farmhouse for a few days. While Will rode into town to send a telegram to his mother, sending the news of Anna's death and burial, Jo and Clara had spent the morning scrubbing the blood from the bedding and the floor in Anna's room. They packed up her clothing, throwing out the bloodstained night dress, not speaking a word to each other. The tragedy was too much to bear.

"I should go home," Clara whispered to herself as she made coffee for the men. It was now noon, and her breasts were full and leaking. She knew Beth needed her. But Joaquin had gathered her in his arms at every opportunity, the weight of his burden resting on her, and she didn't know how to leave. She couldn't abandon him now. Or ever.

"They're near done digging and will bury her. Oh, Clara!" Jo was in a torrent of tears, her face hidden in her hands at the kitchen table.

Clara took her in an embrace. "We must be strong for them. Will is going to need you to hold him when this horrible day is over."

Jo nodded, wiping her face. The two women held hands and went outside just as the men were lowering Anna, wrapped in a sheet, into her earthly resting place.

"Wait!" It was Jo, just as Joaquin was about to shovel the dirt on top of Anna. Tears were flowing freely down his face, leaving a trail in the blood that he had still not washed off.

"My father gave me a Chinese gold coin when my mother died," Jo said, taking a shaky breath. "She died when I was six, in childbirth. I'd like to leave it with Anna."

Clara came and took the shovel from Joaquin. "That sounds lovely, Jo."

"It's still in the room above the clinic, with the rest of my things. Can you wait? I'll ride over and get it."

Joaquin managed a nod. "Will, go with her. While you're there, check the post office to see if your mother has sent a telegram."

Will and Jo left to saddle the horses in the barn, leaving Clara and Joaquin alone. She reached up to wipe the remaining dirt from his face. "While they're gone, I'm going to draw you a bath." He started to protest, but she shook her head. "I'll wash your hair. There's ... blood all through it."

She left him at the kitchen table, staring into a cup of coffee. Then she hauled and heated the water for a bath. It was a laborious job, usually done only once a week, but she couldn't let him bury his daughter without at least washing.

Finally, she placed the large copper tub in the sitting room and poured the heated water in. Then, she went to Joaquin. She took his hand, and he followed her to the tub. His face crumpled, and he again started to grieve.

"I can't," he whispered hoarsely into her hair. "It's too much."

"I know." She held him for a minute, then started to unbutton his shirt. There was blood matted into the hair on his chest, too. Clara looked up into his eyes as she reached for his pants. She had seen him unclothed before, of course, but it had always been when they were love-making in their forest meeting place. Certainly nothing like today.

After he sank into the hot water, he closed his eyes, then dipped his head completely under the water. He emerged, Anna's blood running in rivulets down his face and back. Clara took the cloth she had brought and wiped his face and then his hands. Next, she took a bar of soap and cleaned his chest, carefully prying away the dried clumps. Then she came behind him, washing his hair gently, letting him relax his head into her hands.

"Did you name the baby?" she asked, moving beside the tub once again. He seemed calmer now, some of the sadness washed away by the water.

He shook his head. "I can't think about that now."

She tucked his wet hair behind his ear. "What about Lilianna? Lily for short."

He leaned forward out of the water, sloshing some over the side, and kissed her. "I love it." He sighed, settling back into the tub. His face was grave. "You should go home. Beth needs you."

"I will, in a while. Rebecca is looking after her, I'm sure. I don't want to leave you. I'm going to postpone my trip with my father."

"No." His voice was sharp. "I can't bear for you to be with *him* anymore." He reached out to touch the side of her face. "Please, go with your father. I'll know you're safe there. And I need something to look forward to." He squeezed his eyes shut, fighting back his sorrow.

Clara brought over a towel and helped him dry off. After he dressed, they went to the room next to the library and lay together on the bed. He rested his head against her chest, and within minutes, he was asleep.

Chapter 25

October 1886

AFTER STOPPING AT THE PUBLIC HOUSE AND HAGGLING with the bartender for an ale to quench his thirst, Brendan finally arrived at the clinic; the door was unlocked. He frowned. It was not like Clara to leave it open, but there was no one inside, so he let himself in. He browsed the shelves quickly. McGregor wasn't likely to be interested in any of her medical tools. He found a bottle of laudanum on one shelf and put it into his pocket for later. If he couldn't trade it, it would at least take the edge off the pressure in his head.

Whisky. There was a full bottle hidden out of sight at the back. He uncorked it and drank lustily, consuming a third before wiping his mouth with the back of his hand. This would do him for today, but he still needed something he could bribe McGregor with tomorrow.

He was rummaging through her desk drawer when the clinic door opened. It was Martha Davenport, the old biddy from church. He hadn't forgotten when she'd made him feel like half a man, questioning why he allowed Clara to doctor.

"Clara's not here," he growled. She took a step back, surprise on her face. Her eyes fell on the open bottle of whisky in his hands. He took another slug and slammed it on the patient table.

Her eyes widened in shock, then narrowed with disdain. "Well, I suspected not, with the new baby. But I have some awful corns on my feet that I need filing down. Your wife did a lovely job the last time, but they're back."

Brendan banged the desk drawer shut in reply, and a loose paper fluttered to the ground. Mrs. Davenport leaned down in front of him to pick it up. She opened it and read it, her eyes widening in shock.

"Oh, my." Her face had turned a bright shade of pink.

"What does it say?" The whisky had lit a fire of rage in him. She would answer him, or he would make her pay. He took a menacing step toward her.

"I can't read it. It's quite lewd and ... sinful," she said, reaching for the door handle.

Brendan moved in front of the door, blocking her way. She cowered away from him, and he relished in her fear. "I said, what does it say?"

Mrs. Davenport reluctantly steeled herself and read him the letter. It was from the bastard, quite obviously, describing his desire to have sexual relations with Clara.

Brendan reached inside his pocket. "Read this one." He handed her the letter from the homestead. "And then you may go."

Martha Davenport took a shaky breath.

My Clara, my love,

By the time you read this letter, you will be safely on your way. As much as I am already missing you, I am relieved that you will be out of the grasp of your marriage, at last.

I can hardly remember what my life was like before you came. I never imagined that I could know such happiness, such joy. My only regret is that you did not get to meet my mother. She was sweet and loving, and she would have been so happy for us. You have honoured her by naming your beautiful baby after her. I love you, Clara, and our beautiful daughter, Beth.

I count the days until I see you again. Your place in my heart never wavers.

All my love,
Joaquin

BRENDAN REACHED for the bottle of whisky and took another third of the bottle in a single swig. Martha Davenport hurried out of the clinic, the door banging behind her.

Brendan stared after her, his breathing short and quick. It was true then—not only had his wife given herself to the bastard, but she'd also tricked him into thinking the baby was his. Fury awoke like a demon in his chest, and the whisky burned in his throat. Without another thought, he burst out of the clinic, vengeance pumping through his veins.

Jo OPENED the door to her room, leading out into the clinic. Brendan was gone. She picked up the letters that she had heard Mrs. Davenport read while she had been hidden on the stairwell, barely breathing. Her eyes scanned the details once more and she covered her mouth in shock. She ran out the door, not bothering to lock it.

As she mounted her horse, Will emerged from the telegram office.

"Will!"

He ran over, clearly sensing the urgency in her voice.

"We need to get to your father and Clara. Now."

They left behind a cloud of dust as they took off for the farmhouse.

OUR BEAUTIFUL DAUGHTER, *Beth*. The words were razor-sharp, cutting through every step that Brendan took. She'd lied to him, pulled the wool over his eyes. He was a damn fool.

He took another slug of the whisky, draining the bottle, and tossed it to the side of the road. He'd been used this whole damn time. Even when she'd fled her engagement to the Lieutenant into his gullible arms. He shook his head. Clara Thomas was nothing but a witch.

He staggered into Becca's homestead and found his sister mending Marty's trousers by the hearth.

"Ish hish baby. No' mine," he spat.

His vision blurred as he looked around the room. He jerked the baby—*the damn bastard's baby*—from where Becca had laid her down for a rest next to the hearth.

"Put her down!" Becca's voice was a shriek that made his head pound. "Brendan Murphy, you put her down *now*!"

Becca barreled at him from across the room. She grabbed at his arm. He flung her aside.

"Get away! Mind yer self, Becca." He was going to make Clara regret the day she'd opened her legs and let that filthy man inside her.

"No!" Becca scratched him across the face, her nails drawing blood. "You give me Beth right now, or I will kill you with my bare hands." Her face was twisted with anger and fear. Brendan leaned over and spat in her face.

"You stay outta thish. My wife ish nothin' but a whore."

Becca came at him again, his spit running down into her eyes. His fingers curled into a fist, and he swung. Becca reeled from the punch, stumbled, and her head smashed into the table.

Brendan left with Beth in his arms and went to the barn to saddle a horse. He had something to trade McGregor.

REBECCA CAME TO WITH A GROAN. Her head throbbed, and her vision was blurry. Remembering her brother, she sat up quickly, ignoring the shooting pain that made her stomach heave. Brendan had gone too far this time. She looked around for the baby, panic making her heart thump.

Beth! Rebecca ran out the door to see Brendan leaving the barn on horseback, the baby in his arms. Her niece, the baby she'd promised to protect.

She ran back into the house and into her room. She reached far under the bed, where she'd stashed the gun Brendan had used when he shot McGregor. When he'd meant to shoot his wife. His madness needed to end.

Tying Patrick to her back, she ran out to the barn. Marty was nowhere to be seen, probably far out in the field, gathering whatever harvest had not been destroyed by the storm.

She saddled a horse and rode out, following her brother's trail.

~

CLARA HAD JUST EASED Joaquin's sleeping head off her chest when Jo burst through the door of the farmhouse.

"Clara! Joaquin!"

Clara sat up straight at the alarm in Jo's tone.

"Father!" Will added from behind Jo.

Joaquin sat up. Panic flooded his eyes, and Clara's heart broke anew when she saw the instant that he remembered Anna was gone.

"We're here!" Clara called, pulling Joaquin back into her embrace. She kissed the top of his head as his shoulders started to heave with all-encompassing grief.

Jo came skidding into the room. "Brendan! He was at the clinic."

Clara straightened up, giving them her full attention. "What did he say?"

"He came in when I was upstairs. He didn't know I was there. Oh, Clara! He found your letters!"

Clara felt a wave of panic but then shook her head. "He can't read."

Jo's face was etched with worry. "Mrs. Davenport came in. He forced her to read them. The first was about ..." Jo blushed, and Clara's eyes widened at the realization. "And the second was a letter saying goodbye. About your plans to leave. About Beth being your mother's name, Joaquin."

Joaquin's face went pale, his grief momentarily forgotten. "I wrote that the baby was ours. But I only meant that we would raise her together."

Will leaned against the doorframe. "I saw him leavin'. He looked mighty angry. And I'm fairly certain he was drunk."

Joaquin stood up suddenly. "Son, get the hunting rifle from the barn." He looked at Clara and Jo. "You stay here."

"No." Clara stood and took his hand. "We do this together." She sank back down suddenly as a devastating thought came to her. "Beth! Joaquin, he might harm her!"

Joaquin's face was grim, and he pulled her to her feet. "We'd better hurry."

"I'm coming, too." Jo stood straight.

They left the house. The horses were still outside. Joaquin quickly took off the saddles, lifted Clara onto one, and hopped on behind her. Will came out of the barn with the gun and mounted the other horse with Jo.

They rode quickly through the forest, stopping at Clara's homestead. Taking the rifle, Joaquin went inside with Clara close behind. He looked around the ground floor while Clara dashed upstairs.

"Nothing," he said, shaking his head when she returned. She felt as if she might be sick. Where was her baby?

"We should check Marty and Rebecca's."

It took only a few minutes to make their way there. Clara slid down off the horse and followed Joaquin. They searched the entire house—it was empty. Strange that Rebecca was gone, too.

Clara frowned. "Rebecca? Marty?" She swallowed back

her growing panic. "Where's Beth?" Beth's blanket lay near the hearth. Clara turned to Joaquin in terror. He was inspecting the kitchen table, and he held up his fingers; they were wet with blood.

They ran outside and quickly mounted the horse. Leaning back against Joaquin, Clara quietly sobbed. She was ravaged with guilt as she thought of her baby, left behind with Brendan in the wake of Anna's death. She should have come home to collect her. She was a horrible mother, leaving her baby alone for so long.

"*Where's Beth?*" she repeated, on the edge of hysterics. "What did he do with my baby?"

Joaquin's arm tightened around her waist. "There's only one place I can think of. McGregor's the only person he talks to."

She nodded, and they took off, the horse galloping at such a speed that she clenched her teeth to keep them from slamming together. She would kill Brendan if he hurt her baby.

When they arrived at McGregor's, Clara's heart sank. There was no sign of anyone. *Where is Beth?* She started to sob, covering her mouth to quiet the sound.

"Let's check by the barn. I think I can hear crying," Jo said, sliding off her horse, Will close behind. Clara swung her leg over the horse, and Joaquin caught her as she slid down. They sprinted across the pasture towards the barn, the rifle slung over Joaquin's shoulder.

Joaquin stopped her as they came close and covered her mouth with his hand. The sight was enough to make her scream.

Brendan, in the pasture outside the barn, held Beth in

front of his chest. The sound of her cries made Clara's knees go weak. She struggled against Joaquin, who held her tight against him.

"Stay here. Trust me," he said, leaving her behind, the rifle in his hands.

Clara took a few steps after him. She had now come into clear view of the whole scene—Rebecca stood in front of Brendan, Patrick strapped to her back. Her face was bleeding from a gash on her forehead, and there was a dark swelling under her eye. In her hands, pointed at Brendan, she held Clara's gold-plated pistol.

There was a movement to the side of Brendan. McGregor emerged from the barn, holding a bow and arrow. Clara held her breath. It appeared her husband was surrounded.

Brendan's expression darkened even further when Joaquin approached, with Clara close behind him. He laughed, and the sound sent chills down her spine.

"You thought I wouldn't find out? That you could run away?" He moved his grip around Beth's tiny neck.

"Stop! It's me you want." Joaquin put down the rifle and held up his hands. "Lay down the baby." He nodded towards the rifle. "Take your best shot."

Clara's cry was muffled by Rebecca's shout. "Aye, brother. It's Joaquin you want. Kill him and be done with this."

Brendan looked at his sister, then over to Joaquin, and finally to Clara. "You lied!! This baby is nothin' but a bastard!" His hands shook, and Beth shrieked, her face turning red.

"She's not Joaquin's baby!" Clara screamed, tears

streaming down her face. She got to her feet, her whole body shaking violently. He was hurting Beth. She would strangle him herself.

"Give the lass her baby." It was McGregor. "I'll shoot the damn Spanish bastard myself."

Brendan turned to McGregor. "I want them both dead."

McGregor nodded, his eye on Clara. He couldn't see that far, she realized. He wouldn't be able to shoot them from where he stood. Not with accuracy. "Aye. I'll shoot them both dead, Murphy. But put the babe down. Then we'll have a drink."

Brendan hesitated, looking around at everyone in turn. His eyes were dark and haunted, like the men Clara had seen come in from the battlefield. Then, he lay Beth down on the grass. Jo took a few tentative steps, then ran over and snatched her, bringing her back to where Will stood, a few feet away.

Bang!

The gunshot echoed through the pasture. Rebecca stood, hands shaking with the impact of the shot. The pistol fell from her hands.

CLARA STOOD FROZEN as Rebecca screamed in immediate remorse. "No! Save him! Help him, Clara!"

Brendan fell to the ground, blood spurting from a wound in his stomach. He had fainted but was not dead, his chest rising and falling. The sound of Patrick and Beth's screams filled the air, the infants terrified by the sound of the gunshot.

"No." McGregor came closer, the bow and arrow moving around to aim at each of them with a steady hand. "This is *my* land. If anyone moves, I'll shoot."

Brendan came to, his voice a strangled gasp. "Help. Me."

Clara stared at her husband, bleeding on the ground, and then looked up at McGregor. He had the bow trained right at her. Not at Joaquin. McGregor knew she would be the only one who might try to save Brendan.

Just then, Clara heard a horse trotting into the pasture behind her. She turned, her heart thumping, and blinked in surprise. Getting off a chestnut horse, stalking towards her, was John McKay.

"Hello, Uncle. I see you have company." John's gaze took in the whole scene before coming back to rest on Clara, whose chest seized in horror. "Clara. Looks like I've arrived just in time."

John strode over to where Brendan lay, his blood spreading onto the grass. Rebecca screamed as John approached, running to hide behind Jo and Will. John smirked, pulled a revolver from the holster slung around his waist, and shot Brendan in the chest. Brendan's body seemed to deflate as the last breath left him.

John spat on Brendan's dead body. "I never liked that ass." He looked back to Clara. Joaquin had run back to gather her in his arms, protecting her with his body. "By the looks of things, neither did you." John turned his stare on Joaquin. "Drop the rifle."

As Joaquin placed the rifle on the ground, Beth's cries pierced the air from Jo's arms. Clara wanted her baby with her, but she didn't dare move. Not with John here. He continued to hold the gun, pointing it at Clara as his gaze roamed, falling to Rebecca, on her knees behind Jo. Patrick, still strapped to her back, continued to wail.

"John, my lad. I've not seen you since you were a wee boy. I'm glad you found the place easily." McGregor made his way over to the sound of John's voice and held out his hand for John to grasp.

Clara found her voice underneath layers of shock. "You're his uncle?"

"Aye, great-uncle. On his mother's side. John's come to help me out on the farm now that my eyesight is gone, Mrs. Murphy." He nodded in her direction. "Or, I should say, Widow Murphy."

John sauntered over to Clara and Joaquin. Joaquin stood before her, protecting her with a wide stance. "You were easy to track down, Clara. I knew you wouldn't stop with the doctoring. After you ran away with *him,*" John glanced back at Brendan's body, "and left me with no career to speak of, I decided to have you watched. How convenient for me that you came here, of all places. When Uncle Eunan wrote to me after Christmas telling me that you were lavished in jewels from your father and wearing an expensive gown, the gown I bought you for *our engagement,* I knew I needed to make you pay."

He looked at Joaquin with narrowed eyes, a smirk pulling at his mouth. "From one man to another, and now, yet another. I think there's a word for women like you, Clara. *Harlot.*"

Joaquin reached out to grab John by the collar with a growl.

John wrenched himself free of Joaquin's grasp. "Ah. I see

she's wrapped herself around your manhood already. Easy. I'm not here for her."

John turned and stared at Rebecca. "Uncle said you were here with other Irish folk as well. I seem to remember this one." He strode over to Rebecca. "Stand up."

Rebecca shook her head, clinging to Jo's legs. "No." Her voice was barely audible.

John leaned down and grabbed the front of Rebecca's dress in a tight fist, the revolver in his other hand trained at her head. "I said, stand up."

Rebecca rose to her feet but turned her head away. John grabbed her chin and drew her gaze back to him. John's grip tightened around Rebecca's face. Clara took a step towards them, but Joaquin held her back from advancing further.

"Is that my son?" John's face was close to Rebecca's.

Rebecca shook her head furiously. "It's my husband's babe."

John took a step back, putting his revolver back in its holster. Clara breathed a sigh of relief. He could never know the truth.

Suddenly, John grabbed Beth from Jo's unsuspecting arms. With his other hand, he drew a knife that had been sheathed on his belt.

"Let her go!" Clara screamed. Joaquin picked up the rifle from the ground and aimed the rifle at John.

John moved the baby in front of his chest and laughed at Joaquin. "You'll never make the shot. Not without harming this wee babe." He looked closer at Beth in her soft pink sweater. "She's a real beauty, Clara. Just like her mother."

Clara sobbed into her hands. "What do you want, John?"

John held the tip of the knife to Beth's tiny chest. "Is that my son, Clara?" He thrust his head towards Patrick.

Rebecca sank to her knees, her keening wail adding to the crescendo of the crying children. Clara refused to answer, though her stomach churned.

Joaquin put down the rifle once again and stepped closer to John. "Yes, Patrick's your son. Clara told me all about it when we first met." He held out his arms for Beth. "Give me the baby."

John dropped Beth in Joaquin's outstretched arms and sheathed his knife. "I want half ownership of your father's company, Clara. What should have been mine." He stalked over to her. "If not, I will claim parental rights to Rebecca's child—my son. I will stay here and make your life hell." He leaned in close and raked his gaze slowly over her body. "And I might just take what else should have been mine, too. I'm sure your man here can't protect you all hours of the day."

John turned and pushed aside Joaquin, who stood beside them, his jaw set and nostrils flared. He walked over to McGregor, held out his arm, and the two of them walked back towards the house.

Chapter 26

October 1886

Clara took Beth from Joaquin's arms as soon as John and McGregor disappeared into the house. She ran over to Rebecca, followed closely by Joaquin. Jo, Will, Clara, and Joaquin stared at each other while Rebecca sobbed in Jo's arms.

Finally, Joaquin spurred them into action. "Will and Jo, go get Marty. He'll need to bring the wagon and blankets for …" He trailed off as they all turned to look at Brendan's body, limp in the grass. His face was twisted in a grotesque expression. Clara let out a sharp sob.

Joaquin pulled her into his chest. "I understand," he whispered, though everyone could hear him. She looked up at him—he seemed to have aged ten years in the last day, his face lined and drawn.

"Rebecca, you'll need to come with me to see Sergeant McDonald in town." Joaquin glanced at the house. "After all, that vile man just killed your brother."

Jo and Will took two horses back to Marty. Rebecca rode alongside Clara and Joaquin. Clara held Beth tight against her, with Joaquin's arm around her waist.

"I'm sorry, Rebecca." Joaquin's voice shook, and Clara felt his inner turmoil through his arm. "I couldn't let him harm Beth. Not after Anna."

Rebecca's body shook with sobs. "Can he ... take Patrick from me?"

"No," Clara said firmly, though she shot a worried look at Joaquin. She wasn't sure at all. It would be Rebecca's word against John's, and the courts usually favoured men.

Joaquin dropped Clara and Beth off at the farmhouse. "Stay here. Bar the door. And take this." He held out the pistol. Clara stared at it, but he pushed it into her hands. "I can't handle any more grief today, Clara. I'll ride back to McGregor's with Sergeant McDonald, and then I'll come here to be with you before I ride out to pick up the other children."

Clara nodded and went inside. Beth had fallen asleep during the ride, but Clara woke her to nurse. As she did, the tears began to fall. She mourned Anna's death and grieved for the pain it would cause Joaquin in the months to come. She cried for the man who was the father of her child and for the brief moments she had loved him. She sobbed in relief— blessed relief—that he was gone. And finally, tears fell in worry—worry that Rebecca would lose her son to that damn rapist, John McKay.

For the next two days, Joaquin did not leave her side. They lay hidden in his bed in the farmhouse, Beth between them. They talked very little, turning to each other for physical comfort, trying to nurture their bruised hearts. It was a mix of emotions—heart-wrenching grief blending with the excitement and joy of knowing that they would be free to love each other and, eventually, be married. But for now, they had to remain secretive.

On the third day, they emerged. Laura arrived, and Clara gave them the privacy to grieve together. Joaquin took Laura to the reservation to meet their granddaughter, and after much discussion, Laura took the child home with her. For now, she would raise Lilianna. Clara held Joaquin as he grieved that loss, too, although they both knew it would be for the best.

Clara walked to Rebecca and Marty's homestead, with Beth tied to her back in a sling. Her stomach was tight with nerves. She hadn't seen Rebecca since Brendan's death and wondered how she would move forward with their relationship now that he was gone. A twinge of guilt accompanied her nervousness. Her romance with Joaquin was going to add to Rebecca's turmoil over her brother's death.

She drew a steadying breath and knocked on the door. Even after everything that happened, she prayed there would be no bad blood between them.

Marty answered, dusky shadows under his eyes and new lines etched around them.

"Oh, Clara, I'm so glad to see you." He drew her into a tight embrace, and she felt tears prick her eyes. She started to shake in his comforting arms. "It's all right, lass. Becca's told me everything."

"Everything?" She didn't know what everything entailed. Did he know about her and Joaquin?

"Aye. About your love for Joaquin. Anna's death. Shooting Brendan. And ..." he trailed off, swallowing back his own emotion. "And about that man's threat to take our son."

Clara shook her head. "I won't let that happen, Marty. I don't know how, but he can't take Patrick."

Marty nodded, but his eyes were not convinced. "Becca's out back, making butter if you'd like to see her. I know she'd like to see you."

Clara gave Marty another embrace and then walked around to the back of the homestead. Rebecca was there, pumping the butter churn, her face tight and drawn. Patrick sat on a blanket in the warm October sun, cheerfully gurgling.

"Rebecca?" Clara approached her gently, unsure. Her brother was gone, and Clara couldn't help but wonder if Rebecca blamed her, even though she had been the one to pull the trigger.

Rebecca turned to her, letting go of the churn and covering her mouth with her hands. Tears filled Rebecca's eyes. "Oh, Clara," she whispered. "I'm so sorry, Clara."

Clara walked over and drew Rebecca into an embrace. "I'm the one who's sorry, Rebecca. Please forgive me."

"No." Rebecca pulled away from Clara, her cheeks wet with tears. "I knew he wasn't capable of being a good husband. I should never have let you come with us. But some part of me hoped you would mend him, would encourage him in ways I couldn't."

Clara walked over and picked up Patrick from his blanket. She gave him a kiss on the head before placing him back down.

"I did love him, Rebecca. In the beginning." She took a deep breath. It was time to be honest. "And if I had never come with you, if he hadn't made me unhappy, then I never would have found Joaquin."

Rebecca nodded, wiping away her tears. "Aye. That's true, I guess. How is Joaquin? I can't believe Anna's gone." Tears started to fall again.

Clara blinked away her own grief. "He's ... well, he's broken. But we'll heal together, I guess." She paused. "Will you tell Beth, when she's older, some nice stories about Brendan? I don't have many, but I'd like her to hear some when the time is right."

"Of course." Rebecca reached out to squeeze her hand. "We're still sisters, Clara." She placed Clara's hand on her belly, smiling. "I haven't told Marty yet, but we're finally having another baby. You're the first to know."

"Oh!" She embraced Rebecca tightly. "That's wonderful. I am so very happy."

"Aye, me too." She smiled, her eyes glistening. "Me too."

IN THE AFTERNOON, Clara went to the dressmaker in town and purchased a black gown, so she would look the part of a mourning widow. Already the talk had begun, especially as the Sergeant had John McKay locked in the town jail, waiting for transport to New Westminster. Clara breathed a sigh of relief that she didn't encounter Martha Davenport—try as she might, she hadn't been able to think of any story to sway the old lady from the damning evidence she had read. Only time would tell how vicious Martha would be.

Clara waited by the stagecoach depot, Beth in her arms and her nerves on edge. Her father was due to arrive at any moment. There hadn't been time to send him a telegram with the news, as he had already been on his way, and there was so much to tell.

"Clara!" Jo called, running across the street, her face flushed. "I thought you could use some company."

Clara nodded, her stomach fluttering. Her father would be within his rights to claim her back into his family as a new widow. She wouldn't go—her place was with Joaquin, but she desperately wanted her father's blessing now that everything had changed.

When her father arrived, his face broke out in a wide grin at the sight of his granddaughter asleep in Clara's arms. "I'm so proud of you, Clara," he said, dropping a kiss on her head. "Now I have two beautiful grandchildren." He reached into his vest and brought forth a photograph of her nephew, Wesley, who had been born in May.

"Brendan's dead," she said without preamble as he collected his valise from the back of the stagecoach.

Her father's eyes flew open, and he stared at her. "What—?"

Clara grabbed his hand, and they walked briskly out of town towards her homestead. Jo followed closely behind, offering her silent support. Once they were on the path home, Clara relayed the entire story, starting with Anna's death.

"Oh my." Her father found a log alongside the path and sat, digesting the news. "John was arrested?"

"Yes. He'll be transported to New Westminster to await trial."

"But Rebecca shot Brendan as well?"

"Yes." Clara felt uneasy about that. She had wanted John arrested, of course, but was wary that she might be called to testify. Brendan would have died from the first shot, regardless.

"I can't give him half of the company, Clara."

"I know. And you shouldn't." She felt sick whenever she thought about John's threats.

"I'll hire the best lawyers. But we don't have a strong case against John. Not with everything else you had going on."

They continued to walk, both quiet as her father processed the events. It was all rather shocking. Joaquin was waiting for them outside the homestead, his arms crossed. Her heart leapt at the sight of him, even as he wore the burden of the last days on his face. He was hers, at last.

Her father walked over to Joaquin and threw his arms around him in a tight embrace. Joaquin's face crumpled at her father's affection, though he kept his eyes on Clara. He would need all the strength she could give him in the days to come.

After they had settled inside, Clara and Jo set to making a meal and tea. Joaquin and her father talked, keeping the conversation carefully away from Anna.

As they sat down to eat, her father changed the topic to include her. "Starting tomorrow, Clara will need to enter an appropriate mourning period for Brendan." Her father's voice was firm. He knew of Joaquin's intention to ask for Clara's hand in marriage.

"How long?" Clara asked, coming to sit next to Joaquin.

"Six months. Then you will need to court for a determined time. After that, you may ask me for her hand, Joaquin. I think it will ease all gossip if you wait until a year from now."

"No." Joaquin's response was curt, startling them all. "I won't wait that long." He turned to look at Clara and reached out to touch the side of her face. "I can't."

Her father's expression was soft at their affection. "Six months."

"Three."

Her father sighed. "Four. Even then, tongues will wag."

"Mr. Thomas, with all due respect, Clara and I don't need to court. She's my everything, and I'm hers. The day she becomes my wife will be the happiest in my life."

Her father nodded. "All right, Joaquin. But I do ask that you remain chaste. An unexpected pregnancy before you are wed would be disastrous."

Joaquin reached for her hand. He hadn't touched her since she had given birth to Beth, and four more months seemed like an eternity. "You have my word. But I will ask for her hand after two months. We'll be engaged for another two."

Her father took a cup of tea from Jo. "We'll plan on a wedding for February. Your mother and sister will attend, Clara."

Clara's eyes widened as she took a sip of the steaming tea. The idea of her mother here, in a small rural town, made her nervous.

Her father cleared his throat. "I am exhausted from my travels and will retire early. I assume I'll stay here?" He looked over to the room Clara had shared with Brendan. She had already moved his belongings to Rebecca's and hers to the upstairs room. Mourning or not, she needed a fresh start now.

Joaquin put his hand on her back. "I wish to have Clara's company for tonight. I'll bring her back by morning."

Her father chuckled. "You drive a hard bargain, Joaquin. I think you missed your calling as a businessman." He leaned over to shake Joaquin's hand. "Welcome to the family, son."

Joaquin went to the barn and retrieved the baby bassinette he had been making for Anna's baby so Beth could sleep beside them. Clara stroked the unfinished wood. Maybe one day, their own baby would sleep in it.

He read her mind from across the room. "I'll have to ask you to use your herbal concoction again once we're married." He looked at where Beth lay, his emotions at the surface. "I can't, right now. Not after Anna. I'm sorry, Clara."

She went over to him, and he buried his face in her neck. He hadn't wept since the first day, and he was struggling to keep the tears at bay. "It's all right, Joaquin. I need time, too."

He nodded, and they changed into their bedclothes, turning away from each other, shy with their promise to remain celibate. Clara sat on the edge of the small bed and turned to him with a smile. "I know what I will ask for as a wedding present. If you'll make it for me."

"What's that, Clara?"

"A bigger bed." She grinned up at him, watching as his face broke into a smile. The smile remained with him for a minute, then he pulled her into the single bed with him, her head resting on his chest. She loved being close to him, breathing in the scent of him. The ache and tension of the past months moved out of her like a swift current.

"So, we'll stay then?" He stroked her hair and pulled her up to his mouth for a kiss. "Or do you think we should still move?"

"Stay, please. Unless you still want to go."

"I want to be wherever you are. Always. Forever." He wrapped both of his arms around her.

It was just a few minutes later that he was asleep, his breathing slow and heavy. Clara lay awake for a while, hardly believing that she was here, sleeping in his bed. Then she, too, was pulled into slumber.

WHEN SHE AWOKE BEFORE DAWN, the heat of his body beside her was gone. Raising her head, she saw him in the chair that faced out the window. His shoulders shook in the pale moonlight.

Clara climbed out of bed and went to him, crawling onto his lap. She tucked her feet into the side of the chair and pulled him into her embrace. Grief ravaged his body, and she soothed him until it passed.

"I don't know how to do this, Clara. I don't know how to move on." Exhaustion etched lines into his face.

"Together. We move on together, my love."

He reached for her, his mouth finding solace in hers. Then they sat together as dawn broke, their hearts forged for a new day.

Epilogue

Late November 1886, British Columbia

"Please answer the question, Mrs. Murphy."

Clara had never been so nervous in her life. Even when covered in blood, performing a complex amputation for the first time, she'd managed to remain calm. But today, as she sat on the witness stand with John McKay leering at her, she felt like she might retch. She stared down at her lap, trying to collect her thoughts. So much depended on her answer.

"I'll ask again to refresh your memory, Mrs. Murphy." John's lawyer was a shark, biting with his comments and swift to draw blood. "Why was your husband threatening your baby?"

"My husband was not of a sound mind, sir. He suffered from melancholy and was very drunk at the time."

"Yes, we've been told that by the other witnesses, Mrs. Murphy." The lawyer leaned in close enough that she could smell his cologne. On another day, it might have smelled pleasant, but right now, it made her stomach churn. "What was his motivation, Mrs. Murphy? Husbands are not generally in the business of stealing babies."

"I am sure I cannot tell you what he was thinking." She kept her gaze locked straight into his. Sweat rolled down her back, due in part to the heavy black gown she was wearing, officially still in mourning.

The lawyer leaned back, and Clara let her eyes flit briefly over to where her father sat, next to Joaquin, their backs straight and faces grim. She heard a chuckle, and her sight fell back to John, sitting at the bench across from the stand. He wore the uniform from jail, but appeared at ease, relaxed against the chair with a smug grin. *Damn.* She was about to be attacked.

"I have it on authority from Mrs. Martha Davenport, an upstanding citizen of Langley, that she spoke with your husband just prior to his death. There is strong evidence to believe that your husband thought that the child was, in fact, not his."

Clara smiled sweetly at him. She had been coached by her father's lawyer not to respond. He had not asked a direct question. And there was no evidence. The letters that Mrs. Davenport had read had been destroyed, along with all the other correspondence she had written to Joaquin.

"What is your relationship with Mr. Joaquin Walker?"

"He's our neighbour."

"Where were *you*, Mrs. Murphy, when your husband took the baby from his sister?"

Clara took a deep breath and exhaled slowly. "I was at Mr. Walker's house."

"Why?"

Clara closed her eyes as the memory came flooding back. Anna, covered in blood. "There had been a death. I was called over to deliver the deceased's baby surgically after she passed." Clara kept her eyes trained on the lawyer. If she looked at Joaquin, she would fall apart.

"How many hours were you there, Mrs. Murphy?"

She licked her lips. "I'm not sure."

"What time did you deliver the child?"

She had to answer. Jo had already been asked this on the witness stand, and the judge knew. "Just before dawn."

"Your husband took the baby from his sister and went to Mr. McGregor's house in the early afternoon. Were you at Mr. Walker's residence until then?"

She broke his gaze and looked at her hands. They were tightly clasped together, and her knuckles were turning white. "Yes."

"Doing what?"

"His daughter had just died. I was being a good neighbour."

"By warming his bed?"

She gasped and looked wide-eyed at the judge. The Crown lawyer shouted, and the question was dismissed. Clara stared at John's lawyer, her cheeks burning red. This was far from over.

"According to Mr. Eunan McGregor, you spent the night with Mr. Walker at his residence in the same room."

"Yes. McGregor had us perform a medical procedure and then locked us in the room overnight. We had no choice in the matter." Clara saw her father's lawyer grimace out of the corner of her eye and realized her mistake. She had not been directly questioned.

"When Mr. McGregor opened the door the next morning, he said the two of you were on the settee together in an embrace. Mr. Walker had his arms around you, and you had your head against his chest. Is this true?"

"No. McGregor is blind. His eyesight cannot be relied on to be accurate. He came to me for medical advice on the matter." She let out a small sigh of relief.

"Have you had sexual relations with Mr. Walker?"

Tears came to her eyes as the judge allowed the questioning. Of all the things she imagined lying about on the stand, this was certainly not one of them. "No."

"Are you in a romantic relationship with Mr. Walker?"

She stared at the wall at the back of the room. "No."

"Is Mr. Walker the father of your baby?" There was an objection, but it hardly mattered. The damage was clearly already done.

"Why, Mrs. Murphy, is your daughter named after Mr. Walker's late mother?"

Clara glared down at John. She hated him with every fibre of her body. To him, this was just revenge. "She's not. I just liked the name."

"Who shot your husband before Mr. John McKay arrived?"

"What?" Her heart pounded. She was so flustered and could barely think straight.

"Answer the question, Mrs. Murphy."

"I don't understand." She did, but she needed a moment to think.

"Mr. McGregor says he heard two shots. Your husband's sister screamed and asked you to save him. Who fired the first shot?"

Clara narrowed her eyes. She knew the consequences of lying on the witness stand, but now she was angry. She would not let Rebecca take the fall. "It was McGregor."

The lawyer was taken aback for a second. "Excuse me?"

"McGregor fired the first shot."

"Why would Mr. McGregor shoot your husband, Mrs. Murphy?"

"Again, sir, I can't read minds, but my husband was in debt to McGregor for over a hundred and fifty dollars. You see, that's what happened when Mr. Walker and I stayed the night earlier in the year. A woman had been shot. Bad debt, I guess."

The lawyer hissed and turned to glare at John before turning back to Clara. "Why did you not attempt to save your husband? Both yourself and Mr. Walker are trained physicians."

"McGregor threatened us. Said if we moved, he would shoot us. It was only a few seconds later that John showed up and shot Brendan dead."

The lawyer stared at Clara for a long moment. She stared back and was almost certain she saw defeat in his eyes.

"What is your relationship to Mr. John McKay?"

Clara almost smirked. This was too easy. "A family friend. He was my fiancé."

"And yet you married Mr. Murphy."

"I did. John tried to rape me and broke my nose. He's a serial rapist, sir. Not a nice man."

The lawyer grimaced. He was going to try to smear her again, she was certain. This time, she was prepared.

"Mr. McKay says he saw you kissing Mr. Brendan Murphy while you were still engaged to him."

She shrugged. She hadn't been questioned, but she was going to have her say. "That's true. Now, if I were indeed a mind reader, sir, I might guess that John had a very strong reason to want to kill my husband. Wouldn't you agree?"

The lawyer cursed under his breath. "No further questions, your honour."

A few hours later, Clara was in her hotel room, stripped down to her corset and bloomers. She sat in the chair by the window, feeding Beth. The stagecoach ride from the courthouse to the hotel had been a silent one—both Joaquin and her father had avoided looking at her. Neither seemed to want to talk about how she had been questioned or how she had lied on the stand. Tomorrow, John would be interrogated. Then the lawyers would be able to call back any witnesses for final questioning before the jury made its decision.

A light knock sounded at her door. Clara placed Beth in her cot and pulled up her corset. She quickly slipped on a skirt and blouse, glaring at the black gown in the corner with disdain. After today, she was through wearing it.

She pulled open the door and smiled. It was Joaquin. He glanced in both directions down the hallway before quickly slipping inside her room.

"I'm sorry for lying about our relationship," she said before the door was fully closed. "I want to tell the whole world that I love you."

He silently pulled her into his strong arms, holding her against his chest. The last few months since Brendan's death had been difficult for them both. They had continued to hide their love, with only brief moments like this one to remind them of each other.

His mouth found hers, and she kissed him back eagerly. "I know, my love. You were right to lie." His kisses moved behind her ear and down her neck, and she let out a soft moan. "Though I am not sure anyone believed you."

He pulled away and went to sit in the chair by the window. As much as she wanted to follow and curl up in his lap, she didn't. Joaquin had promised her father that they would remain chaste until their wedding, but it was proving torturous. It was nearly impossible to think of anything else when they were alone, and the air in the room was thick with desire.

"I couldn't let Rebecca be blamed. She was only defending Beth." She bit her lip and came over to stand near him. He put out his arms, and she hesitated only slightly before settling into his lap. He stroked her back, his hands running from her neck down to the base of her spine.

After a minute, he spoke. "Your father thinks it was a mistake to blame McGregor. He thinks ..." Joaquin sighed heavily before continuing. "He thinks you played your card too soon. That *John*," he gritted out the name through clenched teeth, "will come back with a vengeance tomorrow."

Clara reached up and pulled his face down to hers. She kissed his jaw, the rough stubble pricking her lips. He was exhausted—the grief from Anna's death had only begun to fade, and now the stress of the trial was upon them.

"When I think of what he tried to do to you and what he's threatened to do to you ..." Joaquin's arms tightened around her. "I never imagined I could hate anyone more than Brendan, but I do now. If he touches you, I'll be the one in jail."

"He won't. He won't go free." Her eyes blurred with tears because she knew that he would likely be released. He was too manipulative and too conniving to lose this trial. John would make good on his blackmail—if her father didn't give him control of half of Thomas Enterprises, he would stay in Langley and claim parental rights to Rebecca's son Patrick. And John had threatened Clara as well—that he would claim her body one day when Joaquin wasn't around to protect her.

Joaquin rested his chin on the top of her head. "Maybe we should move, Clara. Start over somewhere new, like we planned. Martha Davenport is only going to continue to be a problem, and if John is released—"

"No. Your children won't want to move, and you can't leave Anna." Her voice caught with emotion. Anna was buried on his property, and it would kill him to go. "And there's Will, Jo, Rebecca, and Marty. I won't let John control us. I'm not afraid of him, Joaquin."

He was quiet, rubbing her back once more. One hand drifted around her waist and made its way up to cup her breast. "I'll feel better about it all once we're married." His voice was low, and his other hand moved to her thigh.

She pulled her head back to face him with a teasing grin. "Is that *all* you'll feel better about? Once we're married?"

He chuckled softly. "You're going to beg for me to leave you alone."

Clara gave him a kiss. "Not likely." Removing his hands,

she got up off his lap. "Come. It's time to meet the others for dinner."

THE NEXT MORNING, Clara met Jo and Rebecca in the lobby of the hotel. Will and Marty had returned home to the farms, but Rebecca had needed to stay in case to she was called back to the stand.

"Thank you for watching Beth today," Clara said, handing her over to Jo. Being Chinese, Jo was not allowed into the courtroom except when she had been called to testify. Rebecca was staying behind, too, to keep Jo company. Clara suspected that Rebecca didn't mind, as seeing John likely brought back horrible memories.

Rebecca rubbed a hand over her belly, which had begun to swell. "I'm a wee bit scared, Clara." She didn't elaborate, but Clara understood. She couldn't wait for this to all be over.

"Clara. It's time to go." Her father called her from across the lobby. He frowned as she approached. "What are you wearing?"

"Clothes. I'm finished mourning." She reached for Joaquin's hand, and he slid his fingers into hers. They would separate once they reached the courthouse, but for now, she needed his touch.

"That's a very bad idea. We are in the middle of the trial for your dead husband." Her father scowled at her. She knew he was tired, having travelled back and forth across the country numerous times in the past months. He hadn't wanted to leave her alone at all, but his business needed attending.

"It's been more than two months. We agreed on two months. And to be honest, it impedes my thinking. The gown is heavy and hot, and I refuse to wear it any longer." She looked up at Joaquin to gauge his opinion.

"Clara, as much as I hate seeing you in it, you should listen to your father."

Her father grunted. "We don't have time for you to change. But if you are called back to the stand, you will wear it."

They arrived at the courthouse a few minutes late, and John was already being sworn in on the stand. John's eyes found hers right away, and Joaquin stiffened beside her. His fists clenched as John grinned salaciously. John certainly knew how to get under everyone's skin.

"Full name, please."

"John Charles McKay."

"Mr. McKay, what was your intention in moving across the country to the city of Langley?"

John cleared his throat. His light brown hair had grown longer in jail, and he pushed back the length that fell over his eyes. "My great uncle Eunan asked me to come. He requires help on his farm due to his deteriorating eyesight."

Clara narrowed her eyes. Lies. John knew nothing about farming. He had come for revenge, nothing more.

"Tell me what happened on the day you arrived."

"I arrived the day before, actually. It's a long ride from New Westminster to Langley. I lodged at a hotel in Surrey and left again after breakfast. I stopped in town to ask directions to my uncle's place." John paused, his eyes landing once again on Clara. Her pulse quickened. She had lied to Joaquin; John did scare her.

"As I was nearing my uncle's place, I heard a gunshot, followed by screaming. Babies were crying. When I came into the barn, I saw Brendan Murphy lying on the ground, bleeding from his gut. His sister was crying at his side."

"What did you do then?"

"I walked over. The man was dying, I could see. In my ten years of military experience, I have never seen anyone survive a gunshot wound to the stomach. I did the same that I would do for any fatally wounded soldier. I put an end to his misery."

Clara looked at the judge. To her dismay, he was nodding in agreement. Her heart sank.

"Your uncle, Mr. Eunan McGregor, was he holding a gun?"

"No. He was holding a bow and arrow, trained directly at Clara."

"I see. But you are certain you heard a gunshot?"

"Yes. And I am certain it was a gunshot wound. I walked right up to the poor man. Blood was spurting from his stomach."

"And was anyone at the scene holding a gun?"

"Yes." John's gaze moved to the man beside her. Clara's blood ran cold.

"That man. Joaquin Walker was holding a rifle."

"No further questions, your honour."

No. No, no, no.

Clara couldn't catch her breath, and the room started to spin. Joaquin's steady hand was at her back, pushing her head down between her legs.

"Breathe. In. Out." His voice was a comfort in her ear. She could hear the Crown lawyer in the distance, questioning John. After a minute, her breathing evened out, and she sat up again. Both her father and Joaquin were peering at her, pale and concerned.

She opened her mouth to speak, but Joaquin cut her off. "Not now, Clara," he said in a low tone. He turned his attention back to the trial, but his large hand found hers, and discreetly he rubbed the back of it once with his thumb.

The lawyer finished his questioning, and the court broke for recess. They followed Clara's father's lawyer into a private office, who had come to watch and advise on the proceedings. Clara sank into a chair and covered her face with her hands.

"Mr. Walker, you need to be prepared. There is no doubt that they will call you next. My advice is that you stick to the truth as closely as possible. You ... you may have to reveal that it was his sister who fired the shot." The lawyer's face was grim. "Unfortunately, after Clara's questioning yesterday, it would seem that you had the motivation to kill her husband."

Joaquin and Clara sat in tense silence while Clara's father spoke quietly with the lawyer. From what she could make out, her father was suggesting a bribe to the judge.

She covered her mouth as a sob escaped. "You can't go to jail, Joaquin. I need you."

His face was creased with a deep frown, making the

shadows under his eyes more pronounced. "It will be all right. I didn't shoot him. I'll just be honest."

The lawyer motioned them to the door to head back into the courtroom. Joaquin pulled Clara into his arms just before they stepped back out into the hallway. "I'm sorry for whatever I have to say about us, my love." She tipped her head back to look up at him, and he leaned down and gave her a gentle kiss and then followed her father out the door.

As suspected, Joaquin was called to the stand immediately.

"Full name, please."

"Joaquin George Walker."

"What is your relationship with Mrs. Clara Murphy?" John's lawyer wasted no time getting to the point.

"Clara is my colleague, my friend, my neighbour. And ..." He looked back over at her, locking his eyes with hers. "And I love her. Unfortunately, she doesn't return my affection. I've offered my hand in marriage to her, as she is now widowed, but she did not accept."

Clara looked around, trying to hide her shock. What was he doing? And he had not yet proposed at all. They had agreed that he would ask after her mourning period for Brendan was over.

The lawyer seemed flustered by Joaquin's answer but continued. "Have you engaged in sexual relations with Mrs. Murphy?"

Joaquin raised his eyebrows. "No. But I burn for her, day and night."

Clara's cheeks flamed red. She snuck a glance at her father, who was staring at Joaquin, open-mouthed. The

courtroom was deafeningly silent. Even John looked flab-
bergasted.

The lawyer cleared his throat. "Are you the father of
Mrs. Murphy's baby?

Joaquin gave a low laugh, his eyes sparkling in amusement. "I think I've already answered that question, sir.
Unless you'd like me to explain to you how babies are made."
A murmur of chuckles ran through the courtroom, and the
lawyer's cheeks turned pink.

"Were you carrying a rifle at the scene of the crime?"

"I was. John remembers the rifle because I had it pointed
at him. You see, John snatched Clara's baby and was pointing
a knife at the child. He threatened to kill the baby if Clara's
father did not grant him half his company. He also threatened to rape Clara. Again." Joaquin's eyes were dark as he
glowered at John from the stand.

John's lawyer opened his mouth to ask the next question,
but the judge put up his hand to pause the proceedings. His
gaze fell on John, and the judge shook his head in disgust.

The lawyer cleared his throat, and the judge nodded for
him to continue. "Did you shoot Mr. Brendan Murphy?"

"No. There was another gun at the scene of the crime
that John did not see. A pistol."

"And whose gun was that?"

"It was Clara's. She had been given the gun for protection from her assistant after John tried to rape her about a
year and a half ago. This took place at a military camp in
Saskatchewan, I believe. Clara told me all about it, but I was
not there."

"Did Mrs. Murphy shoot her husband with the pistol?"

"No, she did not have the gun in her possession at the

time. Her husband had traded the pistol to McGregor for moonshine liquor." It was a clever half-truth.

"Who shot Mr. Murphy before Mr. McKay arrived?" The lawyer looked like he was afraid of the answer.

Joaquin looked over at the judge, who was staring back at him with interest. "I'm not sure. I was securing the horses to the front gate when I heard the shot."

John's lawyer gave Joaquin an even stare. "As a medical expert, please give your professional opinion. Was the first shot fatal to Mr. Brendan Murphy? Just a reminder that the medical board will review your answer."

"A gunshot wound to the stomach is not always fatal. It depends on if the bullet has become lodged, hit an organ, or passed through. I would have examined Mr. Murphy regardless of McGregor's threats, but Mr. McKay showed up and shot him dead."

"No further questions, your honour."

Joaquin made to leave the witness stand, but the judge put up his hand again to stop his movement. The courtroom fell silent once again. No one even dared to cough. The judge turned and pointed at Clara. "Mrs. Murphy, come here. I need to speak with you."

Clara's stomach clenched. Was she about to be reprimanded for lying on the stand the day before about her relationship with Joaquin? Leaving her row, she walked up to the bench with shaking legs. "Yes, sir?"

"I would like you to explain something to me, Mrs. Murphy."

She nodded, forcing herself to make eye contact.

The judge leaned forward. "I'm not one to give advice, but I'm going to explain what I have heard, and then I will expect your answer." He pointed at John. "I don't imagine you had much choice when you were engaged to him, but I am glad for your sake that you didn't marry him. Your dead husband, well, from what I have gathered, he was not much better." The judge sat back and adjusted his glasses. "Now, this man over here," he pointed at Joaquin, "seems like a good man. I can tell from his hands that he is hardworking, and his demeanour is kind and honest. Yet he has offered you his hand in marriage, and you have refused?"

Her eyes flew up to Joaquin, still in the questioning box. The corner of his mouth was pulling into a smile, and his eyes twinkled.

"I did refuse, your honour. But I am seeing things in a different light today. I had not realized how much he cared."

"Hmm." The judge peered down at her. "Should we ask Mr. Walker to try again, then, Mrs. Murphy?"

Her eyes widened, and her stomach flipped at the judge's suggestion, but she nodded. "Yes. I think we should."

Joaquin opened the witness box before she even had a chance to look back up at him. Then, he was down on one knee in front of her, holding out his hand.

"Clara Thomas, I love you." Smiling at his use of her maiden name, she glanced out at the courtroom. Everyone was leaning forward in their seats.

"I promise to be a good and faithful husband, to provide for you, to offer you protection." His voice dropped lower for only her to hear. "I will never hurt you. I will not lie. You can always trust me."

"I promise the same," she whispered back.

Joaquin glanced up at the judge, who was looking down at them like a proud father. "Will you marry me, Clara?"

"Yes, Joaquin Walker, I will." She giggled, covering her mouth with her free hand. This was a surreal experience. There was a light smattering of applause from the spectators. Glancing at her father, she saw him smiling and shaking his head.

Joaquin got up from one knee and pulled her into an embrace. They wouldn't dare kiss in front of the judge, but he rested his head in the crook of her neck affectionately.

The judge banged his gavel, startling them both. "Moving on. Court is adjourned until after lunch, after which time I will deliver the verdict."

Clara glanced uneasily at John. He was staring at them from his seat, malice in his eyes.

AFTER COURT ADJOURNED, the group returned to the hotel to eat dinner with Rebecca and Jo.

"John got exactly what he deserves. Being behind bars might make him rethink the way he wants to live his life," Joaquin said after relaying the events of the day to the women.

"But for how long?" Rebecca's expression was tight as she helped herself to more vegetables from the table. Worry etched her features, making her look much older than her thirty years.

"Only two years." Joaquin shook his head, pausing with his fork in the air. "The judge's exact words were: 'You are hardly innocent, Mr. McKay. I don't take kindly to accounts of rape, violence, and threats to kill babies. But of this crime, I cannot convict you of murder.' It was a manslaughter charge, as Brendan may or may not have died from the first shot."

"Aye."

Clara glanced at Rebecca and took her hand in condolence. Regardless of Brendan's wrongdoings, Rebecca had still lost her only brother.

Joaquin cleared his throat, addressing her father across the table. "William, I'd like to take Clara down to the river for a walk after dinner."

Her father nodded. "That's fine, Joaquin. But you board the stage back home in the morning, so make sure you don't stay out late."

"I'll watch Beth if you'd like, Clara," Jo said, smiling at her across the table. Clara thanked her and wondered if Jo was practicing for her own motherhood. Jo and Will had been married since September, but Jo hadn't confided in her about a pregnancy yet.

Joaquin gave Jo a wink. "That would be very nice of you, Jo."

Clara stared at them both; her eyebrows raised suspiciously. Even her father and Rebecca were grinning. What did Joaquin have up his sleeve?

THEY WALKED HAND IN HAND, meandering down to the Fraser River. The evening was clear, although chilly in the November air. They followed a path along the bank of the river and soon made their way out of the busy city centre of New Westminster and into the outskirts of town.

"I like this, walking along with you." She stood on her

tiptoes and snuck a kiss on his cheek. "We've had to hide for so long."

Joaquin smiled, spreading out a blanket that he had brought from the hotel. "For a long time, I never imagined we could." He sat down on the blanket and patted the spot next to him. "Come, my love."

She snuggled next to him, and he wrapped his arm around her. Just when she had relaxed into him, he took her hand and turned to her.

"Do you want me to propose again, Clara? I wasn't exactly planning on asking you in the courtroom of John's trial." He chuckled. "Although it's a story to tell the children, that's for sure."

"It's a story, to be certain. I like it, though. When were you planning on proposing?"

"As soon as you took off that damn black gown." He kissed her deeply, taking her breath away. "I was thinking I might do it on our way back home, at old Tom's apothecary, where we met. But then I also thought our secret forest meeting place might have been nice, too."

He reached into his pocket and held out his hand. A ring sat in his palm. When she picked it up, she saw that it was a thick gold band with roses swirled into the metal. A green emerald sat beautifully in its centre.

"I know it's not a diamond, but it reminded me of the gown you wore to the Christmas social." His voice was husky against her ear as he held her close.

"It was the first night we kissed."

"And the first night we said that we loved each other." He rubbed her cheek with the back of his hand. "Rebecca and Jo helped pick the ring out."

"I love it, Joaquin. It couldn't be more perfect." She shivered as he put it on her finger, and a cool breeze swept in from the river. The sun had set, and the chill dusk air danced between them.

As she settled back into his arms, he spoke again, his voice low in her ear. "You're all right? With a life on the farm?"

She turned her head to grin teasingly at him in the milky night. "Perhaps. Do you promise to love me no matter what roads we take?"

His eyes shone like a fiery ember, and she traced the lines that crinkled at the corners. "You'll have my heart, Clara, all along the way."

Acknowledgments

Crossing 'writing and publishing a book' off my bucket list has been one of the most thrilling experiences in my life! I certainly did not get here alone, and there are many amazing people to thank.

To the team at Rising Action Publishing Collective goes my incredible gratitude. Tina and Alex, you are goddesses. Thank you for believing in Clara's story and giving it an incredible title. I have learned so much during the publishing process. To my publishing siblings at RA, I've loved getting to know each of you and reading your spectacular novels.

When I first saw the cover of Roads, I squealed in front of a classroom of fifth graders. It is truly jaw-dropping, and I will never tire of looking at it. Nat Mack, you are a rockstar!

Jodie Renner, where can I even start? You made me laugh, cry, yell, and I'm pretty sure I cursed at you once or twice. But most of all, you made me start to believe in myself, and for that, I can never thank you enough. Editor extraordinaire!

Carrie and Laura, you have stayed by my side as alpha readers through the writing of two novels, and you deserve more gratitude than I can express on these pages. Carrie, thank you for your knowledge of the Métis and Indigenous peoples, and your eye for historical accuracy and grammar.

Laura, thank you for your encouragement, gently prodding me along through the murky bits and letting me bounce plot ideas off you.

Alina and Becky, my historical besties! Who else can I go to when I need to share a nerdy history tidbit? Thank you for your endless support and helping me answer all my 19th-century musings.

Marie, thank you for helping me get a website together and letting me cry on your shoulder. Arden, our talks have helped me grow into myself more than you know.

Drea, I've enjoyed our friendship immensely. From endless plotting to real-life hard stuff, you've always been there for me. I'll never forget how you read the whole book in one night to help me decide the ending.

Kasha, thank you for your advice on horses and farm life. This city girl had a lot of questions!

To my many other first readers: Carleen, Jaime, Jeannie, Amanda, Corina, Nickie, Joy, Mom, Dad, and Joyanna. There are countless other writers who read scenes and chapters for me while I fumbled through a first draft. Thank you, thank you, thank you!

Is there a better writing group than Moms Who Write? What an amazing collection of writers who offer endless support to one another. I'm so grateful to be a member.

Kim and Janine, your encouragement set me in motion! I'm so lucky to have friends like you. Sarah, thank you for always being willing to help with the not-so-exciting tasks involved with getting a book out into the world. To have people in your corner is one of life's best gifts, and I have some amazing humans in mine.

Mom, Dad, Amy, Joyanna, Liam, Ella, Leyla, Serra and

Ayla—thank you for letting me ramble on and on about Clara. Dad, thanks for always pointing out that scenes in the dark need a full moon to light the way.

Finally, to the women in white coats, the pioneers who came before us, who fought to make their mark in a world tailored for men. We thank you.

The Roads We Take
Book Club Questions

Book Club Questions

1. When Brendan meets Clara for the first time, he notices that she is nurturing like the mother he never had. Discuss how we unconsciously look for qualities in a partner that reflect our families of origin.

2. Contemplate how Rebecca tries to warn Clara off Brendan, calling her soft. Why might Rebecca think this? Compare how privilege and status play a role in both women's lives.

3. When Clara's father catches up with them in Calgary, Clara once again insists on staying with Brendan, despite having seen his true colours. Discuss her reasons for doing so and the turning point of the story.

4. Discuss Brendan's immediate dislike of Joaquin because he's divorced. Back in a time when religious morals dictated society, how would Joaquin have been seen as an obvious outsider?

5. Reflect on when Brendan calls baby Patrick a bastard. Brendan holds prejudice against his sister's baby, though his own parentage is unclear. Think about the idea of being a fatherless child during this time period. Which social disadvantage can you compare with today?

6. Discuss addiction as either a choice or a disease. In a time where mental health was viewed as madness or weakness, did Brendan have any other option?

7. "Brendan has a hard time lovin' himself, so how can he love another?" Reflect on how this statement is portrayed throughout the novel. Can we see this in any other characters?

8. McGregor, Joaquin and Brendan are all men that grew up without fathers. How are their paths different? The same?

9. Speak to Rebecca's need for Brendan not to be left alone, for her to have her own life. Discuss how addiction affects families. At which point does compassion become enabling?

10. Why does the title of the book fit the story? How do the roads we take impact our lives? Do we all find our way in the end, or do some of us wander? What is your definition of having 'arrived'?

About the Author

Christy K Lee is a lifetime writer and storyteller. She is obsessed with stories of women who break all the rules and is sometimes a bit of a rule breaker herself. When she's not writing, she can be found spending time in her classroom, in the local library digging through historical archives, or having a bevvie with a friend.

Christy lives in the Pacific Northwest with her three daughters. *The Roads We Take* is her first novel. Her second, a Canadian historical fiction set during the fur trade, will be releasing Fall 2025 with Rising Action.